"A THRILLING, SHOCKING, NO-HOLDS-BARRED PAGE-TURNER . . .

MacDougal writes about law and politics with an insider's savvy and a breathless pace. You'll wish this book could go on forever. . . . Once you've read *Out of Order*, you'll permanently inscribe Bonnie MacDougal on your must-read-authors list."

—WILLIAM BERNHARDT

"Much more than an ordinary legal thriller. . . . An ambitious, superbly crafted tale . . . Top-notch in every respect."

—*Providence Journal*

"[An] all-you-can-eat buffet of a book . . . A political thriller, a love story, a spy thriller, and a courtroom drama novel by a Philadelphia lawyer who knows how to craft a page-turner."

—*The Register-Herald* (West Virginia)

"MacDougal's third finds the author in ripping form, her writing keener and more glamorous than ever. . . . MacDougal writes with heart. . . . Bravo."

—*Kirkus Reviews*

"Political drama and star-crossed romance mix with the suspenseful action of a legal thriller. . . . Fans of romantic suspense will relish the labyrinthine plot and the dramatic scenes."

—*Publishers Weekly*

Also by Bonnie MacDougal

BREACH OF TRUST
ANGLE OF IMPACT*

**Published by Ballantine Books*

OUT OF ORDER

Bonnie MacDougal

BALLANTINE BOOKS • NEW YORK

This is a work of fiction. Names, characters, places, and incidents are either the product of the author's imagination or are used fictitiously.

* * *

A Ballantine Book
Published by The Ballantine Publishing Group

www.randomhouse.com/BB/

Library of Congress Catalog Card Number: 00-107767

ISBN 0-345-43445-5

Manufactured in the United States of America

First Hardcover Edition: August 1999
First Mass Market Edition: November 2000

10 9 8 7 6 5 4 3 2 1

For Rosemae and Bob,
my parents

1

They moved in a pack, six young males, fit and feral, loping flank to flank with an ice fog swirling at their feet and clouds of hot steam puffing from their mouths. Berms of cindered gray snow rose up on both sides of the road, and they ran between them in perfect unspoken formation, as if cued by some pheromone only they could sniff.

Cam was alone on the narrow country lane, and she slowed as one of the pack suddenly broke formation and surged toward her. He lifted something as he ran, a long ellipse that gleamed to a high polish in the moonlight, and swung it down into the curbside mailbox with a splintering crash.

She flipped on her high beams. Six boys and a baseball bat stood frozen on the road before her, a *tableau vivant* of teenage vandalism, until a second later the headlights scattered them like a laser blast.

"Kids," she muttered.

She was already late, and her nerves were strung tight. She'd spent the last two hours in a frenzy of dressing and undressing, pinning up her hair and tearing it down again, carefully applying makeup only to frantically rub it all off, until at last Doug had mumbled that it might be bad form to arrive late to a party in their own honor. Cam was afraid it was even worse form to arrive separately, but finally she'd insisted that he go on ahead.

Now, watching as the boys dived into the bushes and rolled out of sight, she was glad she had. If Doug saw what she just had, he would have felt duty-bound to stop and do something. It was his nature: if he could do something, he did it. And more to the point, if he knew something, he spoke it. Doug would never have remained silent about the boy who'd just broken the spine of someone's mailbox—the same boy who should have been passing canapés at the party tonight: Trey Ramsay, thirteen-year-old son of their host, United States Senator Ashton Ramsay.

But keeping secrets was an old habit for Cam. She did with this information what she did with most: she filed it away.

She drove on, but a moment later her headlights shone on something else: a dark van was pulled over to the side of the road, and a man stood beside it with a cell phone to his ear. Calling the police, she supposed, and felt some relief that the matter was out of her hands. He was wearing jeans and a ski jacket, respectable enough attire for a Friday night in the suburbs of Wilmington. But there was something in his stance, a dark edge to the way he turned away as she approached. Her eyes flicked up to the mirror as she passed him. For a moment he looked as fit and feral as that wolfpack; for a moment she wondered if he weren't more dangerous than they were.

But only for a moment. She was on the brink of a new life, and no spoiled delinquent or mysterious stranger was going to keep her from it. She kept driving.

A cold February moon shone down on the unbroken snow of the open fields and the hundred-year-old hedgerows that marked off the boundaries of the old Greenville estates. This was the château country of northern Delaware, a region settled two hundred years before by a tribe of Franco-Americans who came to establish a Utopian colony but ended up manufacturing gunpowder instead. Today, the DuPont Company was an abiding presence throughout Delaware. If only six degrees of separation existed between any two people on earth, then only one or two existed between DuPont and any son or daughter of Delaware. Cam smiled as it occurred to her that she was part of that family now, too, a daughter-in-law of Delaware.

The lights were blazing at the end of the Ramsays' driveway, and she turned through the gate stanchions and drove around a circle of snowcapped shrubs to the front steps of the house. It was a decaying old manor of dingy white stucco and faded black shutters, but tonight Cam thought it shone like a palace. Tonight the Ramsays were honoring the newlyweds before what she expected to be the ionosphere of Delaware society.

A valet parker trotted around the side of the house, and madly she shrugged out of her Gore-Tex parka and tossed it in the seat behind her. Her dress was a strapless ball gown of velvet and satin that cost her two months' salary. There was nothing left in the budget for an evening coat after that.

"Evening, miss," the boy said and opened her door.

She hesitated a second, the span of a heart skip and a quick convulsive shiver, then stepped out bare-shouldered into the cold night air.

Twin pillars flanked the front door, each one carved like a headstone with the letter *V*—for victory, Senator Ramsay would have claimed, but first it was for Vaughn. Margo Vaughn Ramsay was the one with the money, and this was her ancestral home. Cam pressed the bell and prepared her smile, and an instant later Margo threw the door open.

"Campbell, darling!" she cried, and scanned the street a moment before she pulled her inside. "You're here at last!"

Margo was wearing yards of green and gold brocade cut something like a kimono, and her steel-gray hair was gathered up in a topknot and shot through with a lethal-looking ivory rod. The first time Cam met her, she'd worn Mao-style silk pajamas, a curious look for Christmas Day, but later Doug explained: Margo spent her childhood in the Far East with her State Department father, and she continued to maintain an affection for all things Asian.

"Mrs. Ramsay, I'm so sorry I'm late—"

"Nonsense. No one's late but Ash." Margo's black eyebrows arched up over flinty gray eyes and high-cut cheekbones. "The train. Again."

Doug had also explained this: the Senator kept a monk's cell on Capitol Hill and commuted home by Metroliner on the weekends. The Tuesday-to-Thursday Club was the derogatory term for such legislators, although, according to Doug, Ramsay adhered strictly to a Monday-through-Friday schedule.

"Everyone!" Margo called. "It's Campbell! At last!"

A buzz of voices rose up, and as the bodies began to spill out into the center hall, Cam felt a stab of her old insecurity. The men were all in tuxedos, and the women in ash-blond pageboys and severe black gowns, while there she stood in a dazzling white ball gown with her hair tumbling long and loose down her back. Once again she'd dressed wrong; once again she was out of place. But quickly she reminded herself: she was the bride and the guest of honor here tonight; this time it was proper to stand out.

A pianist was playing Gershwin in the living room to the left, and a babble of voices still came from the library to the right, while here in the hall, a swarm of guests pressed in close around her. "A pleasure, young lady," someone said. "A pleasure."

"Best wishes to you both!"

A wiry woman seized Cam by both hands. "Oh, I've been so anxious to meet you!" she cried.

"Campbell, Maggie Heller," Margo said.

"Doug's told us so much about you!" the woman gushed. She was overanimated and overthin, as if a hypercharged metabolism was burning off calories faster than she could stuff them into her mouth. "And you know we all adore him, and we wish you all the best!"

"And here's someone you must meet." Margo pulled her free from Maggie Heller and steered her in the other direction, toward a man with pocked skin and deep vertical creases through the hollows of his cheeks. "Norman Finn."

"Congratulations!" he said, stepping forward with the stench of tobacco smoldering from his tuxedo.

Cam shook his hand briefly, repelled by the reek of cigarettes and by that word—*congratulations*—that always struck her as double-edged. "How do you do, Mr. Finn?"

"No, just Finn. Everybody calls me Finn."

"Finn," she repeated doubtfully, then gave a start as a man behind her leaned in too close. She turned to find a video camera zooming in on her face. Strange, she thought, turning away; the society pages could only use stills. Margo continued to pull her along, and Cam continued to clasp hands and murmur greetings as the faces whirled past and the pianist played "'S Wonderful."

"What a wonderful occasion!" the next woman said. "We only wish you'd had your wedding here."

"Yes, why were we cheated out of a wedding?" someone else asked.

Cam smiled and explained. Since she had no family and Doug's mother couldn't travel, they'd kept it a simple affair, a civil ceremony in Florida with only Doug's mother and aunt as witnesses, followed by a honeymoon on St. Bart's.

"I'm sure it was all lovely," Margo said. "But Ash and I decided: if we couldn't have a Delaware wedding, we'd at least have a Delaware wedding reception!"

"Good thing, too," said the pock-faced man, Norman Finn, just Finn. "Gives us a chance to look you over."

Cam gave him an uncertain glance. She didn't know what he meant, nor even what he was doing here. There was something disquieting about him, an undercurrent of crude power, as if he were a plantation overseer or a casino boss.

"Campbell," said the overeager woman, Maggie Heller. "That's such a lovely name!"

"Thank you." A second later Cam winced—*wrong response*—though appropriate enough if they knew the truth.

"You're a lawyer in Philadelphia?"

"Yes. With Jackson, Rieders and Clark."

Finn announced to the crowd, "That's the outfit that acquired Doug's firm last year."

Cam's lips curved in a coy denial. "Oh, not *acquired*, Mr. Finn. Our firm *merged* with Doug's."

"I'd say it's a merger now," he said with a coarse laugh.

"Are you planning to sit for the Delaware bar?" another man asked.

"I already did, last summer. Passed, too!" she added pertly.

"What's your specialty?"

"Oh, I'm just an associate," she said airily. "I do whatever they tell me to do."

"But what department are you in?" the man pressed her.

Her smile dimmed. "Family law," she said after a beat.

"Ahh." He gave a too-knowing nod. "We called that domestic relations in our firm. Until one of our clients thought that meant her husband was having an affair with the maid!"

"I remember that case, Owen," put in a man behind him. "And damned if she wasn't right!"

Cam gave a strained smile through the crowd's laughter.

"No, wait a minute," Finn said. "Doug told us you're an asset-finder."

"Yes," she said, brightening. "I do a lot of that. Executing on judgments, and tracing assets the defendant might have stashed away."

"Oh, I see the connection," a woman remarked dryly. "Since nobody conceals assets better than a man heading for divorce court."

"Damn, is that what asset-finding means?" Finn said. "Here

I was hoping it meant Campbell could help us with our fund-raising."

She gave him a confused look as another round of laughter broke out. He stepped closer and brought a vapor of cigarette stench with him. "Margo, let me take over the introductions here. I got some folks Campbell needs to meet."

"By all means, Finn." Margo relinquished Cam's arm and turned at once to work the crowd. "Why, there you are!" she cried. "How long has it been? Oh, I know—the train! Again!"

More names and faces scrolled past Cam as Finn pulled her along through the hall. *Owen Willoughby; Webb Black; Carl Baldini—you know, Baldini Construction?; Chubb Heller—you met his wife, Maggie, already, didn't you; Ron March—as in the U.S. Attorney Ronald March?—that's right; John Simon, because every party needs a friendly banker.* Cam nodded and smiled and felt a ripple of unease. None of these names was familiar to her, though she'd been following the Wilmington society pages for months. She tried to tune into the snippets of conversation around her. It was the usual party banter that month—the latest movies at the multiplex, the latest White House sex scandal, the latest showdown with Saddam Hussein. A sharper exchange sounded behind her. *Numbers look good. You see that poll yesterday? Yeah, but without the cash, what can he do . . . ?* Margo's voice sounded distantly, its pitch dropping in Doppler effect as she moved to the back of the house. "Yes, Jesse's waiting at the station for him. Trey . . . ? I don't know—he must still be upstairs. He's probably trying to find something to wear. He's been growing out of everything! He's all wrists and ankles these days!"

Finn veered off course and pulled Cam through a cluster of people to reach an old man slumped in a wheelchair. "Jonathan, this is Doug's bride," he announced loudly. "Campbell, meet Jonathan Fletcher."

At last, a name she'd expected to hear tonight. Jonathan Fletcher was a member of Delaware aristocracy, a third- or fourth-generation millionaire. "How do you do, Mr. Fletcher?"

The old man looked up with a squint under woolly white eyebrows and said nothing.

"Campbell—" spoke a woman behind the wheelchair. "Is that a family name?"

"Yes." Cam watched peripherally as Margo picked up the telephone on a console table by the stairs. "It was my mother's maiden name."

"Sounds Scotch," the old man said in a deep rumble that shivered the loose flaps of his jowls.

Cam lip-read as Margo spoke into the phone across the hall: ". . . wondering if you've seen Trey anywhere tonight . . . ?"

"Hundred proof," Cam quipped.

"You don't look Scotch," Fletcher said with a suspicious growl. "More Irish maybe."

She tossed her head and sent her hair cascading down her back. "Aahh, go on with ye," she said in a brogue that brought a loud burst of laughter from the crowd.

The alert pianist made a quick segue into "They All Laughed."

Twenty feet away Margo hung up the phone. The bones showed in her face for a second before her flesh slackened into a smile once more.

"Where do you hail from, Campbell?" someone asked.

"Pennsylvania. Lancaster County?"

"Oh, but tell the rest!" Margo charged across the room so fast that the gold threads sparked in her gown. "Campbell was raised by her grandmother after her parents died in the Philippines. Can you imagine?—they were missionaries there."

Jonathan Fletcher's shaggy eyebrows rose. "Died how?"

"In a Muslim massacre," Cam said. When everyone's faces froze in horror, she added, "But this was almost thirty years ago. I was only a baby."

Finn bent down close to Fletcher's ear. "That's eighteen carat stuff, you know."

The old man nodded and finally pulled his rheumy eyes from Cam to demand of Margo, "Where's that husband of yours?"

"I told you, Jonathan. The train—"

"Where's that husband of mine?" Cam said, almost as querulously as the old man.

She won another laugh from the crowd as Finn pointed her toward the library.

It was a dark-paneled, heavily draped room furnished in a jarring blend of Chesterfield sofas and Japanese silk screens, a dim and dreary room during her previous visits here. But tonight a fire crackled on the hearth, lamps shone from tabletops and wall sconces, and Doug Alexander glowed incandescently in the center of it all.

On any objective tally of looks, he would tot up as average bordering on nondescript. Everything about him could be summed up as *medium*: medium brown hair, medium brown eyes, medium height, medium build, albeit with a slight professorial stoop to his shoulders. But there was something about him that lit up a room, and he was lighting this one up now. From the piano came the strains of one of their favorite songs, "Someone to Watch Over Me." Doug's head came up, and when he spotted Cam in the doorway, he sent her a signal with his eyebrows—*You okay?*—and she sent one back to him with a smile—*Fine, wonderful!*

Standing there, gazing at him, she was. She'd been a loner all her life, but she was half of a couple now, part of a unit, *united,* and she never had to be alone again.

An arm suddenly slipped around her waist and a voice spoke in her ear. "Watch out, babe. You almost look besotted."

"I got news for you, Nathan," she retorted, pivoting in a swirl of white satin. "I *am* besotted." She rose up on tiptoe to hug the tall black man, then stepped back to regard him with a suspicious squint. "What in the world are you doing here?"

"Me?" He feigned affront as he straightened his red bow tie. "I was about to ask you."

But that was exactly her point. Nathan Vance was as much a nobody as she was. That was the basis of their friendship. They'd drifted together in law school the way misfits always do—Cam a poor white orphan girl, and Nathan the son of a family that was black in color only. "No, really," she insisted. "How'd you ever get invited here?"

"Okay, one, I went to school with you." He ticked off the points on his fingers. "Two, I used to work in Philadelphia with you. Three, now I work in Wilmington with Doug. And finally, four, I'm the only one in the world who can claim friendship with both the bride and groom. Thus, I respectfully submit, no one deserves to be here more than me."

It came to her then, the source of all her unease tonight. This was no gathering of Wilmington society. There was no one here from the Beaux Arts Ball committee or the Winterthur point-to-point races or the symphony board. She looked back to the library to see a strange man clapping Doug on the shoulder as another whiff of conversation came her way. *See that trade policy paper he did? A lot of prime stuff in there.*

Nathan's gaze went past her and his shoulders went straight, and Cam turned to see Norman Finn bearing down on them.

"Oh, Finn," she said. "I'd like you to meet my friend, Nathan Vance—"

"Hell, I know Nathan. How's business, young man?"

"Fine, sir. Good to see you tonight."

Lawyers, Cam thought as they shook hands. Of course, they must all be lawyers. It was a logical enough guest list for a party in honor of the marriage of two lawyers, hosted by a former attorney general of the state. But she caught another fragment of conversation: *Yeah, registrations are up, but the fund-raising levels—*

Her bare shoulders shivered as a blast of frigid air shot through the hall, and she turned around as Senator James Ashton Ramsay burst through the front door, larger than life. "Margo!" he roared as the crowd turned his way. "When's dinner? I'm starved!"

A cheer went up, and Cam squeezed back against the wall as the rest of the crowd pressed forward, everyone clamoring for an up-close and personal view of the Senator. He was an imposing figure, tall and barrel-chested, with a hawkish nose and a flowing mane of yellow-white hair that lent him his nickname: the Lion of New Castle County. He peeled off his overcoat and tossed it over a bamboo-backed chair, then pitched himself into the throng.

"Hello, Finn! Owen, Sarah, good to see you! Maggie, my girl, how are you? Ron! How're you doing?"

"Welcome home, Senator!" Finn shouted.

The other guests picked up the cry, as if Ramsay didn't appear in the same place every Friday night. "Welcome home, Senator! Welcome home!"

"Good to see you!" he boomed to them all in return. "Thanks for coming!"

At last Cam understood. These were what Doug called the Party people—by whom he meant not people who liked to party, but rather the people who worked for the Party. She should have realized. The Party was close to a religion for Doug: he tithed, attended regular services, and took an awful lot on faith.

He was working his way toward her through the crowd, and she cut ahead to meet him. "Honey . . . ?" she called.

"Hold on," he said, smiling, and brushed past her.

"There's my boy!" Ramsay yelled and held an arm out to Doug. A path parted, and another cheer went up as the two men pounded each other's shoulders.

The front door opened again and another chilly blast of air came in, this time admitting an unnatural blonde in a lustrous black mink coat.

"Ahh, here's Meredith now." Ramsay pulled the woman front and center before him. "Everyone—I want you to meet Meredith Winters. I coaxed her up from Washington for the weekend, so you folks be sure and show her a good time."

Jesse Lombard, the Senator's longtime factotum, slipped in the door behind them and was there to catch the woman's mink as she poured it off.

"Who is she?" Cam whispered to Nathan as Jesse unobtrusively bore the coats up the stairs.

"Political strategist. Used to read the news in San Francisco. Now she's running Sutherland's campaign in Maryland."

"Wow." Phil Sutherland was a name even a political agnostic like Cam could recognize. He'd been the commander of the armored division in Desert Storm, author of a bestselling autobiography, host of a hugely popular radio talk show, and founder of a Baltimore inner-city mentoring project so successful it was now the model for a dozen similar efforts across the country. His bid for the Senate was the most closely watched race in the country.

"But isn't it kind of early for Ramsay to be interviewing campaign consultants?" Cam asked. "It's more than four years before he has to run again."

Nathan only looked at her.

"Margo!" Ramsay bellowed. "Where are you? And would somebody please put a glass of something in my hand so I can make a toast here?"

On cue, four white-gloved waiters materialized from out of the kitchen and came through the crowd bearing trays laden with flutes of champagne. Margo appeared on their heels and swept to her husband's side. He kissed her with a resounding smack, then snatched a glass off the nearest tray.

"All right, attention, everybody," he said. When the buzzing didn't dwindle, he went to the staircase and climbed up a few steps. The piano music cut off, but there were another few moments of excited humming as the crowd jostled into a semicircle around the base of the stairs. The man with the video camera positioned himself carefully in the front line and kept the tape rolling.

"Good evening, friends," the Senator said as silence finally fell. "I'm glad to see you all here tonight on this wonderful occasion, and I'm proud, too, and I'll tell you why. You all know Doug Alexander. Some of you also knew his father, Gordon Alexander, a man I was lucky enough to call my best friend. We lost Gordon too soon. Way too soon. And when Dorothy got sick and Doug was only a half-grown boy, there he was, facing adversity that most of us couldn't cope with as adults. But he never let it get him down. He took good care of Dorothy. No mother could've asked for a better son. His teachers loved him, his coaches couldn't do without him, and as for me, if I didn't see him at my dinner table every Sunday, I didn't call it a good week.

"Doug grew up into the kind of man who never gave second best and never settled for it, either. He got himself through the best schools, he was hired by the best law firm in town—Sorry, Owen," he said to a man who gave a gracious shrug. "Yours is good, too, but I have to speak my mind here—and he's done nothing but first-class work since he passed the bar. There hasn't been a major real estate development deal in the state that Doug hasn't been a part of. This new waterfront development, every industrialization project that got off the ground in the last decade—they all had Doug Alexander working feverishly behind the scenes to make it happen. The people of this state owe an awful lot to him. And I don't have to tell the people in this room how much the Party owes to him. He's been a good and loyal member and a tireless worker for our candidates.

"But there's always been a missing element to this young man. And it's made Margo and me despair about him more than once."

A few of the guests exchanged uncertain glances.

"But you see, it was the way he was made," Ramsay went on. "He wouldn't settle for second best in a wife, either."

A burst of relieved laughter sounded as Cam's face began to burn.

"But guess what, folks? It turned out he didn't have to! It took him a while to find her, but he got himself a dilly." He peered down into the crowd. "Whoa, hold on. We're missing the bride here. Campbell, where are you?"

"Go on up," Nathan hissed in her ear.

A smattering of applause sounded as she was propelled through the crowd to Doug's side at the foot of the stairs.

"There she is," Ramsay declared, pointing. "You can all see for yourselves her obvious attractions, but folks, I'm here to tell you that she's also smart and sassy and she's gonna keep this boy on his toes for the rest of his life!"

Doug gave her hand a squeeze as the guests laughed and applauded.

"We couldn't be prouder of Doug Alexander if he were our own son," Ramsay said. "But we also know that our proudest day still lies ahead. For tonight it's my honor and privilege to announce to you—and I thank you, Norman Finn, for letting me be the one to announce it—that Doug Alexander is the Party's choice for this November's election to the United States House of Representatives!"

Cam almost buckled at the knees. Doug's hand slipped free, and she looked up through swimming eyes to watch him shaking hands and beaming a thousand-watt smile through the crowd. Ramsay pulled him up beside him on the stairs and threw an arm around his shoulders.

"Friends, I give you Doug Alexander!" He held his glass high. "Our next United States Representative!"

"Doug Alexander!" the crowd roared.

Cam's fingers clenched on the stem of her glass as the guests tossed back their champagne.

"Better get up there with him," a voice said out of a cloud of floral perfume. Cam turned and looked into the sharp features of the blond woman, Meredith Winters. "Go on," she said, and pried the glass out of Cam's hand. "These photo ops don't come cheap."

Cam stumbled toward the stairs, and when Doug reached a hand down, she grabbed it and held on like a woman overboard.

He made a speech, and even in the ice fog swirling around Cam, she could tell that he'd written and rehearsed it in advance. He was lavish in his thanks to the Senator, whom he'd come to regard as a second father. No one could have grown up with a finer role model than Ash Ramsay. He was warmly appreciative of Margo, who'd never failed to make him feel welcome in her home. He was deeply moved and honored by the trust and confidence the Party was showing in him tonight. He singled out Norman Finn and thanked him for the many opportunities to be involved in the Party's work, to make a real difference in the lives of Delawareans. Nothing could make him prouder than to continue that work in Washington.

"As most of you know," he said, "my number one priority is full employment for the people of Delaware. And by full, I don't mean moving names off the unemployment roll and onto the McDonald's payroll. I mean real jobs, with real benefits. Jobs that require the best of your abilities. The kind of job you can spend your life in and raise a family on."

He paused to give a disarming smile. "But much as I'm for full employment, there's one citizen of Delaware who's been employed too long and too far beyond his abilities. And sadly, I think it's time for him to get *on* the unemployment roll. And the man I'm talking about is . . ." He raised his arms like an orchestra conductor, and the entire crowd shouted out in unison: "Hadley Hayes!"

Doug waited with a grin until the laughter and applause died down, then said softly: "You know, I thought the happiest day of my life was the day this incredible woman here beside me consented to become my wife. But then I realized I was wrong, because the happiest day of my life came two weeks ago Wednesday when she looked up at me and said 'I do.' "

Cam looked up at him now, astounded that the man who barely stammered through his marriage proposal was broadcasting his feelings to a houseful of strangers.

"But now, with my wife here beside me, and all of my friends here before me, I realize I was wrong both times, and that the happiest days are those that lie ahead of us—as we win this race and march on to Washington!"

Nathan Vance brought his hands together in a rhythmic, hollow clap, and it caught and swelled into a deafening round of applause. Doug turned to Cam and kissed her, long and lustily, while the cheers echoed through the narrow hallway and roared inside her head.

Outside and a mile away a long, loose line of boys was ambling aimlessly down Sentry Bridge Road. The adrenaline rush of the mailbox-bashing was over, and now they were laughing and stumbling and sticking their legs out to try to trip each other. At the head of the line, Jon Shippen dug his hand in his pocket and turned around with a grin to show the rest. "All right, Ship!" went up the cheer when they saw what he had: a joint pilfered from his brother's stash. He lit it and took a drag, and the sickly sweet odor rose up and swirled through the smell of wood smoke that already hung heavy in the crisp night air.

Trey breathed it all in as he waited for the joint to reach him at the back of the pack. This was his favorite time, after the spree, when all of his senses came alive. Everything seemed sharper to him now. There was an edge to the light that let him see the things he usually missed: the faint quivering of the pine needles; the road slush crystallizing into ice as the nighttime temperature plunged; the hundred different shades of black in the sky. If he could paint this night, he'd use greens so deep and dark they'd blend to black. He'd call it—what else?—*Greenville Night.*

Jason had the bat, and he was dragging it in the snow behind him, leaving a track like an animal with a wounded leg. He passed it over to Trey when the joint reached him. It was down to half an inch by then, and he had to hold it with the precision of a watchmaker to get it to his lips. Trey dragged the bat the same way Jason had and looked behind at the trail it left. For fifty feet, he imagined, a crippled animal had been following them through the night. His gaze drifted upward, to the car that was rolling slowly behind them with its headlights off.

"Shit," he hissed and grabbed Jason by the arm.

Abruptly the headlights flashed on, the siren screeched awake, and the lights started spinning on the roof.

The boys in front of him took off, and Trey dove over the berm and rolled across the snow, then scrambled on all fours through the undergrowth of the hedges. He tore through to the other side, jumped to his feet, and went into a flat-out run across the field. He heard Jason huffing behind him and slowed a second to let him catch up, then side by side they ran on, their boots crunching loudly through the snow until they reached another hedgerow. On elbows and bellies they inched forward through a tangle of branches. Trey raked his hair back out of his face and peered through to the other side. Martins Mill Road lay below them, deserted.

"We lost 'em," Jason said with a panting laugh.

Trey scanned the road. The sirens were still wailing distantly, but there were no cop cars here. He rolled to his side and looked back the way they'd come. The tracks they'd left in the snow looked like a line of black ants marching over white sand dunes.

Jason flopped onto his back, fished a cigarette out of his pocket and lit it. "Want one?" he asked, dragging deep.

Trey didn't answer. The sirens cut off abruptly, and he crawled forward for another look at the road. To the right, where Martins Mill crossed Sentry Bridge, he could see the dim outline of a car. It was waiting there, halfway between him and home, which meant he'd have to go back the way he came, across the field, pick up Sentry Bridge down below, then circle around Chaboullaird and come out farther down on Martins Mill.

He was up on his haunches, ready to start the run back, when a quick beam of light swept over their footprints in the field.

Trey wheeled one way and Jason the other. As Trey burst through the hedges, the headlights flashed on from the cop car at the corner. He spun left and galloped along the shoulder of the road, but it was no use. The snow was dragging at his feet, and the sirens were closing in behind him.

"Hey! Over here!"

Trey's head swiveled left. A man stood beside a van parked in a driveway. The side door was open, and the man was waving him in.

Trey didn't stop to question. He tore up the driveway and dove into the van, and the door slid shut with a crash behind him. He was in a cargo compartment, and there was a wire mesh screen separating it from the seats in the front. A minute later the driver's door opened and closed, and the man ducked his head down low behind the wheel. He didn't speak, and neither did Trey.

The sirens crescendoed to their highest pitch, and for a few seconds the flashing lights of the cop car reflected in a dancing array of red and blue against the sheet metal interior of the van. Trey crouched down low on the floor, until at last the lights passed by and slowly the sound of the siren faded away in the distance.

"Whew." Trey came up on his knees on the carpeted floor. "Thanks, man. I owe you one." He reached for the handle on the sliding door. "Wanna pop the locks?"

The man turned the ignition, and the engine started with a low growl.

"Hey!" Trey didn't know whether he should say more. The neighbors were always going out of their way to do favors for his family; the guy was probably just giving him a lift home.

But when the van backed out of the driveway, the wheels cut the wrong way. "Hey!" Trey lunged for the rear doors, but they were locked, too.

He scrambled forward and yelled through the wire mesh. "Hey! Do you know who my father is?"

The man looked back over his shoulder and locked eyes with Trey.

"Yeah," he said. "I do."

2

It was thirty minutes before Cam was able to slip her hand from Doug's and escape to the back of the house. She went first to the sun room, but someone had been there before her and left behind a haze of stale cigarette smoke that brought another cramp of nausea to her stomach. The caterers had commandeered the kitchen, but the room beyond it was empty and lit only by a fire on the hearth. She stole in.

This was the family sitting room, a homey, well-worn room where Ash watched *Meet the Press* and Margo painted on fans and Trey played Nintendo with his feet up on the furniture. This was where they'd all gathered Christmas Day when Doug first brought her here. A fire burned on the hearth then, too, and she'd felt warm and safe as she snuggled close to him on the dilapidated couch. That was what she'd thought her life with Doug would always be: warm and safe.

She was trembling. She hugged her arms and stood close to the fire, then turned to let the heat touch her back. Over the sofa on the opposite wall hung a Ramsay family photograph. It was an outdoorsy summer scene: Ash and Margo standing with their arms around each other, Trey in front with his head cocked back to flash an impish grin at his father. He was ten or eleven then, with sandy hair and eyes full of mischief and a sprinkling of freckles across his nose and cheeks. Cam knew the photo well: it became the campaign poster for Ramsay's last race. His challenger had been leading in the polls with thinly veiled attacks on the Senator's age, but then the poster came out, and with it a subliminal message: if Ramsay was young enough to father a high-spirited scamp like this one, he surely had enough vigor to keep the Senate in line. He won reelection with a ten-point margin.

But the child in the photograph bore little resemblance to the boy Cam met Christmas Day, the one she'd seen wilding only an hour or so before. The freckles were faded now; his hair was darker and fell to his shoulders; and he had a sullen mouth and a flat, disaffected look in his eye. A lucky thing, Cam thought, that this wasn't Ramsay's election year.

But that only reminded her of whose election year it was.

She sank down on the broken springs of the old sofa. There had to be some mistake. Doug was a good worker bee in the Party hive, but he wasn't the stuff a candidate was made of. He was a real estate lawyer, quiet in his ways and content with a back-room practice. Yes, he was charming, but only because he was so self-effacing. He wasn't one of those glad-handing show-boaters who always craved the limelight. Besides, wasn't there some order to these things? First school board, then city council, then the state legislature? Doug had never run for anything, except, occasionally, the train.

She tensed and rose at the sound of whispers in the hall outside, followed by the rattle of keys and the opening and closing of the back door. She moved to the window and watched as a figure came out on the porch and passed under the light, and when she saw the slash of white scar tissue through the graying buzz cut, she recognized Jesse Lombard, the Senator's all-purpose aide. He limped across the unshoveled snow to the garage, and a minute later the Ramsays' old blue station wagon backed out of the driveway.

At last, Cam thought. The information she'd filed away earlier must have finally been delivered through official channels. The police must have called, and Jesse was being dispatched to fetch the wayward youth. A good man for the job, she reflected. He was a former cop himself, a Vietnam vet who'd joined the state troopers, worked his way through the ranks, and ultimately served as Ramsay's chief investigator at the Attorney General's office. He returned to police duty after Ramsay was elected to the Senate in 1984, but during a resisted arrest a year later, a bullet creased his brain, leaving him with chronic numbness in his left arm and leg and a sporadic twitch in his left cheek. He was retired now, on disability and the Senate payroll.

The station wagon disappeared around the side of the house, and Cam returned to the sagging sofa and to her transfixed stare into the flames. From the front of the house came the sound of a dozen people singing along with the piano, "Strike Up the Band."

Ash Ramsay's booming baritone led the refrain, and when Doug's reedy voice joined in, a chill trickled down her spine.

This was all her own fault. Somehow she'd convinced herself that she could marry into a world of prestige and privilege and not forfeit the anonymity that she'd worked so hard to preserve. In school she kept her grades up and her head down; at Jackson, Rieders, she was doing everything to prosper and nothing to stand out. All she ever wanted was a private life, with the security that came with a certain status and position. That was what Doug already had, and her mistake was in believing that was all he wanted, too.

She sat and watched the flames lick at the edges of the fireplace and reflected on her own campaign, the one that brought her here. She could be honest with herself now that she was two weeks married. She'd set her sights on Doug the night they met, and she'd campaigned for him as single-mindedly as any candidate ever pursued elective office.

It was the summer before, when she was second-chairing a divorce trial in Wilmington against a celebrity divorce lawyer from New York. He had the wife, Cam's firm had the husband, and the husband had a million dollar job running a credit card company.

There were few big-money lawsuits in America that didn't have some corporate nexus to Delaware, and out-of-town lawyers were always swarming into Wilmington with their clients, their cases, and their staggering mountains of paper. Document-baggers, they could have been called. The Delaware courts erected only one small barrier at the gate: a rule requiring out-of-state lawyers to affiliate with local counsel, also known as the full-employment-for-resident-lawyers law.

That summer Jackson, Rieders & Clark decided to take it one better. Rather than affiliate with a Wilmington firm, it would *become* a Wilmington firm. Cashman & Alexander was a twelve-lawyer firm with an eighty-year history, well respected, well connected—and on the edge of bankruptcy. The ink was barely dry on the new partnership agreement before Cam came to town.

One night she was working alone in the offices of the firm formerly known as Cashman & Alexander. She sat in her allotted conference room at a long oval table covered with a thousand pages of paper and almost a hundred volumes of case reporters.

Her supervising partner was dining with the client that evening, and he'd left her with an impossible list of assignments: deposition testimony to cull and mark; exhibits to locate and flag; and four different motions to research and write, none of which the judge would bother to read during the heat of trial, but all of which would vex their opponents and require one of their associates to work late into the following night.

It was after eight, and Cam was exhausted and snappish and longing to be anywhere else, when suddenly the room went dark.

"Hey!" she cried out.

Instantly the lights flashed on again. A man stood in the doorway with his hand on the switch and surprise on his face. "Sorry. I didn't realize anyone was in here."

"Well, someone *is* in here."

"You must be with the team from Philadelphia?"

She nodded and bent to work again.

"Had dinner yet?"

Peevishly she said: "I don't have time for dinner, and I won't have time for sleep, either, if I can't be left alone to finish my work."

When she looked up a few minutes later he was gone.

The next time she looked up, it was because a delicious aroma was wafting toward her. The same man stood again in the doorway, and he was holding a container printed with the name of the Green Room, an elegant, pricey restaurant across the street in the Hotel DuPont.

"It's tonight's special," he said. "Veal marsala."

She stared at him. It was a small act of kindness, but so unexpected she was speechless.

"I hope it's all right," he said, his soft brown eyes showing doubt.

"Great. Thanks." He put the box down on the table, and as the aroma wafted up, suddenly she was ravenous. "You can charge the client account for this," she said.

"I don't think so."

Her head came up and her eyes narrowed.

"I was once an overworked associate myself." He smiled gently. "So I think I'll bear the freight on this. For old times' sake."

He turned to go, and she noticed then that he'd shed his suit jacket and briefcase. "I thought you were on your way home," she said.

"I remembered some work I have to finish." He paused at the door. "I'll be right down the hall if you need anything."

It was nearly two by the time she finished. The corridor outside was in complete darkness, and the man who'd fed her dinner must certainly have long since gone home. She rose stiffly from the table and started to pack up her papers, but her exhaustion made her clumsy, and she knocked over a stack of casebooks that fell to the floor with a crash. Wearily she stooped to gather them up, and when she straightened, he was there in the doorway again, rubbing the sleep from his eyes and offering to walk her to her hotel.

It was only two blocks away. She'd walked far worse streets in her life, and at hours just as bad. But she nodded and rode the elevator with him to the lobby and signed out with him at the security desk and stepped out with him into the summer night.

It was quiet outside, and cooler now that the sun was so long gone. The sky was starless, but Cam liked it that way. The clear night sky always seemed too vast and unknowable to her, but a cover of clouds was a comfort, a feeling like being wrapped in a snug, protective blanket.

They crossed the street on the diagonal and cut through the long grassy rectangle that was so obviously misnamed Rodney Square. It lay along a steep hillside with the state courthouse at its base and the twelve-story, Italian Renaissance–style Hotel DuPont at its summit. The bed she'd longed for all night was waiting there, but now, strolling across the park in the balmy summer air, she found herself longing for it a little less.

His name was Doug Alexander, he told her, and he'd heard a lot about her from Nathan Vance, all good, and he was happy to meet her at last. He was in the real estate department and did a lot of public finance work. Wilmington was his hometown, though his invalid mother now lived in Florida and there was no other family nearby.

At the upper elevation of the park, a broad set of stairs finished the rise from King Street to Walnut Street, and in the middle of the stairs was a statue of a man on the back of a galloping bronze horse. Doug stopped and pointed up at it. "Have you heard the story about Caesar Rodney?"

Cam shook her head.

"He was our first and greatest patriot. One of Delaware's three delegates to the Second Continental Congress in 1776. When the crucial vote came in July, only the other two delegates were in attendance, Read and McKean. McKean was for the Declaration of Independence; Read was against it. McKean knew that Rodney sided with him, so he sent a rider down to his home in Dover with a message about how the vote stood. Rodney got on his horse and rode all night, eighty miles through a thunderstorm, and arrived just in time to cast Delaware's vote in favor of Independence."

"Like Paul Revere," Cam said. "But without the dramatic imperative of the British troops at his heels."

"Well, no, but there was a moral imperative driving him. He got the call that he was needed, and he answered it. That counts for a lot in my book. And look at it this way: if the vote for independence failed, Paul Revere's ride would have been for nothing."

It was two in the morning and she had to be in court at nine, and here she was getting a lesson in history and civics. It should have been corny. No one she knew was this uncynical, this guileless; he was probably the uncoolest man she'd ever met; she should have cut him off and walked away at a brisk and irritated clip. Instead she sat down beside him on the steps and listened as he told her the history of Delaware. He moved his eyes from Caesar Rodney to her, and she could feel the full force of his attention. And then she yawned in his face.

He was more embarrassed than she was. "Look at the time," he said with a chagrined glance at his watch. "And here I am, rambling on." He got up and reached a hand down to Cam.

It happened in that moment. She must have been so exhausted that her emotional guard was down, because right there, at the foot of Caesar Rodney's horse, she stood up and fell in love with Doug Alexander.

"Well, here you are," said a throaty voice, and Margo Ramsay came into the sitting room.

Cam lurched to her feet. "Oh, I'm sorry. I just needed a moment—"

"Sssh." Margo waved her down and collapsed on the sofa beside her. "I need the same moment myself. It's absolute madness out there." She put her feet up on the battered coffee table and placed a leathery hand over Cam's.

Cam had been motherless too long. That simple gesture made her long to plunge her face against Margo's shoulder and sob out all of her troubles. But of course, she couldn't tell her troubles to anyone, least of all to Margo Ramsay, and so they sat long moments in silence, listening to the hoots and hollers of the Party people and the crackling of the logs in the fireplace.

"He wanted to surprise you, I imagine," Margo said at last. "That's why he didn't tell you beforehand. He must have thought the surprise was worth more than the opportunity to prepare yourself. But I can easily see how it would be the other way around."

Cam let out a weak laugh. "Is there ever enough time to brace yourself for something like this?"

"Oh, you'd be amazed at the power of time."

"Heals all wounds?" she murmured.

"Yes, that. And allows you to adjust to almost anything."

Cam's gaze moved up from the fire. Over the mantel hung an oil portrait of a young woman, a fragile beauty with pale hair and clouded eyes. The first time Cam came into this room she saw how Doug's eyes were drawn to that portrait, and she made it her business to find out who she was. She was Cynthia, the Ramsays' daughter, who'd grown up with Doug and who would have been the one on his arm tonight if there were any kind of natural order to the world. There'd been a certain expectation—if not quite between them, at least about them—and it might have come to something if only Cynthia hadn't loaded up on speed and wrapped her car around a telephone pole one cold night ten years ago.

"No," Margo said sharply. "I know what you're thinking. But you're wrong."

Cam flushed. "It's just that she would have been so much better suited—"

"Not at all. I've been watching you, dear. You're tough, and you're resilient. Whereas Cynth—" Margo's own gaze moved to the portrait. "She was a lovely girl, and so sweet!" She caught her lip in her teeth and took a shaky breath. "But she didn't cope well with adversity. She could never bend and snap back the way you can. She could only snap."

Cynth. The name reminded Cam of the hyacinth, the headyfragranced flower whose stem was too weak to support its own blossom.

Margo dabbed at the corners of her eyes. "Ash spoke the truth out there," she said. "We had our doubts about running Doug this year until he showed up with you Christmas Day. You were the best present we could have asked for."

"But Mrs. Ramsay, I come from a different world. I don't know these people—"

"Darling! Don't you see? That's the beauty of who you are: you don't bring any baggage with you. Cynth would have, you know. How could Doug ever hope to distance himself from Ash if she were in your place tonight?" Margo put her hand under Cam's chin and bent to meet her eyes. "You're that very rare commodity these days, Campbell—a woman without a past."

Cam's eyes shifted. "It's just that I never expected—"

"Oh, Doug should have told you. I can see that now. You need time to get used to the idea. But darling, you'll have it! By the time Doug announces—you'll see—the excitement will start to build, and you'll realize how very much you have to contribute."

Cam's excitement started to build the moment Margo mentioned Doug's announcement. That had to mean his speech on the staircase didn't qualify. Which meant she still had time to stop this.

"Thank you so much, Mrs. Ramsay." Cam gave her a quick hug, then stood up and shook out her skirts. "I'd better get back to the party now."

"There's the spirit!" Margo declared and shook a knobby fist in the air.

Thirty miles away Gloria Lipton sat alone at her secretarial station in the hushed and darkened headquarters of Jackson, Rieders & Clark. It was her favorite time, Fridays at nine, when the frantic beehive buzz that persisted all week long inside a major law firm finally came to an end. Now there was only the great swelling silence of the emptied corridors and the abiding hum of the computers that no one bothered to turn off anymore.

The silly young secretaries had departed at the stroke of five, all hard and bright and shrill as they poured into the elevators amid packages and giggles. Their kind never remained at their desks after hours without a direct order from their bosses and an assurance of overtime, and not even with that on Fridays. No, they had more important things to do. They had to rush home to change into skintight polyester, then hurry to the clubs to bare their midriffs for loutish young men in dirty jeans and work boots.

It was all so very different when Gloria was a young secretary. She went off to parties, too, she and her friends at the agency, but they wore hats and gloves and airs of subdued refinement. The receptions they attended were elegant and important affairs, and the men they sometimes took home with them were diplomats and undersecretaries and even congressmen. No one ever needed to slip packets of powder into the girls' drinks in those days; the power those men wielded was aphrodisiac enough.

But that was another city and long ago. Gloria no longer wore hats and gloves to work, and the powerful men who surrounded her today didn't have the power to start a war or end a depression, but only to start a lawsuit and suffer from depression. Still, she tried to keep her standards up. She dressed every day in pearls and sensible suits, she kept her desk and her files immaculate, and she remained firmly seated at her station every night until she was certain that Mr. Austin no longer needed her.

He always needed her on Friday nights, though he routinely departed by six, for this was when Gloria attended to his desktop and files. It was her only real opportunity, since he spent so much of the day in closed-door meetings. It was a delicate and difficult job, being chairman of a major law firm, a first among equals expected to somehow keep a hundred intractable partners under control, and he couldn't have done it without her.

Gloria went into Austin's office and sat down in his chair. First she slowly read and memorized each confidential memorandum before locking it away. Then she retrieved a tape of dictation from the pocket machine she unearthed from under a mountain of billing reports.

There were only three items on tonight's tape, she discovered back at her own desk with the headphones fitted to her ears: a letter to opposing counsel in a securities fraud case; a memo to all partners reporting and slightly exaggerating the last-quarter profit figures; and finally, a message to her—"Gloria, please order flowers for Campbell Smith. I just learned that she was married two weeks ago."

Campbell Smith—the name meant nothing to Gloria. She reached for the firm directory and flipped through the glossy pages until she came to the photograph. Oh, yes, now she remembered—a girl with an unruly mass of gold-streaked hair and skirts that ended a good eight inches above her knee, which was hardly appropriate attire for a lawyer in the firm of Jackson, Rieders & Clark. But according to the directory, that was what she was: a graduate of Michigan Law who'd been an associate in their family law department for almost four years.

Gloria slid her reading glasses down her nose and looked more closely at the photograph. There was something awfully familiar about this girl, and it was more than fleeting encounters in the elevator would explain. She was a saucy-looking thing, but perhaps with her hair pinned up and a crisp white blouse and a string of pearls at her throat—

Gloria blinked as the picture formed in her mind. It couldn't be. Could it? No—of course not, it wasn't possible. This was what came of reminiscing about the old days in Washington. Her eyes were playing tricks on her.

She slammed the directory shut and posted a note to remind herself to order the flowers Monday morning, then bundled herself up for the walk home.

Fifty stories down, a cold wind was gusting through the streets of Center City. A few businessmen were running for the train on Market Street, and some hardy restaurant-goers were strolling arm in arm on Chestnut and Walnut. But south of Walnut the lights grew dim and the streets fell quiet. Gloria walked briskly, her mind brimming with happy thoughts of the weekend ahead. Saturday brought a week's worth of C-SPAN tapes to review, while Sunday, blessed Sunday, brought the Sunday *Times*, *Face the Nation*, *Meet the Press*, and *Firing Line*. There was no more devoted follower of national affairs than Gloria Lipton. If the law was her vocation, then lawmakers were her avocation, and she prided herself on believing she was equally astute in both arenas.

On South Eighteenth Street a man was struggling to unlock his car while balancing a long box under his arm. He looked up from his keys at the sound of Gloria's footsteps, and she nodded a stern greeting at him. He gave a pleasant nod in return, then opened the rear door and laid the box inside.

Roses, Gloria thought as she passed him. How very gallant. And what fine upright posture he had. One seldom encountered good posture these days. Now this—she thought, walking on—was the kind of man a secretary *ought* to be preening for.

The thought of flowers made her think again of Campbell Smith. It was so very strange, the way the girl's photograph had suddenly reminded her of—

A crushing blow struck against the back of her legs, and with a gasp Gloria lurched forward to the pavement. The bones snapped in her wrist as she tried to block her fall, and her forehead cracked hard against the concrete. Dizzily she looked back as the long ellipse of a baseball bat zoomed in toward her. She opened her mouth to scream, but before the sound came out, a mushroom cloud of dank dark pain exploded through her head and silenced her.

She woke sometime later to the sticky weight of pain at the base of her skull. Her eyes fluttered open and she blinked away the heavy fog until she could distinguish above her the ceiling and window of a car. She was lying on her back in the rear seat of a car. She struggled to rise up on her elbows, but the pain in her head seemed to glue her to the upholstery. Then she felt the hands on her thighs and the hot pressure of penetration between her legs, and she gave up the struggle. She understood now. There was nothing to get alarmed about. She was a spinster, not a virgin. If she didn't struggle and she didn't look into his eyes, it would all be over quickly.

But it wasn't what she expected. He didn't grunt and root like a pig on top of her. There was something cold and methodical in the way he moved, and he seemed to be taking no more pleasure in the act than she was, which made her wonder furiously—what was the point? At last she felt the hot spurt and heard his breath expel as if he were as relieved as she that it was over. But of course, it wasn't over, and she braced herself for the next phase, in which she expected to be unceremoniously hurled out onto the sidewalk. She half rose to assist in the effort.

"Lie down," he said softly. "And close your eyes real tight."

Of course that only made them open wide, and just in time to see the cold white flash of the blade before it sliced through her throat.

3

Meredith Winters was watching from across the room when the candidate's wife rejoined the party. She sidled up to him with a bright smile and tucked her arm through his, and he gave her a fond glance as he resumed his remarks. "I like to call it a jobs program," he said. "Trade policy might be the cause, but the shortage of decent jobs is the problem, and that's what we should keep our eye on."

Better he should keep his eye on his wife, Meredith thought. From twenty feet away she could spot all the symptoms of a reluctant political spouse.

"Well, Meredith," Norman Finn was saying beside her, "we're awfully flattered that you're considering doing a race in our little state."

"It's not little to me," she said as Senator Ramsay came up to join them. "Delaware's a statistical microcosm of America. From the wealth and industry of the north to the inner city problems of Wilmington to the poor chicken farmers of the south—why, you have a virtual cross section of the country. Then add the fact that you only have one seat in the House. With the congressional district covering the entire state, it means this campaign has to be run exactly as if it were a Senate race. But since there's no major media market here, every national campaign has to be run as if it were a local one—" She broke off with a silvery laugh. "Why, gentlemen, it's a strategist's dream."

"The lady's done her homework, Ash."

"So I see. So I see."

"I've been studying *your* last election results, Senator," she said. "A very impressive margin. Senator Tauscher's never come close to those kinds of numbers."

"No, you're right," he said, pleased and expansive, and Meredith kept her eyes full on him while he explained why he did so much better than his fellow Delaware senator.

"Because trade policy sounds too far removed from ordinary life," the candidate was saying across the room. "We have to bring it down to a bread and butter issue. We have to put it right up there on the blackboard: these policies have cost America its jobs."

He wasn't bad, Meredith thought. A little too much George Bush preppiness, maybe, but she could work on that, particularly in light of his other attributes. He had an aw-shucks earnestness that still played well in most markets, and he also showed signs of that magical Clintonesque knack of focusing all his attention as he listened, of showing fascination in everything the speaker had to say. And that was the first law of politics: make people think they're important, and they'll return the compliment a thousand times over.

Across the room the candidate was saying, "And here we've got Bill Gates bragging—*bragging*—about the number of software design jobs that are being shipped to India. Where, by the way, the Indian government provides the office space, the electrical power, satellite hookups, and tax exemptions. So a job that paid sixty thousand in Seattle goes to a programmer in Calcutta who's making six thousand. And Gates touts this as a good thing? Good for Microsoft maybe, in the short run. But disastrous for America."

Not bad, Meredith thought again. A billionaire monopolist on the other side of the continent made a pretty good straw man to knock down. She nodded at the Senator as she watched Alexander move to address the old man in the wheelchair again.

When Ramsay was called elsewhere, she hooked Finn's elbow. "Who's that man Doug's talking to?"

"Hmm?" He turned to look. "Oh, that's Jonathan Fletcher. A major contributor and fund-raiser." In case she missed it, he repeated the key word: "Major."

"Ahh."

"He was the one who wanted most to vet Doug's wife. But I gotta say, it looks like she's won him over completely."

Meredith nodded, flabbergasted that any of these people could possibly see the wife as an asset to the campaign. They just didn't get it, they never did when it came to wives. Voters never wanted a candidate's wife to be too smart or ambitious, and this girl had yet a third strike against her: she was sexy. Even in her ridiculous debutante get-up, she was clearly a hot little number, with her cupid's-bow mouth and tousled hair and lush, exaggerated curves. There wasn't enough navy-blue and Arnold Scaasi in the world to tone this one down.

Meredith accepted another canapé and mused on the problem. There was only one solution: pregnancy. The wife would have a hard time looking smart and sexy if she were carrying a good-sized belly on her. Meredith calculated the months. Late February to early November. Perfect, if she could get them started right away.

An agitated woman was fluttering at Finn's elbow. "Oh, hello, Maggie," he said. "Have you met Meredith Winters?"

"No," the woman gasped. "I mean, yes! But I was wondering? Could I have your autograph?"

Meredith did a little feint. "Mine? Oh, well, sure, if you like."

Dutifully she scrawled out her name while the woman gushed: "I read all about you in the *Post*, and oh, it would be such a thrill to work with you on this campaign! I do hope you'll do it!"

"Well, knowing there're people like you involved certainly tips the scales that way."

Though of course there were always people like her—political groupies who volunteered for every menial job there was in hopes of a two minute eye-to-eye with the candidate. Meredith had known a hundred Maggies before, typically insecure women who tried to prove their worth by toiling on issues they didn't understand. Maggie would be the kind of loyalist who deified the Party's candidate and demonized the opposition and never had a clue how little difference there was between them. Meredith knew her type very well. They were the backbone of the Party.

It reminded her of the second law of politics: never underestimate the power of stupid people in large groups.

Ramsay was approaching again, and she scoured her brain for another topic that would let him shine while she continued her surreptitious study of the candidate. It came to her by the time he reached Maggie Heller's side.

"Senator, I see your committee's having another go at that tort reform bill."

"Yes, it was referred to Judiciary last week."

"What's this?" Maggie asked, insinuating herself between them.

"It's a bill to reform product liability laws," Ramsay said. "Limit punitive damages, relieve manufacturers of liability when the product's more than fifteen years old, and so on."

"Oh." Maggie's mouth hung open uncertainly, and her eyes darted nervously to Meredith, who knew she was dying to ask: *Are we for it or against it?*

"You voted in favor the last time, didn't you, Senator?" Meredith asked, ending Maggie's misery.

"Along with almost two-thirds of my colleagues."

"Which wasn't quite enough to override the President's veto, was it?"

"Oh," Maggie said, blinking. "Then why is it coming up again then? Is it different somehow?"

"It's a different Congress," Meredith said. "And that means a whole new ball game." She inclined her head in the direction of the candidate. "Can we assume that Doug Alexander supports tort reform as you do, Senator?"

"Whoa, hold on," he protested mildly. "Like you said, this is a whole new ball game. I'm not even sure how I'm gonna swing next time I'm up at bat. As for Doug"—he gazed proudly across the room—"he's his own man entirely."

Cam kept herself glued to Doug's arm for the balance of the evening, smiling until her jaw trembled at all the expressions of congratulations that she now knew were double-edged. After midnight a few couples cleared a circle on the living room rug and shouted out for dancing, and Cam put on a pretty pout and enticed Doug onto the floor. A smattering of applause sounded as the newlyweds appeared in the center of the room, and the pianist obliged with a ballad, "The Man I Love."

Cam twined her arms around Doug's neck and pressed her cheek against his shoulder, and as they swayed slowly to the lingering rhythms of the song, her thoughts raced a mile a minute. Tonight she was learning what every politician eventually had to—that she could never stop running. She'd won her campaign to marry Doug; this should have been her victory party. But instead it would have to be the kickoff for her next campaign, the one to keep him.

"You look so beautiful tonight," he whispered against her ear as they danced. "Look how tan you still are from St. Bart's. It's like the sun kissed your body."

"Mmm. I think you kissed this body a lot more than the sun did."

Softly, he laughed. "I remember."

Deep folds of satin separated them, but she moved her hips against his, long enough and close enough to feel the stirrings of his response. He cleared his throat and whispered again, hoarsely, "I can't wait to get you home."

No formal announcement was required; her campaign could kick off immediately. She put some mischief in her eyes and rose up on tiptoes to breathe in his ear: "Then don't."

Their separate arrivals to the party necessitated separate departures, and Cam's Honda was brought around first. As soon as she was out of the Ramsays' driveway and around the bend of the road, she pulled over and reached back for her parka. She was shivering so violently that she could barely push her arms into the sleeves, and she was still struggling with the zipper when a flash of headlights washed over the hood of the car and into her eyes. She dimmed her own lights, and as the approaching car did the same, she saw that it was Jesse Lombard in the Ramsays' station wagon.

He slowed to scan her Honda as he passed, and Cam gave him a wave as she scanned his. She was surprised to see that he was alone. When he left the house three hours ago, she assumed he'd come back with Trey in tow. So where was Trey? Still running wild with his friends? Or in a holding cell somewhere? She couldn't believe that the police would keep anyone's son jailed overnight for vandalism, let alone the son of Senator Ashton Ramsay. But maybe there was a protocol to these things. Maybe Jesse had to go back and report Trey's situation, and Ramsay had to pick up the phone himself and call in a few chits or give an IOU or two to gain his release.

Jesse gave her a little salute of recognition and drove on, and Cam finally got the parka zipped and headed for home.

Home was two miles away, in the house that belonged for thirty years to Doug's parents and now belonged to Doug and her, thanks to the deed his mother signed over as their wedding gift. Its vintage was the same as the Ramsays' house, and so was the air of decayed gentility, though the Alexanders' house was a little less genteel and a lot more decayed. It sat on four overgrown acres, and behind it was a scattering of dilapidated outbuildings: a one-car garage, a toolshed, a potting shed, a springhouse, and back in the ruins of the old garden, a crumbling two-story summerhouse they called a folly.

She parked and dashed through the cold to the kitchen door. Inside she shed her coat and turned on the lights on the shabby interior. Little had been done to maintain the house since Doug's father died, and it was furnished only with the odds and ends his mother didn't want in Florida and the few pieces Doug and Cam had brought with them. The best room was Doug's study, and she lit a fire there and switched on the lamp beside the leather sofa. Upstairs in their bedroom she lit another fire and turned down the covers. She kicked off her shoes into the closet, but kept the dress on—a signal that she wasn't ready for bed yet, that they should talk first. Back in the kitchen she put on a pot of coffee for the same purpose, then waited by the window and prepared her case.

She'd have to begin with some concessions: the news was incredibly exciting; she was enormously proud of him; what a thrill it was to be married to a man so honored. But—they were only just married. This was their honeymoon year, and she couldn't bear the idea that they'd be apart so much during the next nine months. And that was only through the election. If he won—*when* he won—and had to go to Washington, she couldn't be a weekend wife like Margo Ramsay. And she couldn't go to Washington with him, either, not at this point in her career, and not in the state of their finances. The house desperately needed work—basic things, like a new roof and windows and plumbing and electrical repairs. Doug's income had foundered these last few years as his firm's fortunes declined, and he was supporting his mother's household, too. As for Cam, her career prospects were uncertain, and she had expenses of her own. Could they really afford for him to take a year off from his practice, and then, when he won, to take the cut in pay that he would have to as a congressman? Not to mention the rent in Washington and the weekly commuting expenses?

The crunch of gravel sounded in the driveway, and a moment later Doug burst through the door and grabbed her and spun her through the kitchen.

"Cam! Isn't it great? Can you believe it?" His fingers were

like icicles on her back, and his mouth was barely warmer as it crushed down over hers.

"Honey!" She laughed and tried to dance free. "You're freezing—let's get you warmed up. I have some hot coffee—"

But he pulled her tighter to him and kissed her again.

"Doug—" She pried at his icy fingers.

"Oh, God, Cam," he groaned and plunged his face into her neck. "Oh, God! What a night!"

His fingers found the zipper at her back, and he pushed the gown down over her hips until she was standing in a puddle of satin wearing nothing but lace panties and thigh-high stockings. His cold hands clamped over her breasts. "Oh, Cam," he said again, his voice gone thick, and he bent his head to grind his mouth against hers.

He was still flying high from the party, she realized, and it would take more than a few breathless protests from her to deflate him. Besides, her conscience tugged at her. It wasn't fair to catch a man by playing sex kitten only to turn into an aloof house cat after he was caught. Later, she decided. They'd talk later.

She made herself go soft and pliant in his arms. A rumble sounded deep in his throat, and he bent and lifted her out of the puddle of her skirts and into his arms. "Honey," she began with a laugh as he headed for the hall, "let me—"

He stopped her with another kiss and carried her up the stairs to their room, where he deposited her on the bed and peeled off his clothes and entered her in one smooth motion.

Cam lay back, astonished at the easy rhythm he found. When she first took him to her bed last fall, he was a shy, fumbling lover, always afraid of hurting her or overstepping his bounds. But now he moved confidently, afraid of nothing, entitled to everything. She supposed the credit was hers. She'd made him the master of her body, and now he believed it.

It was essentially the same thing that the houseful of Party people had done to him tonight.

She opened her eyes and looked bleakly past him to the spiderweb cracks in the plaster ceiling. Not only would it be hard to bring him down from this high, it would be cruel. It wasn't his fault that marriage to her ruled out politics for him. But he was the one who would suffer for it.

She stroked his hair and trailed her lips over his face and neck as he quickened his pace. Although she was numb from the brain down, she paid attention to where he was, and at the right moment let out the cry he was waiting for. He came a moment later with a gasp.

Now, she thought, as they lay together afterward. Now, before he falls asleep. Not here, though. She had to entice him downstairs, she had to pour him a cup of coffee and snuggle beside him in front of the fire. His fingertips were brushing sleepily over her shoulders, he was already fading.

Cam cleared her throat. "Doug, sweetheart . . . ?"

The bedside phone rang in a shrill alarm, and he heaved over and picked it up.

"Yeah?" he mumbled, then—"Margo? What's wrong?" He sat up straight and swung his feet to the floor. "Of course. No, I'll be right there."

Cam rose up on an elbow as he hung up. "What is it? What's wrong?"

"Trey never came home tonight." He turned and gave her a bewildered look. "They think he's been kidnapped."

4

Trey woke with a violent jerk, as if he were falling and it was only the act of waking that saved him. His heart ricocheted inside his chest for a minute until he remembered where he was—on the floor in the back of a van—then he lifted his head and cursed himself. He hadn't meant to sleep; he meant to stay awake and alert and ready to make his break the second he got his chance. But the van was too warm and the engine too loud and lulling. He'd peeled off his coat and balled it up for a pillow and drifted off despite himself.

The van was stopped now; that was what woke him. It was still dark out, and sodium vapor lights shone an eerie amber glow over an empty parking lot. He rose up and looked outside at the plate-glass windows of an all-night restaurant, then inside at the driver's seat, and when he saw it was empty, he lunged for the door, side first, then rear. Both locked.

He slumped back on the floor. What an idiot he was. A five-year-old knew better than to get into a stranger's car, but he jumped right in. He even said, "Thanks, man. I owe you one." To cap it off, he shouted, "Do you know who my father is?" Like, if the guy didn't already have a good enough reason to kidnap him, he had to go and draw him a picture.

Trey flopped over on his side and found himself eye-to-eye with a black nylon duffel bag. He sat up and unzipped it. Inside were socks, underwear, several flannel shirts. No gun or knife or cell phone. But his hands closed around a shaving kit. *Yes.* He tore the zipper open and found the razor. It was only a plastic disposable, but it might come in handy. He popped out the cartridge and tucked it in his shirt pocket before he zipped up the duffel again.

The side door groaned on its track, and Trey scrambled backward so fast that he slammed against the wall.

"Whoa," a voice said with a chuckle. "Take it easy."

It was the man, the kidnapper, and he stood silhouetted in the doorway with his arms braced on either side of the opening, blocking it. "Hungry?" he said.

Trey nodded.

"Come on. We'll talk inside."

Trey started for the door.

"Don't forget your coat. It's cold out."

Trey pulled on his jacket and jumped to the macadam. It was a turnpike rest stop, he realized from the roar of traffic on the highway, and the parking lot lights gave him his first good look at his abductor. He was thirty or forty, and he was wearing a green ski jacket, jeans, and work boots. Nothing ominous there, but he had a day's growth of black beard that made even his smile look menacing. He slid the door shut and took Trey by the arm. He thrust his other hand in his coat pocket, and with a jolt Trey realized that was where the gun was.

PLEASE SEAT YOURSELVES, a sign read as they came through the double glass doors into the restaurant. The place was almost empty. Two lone men were nursing cups of coffee at the counter, and one booth was occupied by a couple, the woman with smeared makeup and the man talking in a loud, slurred voice. One waitress, one cashier, and probably one cook rounded out the crowd.

The man steered him to a booth in the corner, far from the other customers, then dropped Trey's arm and took the seat across from him, where he could keep his gun trained.

The waitress strolled over to their table. "Morning, boys. Ready to order?"

"I am. How 'bout you, Jamie?"

Trey stared at the Formica and didn't answer.

"He's still half asleep. I better order for both of us. Serving breakfast yet?"

"Never stopped."

"We'll have sausage and eggs. Two apiece, over easy. Coffee for me, and a glass of milk for my friend here."

Friend? Trey threw a stricken look up at the waitress.

"Okey-doke. Be right back with your drinks."

Trey followed her retreating back with panicked eyes.

"Listen, Jamie." The man put his elbows on the table and leaned in closer. "Let me explain what's going on here."

"Not Jamie," Trey said in a choked whisper.

The man cocked his head at him, then suddenly seemed to wince. "Sorry. I don't know why—somehow I've just been thinking of you that way. So what is it you go by? Jim?"

"Trey."

"Excuse me?"

"I'm called Trey."

He looked blank. "How come?"

"You figure it out," Trey said darkly.

The waitress returned and set down the coffee and milk, and as she left, Trey sat up straight. "I gotta go," he blurted as the idea came to him. "You know—to the bathroom."

"Sure." The man stood up. "Me, too."

There was the man's hand, on his elbow again. Trey's heart fell as he got to his feet.

At the cash register up front, a gray-haired woman sat counting out bills, snapping each one crisply, her lips moving with the count. Trey eyed her as they rounded the counter, and he lurched to a halt in front of her.

"Lady, you gotta help me!" he cried out. "This guy kidnapped me!"

The hand squeezed tight on his elbow as the cashier looked up. Her eyes darted from Trey to the man then back to Trey again. Slowly she pursed her lips. "Too bad for you," she said as she picked up the stack of bills to start her count over again, "that you're the spittin' image of your daddy."

Trey stared at her.

"Come on," the man said on an expulsion of breath and pushed him on toward the rest rooms.

"Tough age," the cashier called after them.

The man laughed over his shoulder. "Tell me about it."

But he wasn't laughing when they reached the men's room. He swung the door in, and Trey stumbled through and backed away to the far side of the tiled space.

"Jamie—*Trey*." He came toward him. "Listen to me."

Trey looked wildly around him, at the wall of stalls, the wall of urinals, the wall of mirrors over the sinks, the wall of tile pressing against his back. The man came closer, and the mirror caught the two of them in one quick freeze frame like a flash camera.

"I really gotta go!" Trey blurted. He darted into one of the stalls and slid the bolt shut, then leaned back against the door and covered his face with his hands.

"Trey, I'm sorry," the man was saying on the other side of the door. "I never should have grabbed you off the street like that. But I couldn't think of another way, and there wasn't any time for explanations."

"No," Trey said. His face was wet with sweat, and as it trickled through his fingers, the flash image from the mirror started to develop like a Polaroid snapshot in his mind. He could see the dim outline of himself backing away, and of the man closing in after him.

"Listen to me. My name's Steve Patterson and—"

Trey clapped his hands over his ears. "No—stop."

"—I'm your father."

The Polaroid of their faces went sharper and so did the resemblance until it burned like a branding iron through his eyes into his brain. "No!" he screamed. "My father is Ash Ramsay. Senator James Ashton Ramsay, Junior. My name is James Ashton Ramsay the Third, and you can't be my father because I'm not adopted! Because nobody ever told me I was adopted!"

There was a sudden awful silence on the other side of the door.

"So you're nobody to me!" Trey shouted as the sob ripped out of his throat. "Nobody!"

He didn't hear the lock jiggling, and when the door suddenly gave way behind him, he fell back flailing out of the stall. The man caught him and sank with him to the floor, and everything blurred out of focus as Trey's eyes flooded with tears. The man's arms were around him, and Trey wanted to shake free, but all he could do was duck his head and hide his eyes.

"So you're nobody!" he strangled out one more time.

But the man wasn't listening. He was rocking him and saying again and again, "Oh, God, I'm sorry, Jamie. Oh, God, I'm so sorry."

The lights were still blazing at the Ramsay house, but this time it was Jesse Lombard who threw the door open. He looked at Doug and Cam with blank disappointment and shuffled aside to let them in.

"Any news?" Doug asked him.

He shook his head. A muscle was jumping wildly on the left side of his face; Cam remembered hearing that his injuries were exacerbated by stress.

He turned and led them to the back of the house. The detritus of the party was everywhere. Glasses and plates and napkins were strewn about the living room, and the dining room table was still spread with the remains of the buffet. From the looks of the kitchen, the caterers had been sent home before they could clean up.

Cam's guilt bored deeper as she followed. She should have called the Ramsays the moment she recognized Trey in the pack of boys, or she should have done what Doug would have and jumped out of the car and shouted for him to come with her. At a minimum, as Doug said repeatedly during the drive over, she should have told him what she saw the moment she arrived at the party. He was right, of course, though he was wrong about her motive; he thought she'd acted out of some misguided desire to protect Trey. He didn't know her well enough yet to realize that she hoarded information the way a miser hoards gold coins.

The fire in the family sitting room had died to orange embers, and the Ramsays stood at polar ends of the room, staring out of separate windows.

"I'll go outside, look around some more," Jesse said.

"Yeah, you do that," the Senator mumbled.

As Jesse limped away, Margo turned from the window, and the skin stretched tight over her face when she saw Cam. "Oh, Campbell! We didn't mean for you to come, too."

Cam read the subtext: she wasn't family yet, not enough to be in on this.

"Campbell has some information we thought might help," Doug explained and pushed her forward into the room.

"I saw Trey earlier tonight," she said. "When I was driving here. He was with some friends on Martins Mill Road."

"When?" Ramsay said at the same time that his wife cried, "What friends?"

"About eight o'clock. The only other boy I recognized was the one who was here Christmas night. The dark-haired boy?"

"Jason Dunn?" the Senator said.

"That's the one."

Margo's shoulders slumped. "I called Jason already. He hasn't seen Trey since school today."

She reached up and pulled the ivory rod from her topknot, and as her gray hair fell loose to her shoulders, she suddenly looked her age and older. Cam thought how hard it must be to have a child so late in life, to be storing the Flintstones vitamins beside the estrogen supplements in the medicine cabinet, and to have no recollection of the workings of a kid's mind.

"Would it be all right if I called Jason?" Cam asked.

"Honey, Margo already—"

"They were doing something they shouldn't have been," she said abruptly. "I don't think Jason would freely admit anything about his whereabouts tonight."

"What?" Margo said. "What were they doing?"

Ramsay brushed past her and flipped through the telephone book. "Here," he said to Cam, pointing out the number.

The line connected on the second ring.

"Yeah?"

The boy's voice sounded like Trey's, deep-pitched and carefully expressionless, as if the slightest animation might screech it up into soprano again.

"Jason? This is Campbell Alexander. I'm a friend of the Ramsays. Trey never came home tonight, so it's very important that you tell me where you last saw him."

"Hey, I already told his mom. I haven't see him. Not since school."

"Look, Jason. I saw you tonight. Okay?" She turned her back to the Ramsays and lowered her voice. "I know all about the mailboxes, so unless you want me to supply the cops with some names and addresses, you better cut the crap. You got that?"

"Uh—could you hold on a minute?"

Whispers came from the other end of the line. His mother must have come into the room, and he was trying urgently to get her out.

"Okay, look," he said, returning to the line. "We all took off when we heard the police sirens. Trey, he headed back down Martins Mill. There was a guy there in his driveway, and he called out to Trey, 'Get in, hurry up.' Then they took off."

"Who was he? Somebody from school?"

"No way. He was an old dude. You know, middle-aged."

"How do you know it was his driveway?"

"Uh, he was parked in it."

"What was he driving?"

"I don't know—what do you call it? Not a minivan, but like that. You know, like a plumber or something."

"A closed-panel van?"

"I guess."

"What color?"

"I don't remember."

He didn't have to. Cam remembered it herself, the black van pulled over to the side of the road, the man standing beside it with a cell phone in his hand.

"And they drove away together?"

"Yeah. Trey jumped in the back, and they took off down Martins Mill."

Cam braced herself as she hung up and turned to face the Ramsays. She hardly knew what to tell them. All of the awful possibilities swirled through her mind: Trey snared by a sexual predator, or captured by international terrorists, or kidnapped for ransom and thus already dead. Their worst fears realized, and she was the one who could have prevented it.

"There was a man parked in a driveway on Martins Mill Road," she said. "He lured Trey into his van and drove off with him. Jason saw it happen. And I'm afraid I may have seen the same man earlier myself."

She waited for them to collapse, but Margo said nothing, and Ramsay's expression only sharpened. "What did he look like?"

"Mid-thirties. About six feet tall. Dark hair, a little on the long side."

"Did you get a look at his face?"

Cam hesitated, searching for a descriptor, but the ones that came to mind—dark, edgy, unsettling—were not helpful. She nodded.

Ramsay pivoted. "Margo, where's that—"

But his wife was already flying across the room to tear through a drawer in the cabinet against the wall.

"Forgive me, Senator, but shouldn't we—"

"Here," Margo said, and thrust something at her husband, which he then thrust at Cam.

She turned and held it to the lamplight. It was a snapshot of three college boys in red football jerseys, and for a second she wondered if the Ramsays had lost their senses after all. But then she noticed the figure on the right. He was a dozen years younger and he wore an easy and open grin on his face, but there was no doubt he was the man she had seen on the road.

Cam looked up in amazement. "Yes, that's him."

Margo moaned and hugged her arms tight to her ribs, and Ramsay stood contemplating a spot on the floor in front of him. A long moment passed, and Cam sent confused looks at each of the Ramsays in turn and finally at Doug.

"It's him, isn't it?" Doug said heavily. "His father."

"What?" Cam said.

Doug didn't answer her, and Ramsay didn't answer him. He dragged himself to a chair and gripped the armrests to sink down into it.

"You knew this was coming?" Doug said.

"Of course not!" Margo glared at her husband, then stormed to the window and stood with her fists clenched at her sides.

Ramsay lifted his chin from his chest and gazed bleary-eyed at his wife's back. "We've had a few letters," he admitted.

"What's he want? Money?"

"God, no," the Senator said with a bitter laugh. "Nothing so easy as that."

"Isn't it obvious?" Margo cried. "He wants Trey." In a smaller voice she said, "And now he has him."

Cam felt like the stupidest pupil in class. She never realized that Trey was adopted, and even now as she glanced from brother to sister in the room's portraits, she never would have guessed. But slowly the family law lawyer in her awakened, and she said: "It's still a crime. I mean, assuming his parental rights were terminated—"

"They were," Ramsay said.

"Then it's the same as if a stranger kidnapped him. You have to call the police. Or, no—" Curious that she would forget this jurisdictional detail. "The FBI."

"No," Ramsay said. "We can't do that."

Margo whirled from the window. "Ash, what about Ron March? He's the U.S. Attorney. Isn't he in charge of the FBI?"

"Not exactly," Ramsay said. "Not enough. We can't risk it, Margo."

Cam turned to Doug, mystified.

"The scandal," he said to her. "The newspapers would have a field day. Not to mention the opposition."

"Besides—" Ramsay spoke beseechingly to his wife. "It's not like the boy's in any danger. Margo? We know that much. He wouldn't hurt him."

"No," she said finally, tightly. "I suppose not."

"So—" He clasped his hands together. "—we'll keep this to ourselves. Doug?"

"Of course." The two men exchanged a look that Cam had no trouble interpreting. Doug was to ensure her silence.

Ramsay rubbed his eyes, then took both hands and raked his fingers through his hair until it stood out like a mane around his head. Now he really did look like the Lion of New Castle County, although an old and tired one, toothless and declawed.

"We have to deal with this ourselves," he said. "We'll hire somebody, make some inquiries. . . ." His voice trailed off wearily.

"I know who you should hire," Doug said. "She's standing right in front of you."

Cam's jaw dropped.

"Campbell?" Ramsay said.

"It's her specialty. Tracking people."

"Assets," she corrected him, though it was true that one usually led to the other.

"She's done it a hundred times," Doug went on. "She's got access to the best resources. I can open an account for her to log her time against, and no one ever has to be the wiser. It'll never leave this room."

Ramsay looked to Margo, who gave a short, helpless nod. He turned to Cam. "Will you do it, Campbell? I don't have to tell you how much it would mean to us."

Doug was urging her with his eyes, and she could see exactly how much it would mean to him. He wanted to ingratiate himself even more to the Senator, to win not only the love and support he already had, but also his undying gratitude.

But once again it was her guilt that persuaded her. Not only for what she'd already done to the Ramsays, but for what she was about to do to Doug. He didn't know it yet, but his dreams of political glory were soon to end. The least she could do for him was this.

"Of course," she said. "I'll do whatever I can."

The back door opened and Jesse Lombard came into the doorway. Hopeful looks were exchanged all around, but when everyone's head shook sadly, the Senator said, "It's what we thought, Jess."

His broken body went tense. "You want me to . . . ?"

"No. Campbell's going to track him down for us."

"I'll need some information—" she began.

"We'll let you talk," Doug said.

Jesse lingered unhappily in the doorway until Doug clapped a hand on his shoulder and steered him out of the room. As Cam took a chair beside the Senator, she could hear them pitching into the party clean-up in the kitchen, and she thought how wise and sweet it was of Doug—what Jesse needed most was to feel useful.

What she needed most was information, and over the next hour she did her best to extract it from Ash and Margo. They sat side by side on the sagging sofa beneath the family portrait that later became the campaign poster, and Cam couldn't help but see the irony: the little scamp who won Ramsay's last election for him turned out to be somebody else's little scamp.

His name was Steve Patterson, and they'd heard nothing from him or about him since he signed the adoption papers. Until one day out of the blue they got a letter from him. It arrived soon after Ramsay's last reelection, a year ago last November, and was followed by three or four more letters, the most recent during the last Christmas holidays. But they'd destroyed them all—whether out of anger or fear that Trey would discover them, Cam couldn't pin down. Each was handwritten, a page or two long, but they couldn't recall anything Patterson had to say beyond the fact that he wanted his son. The letters each demanded a reply and provided an address, but all they could remember of it now was that it was in Rehoboth Beach, a resort town on Delaware's little stretch of Atlantic coastline.

Cam pressed them for more details about Patterson, but they were too tired or too distraught to dredge up much. He'd been a student at Cornell, though they didn't know if he'd ever graduated. He might have been studying architecture.

"What about Trey's birth mother?" she asked. "Is there any chance he'd be in contact with her?"

Now they looked completely helpless. Perhaps, but they knew even less about her. In fact, they couldn't even remember her name.

* * *

It was almost four o'clock before Cam and Doug were home and in bed again. The fire had died, and the sheets were freezing, and no sooner did their body heat begin to warm them than Cam had to dash out of the covers to set the alarm clock.

"What's that for?" Doug asked, tucking her in again.

"I better get to the office first thing to see what I can find out online about Patterson."

"When do you think you'll be back?"

"Early afternoon?"

"I'll probably still be here in bed."

"Good." She snuggled close to him. "This is just where I want you."

His laugh stirred a soft breeze against her neck.

They nestled down deep in the blankets, and on the edge of sleep, she asked him, "Honey? How come you never mentioned Trey was adopted?"

"I don't know." He yawned and wrapped an arm tighter around her. "I guess that's what marriage is all about, right?"

"What?"

"Discovering each other's secrets."

"Oh." Cam lay wide-eyed as his breathing went deep and slow and even. "Right," she said to the darkness.

5

In the morning, Cam drove thirty miles north to center city Philadelphia. A billboard looked down over the interstate where she crossed the city limits, and every morning since she moved in with Doug it had been asking her the same question: DO YOU HAVE A WOUND THAT WON'T HEAL? FOR TREATMENT OF YOUR CHRONIC WOUND, CALL THE CROZER CENTER FOR WOUND HEALING. The same question, every day.

She parked in a six-dollar all-day lot and walked five blocks south and east. Her building was fifty stories tall and sheathed in reflective glass like a highway cop's sunglasses. This morning it reflected the steeples of the city architecture under clouds that hung low and ominous in the sky.

The usual Saturday security guard was on duty at the lobby console, but today he was flanked by two uniformed cops, and two more cops were stationed by the elevator banks.

"What's going on?" Cam asked.

The guard shrugged and handed her the clipboard with the weekend sign-in sheet. She scribbled her name, and one of the cops spun the clipboard around to read it. "You Campbell Smith?" he said sharply.

"Yes, why?"

"Come with me."

She threw a look to the guard, but he only bugged out his eyes at her.

"What's going on?" she said again as the cop led her into an elevator and pushed the button for the fiftieth floor.

"Lieutenant Thaddeus wants to see you."

"Why? Who's he?"

He didn't answer.

The doors opened on the fiftieth floor, and the cop waved her out and down the hall toward the executive wing of the offices. Two men stood in the corridor outside Clifford Austin's office. One of them was another uniformed cop, the other a broad-shouldered black man in a tight-fitting suit.

The cop beside her called down the hall, "I got Campbell Smith here, Lieutenant."

The man in the suit turned and stared at her. He had a thrusting jaw, a receding hairline, and watchful eyes. "Lieutenant Thaddeus," he said, not offering his hand. "You Miss Smith?"

"Yes, why?"

He jerked his chin at the uniformed cops, a signal to leave.

"What's this all about?"

He turned and studied her a moment before he spoke. "One of your coworkers was killed last night."

Her breath caught. "Oh, no—who?"

"Gloria Lipton."

The name meant nothing to her. She started to shake her head, but suddenly remembered where she was. "Oh, God—is that Cliff Austin's secretary?"

"That's right."

She looked over the cubicle walls of the secretarial station. Everything on the desk was in order: a dust-free keyboard and monitor, and a neat lineup of stapler, scissors, tape dispenser, and message pads. Black-and-white photographs were mounted to the desk surround, all political vanity shots of people posing with Lyndon Johnson and Gerald Ford and a very boyish Ted Kennedy. The same young woman appeared in each, wearing a pillbox hat, a prim suit, and a nervous smile. Now Cam could put a face to the name. Gloria Lipton.

Thaddeus walked around to stand beside the desk. "Do you recall what time you last saw her yesterday?"

Cam frowned. "I don't recall that I saw her at all yesterday."

He stared at her, then pulled a three-ring binder forward on the desk. It was the firm's directory of lawyers, a slick compilation of photos and bios that was occasionally exploited for marketing purposes but was really designed so that the lawyers could identify one another. Cam leaned over the cubicle to see what he was pointing out, and realized halfway down that the page was turned to her own photo. Stuck beside it was a little yellow Post-it marked with a big red question mark.

She looked up in confusion.

He pointed again, this time to Gloria's computer monitor. Another Post-it was stuck to the screen. It read: *Campbell Smith.*

"I can't think why—" she said.

"Try."

Her stomach lurched. "I—I don't know. I didn't know her. I can't imagine—"

"Campbell? What are you doing here?"

She spun around with a guilty start. Behind her stood Clifford Austin, the chairman of Jackson, Rieders & Clark. He was a man of sixty with a high domed forehead and a stiff, formal air. Even now, on a Saturday morning, he was wearing a three-piece suit with a gold watch chain strung across his vest.

"I—I don't know," she stammered, pushing her hair out of her face with a flustered hand. "Your secretary had my name posted on her desk. I can't explain—"

Austin gave an imperious look to Thaddeus, who obligingly showed him the directory and the two Post-its.

"Well, I can," he said peevishly. "Yesterday I heard the news about Campbell's marriage, and I asked Gloria to send her some flowers on behalf of the firm. Obviously she looked her up in the directory and jotted herself a reminder."

Cam felt a warm flow of relief and darted a quick glance at Thaddeus to see if it was justified. At his abrupt dismissive nod, she turned and hurried for the elevator.

Too close, she thought, her heart hammering as the doors snapped shut. It was only an innocent inquiry in a routine investigation, but it was too close.

She sank down to the forty-sixth floor, where the family law department was housed. Though *antifamily law* was how she thought of it—a more accurate term, she felt, for the state-sanctioned rupture of husband and wife and parent and child. She never meant to specialize in it, but the firm's prestige departments—litigation, tax, corporate finance—required associates to compete for openings. She chose not to, and ended up in antifamily law by default.

She opened the door on her ten-by-ten-foot office, threw her coat on a chair, and sat down behind her desk. Her hands were still trembling from the encounter upstairs, and she picked up a pencil and twirled it while she willed herself to calm down. A bookcase stood against the opposite wall, and on its center shelf was a photo of Doug. His smile touched her from across the room, and slowly she smiled back until she felt herself begin to relax. Gloria Lipton meant nothing to her, but Doug meant everything, and if she wanted to keep him, she knew she'd better focus on what she'd come here for: Steve Patterson.

She began with the lowest-tech approach and dialed directory assistance. The name was a common one, but Rehoboth Beach had a small year-round population, and she was given only three listings: for Stephen, Steven, and S. The last was almost certainly a woman, so she dialed it first and asked for Steve. "You got the wrong number," came the expected female reply.

Next she tried Stephen, and asked for Steve.

"Hi, Mr. Patterson," she said to the man who came to the phone. "My name's Camille Smith, and I'm with the Cornell University Treasurer's Office?"

"Not interested—"

"No—wait. We've just completed an audit that shows you're entitled to a tuition refund of five thousand dollars."

"Oh?" The man's voice rose half an octave.

"If you could confirm the years you matriculated here?"

"Umm. I guess it was 1992 to 1996?"

Not a bad guess, but not her man. She hung up and dialed Steven. A recording answered: "We're sorry. The number you have dialed is no longer in service. Please check the number and try again."

Time now to go high-tech. She turned to her computer and loaded a CD-ROM that contained the current reverse telephone directory for Delaware. The number yielded a listing for Steven A. Patterson, and a street address of 132 Lake Drive, Rehoboth Beach. She checked the directory for the previous year and found the same listing, but there was nothing for the year before that. Next she logged online, entered her password, and was admitted into a database service, one of several the firm subscribed to. This one compiled information from tens of thousands of credit bureaus, insurance companies, motor vehicle departments, and courthouse recorders. Cam ordered a search for *Steven A. Patterson, 132 Lake Drive, Rehoboth Beach, Delaware.* If he ever used that address to register a car or to make an insurance claim or even to buy a dog license, the database should have captured him.

It had. In five minutes she had a printout showing Patterson's date of birth, April 3, 1964; his Social Security number; a

Delaware registration for a 1995 Ford Explorer; and a checking account at PrimeTrust Bank.

Cam called directory assistance again, this time for PrimeTrust Bank, then dialed its Dover branch.

"Hello, this is Camille Smith calling from D'Alessandro Plymouth Dodge. I'd like to verify funds please?" She gave Patterson's name and account number and decided he was paying two thousand down on a used car.

"I'm sorry," the clerk said. "That account has been closed."

"When?"

There was another clatter of keys. "The seventeenth."

Last Tuesday. She hung up. The bank account closed and the phone disconnected—this obviously wasn't an impulse kidnapping. She went back online and searched the real estate records for 132 Lake Drive. After a minute the answer flashed on the monitor. The record owners: George and Marcia Westover, with a permanent address on Rittenhouse Square in Philadelphia. About six blocks from where she sat.

Cam was so surprised by the coincidence that she immediately looked up their number and dialed it.

"George Westover, please?" she said when a man answered.

"Speaking."

"This is Camille Smith from PrimeTrust Bank of Delaware—"

"Sorry, not interested."

She frowned at the buzzing phone in her hand. Telemarketers were ruining investigative work; it was becoming harder and harder to get anywhere with pretext calls. She dialed again.

"Hello?"

"Please don't hang up. I'm calling about Steve Patterson."

There was a beat of silence. "Who did you say you were?"

"Camille Smith, PrimeTrust Bank. Mr. Patterson had an account here until last Tuesday."

"What about it?"

"We discovered a posting error that resulted in an unremitted balance in the account. But he neglected to leave a forwarding address. We thought perhaps he gave you his new address . . . ?"

"Where did you get my name?"

"Mr. Patterson listed you as a reference when he opened the account."

A short unpleasant laugh sounded over the line. "Look, young lady, Miss—Smith, was it? I started my career in banking operations thirty years ago, and I never heard of any financial institution that requires a personal reference to open a checking account. Nor have I ever heard of a bank making any effort to trace the owner of an abandoned account after only five days, and certainly not by personal telephone call on a Saturday. So why don't you drop the pretense and tell me what this is really about?"

Cam was glad he was so bombastic; it gave her time to come up with a new cover story. She considered the jilted lover routine, performed with a breathless little choke in her voice, but George Westover struck her as too flinty a character to care very much if her heart were broken. Better to skate a little closer to the truth.

"I apologize, Mr. Westover. My name is Campbell Alexander, and I'm an attorney with the firm of Jackson, Rieders and Clark. Mr. Patterson may be an important witness in a matter I'm handling, and I need to discuss it with him urgently."

"What matter?"

"I'm sorry, I'm not free to discuss it."

"Well, I'm not free to give out his address. Even if I had it, which I don't. However, if you care to leave your number, and if Steve happens to call, I'll relay the message."

There seemed little point in withholding her number at this point. She recited it and added her car and home numbers for good measure.

"Mr. Westover, I hope you'll impress upon Mr. Patterson the urgency of this matter," she said, hoping to impress upon Westover that he should call Patterson sooner rather than later.

"What I intend to impress upon him, young lady, if and when I hear from him, is that you engaged in a cheap ruse and that he should feel no obligation whatsoever to deal with you. However, as Steve is one of the most honorable men I've had the privilege to know, I expect he'll follow his own good judgment on the subject."

He was scolding her, he wanted her to feel ashamed, but all he succeeded in doing was arousing her curiosity. "Mr. Westover, I have to confess—I've never known a landlord to be so supportive of a tenant."

"Landlord?" He hooted. "Young lady, you haven't done your homework at all."

He hung up, and Cam immediately ran a new database search.

Five minutes later she did feel ashamed. George Westover was a senior vice-president of Bradley & Hunsinger, the biggest investment banking firm in Philadelphia. If she'd known that, if she'd stopped for two minutes to check him out before she called, she never would have used the bank clerk pretext on him.

She let her head fall back and spun around in her chair in disgust. She never acted on impulse, not since she was fifteen years old, but she'd called Westover on little more than a whim and ruined any chance of getting information from him. The odds of Patterson returning the call were nil. Even if Westover relayed the message, and even if Patterson fell for her cover story, he was too busy kidnapping Trey to return phone calls. And if he figured out the Ramsay connection, she'd be the last person he'd want to talk to.

She drummed her fingers on the desk for a moment, then leaned forward and entered another search on the computer. *Abigail Zodtner Johnson,* she typed, along with every permutation of the name she could imagine. Date of birth: *09/12/47*. Social Security number: *199-56-1039*.

It was a search she slipped in almost every time she had the database open, as a test of faith perhaps, or of the comprehensiveness of the database service. But today, as always, the test was failed. The search results came back: *Not found*.

A knock sounded on the door, and Cam sat up straight and tense. "Yes?"

The door opened to reveal Clifford Austin on her threshold. "A moment, Campbell?"

"Oh—of course," she said, scrambling to her feet. Austin was the chairman of a 250-lawyer firm; he seldom dropped in on lowly fourth-year associates. She scooped an armful of papers from a chair, then retreated behind her desk.

"I wanted to apologize for that episode upstairs," he said, sitting down rigidly across from her. "Are you all right? You looked a bit shaken."

"Oh—it was just the news about Gloria. I mean, how awful."

He gave a grim nod.

"Do they know what happened?"

"Her body was found in a stairwell on Twenty-second Street near Pine. Apparently she'd been sexually assaulted, and her throat"—he paused to clear his own—"was slit."

"Do they have any idea who . . . ?"

He shook his head. "There were no witnesses, and there's no trace of the murder weapon. And no fingerprints. It seems they do have DNA and some sort of fibers. But with no suspect to match those things against . . ."

His voice trailed off as her phone rang. She pressed a button to route the call to voice mail, but still his silence persisted. Cam felt a growing anxiety. Cliff Austin didn't pay social calls on associates, and she didn't believe that he simply wanted to share the grisly details of Gloria's murder.

He shifted his weight in the chair. "I did wish to offer my best wishes on your marriage, Campbell. I offered my congratulations to Doug as soon as I heard the news yesterday. A most auspicious match, I'm sure."

Now she understood. Jackson, Rieders & Clark had an anti-nepotism rule that prohibited the employment of lawyers who were related by blood or marriage to any of the firm's partners. The idea was to prevent factions and favoritism and the rise of mini-dynasties within the firm; it was known as the Malloy rule, in honor of a former partner who'd had eight sons. Austin was here to make sure she comprehended that the rule applied to her even though her employment predated Doug's partnership.

"Thank you, Cliff," she said warmly, relieved that this was the extent of his mission. "I'm only sorry that I'll have to be leaving the firm. Is it sixty days or ninety?"

But he waved his hand in the air. "Don't even think about leaving us, Campbell. Now, more than ever, we regard you as a valuable asset."

Puzzled, she said, "But the rule—"

"You'll be the exception."

With a cold-lipped smile, Austin pushed to his feet and left Cam staring in bewilderment long after he closed the door and was gone.

The red light was blinking on her phone, and she finally stirred as she remembered the call she'd routed to voice mail. She dialed in for the message.

"Hi, sorry I missed you." Doug's warm voice flowed like a balm into her brain. "Listen, Owen Willoughby just called to invite me to lunch down at the Green Room, and I'll probably stop by the office afterward, so don't hurry home on my account, okay? And be careful on the roads. They're calling for snow later. I love you."

Owen Willoughby was a lawyer, and the Green Room was a popular Wilmington restaurant, so for five or six seconds Cam let herself believe it was nothing more than a lawyers' lunch. But Willoughby was also a Party leader, and the Green Room was in the lobby of the Hotel DuPont, where Meredith Winters was residing for the weekend.

Cam called home, but she was too late; Doug had already gone.

She stared at her desk a while, at Steve Patterson's credit report and the property owner's report for 132 Lake Drive, then swiveled her chair around and gazed out at the southern sky. There was still no sign of snow, and it was only twelve o'clock. She could make it to Rehoboth Beach and be home in time for a quiet supper with Doug, followed at last, she hoped, by a little fireside conversation.

She grabbed her parka and headed for the elevator.

Trey was staring feverishly at the passing roadside along the interstate. *Okay, so he was adopted, so what? He probably halfway knew it anyway. And it explained a lot, like why he had the oldest parents in the universe and why they waited twenty years between kids and why the old man looked at him sometimes like he was the neighbor's kid who forgot to go home. So okay, he was cool with all that. Big deal anyway, right?*

What was harder going down was the idea that this guy beside him, the one wearing jeans and Ray•Bans who was young and tough and even kind of cool, that this guy was his father and thought he could just show up one day and say, hey, you're mine, hop in, we're going home.

That was the part that was sticking in Trey's throat and making his eyes burn.

He was up front now, passenger side, strapped in and buckled up by this guy Steve—*who had a father named Steve?*—like he didn't know how to do it himself just because he sat there a couple minutes without moving. He rode with his face to the window and his body twisted so far in his seat that the webbing of the shoulder harness sliced into his throat.

"Feel like talking?" Steve asked for the third time.

Trey didn't answer, which should have been answer enough.

So far they'd traveled the length of the New Jersey Turnpike, looped around New York, and shot across most of Connecticut until they hung a left for Massachusetts. They were heading into their fifth hour of silence when the snow started to fall. Steve reached for the radio again and picked up a local newscast with a weather guy droning on that the storm center was over the Berkshires and heading south.

"Looks like we'll pass right through it," Steve said, and when again Trey said nothing, he returned to the radio and blipped through several frequencies until he landed on some rock music. Steve liked to surf the stations the same way he did, which didn't help, and sometimes he'd even hum along or sing little snatches of Smashmouth or the Beastie Boys, which nobody's father was supposed to do. Trey shifted sideways in his seat, but only long enough to send him a scathing look before he turned back to the window.

"I'm sorry," Steve said for the ninth or tenth time. "I never thought— If I'd known, I never would have—"

He was still apologizing for the wrong thing, the part that wasn't his fault instead of the part that was.

Toward noon he took an exit off the interstate and a right at the stoplight at the base of the ramp and headed into a zone of gas stations and minimalls. They were stopping for lunch, Trey supposed, and he decided to say he wasn't hungry, though in truth he was starving. They never did get around to eating breakfast that morning, and he never exactly had dinner the night before either, only a bag of chips at Jason's and a couple tacos from the 7-Eleven. But no, he wasn't going to eat with this guy; he wouldn't give him the satisfaction.

Ahead on the right he could see a group of dark figures milling around against the white of the snow, and as they came closer he realized it was a bunch of kids playing hockey on a frozen pond. It was Saturday, he remembered; he could have been playing hockey himself, except that the ice never froze thick enough in Delaware to skate outside, which meant you had to have rink time, which meant you had to be in a league, and he'd dropped out of Peewee hockey a couple years ago, right after the father-son banquet. The old man never made it to the games, but he said he wouldn't miss the banquet, and at the last minute he even pulled some strings to get it rescheduled to better suit his calendar. He hadn't been home yet when it was time to go, so Jesse drove Trey to the restaurant by himself and said he'd bring the Senator straight from the train station. Trey had eaten his dinner next to an empty chair, watching the door and waiting while he avoided a roomful of resentful glances. The old man never showed.

But neither did this guy, Trey thought, darting him a look. *The old man at least had an excuse. What was this guy's?*

They drove past half a dozen fast food places, and when they finally turned, it wasn't into a restaurant at all. It was a Hertz rental lot.

"I thought we'd trade in our wheels," Steve said, shutting off the engine. "What's your favorite car? Some kind of sports coupe?"

Trey didn't answer. He wasn't going to give him that satisfaction either.

"Well, I'll see what they got." He opened his door. "Won't be long."

He swung out of the van and through the door of the rental office, and he was gone a full minute before Trey realized what just happened here.

In a flash he was out of the van and across four lanes of highway and galloping over a field to a patch of woods beyond. The snow was falling hard and steady. It wouldn't be long before his tracks were filled in, and Steve wouldn't have a clue where he'd gone. He'd head—where? Not home, not now, but somewhere. Maybe Boston. Or New York. Yeah, New York, the biggest city on the planet. He could get lost forever in a place like that.

His jacket was unzipped, and the snow was blowing inside around his ribs and up into his sleeves, but he couldn't stop to zip it now, especially not now, because now he could hear Steve yelling behind him.

It was only another hundred feet to the woods, but it was hard to run in this snow. It was a different kind of snow from the hard, crunchy stuff in Delaware. This snow was like a fine powder that went all slick under the soles of his Nikes. He had to slow up to keep his traction, but it was still okay, he had a huge lead, and besides, no thirteen-year-old guy had a father who could outrun him.

"Jamie! Come on, wait! Please!"

The shouts sounded right behind him, and in the next instant the world inverted and Trey was facedown in the snow.

It was no use trying to fight—Steve had him pinned, and the wave of hopelessness that rose up inside him hit him harder than the tackle. The air left his lungs in a whoosh of defeat, and he lay there not moving, barely breathing, until Steve rolled him over onto his back.

"Jeez," he said, panting hard. "I haven't run—that hard—since college. Let me—get my breath here a minute." He flopped alongside him in the snow and leaned back on his elbows. He sucked in a few big breaths before he spoke again. "You got—friends in Worcester or something?"

Trey looked at him.

"I mean—where'd you think you were going to go?"

"Anywhere," Trey spat out. "Away from you."

Steve recoiled a little, then tried to recover with a laugh, like it was all only a joke. "What, and abandon me here?"

"Why not?" Trey said with a sneer. "You did it to me."

Steve's breath sucked in again, with a different sound this time. "God, Jamie—*Trey*. Is that what you think? That I abandoned you?"

Trey stared up at the sky, and felt the snow soaking into his back and legs.

"Look at me," Steve said, and when Trey didn't, he took him by the chin and forced him to. "Listen to me. I never wanted to give you up. They *stole* you from me. And it took me thirteen years to find you."

Trey stared at him. The snow was melting fast beneath him. It made him feel like he was sinking in a tub of ice water.

"No shit?" he said finally.

"Swear to God."

The world inverted yet again, and all he could think to say was, "Oh."

"Come on." Steve got to his feet and pulled Trey up after him. "Let's find a motel and get you a hot shower and something to eat."

"Pizza?"

"You got it," Steve said.

6

Rehoboth Beach was a seaside resort a hundred miles south of Wilmington. It lay on a pine-forested headland that stretched out into the Atlantic between Delaware Bay to the north and Rehoboth Bay to the south. Though it could never rival the Jersey shore as the favored vacation spot for Philadelphians, it was popular enough that on a Friday afternoon in August, the trip was a long crawl. But on a Saturday afternoon in February, Cam was able to keep the needle close to sixty almost all the way there. She stopped only once, at a florist shop in Dover, where she bought a thirty-dollar arrangement of stargazer lilies. By two-thirty she was turning off Route 1 and heading for the ocean.

The sky hung low, the color of dingy sheets hanging on the line in a coal town, and when the ocean appeared in fleeting glimpses ahead, it was the same dull gray as the sky. The wind was roaring in, and it lashed the water into foamy white swells that crested and crashed against the gray sand beach.

Both sides of Rehoboth Avenue were lined with shops and restaurants, some of them boarded up and all of them closed for the season. It was a summer resort in winter hibernation, and like all things in hibernation, it seemed lifeless. Cam's Honda was the only car on the street, and there wasn't a pedestrian in sight. But a glow of lights appeared in a storefront window ahead, and when Cam saw the realtor's sign, she pulled over into the parking space in front of it. The wind tore at her coat and howled at her ears as she got out of the car, and somewhere down the street a loose shutter was banging disconsolately against a window. A cold hard rain began to spit, and she flipped up her hood and ran for the office.

"Hello?" a woman's voice called from the back. "I'll be right with you."

"Take your time," Cam called back.

She scanned the rack of brochures on the wall, and when she spotted a local street map, she grabbed it and dashed back outside. The realtor's face appeared at the window as Cam ducked into the car, but she ignored her and settled in behind the wheel to study the map. Two minutes later she backed out of the space and left the woman wondering.

The rain began to streak the windshield, and she switched on the wipers and drove south, through a neighborhood of tree-lined streets and modest little houses that rented for three thousand a week from Memorial Day to Labor Day then sat empty for the rest of the year. The road took a curve, and as Silver Lake appeared ahead, all modesty disappeared. Here the houses were big and lavishly appointed, a few with docks and gazebos perched at the edge of a tidewater basin. A road looped around the lake; the sign said Lake Drive.

This was the last place Cam would have looked for Steve Patterson. She'd pictured him first in a battered fishing shack on the bay; after she uncovered the Westover connection, she'd upgraded him in her mind to an ocean-block condo. But she never imagined him on a street like this.

The road took her over a narrow strip of land between the ocean and the lake, and the street numbers rolled past—82, 88, 106—until an enormous oceanfront house loomed ahead. It was a Shingle Style house three stories high, and newly constructed, judging from the unweathered cedar-shake siding. A deep veranda made a bold sweep around the house, and all of it was trimmed out in gleaming white columns and rails.

Cam knew nothing about architecture, and until this moment cared less, but suddenly she thought this must be the most beautiful house in the world. She could barely pull her eyes from it as she drove past, and she was three houses away before she read another mailbox number and realized she'd passed 132. She swung a U-turn and paid closer attention on the return trip. When the Shingle Style house approached this time, she kept her eyes on the mailbox. The number was 132.

She cut a sharp turn into the driveway and sat gazing at the house until a hard gust of wind blew up off the ocean and made the Honda shudder on its axles. She picked up the floral arrangement from the seat beside her, tucked it inside her coat, then dashed out of the car and up the broad steps to the entrance portico.

The wind stilled when she reached the lee of the house, and she brought out the flowers and held them carefully in front of her as she rang the doorbell. No one answered, and she rang a second time, then peered in through the sidelight. A barrel-vaulted ceiling rose up eighteen or twenty feet, and a long expanse of shimmering hardwood floor stretched ahead until it reached a wall of French doors overlooking the ocean. The space was open as far as she could see. It was also empty. No people, no furniture, no signs of life at all. The house looked as if it had never been occupied.

She rang the bell again and called out a perky "Hello! Flower delivery!"

Still no answer. She tried the knob—locked—then ran out to the street and opened the mailbox. Empty. She returned to the house and followed the veranda around its perimeter, stopping to peer in all the windows as she went, but everywhere it was the same. Spectacular and empty. She came around the corner on the ocean side and had to turn and crouch against the battering of the wind as it swept in off the sea. A two-story glass semicircle curved out from the main block of the house on this side. Upstairs it probably was a wing of the master suite; on this level Cam guessed that it was a breakfast room. It was a dazzling space, with windows from floor to ceiling like an English conservatory—a beautiful, gracious room in a beautiful, gracious house. For a second she tried to picture herself in this room, drinking early morning coffee while she watched the sun rise over the Atlantic. It was quite a leap of imagination for a girl who grew up in a house trailer behind a highway filling station, and after a moment she moved on.

The next room was the kitchen, and here she could see a few signs of life: a pair of stools pulled up to a granite-topped center island, a coffee maker plugged in on the countertop, and a note pinned to the refrigerator with a magnet. She squinted through the glass, but the writing on the note was too small to read from where she stood.

She continued down the oceanfront wall of French doors until she reached another barrel-vaulted space. This one had a massive stone fireplace, and a futon mattress lay on the floor by the hearth. Against the wall stood a computer desk and hutch, though there was no sign of a computer. Cam rattled all the knobs here, too, but the whole row of doors was locked up tight.

She flopped back against the cedar shakes and let the wind sting her face. This was clearly a job for the authorities. The police could put out an APB on Patterson's Ford Explorer; they could break down these doors and read the refrigerator note and search the house for other leads. Two easy routes, both closed to her.

It still made no sense to her, that the Ramsays wouldn't call the FBI. A strange man snatched their son off the street in the dead of night. The fact that he was the boy's biological father was irrelevant. They didn't know him, and they didn't know whether he was sick or violent or mercenary. And so what if there were a news leak? The press couldn't be anything but sympathetic to them under the circumstances.

There was a second's lull in the wind, long enough for Cam to hear a car out on the street. She peeked around the corner of the house and saw a silver Mercedes coupe turn into the driveway of the place next door. She put the flowers down on the floor of the veranda and ran out into the rain. A second later she came back and tore off her parka and tucked it out of sight, too.

"Hello? Excuse me?" she called as she dashed across the dunes to the neighboring house.

A man was lifting a bag of groceries out of his trunk, and he turned as Cam arrived shivering and breathless in his driveway.

"Please ex-excuse me," she panted. "I'm Cammy Smith, the Westovers' new tenant next door? And I can't *believe* I did this, but I just locked myself out of the house."

He was a distinguished-looking man in his forties or fifties, with gentle eyes and a brush of silver at each temple. "Oh, too bad," he said. "And on a day like this! You better come on in out of the weather."

He led her up the steps and opened the door into another grand beach house. This one was Mediterranean in style, done in stucco walls and glazed tile floors. The air inside was fragrant with garlic and basil.

"Oh, no, please." She hesitated on the threshold. "I don't want to intrude. I was only hoping maybe the Westovers left a spare key with you . . . ?"

"Gary?" came a voice from down the hall. "Did you remember the portobellos?"

A younger man turned the corner and pulled up short when he saw Cam. "Oh—hi!" he said. His sleek young body was shown off to good advantage in a tight white tank top and jeans, and he wore a red shirt tied around his waist like the back half of a breechcloth.

The older man closed the door. "Derek, this is—"

"Cammy Smith," she said. "Please forgive me for barging in on you. I'm renting from the Westovers next door, and I was just unloading my car when the wind banged the door behind me and I locked myself out."

"Bummer!" the young man said.

"I was wondering if George and Marcia might have left an extra key with you for safekeeping?"

"Sorry," said the older man, Gary, as he shifted the bag of groceries into Derek's arms. "We don't really know them that well."

"Oh." She bit her lip. "I can't believe what a klutz I am. Though the way things have been going"—she raked a hand miserably through her rain-streaked hair—"it's about par for the course."

"Why don't you come and sit by the fire a minute?" Gary said. "You can dry off at least."

"And how 'bout a nice hot cup of tea?" Derek said.

"That would be wonderful."

"Go on in and sit down. I'll be just a sec."

Derek turned a corner to the right, and Gary took her ahead to the living room. A fire burned brightly on a hearth of terra-cotta tiles, and a wall of glass opened onto the ocean. Gary sat down on a suede love seat and crossed his legs. "Did you come very far?"

"Mmm." Cam perched on the edge of a chair that was positioned to capture the view. "From Philadelphia."

"Unusual time to be renting a beach house."

"Yeah, well—" She gave an unhappy shrug. "I really need to be alone for a while, and George—he's a friend of my father's?—he thought it might do me some good to spend a couple of months here."

Derek came into the room with two steaming mugs, and his

eyebrows shot up as he heard the last of her remarks. "Sounds like man trouble."

She laughed. "That obvious, huh? I guess I must look like the walking wounded."

"You look fine." He handed her a mug. "Here you go—Cammy, is it?" She nodded, and he settled onto the love seat beside Gary. "It's just that, believe me, I know all the signs."

She lifted the mug to her lips. "I'm lucky the house is even available. I mean, I guess the last tenant just left?"

They looked at each other. "I wasn't aware they ever rented that house out," Gary said.

"Oh." She took a sip while she regrouped. "I thought George mentioned someone—Patterson, was it?"

"Oh, you mean Steve!" Derek turned to Gary. "You know—the architect."

"Oh, yes, the guy who remodeled the place."

Cam's head swiveled to the window, and she looked across the undulating dunes at the Shingle Style house. It wasn't new, then, merely timeless, and somehow she felt its beauty even more.

"But I can see where you'd think he was a tenant," Derek said. "He lived there the whole time he worked on the place, and gosh, it must have been a year or so."

"Wow," she said. "Some remodeling job."

"It was pretty extensive," Gary said. "He probably spent the first three months just drawing up the plans."

"But you know the amazing part?" Derek said. "He did a huge amount of the construction himself. Hands on."

"That is amazing."

"A very talented guy. And really, really nice."

Cam did a mental double-take at the way he said that. It suddenly occurred to her that Steve Patterson might also be gay. If so, it would explain a lot—his willingness to sign away a baby who was obviously a mistake; his long-term residence in a popular gay resort town; perhaps even George Westover's fierce loyalty to him.

Gary turned to Derek with one brow raised. "When did you two get so well acquainted?"

"When you were in Washington," Derek said peevishly. "And I was here alone all week. What do you think?"

Gary laughed and laid a placating hand on Derek's knee.

"What is it you do in Washington?" Cam asked.

"Oh, I'm afraid I'm the lowest form of life."

"A lawyer?"

"No, you have to go lower still, even below politician."

"Oh. You're a lobbyist."

"Smart girl," he said with a good-natured smile.

Cam drained her cup and put it down on a marble coaster. "I guess I'll do all right here," she said to Derek. "I mean if you don't mind living alone during the week, and the architect didn't mind living alone next door—"

"Oh, Steve wasn't alone. His girlfriend was there, too. What was her name? Beth maybe?"

First hypothesis swiftly disproved. Cam turned again to the window. "He sure did a bang-up job on the house. I only wish I could get inside to enjoy it."

"Sorry we can't help you there," Gary said. "But you're welcome to use the phone."

"Thanks. I better call the Westovers."

They pointed her to a phone in the hallway, and she dialed her own voice mail number at the office and played out a chagrined confession of her ineptness and a plea for rescue. "Oh, thanks," she said to the silence. "I'll see you there in about two hours."

The two men were on their feet in the doorway when she hung up. "George is meeting me in Wilmington with another key," she said, heading for the door. "Thanks so much. You've been awfully kind."

They saw her to the door, and she ran down the stairs into the cold drizzle. Halfway to the Westover house, she turned back to wave goodbye, but the door was safely closed. Nonetheless she circled the house and went up on the far side of the veranda to retrieve her parka. But she left the flowers where they were, her own small tribute to the beauty of the house.

Before she left town, she stopped at the library and spent fifteen minutes with the local yellow pages, then another thirty on the car phone with every building supply house in a fifty-mile radius until she found three that had traded with Steve Patterson. She was Camille Smith again, credit manager for All-State Appliances, and had received an NSF check from Mr. Patterson. She was sure it was an honest mistake that he could quickly clear up, but she didn't have a current address or phone number?

Neither did they, and they all reported that he'd satisfactorily cleared his accounts with them.

Cam stared through the windshield as the rain started to change over to sleet. She'd learned so much, yet knew so little. She knew where Patterson had lived for the past year or two, and she knew why. She knew that he created structures of amazing beauty, of his own design and largely with his own hands. She knew he was liked and admired by stodgy old investment bankers and hip young gay men alike. She knew he had a girlfriend and she knew he had a son. She just couldn't figure out where he'd taken them.

Them? She sat up straight behind the wheel as it suddenly came to her that the woman who was Patterson's partner on the futon might also be his partner on the road.

Cam had a credo in investigations like this one, which roughly came down to four words: *go after the woman*. The men she tracked usually did a good job of concealing their trails, but nine times out of ten their wives or girlfriends dropped a few bread crumbs to mark the way back. There was a famous case in Philadelphia in the Eighties: a yuppie drug dealer skipped bail with his wife and child and swept his trail so clean that a year-long, coast-to-coast manhunt came up empty. But his wife couldn't sever the home ties so easily. She wrote often to her mother, and though she carefully followed her husband's mail drop instructions, she wasn't so careful about what she wrote. One of her letters, intercepted by the FBI, described her child's birthday party at a chain restaurant which was then in only a handful of markets in the country. The FBI narrowed their search to those markets, and within weeks they had their man.

Steve Patterson might have swept his trail clean, Cam thought, but there was a chance that his girlfriend left a crumb or two behind.

Her first task was to figure out who she was. Beth maybe, Derek said. Beth Maybe. Almost at once another possibility struck her. She grabbed some quarters and ran through the sleet to a phone booth on the corner and dialed the Ramsays' number on the land line. Jesse Lombard answered, and as he announced her name, she heard the Senator direct the call to his library. A minute later he picked up.

"Campbell?" he said in his big booming voice.

"Hello, Senator. Any word on your end?"

"No." His voice quickly deflated. "I suppose that means you haven't had any luck."

"Not much." She gave him a one minute update, then said, "Senator, unless you've changed your mind about calling the authorities—"

"We haven't."

"Then I can only think of one more avenue to explore. Trey's birth mother. She may have stayed in contact with Patterson. She might even be with him now."

"No, I doubt that."

"I need to see the adoption records—"

"They're sealed."

"Senator—" She stifled her impatience. "I'm speaking of your own copies, not the court file."

"Oh. Hold on—excuse me a minute. What is it, Jesse?" The last sentence came out muffled, and her three minutes were nearly up when Ramsay finally returned to the line. "Let me get back to you on that," he said.

"I'm about out of ideas, Senator—"

"I'll call you tomorrow."

The sleet changed over to snow as she headed north again, and the road grew slick. She had a lightweight car and four bald tires and it felt as if there was nothing holding her to the road, not traction, not even gravity. She didn't dare let the needle go above forty. It was almost eight o'clock by the time she turned onto Martins Mill Road for the home stretch.

Two inches of unmarked snow covered both the road and their driveway. She tapped the brake to make the turn, and suddenly the Honda's rear end was fishtailing across the road. She slammed on the brakes and made it worse, then jerked the wheel hard to the left, but not in time. All four tires skidded off the road, and the car was left floundering in the ditch.

She tried all the tricks—first gear, reverse, then forward, then back again—but no amount of rocking or spinning was going to get her up on the road tonight. She sat a moment in a weary slump against the steering wheel, then finally shut off the ignition and trudged through the snow across the road toward home.

The house was in darkness. She hit the light switch in the kitchen and called out, "Doug? Honey, are you home?"

All that greeted her was a cold damp chill in the air. She searched for a note, but the only message was the one left on the answering machine at 5:35 P.M.

"Cam, honey. Sorry I missed you. I was hoping you could join us for dinner tonight. A bunch of us are getting together at the Wilmington Country Club. If you can make it, come on down. If you can't, don't wait up, 'cause we'll probably go late. I love you."

A bunch of us. Doug's euphemism for the Party, which meant tonight's dinner was one she couldn't afford to miss. She found the number for the club and reached a hostess who transferred her to an assistant manager who put her on hold. After five minutes he returned to the phone and said, "I'm sorry, Mrs. Alexander, but your husband just got up to give a speech. Could I have him call you later?"

"No. Thanks anyway."

She hung up and went to the front window. Across the road her car sat askew and alone in the ditch. And here she was, only two and a half weeks married and already spending Saturday nights alone. It was almost funny.

She changed into a heavy robe and slippers and wandered the house from room to room, stopping to gaze out each window as the snow fell soft and silent and deep. At ten o'clock, too tired to pace any longer, she went upstairs and lit a fire in the bedroom and curled up on the rug beside it, hoping the hard floor would keep her from falling asleep. But the warm fire made her drowsy, and as the heat seeped into her bones, her eyes fell closed and her thoughts drifted in and out of focus, then faded to black.

When she found the phone in her hand, she wasn't even sure it had rung. "Hello?" she murmured as her eyes sank shut again.

"Campbell Alexander?" It was a man's voice, youthful, with a husky edge.

"Hmm?"

"This is Steve Patterson."

Her eyes flashed open. "Mr. Patterson, I—I—" She scrambled to her feet. "Mr. Westover called you?"

"He doesn't know where I am. I called him to find out if the cops were looking for me. Instead I found out you were."

"Oh. Well—thank you for returning my call."

"I wasn't going to. Until Trey told me who you were."

Her first reaction was surprise that Trey knew—he'd given little more than a grunt when they were introduced. Her next reaction was dismay. If Patterson knew who she was, then he had to know everything else, and that meant there wasn't any ruse she could hide behind.

"I guess you know why I want to talk with you," she said.

"I don't believe you do," he said. "Or the Ramsays, either. If they wanted to talk to me, they could have answered my letters. Or picked up the goddamn phone once in sixteen months."

"Mr. Patterson—"

"All they want is to know where I've taken my son. Right? That's what you're trying to find out."

Cam cradled the phone and didn't answer.

"But you've gone as far as you'll get," he said. "You won't be able to find us."

She watched the snow fall as he spoke. The timbre of his voice was almost hypnotic, and she had to rouse herself to respond. "That's not all they want. They're desperate to know that Trey's all right."

"Give me a break," he snapped. "They let that kid run wild. So I'm not buying any of their concerned parent bullshit."

"What is this?" she snapped back. "The voice of parental wisdom? After what? Twenty-four hours' experience?"

She was surprised by her own outburst, and even more surprised when he laughed. It was a soft sound, reluctant and a little chagrined, and after a moment he said, "Okay, tell the Ramsays that he's all right."

"Is he there? Can I talk to him?"

"He's asleep."

"Can't you wake him?"

"Now who's the voice of parental wisdom? Believe me, by the time you get a kid to go to bed, the last thing you want to do is wake him." In a lower voice he said, "Especially after the day he had."

She jumped on that. "So he's not all right!"

"Hey—listen, it would be a lot for anybody to absorb in a day. But you can blame the Ramsays for that. I'm not the one who lied to him for thirteen years."

"Maybe if I talked to him . . . ?"

"Forget it."

"Please." She pulled out a trump card. "His mother's been worried sick."

There was a beat of silence, and when Patterson spoke again, it was in a different voice. "His mother's dead."

A click, and the phone buzzed furiously in her hand.

7

The dinner went on interminably, five courses and six speeches and long tedious lulls between each one, but at midnight the chairs scraped back from the tables and the guests creaked to their feet. Meredith Winters retrieved her coat from the check-room and made a beeline through the milling crowd for the porte cochere at the front of the country club. The snow was still falling and she clutched the mink tightly around her.

A black Lincoln looped around the parking lot and pulled up at the entrance, and Norman Finn leaned across the seat and opened the door for her.

"Thanks for the ride," she said, sliding in.

"My pleasure."

He lit a cigarette and drove out the long lane of the country club, between the orderly lines of trees and past the snow-covered golf greens, then turned for downtown Wilmington. Meredith opened her window a crack and watched the countryside roll past. God, it was like a wilderness out here. Philadelphia was only a stone's throw away, and Baltimore only a little farther in the other direction, but no one would ever believe it on this lonely road tonight.

"Quite a successful evening," Finn said.

"Yes," Meredith said noncommittally, because she knew he was looking for a commitment. That was the way it worked: as soon as a political strategist of any prominence signed on for a campaign, the candidate acquired overnight credibility and the contributions began to pour in—enough at least to pay for the strategist. It was the circularity of politics.

"So you're doing the Sutherland race over in Maryland."

"Yes."

"Quite a comer, Sutherland."

"He doesn't have to come very far," she replied tartly. "He's not only a national figure, he's a national treasure."

He gave her a sly wink. "Easy race, then."

She saw where he was going and laughed out loud. "Not so. He's up against a two-term incumbent. And I don't have to tell you about the advantages of incumbency."

"Yeah. What're the latest statistics on that?"

"Ninety-eight percent of incumbents hold their seats."

"Yeah, familiarity breeds votes, I guess."

"But that's not all. Look at everything the incumbent has to work with. The staff and office allowances, the franking privilege, free use of the radio and TV studios on Capitol Hill to produce their news clips. And of course the biggest perk of all: the power to exchange current favors for future campaign contributions." She waited a deliberate beat, then said, "Hadley Hayes has all of that, you know."

"You're not letting that scare you away from this race, are you?"

She smiled. "Nothing scares me, Finn."

After a few minutes the skyline of Wilmington rolled into view. Like Washington, it was a low-rise town. Unlike Washington, it was the size of an inkblot on the landscape.

"Tell me about Jonathan Fletcher," she said. The old man in the wheelchair had not appeared tonight, but his name seemed to be on everyone's lips.

"Jon?" Finn's eyes flickered up to the mirror as he cut across two lanes of traffic to make his turn. "Oh, there's a lot I could tell you about Jon. But there's only one thing you really need to know. His middle name's DuPont."

Her eyebrows arched. "Can you count on much from him?"

"Yep. Ash'll see to it."

"Mmm. That was quite a lavish promise the Senator made tonight."

"He'll deliver on it."

She considered that response while Finn lit up a second cigarette. "Exactly what is the Senator's interest in this race?"

"Just what he said. He's got a real affection for Doug. He believes in him."

"And . . . ?"

"And . . ." He shrugged. "Some folks see Hadley Hayes challenging Ash the next time around."

"Ahh." She tilted her head back against the upholstery. "Not much of a challenge if the guy loses and has to sit on the sidelines for four years."

"Nope."

"Nor if Hayes has to deplete his war chest twice over just to hold on to his seat. Isn't that equally true? So long as Hayes is forced to spend big enough, Ramsay gets the same result. Whether Doug wins or loses."

"Hey, nobody's looking for Doug to lose."

She had her doubts. "I was surprised the governor wasn't there tonight," she said after a moment. "Or last night, for that matter."

Delaware had only four major statewide offices: the two senators, Ramsay and Tauscher; the current representative-at-large, Hadley Hayes; and the governor, Sam Davis. For generations the voters of Delaware had equitably divided the four offices between the two parties. Senator Ramsay and Governor Davis were the current representatives of their Party, which should have meant that Davis would make an appearance on behalf of the Party's latest candidate.

Finn shrugged. "Sam's a busy man."

She nodded. Just as she'd thought.

The long snow-covered rectangle of Rodney Square appeared ahead, and Finn slowed to a stop at the doors of the hotel. He laid his arm over the seat back and turned to her. "So, what do you think, Meredith?"

She reached for the handle as the doorman approached. "I think I need some more convincing." She stepped out, then turned back and ducked her head in. "Because regardless of what the Party does, Finn—I only back winners."

Her room was a small suite decorated sedately in dark antiques and floral prints. It seemed even smaller to her now that she was facing her second night here. She made a mental note: if she signed on to this race, the budget would have to include a room upgrade. She kicked off her shoes and hurried to the bathroom. It had been a typical working party for her: five club sodas and not a moment to extricate herself to find the john.

Afterward she leaned close to the mirror and made an almost clinical inspection of the bags under her eyes and the slackening skin along her jawline. She was forty-two years old, and while her face might still be her fortune, its net worth was clearly declining. Ten years ago she was being touted as the next Diane Sawyer, but the national opportunities never quite gelled and the closest she got to a network was the web of fine lines that began to radiate out from the corners of her eyes. Five years ago people started to speculate about how long she could hold on even as local news anchor.

It was the price of being a woman in this business. No one ever worried about the resiliency of Dan Rather's skin, and Ted Koppel's hair was merely a joke, not a factor in negotiating his next contract renewal. The strain began to tell in her face, and when she fainted one day from the latest diet to keep her weight at a camera-pleasing fifteen pounds under ideal, she knew it was time to choose a new career. She had two key talents: an understanding of how to shape media perceptions, and the ability to entice men to do her bidding. Party politics was a natural fit.

She'd done well enough so far. She had contracts and connections and a million dollar house in Georgetown. But she wasn't yet where she needed to be, and as she gazed at her reflection, she was all too aware that time was running out. The next presidential election was only two years away. If she didn't have a candidate in that race, she never would.

She switched off the bathroom light and returned to the living room of the suite. It overlooked Rodney Square, and she went to the window to decide if the view merited another nine months of Wilmington lodging. The drapes were open but the undersheers closed, and she held one side back to look out over the block-wide park. Public buildings and corporate headquarters surrounded it: a courthouse, the library, a big credit card company. All very impressive, all very staid. Win or lose, nine months in this burg and she'd die of boredom.

She needed a drink, a real one now, and as she turned from the window in search of the minibar, a shape lunged out at her from behind the drapes.

The scream strangled in her throat as a hand clamped over her mouth and an arm squeezed hard around her ribs. She froze, though her eyes moved wildly through the room, searching for a weapon or escape route. But then a soft laugh sounded in her ear and she was free.

She whirled and stopped short at the flash of shaggy blond hair. "Bret!" she gasped. Her hand swung out at his face, but at the last instant she remembered who he was and pressed it to her heaving chest instead.

His dark eyes were dancing with laughter. "Did I scare you, merry Meredith?"

"What are you doing here? How did you get in?"

"Uh-uh." He held up a hand of warning. "You don't want to know. Your rule, remember? The end justifies the means only if you don't have to know too much about the means."

That *was* her rule, and she remembered now that Bret had been in the Sutherland for Senate headquarters the day she pronounced it before a new group of campaign volunteers.

"Does your father know you're here?" she demanded.

He shook his head with his maddening bad-boy smile. "Haven't you figured out how we work yet? I watch Dad's ass. He doesn't watch mine."

"Yeah? So who's watching yours?"

His mouth curved mischievously. "I had the feeling maybe you were."

Her face went tight and she brushed past him to the minibar. She pulled out the tiny bottles of vodka and tonic and while she mixed her drink she carefully considered her response. A righteous how-dare-you came first to mind, followed by a withering you-wish! She turned around and regarded him coolly as she took her first sip. He was barely twenty-four, drop-dead gorgeous, and with a swagger in his walk that showed he knew it. He had the same military bearing as his father, and it was only an attention deficit disorder that kept him from following in his footsteps to West Point.

"So," she said finally. "You figure a cute butt's all you need to barge into somebody's hotel room?"

He raked his eyes over her body; there was no deficit in his attention now. "I bet yours has gotten you into a few."

"How dare you," she said, though she forgot to put any rancor in her tone.

He came closer, and she forgot to move away. He took the glass from her and set it down, then took her by the shoulders, and when he kissed her, she felt a wild tingle spread through her. He was too young, the situation was too dangerous.

"What if he finds out?"

"He won't."

Her eyes fell shut as his lips moved to her earlobe. "But what if he does?"

"Dad's like you—there's some things he'd rather not know about. And my sex life is at the top of the list."

She pried his hands loose and stepped free, then crossed the room to pick up the phone.

"Are you calling him?" he asked, suddenly nervous.

"No." She dialed four digits. "I'm arranging for you to spend the night."

His face lit up, and he took an eager step toward her.

"This is Meredith Winters in 807," she said to the desk. "Do you have another room available? On another floor?"

A brief flare of frustration passed over Bret's face, but by the time she hung up he was laughing again.

"Get a good night's sleep," she said, leading him to the door. "And you can go to a Party brunch with me tomorrow."

"I promised myself that one way or the other, I was going to have breakfast with you tomorrow." He made a rueful face as he stepped out into the hall. "Too bad it had to be the other."

"Meet me in the lobby at ten."

She started to close the door, but he ducked his head through and kissed her again, a steamy kiss that left her gasping for breath when he pulled back.

His black eyes were dancing. "Sleep well," he teased.

"You, too," she said hoarsely.

She sagged into the door to click it shut, and as she hurried to pull the chain, she could still hear him laughing in the hall.

8

There was a whisper in Cam's ear and a nuzzle against her neck, and she rolled over to find the sunlight streaming through the windows and Doug smiling down at her. "About time," he said, and kissed the tip of her nose. "Sleepyhead."

"Mmm." She reached her arms up in a delicious stretch that ended in a hug.

"Though after that performance last night," he said against the wild tangle of her hair, "I'm not surprised you're worn-out."

Her cheek was pressed to his, so he couldn't see the confusion on her face and the slow dawning recollection of all they'd done during the night. It was like a dream when he'd come to her. She'd been in a deep heavy sleep with the voice of Steve Patterson still echoing in her mind, and when she stirred it was only into that hazy unreal world between sleep and wakefulness. Her eyes never opened but her body did, with a fierce hunger that made her flush to remember it now.

"How did it go yesterday?" Doug asked. "Any luck?"

Somehow it didn't seem right to tell him about Patterson's call, to speak the words out loud after they'd been echoing in her mind all night. "I have a few leads," she said.

"Good," he murmured, and snuggled closer.

They lay together with their arms and legs entwined, and Cam realized that the moment had finally arrived, the one she'd been waiting for and dreading since Friday night. She combed her fingers through his hair. "Doug, sweetheart?"

"Cam, sweetheart?" he echoed, teasing her.

"Can we talk a minute about the campaign?"

"Sure." He sobered at once. "You bet. I'm thrilled that you're taking an interest in it."

A bad start. "Well, I do have some reservations."

He waited.

"I mean—financially, it'll be so hard—" No, that wasn't the opening she'd planned. Frantically she tried to backpedal. "You know, we only just got married—"

Too late. He was rising up over her with laughter in his face. "You really *were* out of it last night, weren't you? You didn't hear a word I said."

"No, but, honey—"

"I wish you'd been there with me. It was the greatest moment of my life. Ash stood up at the head of the table—"

"He was there?" She'd expected Ramsay to be home with Margo last night, both of them wringing their hands over Trey's abduction. Instead he was out making political speeches while Steve Patterson worried about how much sleep his son was getting. She was surprised at how much it rankled.

"Uh-huh. And he stood up in front of everybody and made a pledge to raise two million dollars for my campaign!"

It took a second to sink in. "Two million?" she said.

"I know! Can you believe it?"

"How?" she asked, to keep from asking *why*. "I mean, how can he raise so much?"

"Contributors are willing to give money to an incumbent that they'd never risk on a newcomer." He flopped back on the pillow and folded his arms under his head. "So Ash tells them to give it as soft money to the Party, and the Party pledges the lion's share of that to me."

"Soft money—that's where there're no limits on contributions?"

"Right."

"I thought they were going to ban that."

He snorted. "That bill will never pass. Even the members who signed on as cosponsors are working behind the scenes to get it tabled. And the lobbyists—" He let out a harsh laugh. "They must be hustling twenty-four/seven to kill it. Finance reform would put them out of business."

Cam looked at him. *When did he ever laugh like that?*

"Whoa—look at the time." He rolled over and swung his feet to the floor. "I better hit the shower. A bunch of people are coming over for a brunch meeting."

"What?" Cam bolted up in bed. "Doug, the house! And food—we don't have food—"

"Relax. Maggie Heller's taking care of everything. This is the way it'll be from now on, sweetheart. You won't have to worry about anything anymore."

Cam was still scrubbing the kitchen counters when Maggie arrived with three college-age kids and four bags of groceries. Two of the kids were immediately dispatched to shovel the driveway; the third Maggie brought with her to the back door where Cam was waiting.

"Oh, here she is now!" Maggie exclaimed. "Campbell, I was just telling Gillian all about you!"

Gillian was a pretty young coed in a plaid kilt, who wore her blond hair held back with a velvet headband. She was a sophomore at the University of Delaware, she told Cam sweetly, and though she'd yet to vote in her first election, she knew that Doug Alexander was the best candidate to run for Congress since—well, since ever.

Cam made her escape as they started to unpack the groceries, but only as far as Doug's study down the hall. Today would have been the perfect day to hide out at her office, but with her car snowbound, there was no chance of an inconspicuous getaway.

Besides, she thought, sinking into Doug's chair, there was nothing for her to do at the office. She'd already run to ground every possible lead on Steve Patterson. Trey's birth mother was dead, he'd said, and the heavy edge in his voice left her no doubt that it was true. So that meant that his current girlfriend, Beth Maybe, wasn't Trey's mother, which meant that even if she could get her hands on the adoption records, they'd be no help.

Cars began to arrive, their doors opening and slamming shut in the driveway, and on the other side of the study door Cam could hear the stomping of feet and the buzz of voices, with Doug's voice cresting over them all. "I like to call it a jobs program," he was saying once more. "You know, as recently as 1960, forty percent of the jobs here in the Delaware Valley were manufacturing jobs. You know what it is today? Sixteen percent."

A memory washed back in her mind, of another Sunday morning, early in their courtship, when she'd helped him draft a report for some Party research project. She remembered wearing one of his shirts (and nothing else) and typing from his notes while he nuzzled her neck and murmured things like, *Maybe that should be a separate bullet,* and *Could we boldface that line there?* The final product was a treatise full of dry statistics and tentative conclusions. She never imagined she was helping him put together a manifesto.

She turned back to her own notes and circled Beth's possible name in red. *Go after the woman,* she reminded herself. Beth was the woman in Patterson's life whether she was Trey's mother or not.

From the dining room came the clink of the china and the rattle of the silver, and the steady drone of voices in the hallway began to drift that way.

So how to learn Beth's name? George Westover was a likely source. Cam contemplated the telephone for a moment, wondering what ruse might work this time. She could be a good Samaritan who'd found something nearby—a piece of jewelry, perhaps—and wanted to return it to its rightful owner. Or maybe she could be a reporter for *Architectural Digest* looking to do a feature story on the Lake Drive renovation, with an up-close and personal view of the architect and his significant other.

But she knew it wouldn't work, even if she disguised her voice or asked someone else to place the call. Westover wouldn't be susceptible to any kind of ruse so soon after her blunder yesterday. It would be weeks before his suspicions faded enough for him to give up any information. If he even had any.

What else? Patterson might have named his girlfriend as an additional driver on his auto insurance policy. In the morning she could call DMV for the name of his carrier and then claim that she'd been in a fender-bender with a woman driving that vehicle. But that seemed a long shot, and in any event, a day away.

What could she do today? She could go back to Rehoboth Beach and try a door-to-door canvass of the neighbors, people Steve and Beth might have socialized with, nearby shopkeepers they patronized. But she remembered the deserted streets and boarded-up windows of the hibernating resort, and then she remembered her car marooned in the ditch, and she crossed that idea off her list.

Doug's voice rose again. "We've taken millions of good solid American jobs and shipped them all overseas. We've given foreign manufacturers unlimited access to the wealthiest consumer market on earth without the slightest effort to make it reciprocal."

She tried to tune him out, then realized with a pang that only a few days before she would have been straining her ears for the sound of his voice.

The wheels of another car crunched in the driveway, and when she saw Nathan's Tahoe through the window, she got up with a cry of delight. Here was a welcome distraction, a guest of her own, and one who would be happy to huddle in here with her and crack jokes about all the Party people outside.

She went out into the hall to open the door for him, but he was already crossing the threshold with Norman Finn.

"Morning, Campbell," Finn said. "I was just saying to Nathan here, hell of a thing about that secretary in your firm getting killed."

"Yes, awful."

"You see what the papers are calling it?" Nathan said. "The Center City Secretary Murder. Bad news for Philadelphia. They already lost a big chunk of their tax base when the heavy industry moved out. Now if the secretaries don't feel safe, it won't be long before all the banks and law firms move out, too."

Finn gave a grim nod. "We ought to take a look, make sure we don't get any echo effect down here in Wilmington."

"Good idea. Form a blue-ribbon panel."

"Packed full of working women."

"Want me to get it started?" Nathan said.

"No, leave it to me. You got enough on your plate this year. Speaking of which"—Finn started for the dining room—"there's a bunch of folks waiting to see you down the hall."

"Great," Nathan said, shrugging out of his coat. "I'll be right there."

Cam took his coat to the closet. It was packed full of wet wool and stiff leather, the coats of people she didn't know. She turned back to Nathan and wondered if he were a stranger, too. "You're really going all out to show the flag here, aren't you?" she said.

"Nice to see you, too," he drawled, and pecked her on the cheek. "Missed you at the country club last night."

"You were there?" She tried to mask her surprise with a joke. "Jeez, Nathan—you already have Doug's vote for partnership. You really don't need to suck up this much."

He laughed and left her to join the crowd.

She felt a sting of betrayal as she watched him go—deserted by her best and oldest friend. Old friends were a luxury she seldom allowed herself, and at almost seven years' duration, her friendship with Nathan was a record.

She went back into the study, alone, and studied her notes

again. *Go after the woman.* But she couldn't go after the woman if she couldn't find out who she was. This time her credo led to a dead end.

Dead. *His mother's dead.*

It came to her then that there was another woman to go after. Dead or alive, Trey's birth mother could have left some kind of trail that would lead to Patterson. Her parents, for instance. Maybe they'd stayed in touch with Patterson, or maybe they knew his parents.

Which led her back to the adoption file, the one Senator Ramsay was supposed to be searching for, when he wasn't busy attending political meetings.

At least he wasn't attending this one.

The drone of voices drifted out of the dining room and settled in deep in the living room, and when the volume of voices diminished, Cam guessed that the official meeting was under way. She stole down the hall and into the dining room. The table had been cleared of everything except the coffee service and a plate of bagels. Cam helped herself to a bagel and a cup of coffee, and headed for the kitchen, but a different set of voices came from the other side of the door; Maggie's volunteer brigade must still be at work. Cam stayed in the dining room to eat, at an inconspicuous post by the window.

Outside, the line of cars filled the driveway and wrapped around the roadside in front of the house. She studied the makes and models and played a little game of guessing which belonged to whom. The minivan by the back door was certainly Maggie Heller's, and Cam already knew Nathan's Chevy Tahoe, so that didn't count. The green Range Rover looked familiar; she thought it might belong to Webb Black, a slight, anxious-looking man who was an old friend of Doug's and also a Wilmington lawyer. The black Lincoln—she'd bet anything that was Norman Finn's. He was taking a risk, driving a car like that on snow-covered roads, but he was probably the kind of man who liked to take risks—Doug Alexander being a case in point.

A deep sigh escaped her.

"I know who you are," a voice spoke in her ear.

She spun around, bobbling the cup until the coffee sloshed over the rim and scalded her hand. A man stood before her with a guileful grin on his face, and she backed away from him until the edge of the windowsill cut into the backs of her legs.

"You're Doug's wife. Campbell, right?"

"Oh." She breathed again. "Yes. Yes, that's right."

He was a young man with blond hair swept over his forehead like the surfers in the old beach blanket movies of the Fifties. His eyes were black, in startling contrast to his pale hair.

"Hi. I'm Bret Sutherland."

After a beat she said, "Phil Sutherland . . . ?"

He nodded. "I guessed who you were the minute I saw you. Meredith Winters described you perfectly."

"Oh? How's that?"

"A vision trying to be invisible."

Cam blushed, embarrassed equally by the compliment and the fact that she was so easy to read. "Well, I'm afraid it's all a little new to me."

"My mother hates it, too," he confided. "I think she'd rather go through Desert Storm all over again than have to appear at another political event. You know what she does after every dinner Dad drags her to?"

"What?"

"Vomits." He grinned.

Cam stared at him until a clattering of heels sounded in the hall and Maggie Heller burst excitedly into the room. "Oh, Bret, there you are! Meredith was wondering where you got to. Campbell, did you meet Bret Sutherland?"

"Yes, just now." Cam put her cup down on the table and mopped her hands on a napkin.

"It's such a thrill for us to have you here!" Maggie gazed up adoringly at him. "Your father is such a wonderful man, and we all admire him so much!"

"Thanks. Me, too."

"What it must have been like, growing up with him!"

"It was an honor," he said. "And a privilege."

"Why, you really mean that, don't you?"

"I do. He's not only a great American, he's the hero of my life."

He spoke with the fervor of deep feelings and without a trace of embarrassment, and Cam listened in astonishment, that anyone of her generation could speak of a parent that way. He must have felt the force of her gaze on him, because he turned and smiled at her. "Well, I'm sure Mrs. Alexander feels the same way about her candidate."

She flushed.

"Oh, Campbell, speaking of which," Maggie said, "you still need to register to vote in Delaware. I brought you a mail-in form."

"Great, thanks," she said faintly.

"Oh, and I almost forgot!" Maggie dug into the pocket of her cardigan and came out with a computer diskette. "Here's that file Doug wanted. Could you put it in a safe place?"

Cam took the diskette. "What is it?"

"The voter registration rolls. I pulled them together statewide. And made them fully searchable, I might add." Her eyes went suddenly round as a smattering of applause came from the living room. "Oh, Bret, we better get back."

He made an imposed-upon face at Cam before he turned to smile at Maggie as she bore him off to the living room.

Cam cleaned up the coffee spill and was heading back to the sanctuary of the study when she heard Doug's voice, announcing that Webb Black would be his campaign chairman and John Simon the treasurer. "And for campaign legal adviser," he said as Cam's steps slowed outside, "first I considered myself, but Owen told me I'd have a fool for a client if I did that. Then, of course, I thought of Campbell, but I figured, no, one of us better bring home a paycheck this year."

Cam shrank back from the ensuing gale of laughter.

"So finally I decided to pick somebody who's not doing much of anything else this year, except maybe billing three thousand hours. Also somebody who couldn't say no. My friend and associate, Nathan Vance. Glad to have you aboard, Nathan."

Cam froze through the burst of applause.

"So those are our officers," Doug went on. "In terms of volunteer activities, the irreplaceable Maggie Heller has volunteered to supervise and coordinate for us."

As Maggie led her own cheer, Cam turned and stumbled up the stairs and down the hall to the bathroom, where she leaned over the toilet and vomited a stream of coffee and bagel chunks into the bowl.

Thirty minutes later she was sitting on the front porch steps, huddling inside her parka and drawing slow, deep breaths until her stomach at least felt calm. When the door opened behind her, she closed her eyes and made a wish that it would be Doug, that he'd realized her distress and come to comfort her, and as long as she was wishing, that he'd decided to quit politics and send all these people away.

"Hey, there, beautiful."

She didn't turn around, not even when Nathan came up and stood behind her. She knew her resentment made no sense. He wasn't her husband, only her friend. But he was her only friend; that was the problem.

He looked out over the front lawn and chuckled when he spotted her car in the ditch. "Now I see why you didn't show up at the dinner last night."

"And now I know why you did," she said bitterly. "Campaign legal adviser, huh?"

"Yeah, how 'bout that?"

"Is this why you wanted to transfer to Wilmington?" she asked suddenly. After their law firm merger went through, Nathan was the first in line to volunteer for a transfer, a move that baffled her at the time. "So you could get into Delaware politics?"

"Yep."

She turned to stare up at him.

"You know, little pond, big fish, all that." He shrugged. "In Philly there were too many other brothers, all of us Mau-Mauing each other all the time. I was never going to break in there."

She sat stunned. It was bad enough she hadn't known Doug was interested in politics, but Nathan was her best friend and she'd never suspected.

"You should have come to the dinner last night, Cam. You need to stay in the loop so you don't get blindsided."

"I couldn't come. Even if I'd gotten any notice."

"Hey, nobody had much notice. A lot of this is gonna play like pickup basketball. You have to be able to roll with the punches."

Irritably she said, "Stick with a metaphor, would you, Nathan?"

He laughed and reached down to pull her to her feet. "Come on. Let's go haul that little Jap car out of the ditch."

She walked with him down the driveway with her hands thrust deep in her pockets and her shoes scuffing against the clean-scraped surface of the driveway. The sun shone a dazzling pale gold against the new snowfall where it lay untouched over the lawn.

"Doug did tell me the big news of the night," she said. "About the money."

"Impressed?"

"More like appalled. I mean, how many registered voters do you have in this state anyway? Three hundred, four hundred thousand?"

"Fewer than that in play. Since it's not a presidential year—it's not even a senatorial year in Delaware—it'll be under two hundred thousand who actually turn out to vote."

"Two million for two hundred thousand votes."

"Worse if you want to get technical. In any race, anywhere, only about seven percent of the voters really decide the outcome, because everybody else votes the party line. So basically we have—what?—fourteen thousand votes in play. And you gotta figure old Hadley will match us dollar for dollar."

"So we're really talking four million dollars for fourteen thousand votes?" Cam stopped and did the math. "That's almost three hundred dollars a head. God, Nathan—don't you think they'd all rather skip the election and take the cash?"

He laughed.

"I don't get it," she said. "Why are all these people rallying around Doug? All the Party has to do is point at somebody and suddenly everybody thinks he's the greatest thing since sliced bread?"

"Happens I do think that. He's got some really exciting ideas, Cam. Stuff nobody mainstream has the balls even to mention, let alone do something about."

"And you thought so even before the Party anointed him?"

A door banged behind them, and Norman Finn came out on the front porch and lit a cigarette.

Cam grimaced. "Speak of the devil."

"You remember that Emerson quote," Nathan said. " 'A political party is an elegant incognito, designed to save people from the vexation of having to think for themselves.' "

"That's just it!" she cried. "They don't even know who the hell Doug is. And as long as the Party backs him, they don't care."

"Yep. It's the cognitive filter at work."

"What?"

"Didn't you take any poli sci back at Michigan? That's what

they call the psychological process that governs the whole political process. Cognitive filter, or perceptual screen. It means that once you decide to align yourself with a party or a candidate, you project your own beliefs onto them, and you screen out anything that doesn't mesh. It's why the Clintonites never bothered to read the Gennifer Flowers transcripts. Or why the Reaganites refused to follow Iran-Contra. It's a self-protection mechanism. Your brain blocks out anything that doesn't square with your perception of your candidate."

"Nathan, listen to yourself. Can't you hear how awful that is?"

"Come on." He took her by the arm and propelled her out to the road. "You were a pretty smart chick in law school. Don't go dumbing up on me now."

"What's that supposed to mean?"

"You used to know how things stood. But now you're acting like some silly virgin who wanted to have sex but had no idea she'd have to lose her cherry to do it."

She jerked her arm free, and when they reached the car, she got behind the wheel and slammed the door. Nathan went around to the front of the car, and she started the engine with a roar and put it in reverse. He braced his shoulder against the bumper and pushed hard, and in a minute all four wheels were back on the roadway.

Cam lowered the window as he climbed out of the ditch. "I never knew Doug wanted to run for office," she said tightly.

He looked at her as he brushed his hands clean. "Sounds like you're the one who doesn't know who the hell he is."

She put the car in gear and cut sharply around him to pull into the driveway. Finn was watching from the porch, and he gave her a little victory salute as she passed.

The afternoon wore on until the sun beamed long glaring rays through the hazy windows and cast shadows like shrouds in the corners of the rooms. At five o'clock Maggie Heller packed up her troops and left the house in a hypercharged flurry that left Cam feeling as if a tornado had passed through and it was finally safe to come out of the root cellar. The other guests gradually departed, and Cam stood waiting in the hallway as Doug saw them off.

Meredith Winters was the last to leave. "Maybe by the end of the week," she said. "I should complete my research by then."

"Research into what?" Doug asked with a smile. "Maybe I can save you some time."

She gave him a frank look. "I want to be sure you can win this thing."

His smile disappeared. "Let me tell you something," he said. "If I didn't think I could win, I'd get out of this race tomorrow."

Cam waited while he walked Meredith to Webb's Range Rover, and when at last he returned and the door was finally closed for good, she went up to him and into his arms.

"Went well, didn't it?" he said.

"Mmm." She leaned closer.

After a moment she felt him lift his wrist behind her back. "Oh, look at the time," he said, and pulled her arms loose. "I have to call Ash before he leaves for the train station."

"Oh—I need to talk to him, too," she said. "Put me on at the end?"

"You bet."

But an hour later he emerged from his study with the call already ended. "Ash had to run for the train," he explained. "But he asked me to give you a message. He said they can't find their copy of the adoption file."

"Oh."

"And he thinks it would be a dead end, anyway. But meanwhile"—Doug's face lit up—"he had lunch with Jonathan Fletcher today, and apparently Jon was very impressed with us Friday night. And you know what that means."

He grabbed her and spun an exhilarated circle through the room, then fell back on the sofa and pulled her down on top of him.

She collapsed on him in a dizzy, defeated slump. There was nothing she could do to change his mind. On one side of the scale was his personal ambition, two million dollars, and a truckload of Party loyalists. On the other side was her. By herself.

There was nothing she could do to counterbalance all that, and nothing she could say. Except the truth, and that was the biggest dead end of all.

9

They hit the road early Sunday morning, stopping once at the airport in Portland to turn in the rented Mustang and cash Steve's Explorer out of long-term parking, then again in Freeport, where they spent an hour in the L.L. Bean outlet. Steve grabbed clothes off the shelves and thrust them at Trey in stacks: flannel shirts and thermal Henleys, jeans and Thinsulate wind pants, waterproof boots and arctic parkas.

"Where are we going? The North Pole?"

"Feels like it sometimes when the wind kicks up." Steve pushed him into the dressing room. "Go on, try those on."

The register totaled over eight hundred dollars, and he rolled out a wad of cash to pay it.

They cruised a different outlet store for underwear, then a drugstore for a toothbrush and comb. "You shaving yet?" Steve asked him, and smoothed a hand over his jaw to judge.

For a second Trey was mortified and ducked his head away. But then he quipped, "Only my head sometimes."

Steve cracked up and made a grab for him, and they tussled a minute in the aisle—until the cashier cleared her throat with a disapproving growl.

"Busted," Steve said under his breath, and Trey had to fight to keep a straight face until their purchases were rung up.

They were heading back to the Explorer with their packages when Steve stopped and pointed his chin at a phone booth on the corner ahead. "Last chance," he said.

Trey eyed it for a minute. "You already told Campbell Alexander, right?" he said finally. "That I'm okay?"

"Yeah, I told her."

"Then I got nothing else to say to them."

"Make sure now. Any closer than this, and we can't risk it."

"I'm sure," Trey said.

They stowed the bags in the back of the Explorer and headed north again. Another few hours and they'd be there, Steve said. Or at least they'd be to Baxter Bay and the boat that would take them there.

"Is it a motorboat?"

"Be a pretty long haul in a rowboat. The island's twelve miles out to sea."

"Wow." Trey studied the map until he located it again, a little sliver of land that floated like a ghost ship off the coast of Maine. It was so tiny that its name had to float by itself in a box alongside. Maristella Island. It looked like the end of the world.

"And nobody lives there but you? For real?"

"For real, except that the population's about to increase by fifty percent."

Fifty percent? Trey did the math. Oh, right, Beth lived there, too. A "friend" Steve called her, which he assumed meant they were screwing each other, who was "trying her hand at writing," which he wasn't as clear on.

"How'd you ever find this place, anyway?"

"They found me," Steve said.

Trey looked over. A sun glare was coming in through the driver's side window, and Steve had the visor turned and his sunglasses on.

"What are you, famous?"

The corner of his mouth twitched. "Obviously not."

"No, I mean—you know."

"I've gotten a few good notices. Won an award or two, for whatever that's worth."

"Wow," Trey said again.

Late in the afternoon they turned off Route 1 and descended over a steep winding road to a little coastal village of weathered clapboard houses with brick chimneys. At the base of the road the harbor opened up in front of them, and beyond it lay all of the ocean, black and sparkling in the cold sunlight, with white gulls above it, soaring and dipping against the pale blue sky. Fishing boats were crowding up against the docks, and fathers and sons in heavy rubberized gear were shouting to each other and jumping to the wharves with lengths of cable and rope.

"There she is," Steve said, pointing down. Tied up low to the wharf and bobbing like a toy among all the big deck boats was a twenty-foot motorboat of gleaming white fiberglass.

"Cool."

Steve climbed down the ladder on the bulkhead, and Trey passed the L.L. Bean bags down to him. Steve stowed them all under the tarp, but he pulled Trey's new parka out of one of them. "Better trade coats now," he said. "The trip across the water'll freeze your butt off."

"Nah, I'll be fine."

They got back in the Explorer and drove out of the harbor and south a few blocks, to a big old house that perched on the edge of the seawall, behind a sign that read BREAKWATER BREAKFASTS AND BEDS, TOO. Steve circled to a parking lot behind the house and backed into a space until the rear bumper nudged the retaining wall.

"Beth stayed here for a few days while I was scoping out the place," he explained as he shut off the ignition. "The owners told her we could leave the car here."

Trey climbed out after him and watched as he went around to the rear bumper with a screwdriver. When he came back he had the license plate in his hand. He stowed it in the duffel bag and slung the bag over his shoulder.

They headed back to the harbor on foot, along the edge of the seawall. Trey gazed out to sea and wondered if the island could be seen from here. Twelve miles out; it was incredible. A blast of wind blew off the water, and he gritted his teeth to keep them from chattering. But he wasn't cold; he was too excited to be cold. "I've never been on a motorboat before."

"No?"

"Uh-uh. Jesse took me fishing in a rowboat a couple times, but he'd never get in a motorboat. He said he had enough of that in Vietnam."

"He was in the Navy?"

"Yeah. He called it the Brown Water Navy. It was this special task force that patrolled the rivers. One day they got ambushed, the whole flotilla. Jesse was like the only guy who survived."

"Jeez." Steve glanced at him as they walked in step together, and after a minute he said, "You spent a lot of time with this guy?"

"Jesse? I guess. He was always sort of around. He even had a room in the house for a while, but he kept waking everybody up with his Vietnam nightmares, so they built him a room over the garage."

"How was he to you?"

"What d'you mean?"

They reached the wharf, and another gust of wind came off the water, so cold this time that Trey had to turn and hunch his back against it.

"I mean, did he treat you all right?" Steve started down the ladder to the boat.

"Sure." Trey went down after him and vaulted over the gunwale.

"He was somebody you could talk to?"

"You mean, was he like my buddy or something?"

Steve looked out to sea. "Something like that."

"Nah. No way. He was a staffer."

"What?"

"You know," Trey explained with pained obviousness. "On the payroll. The staffers know not to cross any lines. They just do what they're told."

"Is that right?" Steve cracked a smile. "Hey, guess what?" He reached under the tarp for Trey's new parka and tossed it at him. "You just became a staffer. Put that on. Now."

Trey made a face and pulled on the parka.

Steve started up the engine and they chugged out of the harbor until they were past all the moored work boats and the channel buoys, then he opened up the throttle, the bow lifted out of the water, and they were shooting out into the open sea.

Trey swiveled in his seat and cupped his hands over his eyes to watch the land fall away until there was nothing left to see. He swiveled all the way around. The ocean seemed to stretch out forever in all directions, and everything seemed vast and open. Steve reached over, flipped up the hood of Trey's parka, and motioned for him to tie it. The hood muffled the roar of the engine and the sounds of the sea, and it was funny how it made him feel—like he was wrapped up in a cocoon, yet hurtling into the biggest adventure of his life.

The island appeared at last, a low swell on the horizon. Trey cupped his hands to his forehead and squinted until he could make out the steep headland that tapered down to a low rocky beach on the leeward side. The island was half a mile long, Steve told him, but only a hundred yards wide at its widest point, just a narrow finger of land rising up out of the water. *Maristella* meant *Star of the Sea*, Steve said, and Trey could see how the sun glittered off the silica in the sand and rocks; at night, in the moonlight, he imagined a galaxy of stars floating in the ocean.

They tied up to a deepwater dock on the southern tip of the island, and Trey followed Steve's long strides up a boardwalk path from the water's edge to another path of packed earth that cut through a dense stand of spruce trees. After a hundred feet it emerged onto an open hillside. At the top of it stood the house looking out to sea. It was a battered wooden building with steeply pitched roof lines and something like a clock tower steepling up into the sky.

"Gothic Revival," Steve said. "Pretty awful, huh?"

"Butt-ugly," Trey said happily, thinking that it looked like a haunted mansion.

"We'll see what we can do about that."

A light glowed from inside the house, and as they came up the hill, the door opened and a woman emerged, clutching an afghan around her shoulders. She was small, with pale wispy hair and sloping shoulders.

"At last!" she called. "I was expecting you hours ago!"

"Sorry," Steve yelled back. "We had to stop and do some shopping." He held up the bags as evidence.

Steve gave her a quick kiss at the door, then reached for Trey and pulled him front and center. "Beth, this is Trey."

She was starting to smile, but stopped and gave Steve a puzzled frown. "Trey? But I thought—"

"Jamie's cool," Trey said.

The sun was sinking over the mainland when Steve took him upstairs to his room. The main staircase rose up majestically through to the second and then the third floors, but on the third floor Steve opened a door and revealed another smaller, steeper set of stairs. At the top, he opened another door on a small room, about twelve feet square, with windows on each of the four walls, and an ocean view from every window.

It was the tower room, Trey realized, and hands down the coolest room in the house. He went to the seaward side and looked down. From here the flagstone terrace looked like it was carved out of granite, and it felt like it was hanging in the air. It must have been a drop of thirty or forty feet to the terrace, and from there a sheer cliff dropped another hundred feet almost straight down to the sea. The surf was crashing into the boulders below, and the spray rose up like a geyser.

"Awesome," he said and spun to another window, where an orange sun was sinking down through a pink-streaked sky. "This is my room?"

"If you like it."

He pretended to give it some thought, then shrugged and said, "It's okay, I guess."

Steve faked a tackle, and Trey dove and rolled across the bed and came up laughing on the other side.

An hour later he was sprawled across his bed with a stubby pencil and some paper he snagged from a dresser drawer. He was trying to capture the look of the island as he'd first seen it rising out of the sea. The spruce forest went down fine, with heavy dark slash lines picking up the trees, and the house loomed up okay on the top of the hill, but he was still struggling to capture the ripple of the light on the water when Steve came in behind him.

"My God," he whispered.

Trey rolled over. Steve was staring down at him with a strange look on his face. "What?"

"Can I see that?"

Trey flushed. "I was just fooling around."

"Please."

Reluctantly he handed it over, and Steve stood a moment staring at it.

"You have your mother's eye," he said finally.

"Huh?"

"You see things the way she did. Look." He sat down beside him. "Here? The way you have the sunlight pooling here on the surface of the water? Then forming into an eddy over here?"

"Yeah, I know. I suck at reflections."

"She would have sketched it exactly the way you have. It's amazing."

"Was she an artist?"

"She could have been. But she was like you." Steve gave him a look. "She thought she sucked."

Trey laughed and flopped back with his arms folded under his head. For the first time he noticed a recessed square in the ceiling above him. "Hey, what's that?"

Steve looked up. "Oh. That's the trapdoor to the widow's walk."

"Huh?"

"It's an old seaboard tradition. A viewing platform on the roof, for observing ships at sea. But listen, don't go up there. The wood's all rotted out. I have to rebuild it. Either that or shear it off."

"No, keep it."

"You're the boss." Steve came over and ruffled his hair. "Hey, you doing okay?"

"Great."

"Really?"

"Really."

"Then I'll let you get some sleep. Where's your laundry? I bet it's pretty gamy after three days."

"On the floor over there." Trey waved a hand, then rolled over on his stomach and scrunched up his pillow.

Steve scooped up the discarded clothes and was heading out the door when something clattered to the floor. Trey's eyes opened, and a second before Steve picked it up, he recognized it and sat up straight. It was the razor cartridge from Steve's shaving kit in the van.

The clothes spilled out of Steve's arms.

"Wait—I can explain," Trey said. "It was yesterday morning when I took that. I mean, I didn't know—"

"I understand. It's okay."

He thrust his hands in his pockets and paced to the window, the one that looked back to the mainland. It was too dark to see anything now, but he stood there anyway, looking out at nothing.

"I'm sorry," Trey said.

"No, don't be. I don't want you to feel sorry. And I sure as hell don't want you to feel scared or threatened."

"I don't, I told you, that was yesterday—"

"Look, I know I didn't give you any choice the other night. How could I? You didn't have anything to choose between, not until you knew who I was. But now—" He crossed the room and hauled Trey out of bed. "Come on. I want to show you something."

He led the way down the tower stairs, and opened a door on the third floor and hit the light switch. The only furniture in the room was a table and chair. Centered on the table was a short-wave radio set. "This is our link to the outside world."

"Yeah, so?"

Steve sat down with his elbows on his knees and his hands clasped together. "I broke the law when I took you," he said, looking up at Trey. "I may not agree with it, but it's still the law and I broke it. Big-time. There's a lot of people who'd say I had no right to do that. And there's a lot of people who'd put me away for it. If you ever feel the same way"—he pointed to the radio set—"this is your ride home."

"Hey, come on." Trey backed toward the door. "I don't need to know this."

"Get back here and pay attention." Steve swiveled around and reached for the controls. "Here's the power button. We're already set to the emergency channel. See? And you push this button to transmit."

"Come on, man. Cut it out!"

Trey wheeled out of the room, galloped back up the tower stairs, and dove into bed.

Steve followed more slowly, and only as far as the doorway. He hooked his fingers overhead on the door frame and stood there a long moment. "I just wanted you to know," he said finally. "You have a choice now. Better than a choice."

He switched off the light and spoke his last words in darkness. "You're holding all the cards."

The lights were switching on all over Washington Sunday night as the residents returned from their home districts, their junkets, and their weekend escapes. Meredith Winters got a cab at Union Station, and from the backseat watched the city light up like a Christmas tree. It was barely 120 miles from Wilmington to Washington, but it seemed like another world. Saturday's snow hadn't ventured this far south, and the streets lay under the same gritty black crust she'd left on Friday.

Her town house was still in darkness as the cab pulled up to the curb. It was brick, three stories tall, narrow and deep and mortgaged up to the second-floor windows. The doorstep was piled high with the weekend editions of the *Times*, the *Post*, the *Tribune*, and for old times' sake, the *Examiner*. An intern from the office had been assigned to collect the papers while Meredith was out of town. Obviously he or she hadn't, which meant that somebody's head was going to roll tomorrow.

Inside she touched a switch, and the house lit up in a gentle wash of cool light through the hall and up the stairs. The house was exquisitely understated in natural linen fabrics and handcrafted woods; Gustav Stickley furniture, and sisal rugs. It was an unusual decorating scheme for Washington, drab by its standards of gilt and chintz, but the pure American provenance played well with her clients, just as her cellar of fine California wines did. She moved from room to room, hitting light switches as she went. Doug Alexander would love this house, he with his buy-American mind-set.

That thought stirred an idea, and when she reached her study, she picked up a palm-sized computer. "Funnel a message to the Alexander campaign," she spoke into the chip. "The wife needs to lose her Japanese import."

Upstairs she started the bath and tapped in an ounce of gardenia-scented oil, then undressed and slid wearily into the foaming water. Another exhausting weekend, but not a wasted one. She was growing more and more sanguine about the Alexander campaign. He might be on a crusade where his trade program was concerned, but he was showing some admirable flexibility when it came to the rest of the issues. She could work with a mind like that.

Meredith extended her toes to turn off the faucet and sank back blissfully into the silken bubbles. Even the wife was diminishing as a worry. Today she'd exhibited no signs that she wanted to control the campaign, her husband, or even her own household. In fact, if she were any mousier, they'd have to put her through some assertiveness training before she hit the campaign trail.

The telephone rang. Meredith glanced at the clock on the vanity. Exactly on time. He was as predictable as the dawn. She reached for the tubside extension. "Hello?"

"I'm right outside."

"I'm waiting," she purred.

She toweled off and pulled on a robe, then ran downstairs and turned the dead bolt in the back door. She was in the living room and had his scotch poured by the time he slipped through the door.

He was dressed all in black, which was his idea of nocturnal urban camouflage. He shrugged out of the black leather coat and pulled off the black knit cap and tossed them both on a chair, then accepted the offer of a drink and her mouth in one fluid motion.

"Miss me?" she asked.

He made a gruff noise in his throat and gulped his drink. He had no patience with romantic palaver. He was a man of action, not talk. He took in her robe and her damp skin. "What'd you do, start without me?"

She smiled seductively. "I'd need a considerable head start if I were ever to catch up with you in that department."

His eyelids drooped with arousal. The joy of sleeping with a man who'd surrounded himself with toadies all his life was that he accepted such statements at face value. He tossed back the rest of his drink, then took her by the hand and propelled her up the stairs ahead of him.

He was not a generous lover, but he was usually a vigorous one, and in Meredith's experience, one often compensated for the other. Tonight, though, he was slow to start and quick to finish, and as she lay in his arms afterward, she couldn't keep her thoughts from drifting to Bret. What a delicious gift he would have been, a secret splurge like bonbons hidden in a desk drawer.

No—more like a hidden bag of cocaine. He was a danger to her, and one she'd have to stay well away from.

"Your mind's somewhere else tonight."

"Oh? Well, I suppose it's still in Delaware."

He sat up with a scowl and switched on the bedside lamp. "I don't see why you had to go traipsing up there anyway."

"I have to have more than one candidate this year."

"Why? You're being paid enough."

"There's no such thing as enough. Besides, I need to spread my name around. That's how this business works." When he continued to scowl, she scooted closer and ran her nails across his chest. "Anyway, the advantage of Delaware is that I won't have to go far. Or be away from you for long."

"What's the story on this guy?" he said grudgingly. "You like his looks or not?"

"Maybe. I'm starting to think he can win, but the important thing is that no one else seems to agree."

He looked askance. "And that appeals to you?"

"It does if I'm right and they're wrong. If we get the upset I think we can, it'll make national headlines." She gave him a coy look through her lashes. "Along with the reputation of a certain strategist we both know and love?"

He laughed and slapped her on the rump. "I want a look at this guy who's trying to steal you away from me."

"Here." She rolled over him and picked up the video from Friday night's party. "You can watch him in living color while I go shower."

She slid the cassette into the VCR and pushed Play, then hurried into the bathroom before he took too close a look at her sagging buttocks. She was twenty years younger than he was, but there was something in the sexual equation that gave men the right to be critical in this respect. Probably the fact that they could always get someone younger still.

She bathed for the second time that night, and when she returned to the bedroom, he was dressed and sitting on the foot of the bed with the remote control in his hand. "Come here a minute," he said, watching the screen intently as the tape rewound.

She perched beside him and nibbled his earlobe, but he paid her no attention. "There." He pushed the Play button. It was the big moment on the Senator's staircase when the candidate reached down and plucked his wife out of the crowd.

"Who's that?" he demanded as the wife appeared with that Dan-Quayle-in-the-headlights look she wore all night.

"The candidate's wife. Campbell Smith."

"What do you know about her?"

"Not much. They haven't put together their bios yet."

"Just tell me what you *do* know."

She stiffened at his tone of voice. "She's a lawyer with one of the big firms in Philadelphia. Someone said her parents died and she was raised by her grandmother in Pennsylvania. What's this all about, anyway?"

"There's something awful familiar about her."

"What?"

"I can't place it." He bent over to tie his shoelaces, then rose to his full imposing height. "Find out everything you can about her. Maybe it'll come to me."

"All right."

He reached for his gun on the nightstand and slid it into the holster at the small of his back.

"Can't you stay longer?" Meredith always waited until he had his gun packed to extend the invitation; it decreased the odds that he'd accept.

"No, I'm meeting Bret for a drink down at Clyde's."

Her eyes went wide and she surged to her feet. "You didn't tell him you were coming here?"

He gave a disgusted grimace. The question was too ridiculous for him to dignify with an answer.

"But if he's meeting you at this hour here in Georgetown, he might—"

"He might, but he won't. The boy never makes a move without my say-so, in case you haven't noticed."

"No, I guess not," she mumbled.

"Come on. Walk me out."

She went with him down the stairs and to the back door, but this time she switched off the lights as they moved through the hall, and by the time General Phil Sutherland kissed her at the door, they were in total darkness.

10

DO YOU HAVE A WOUND THAT WON'T HEAL? the billboard asked as Cam drove into Philadelphia Monday morning, and this time she answered it, *Yes, but if I keep it wrapped up tight with gauze and tape, no one ever needs to know.*

She found her secretary deep in conversation with Grant Peyton, the first-year associate Cam shared her with. Helen sat in a grandmotherly sprawl at her desk while Grant hung over the half wall of her station and munched his way through the buffet of homemade pastries she laid out every Monday morning.

"Oh, Campbell," Helen called as she rounded the corner to her office. "Did you hear about Gloria Lipton?"

"Yes. How awful."

Grant brushed some crumbs from his mouth. "I was just telling Helen that from now on I'm going to walk her to her bus at the end of the day."

Helen beamed up at him so happily that Cam refrained from pointing out that there was nobody to walk her home when she got off the bus on the other end, in a far worse neighborhood than Center City. "How nice," she said.

She went into her office and powered up her computer. A fragment of conversation had been looping through her mind all morning: *If I didn't think I could win, I'd get out of this race tomorrow.* She'd gone to bed disheartened last night, but woke up this morning with that phrase echoing in her head. There was something there, she knew it, and it felt surprisingly like hope.

She logged online. It would be political research today, a new field for her, but the techniques had to be the same.

Where to start? After a second's deliberation she typed into the search field: *Hadley Hayes*.

* * *

Tuesday night Doug parked in the garage and trudged up the steps to the back door. He gave Cam a preoccupied kiss as she took his coat from him in the kitchen.

"How was your day?" she asked.

"Okay." He picked up the mail on the counter and flipped through it with little interest. "Webb held a lunch at his office so that I could court some of his partners, and Owen did the same with drinks at his firm tonight."

"How'd it go?"

"I don't know. I made my pitch, and they asked some questions, and that was about it. I didn't get one solid commitment from the bunch." His brow creased. "These people ought to be my core supporters. They're Wilmington lawyers like me, they're partners of Party leaders, and they've all got their lives invested in the economy of this state. It shouldn't be a hard sell. I mean, if they won't wave the flag, who will?"

It was the first time since Friday night that he'd come down even a few feet off the cloud of his nomination. Cam's heart pinched to see him so dispirited, but at the same time her own hopes rose. He was in the best possible mood for her purposes.

"I'm sorry, sweetheart. Why don't we have a nice dinner and you can try to relax?"

At that, he stopped and took in the aroma-infused kitchen, the lush classical music playing in the dining room, and Cam standing before him in a black bodysuit and flowing silk pants.

"Wow!" he said, slowly blinking his way to a grin. "What's the occasion?"

"Our anniversary," she replied tartly.

He laughed.

"But it is. Twenty days today. It's only when you've been married forever that you measure it in years." She moved closer and lifted her face to his. "For us it's still days."

"Mmm." He kissed her. "And sometimes still hours."

She led him into the dining room. The table was one of his mother's left-behinds, a battered mahogany that seated ten, and she'd set it with fresh candles and his grandmother's best linens. Doug's place was at the head, her own on his right.

She returned to the kitchen for the salmon soufflé, and when she came back, Doug had removed his coat and tie and shifted his place setting to the seat opposite hers. "I want to be able to see you," he explained with a smile.

She sat down at the reconfigured table, feeling as if she were about to take his deposition, or maybe he hers. It served to remind her: this was business, not pleasure.

"To us," Doug said, and lifted his glass.

She kept the wine flowing and the conversation as light as the soufflé throughout the appetizer course. But when she brought out the dinner plates, she sat down, picked up her fork, and said, "How long does Governor Davis have left in office?"

"Two years," Doug said, sawing off a portion of duckling.

"And then he's constitutionally prohibited from seeking another term?"

"Ohhh." Doug moaned as the first forkful of duckling passed his lips. "Cam, this is fabulous."

"He's only fifty, isn't he? What will he do then?"

"I don't know. There're a lot of options for a man with his talent and experience."

"Are there? The way I see it, there're really only three. He could challenge Tauscher for the Senate. Or he could sit out two years and inherit Senator Ramsay's seat, assuming he doesn't want to keep it himself. Or he could run for the House and not have to sit out at all."

Doug put his fork down and looked at her.

"So here's the thing," she said. "If Davis has his eye on the House seat, would the Party really be looking to win it for you, only to pull it out from under you in two years and hand it over to Davis?"

"They're running me, aren't they?"

"Sure, but they can hardly let Hadley Hayes run unopposed. He's already raised a million dollars for this year's campaign. If he gets to sit on that money for two more years, he'll have quite a war chest to use against Governor Davis."

"Cam." Doug stared at her. "Where's all this coming from?"

It was coming from the last two days, in which she'd surfed through every available newspaper and magazine database for references to Hadley Hayes, then through the *Congressional Record* and committee conference reports, and then into a broadcast database for transcripts of all his speeches and remarks. She ordered up archives of his constituent newsletters and press releases, and of his financial disclosure reports and campaign finance records. Then she'd run the same kind of search on Sam

Davis. The results were summarized in a twenty-page memorandum in her briefcase.

"I've been thinking about it a lot," she said, and braced herself to deliver the bad news. "Honey, I'm afraid the Party might be running you just as a place holder for Davis."

He stared at her a minute, then let out an astonished laugh. "Campbell, I am impressed. There're Party people on the executive committee who haven't figured that one out yet."

Her eyes opened wide. "You knew?"

"Give me a little credit."

"It doesn't bother you? I mean, they're making you their sacrificial lamb."

"Don't worry." He picked up his knife and fork again. "It's not going to happen."

"But if Governor Davis—"

"He'll find some other office to run for."

"What makes you think so?"

"Because I intend to win Hayes's seat myself, before Sam gets a shot."

This was the overconfidence she needed to shake. "But without the Party's full support—"

"I've got two strategies around that. First, I'm trying to convince Sam that he should go after Tauscher's seat. After all, that's the one he really wants. If he backs me for the House, I'll back him for the Senate in two years."

"Is he biting?"

"He still has to be convinced that Tauscher's vulnerable."

"And if you can't convince him?"

He smiled. "Then I'll have to convince the Party that Sam's pretty damn vulnerable himself."

Cam stared at him as he polished off his duckling and scraped his plate clean.

She scraped her own clean into the garbage can in the kitchen. This wasn't proceeding according to plan. She needed to regroup. No, she needed a cheat sheet. She opened her briefcase and pulled out the memorandum, and when she returned to the dining room with their salad plates, it was tucked out of sight under her arm.

"Maybe the real issue isn't how vulnerable Sam Davis is," she said, taking her place at the table again, "but how vulnerable Hadley Hayes is. I'm afraid the answer is, not very."

Doug shook his head dismissively as he picked up his salad fork. "He's a dinosaur. He hasn't had a new idea for thirty years. All he harps on is defense and national security. He never got the memo that the Cold War's over and we won."

"But remember, that stuff plays pretty well in Dover. The Air Force base employs close to seven thousand people. And with Hayes on the subcommittee for military construction projects, he's brought even more jobs than that to the area."

"You've done some research," Doug said.

She nodded and flipped through the pages of her memorandum. "Hayes won his last reelection by a thirty-point margin. And in an omnibus Gallup poll last year, Hayes got an approval rating of eighty-two percent. That was one of the highest in the whole Congress. Honey"—she sat back, point proven—"the man's enormously popular!"

Doug was squinting across the table. "Can I see that?" He pulled the memo out of her hands and looked at the cover. "What is this?"

"Just a few notes I put together. An analysis of Hadley Hayes and his prospects for reelection."

"You're starting to get into this, aren't you? And here I was afraid you'd never share my interest in public life."

"No, Doug, I—"

He held up a hand to silence her as he turned to the first page and started to read. After a moment he forgot his salad, put down his fork, and half turned in his chair as he continued reading.

Cam got up and opened another bottle of wine and refilled their glasses. She sipped nervously at hers. An awful silence seemed to fall over the room, and when she realized that the CD had ended, she got up and put on another, a jaunty medley of Old English folk tunes.

She returned to her seat. He was still reading, and she tried to guess by his expression where he was in the memo. The first section dealt with Hayes's popularity, his principal and very prominent supporters, and his campaign war chest. The second was a statistical analysis of the advantages of incumbency. The final section detailed the failure rates of candidates for national office who'd never previously held elective office.

It was the last section she now wished she could revise. She'd presented the facts coldly, and maybe even harshly. Unless the first-time candidate was buoyed by some freak of publicity or his own private fortune, his chance of winning was nil.

Fifteen minutes passed before Doug closed the memo. He stared at the arrangement of greens on his plate, then at the glow of the candlelight through his untouched wine. He reached for the glass and drained it in one swallow.

"This is what you think of me?" he said.

"No! This has nothing to do with you. Only with the unlikelihood of anyone in your position beating Hayes this year."

"I'm not anyone."

"No. You're the man I love. And I can't bear to see you get hurt."

It was the truest thing she'd ever said, but it wasn't true enough, and the thought of all she was withholding from him made her break her eyes from his and stare down at the blank white cloth on the table.

"No?" he said softly. "Well, guess what? I am hurt."

"But you said you didn't want to run if you didn't think you could win."

"That's the point: I think I can. You're the only one who seems to think otherwise."

He pushed his chair back from the table and went down the hall with her memo rolled in his fist.

After a moment she got up and killed the music.

The grandfather's clock chimed the passage of another fifteen minutes. Cam looked at the creeping hands on the clock face and wished she could move them the other way, back to the moment before she gave him the memo. She cleared the table and cleaned the kitchen, but after another fifteen minutes passed, she couldn't wait any longer.

Doug was sitting at his desk in the study. He must have heard her footsteps in the hall, but he didn't look up, and the tears she'd been fighting wouldn't hold back any longer. They welled up in her eyes, and her words came out in a choke: "Doug, I'm so sorry."

He shook his head. "No, it's my fault. Margo told me—in fact, she reamed me out about it. I should have told you before. I see that now. I should have given you time to adjust." He looked over at her and opened his arms. "Come here."

She rushed across the room to curl up on his lap. He felt warm and solid around her, and she would have been happy to spend another fifteen minutes of silence there. But too soon he spoke again.

"Tell me what you're so afraid of."

"I don't know."

"Come on. Explain it to me."

She took a deep breath. "I think it might be the fanaticism. I mean, a lot of terrible things are done in the name of political fanaticism. Just like religion. But nobody stops to think how bad it is because they're all caught up in the frenzy of their cause. Every time I watch the presidential conventions, there're all these people lathered up and delirious, like they're having a group orgasm. And I always think: this is too important. This should be a rational, intelligent decision-making process. These people should be sitting around a conference table with a stack of position papers in front of them. Not screaming and waving signs and blowing noisemakers."

"But that's all for show. I was a delegate to the last convention, and I can tell you that the real decisions *were* made in a conference room."

"But then—isn't that even worse?"

He was thinking of something else. "You're right, though. It is like religion. But isn't mankind better off for having something to believe in?"

"What if they believe in human sacrifice? Or genocide?"

He leaned back and gazed at her a long moment. "I know where this is coming from," he said at last. "It's your parents, isn't it?"

Cam went very still. "What?"

"Their call to become missionaries. They left you to answer that call, and they never came back. And you're afraid that if I answer my call the way they did, you'll lose me, too."

"Oh." She turned her face and pressed her cheek against the top of his head. "Maybe."

"I understand, sweetheart," he said, stroking her hair. "But it won't be that way for us. You won't lose me. I promise."

Her face was hidden from him, but there was nothing she could do to hide her shiver.

"Cold?"

"A little."

He tightened his arms around her. "Hard to believe that only ten days ago we were on the beach in St. Bart's."

"Mmm."

"We should go back sometime."

"I'd love that," she said, and had an inspiration. They'd go in November, before the big holiday crowds, during election week, and she would do her utmost to keep his mind off the race he wasn't in.

"Cam, if only you understood what it means to me, to be in this election."

"Explain it to me."

"It goes back to my father. He wanted this so much."

"For you to go to Congress?"

"Not me. Him. It was his life's ambition, and he worked hard for it. He volunteered for the Party candidates year after year, he gave money we couldn't really afford to give. But the payoff never came. One year—I was about ten—Dad lobbied hard for the Party's nomination for Congress, and he came close, but they gave the nod to a friend of his instead.

"Dad threw himself into the campaign anyway, no hard feelings, and on election day he took me along to do poll duty for our candidate. It was raining that day, but we stood there handing out leaflets and calling out our guy's name to every voter who went past. The downpour got so bad that all the other poll watchers packed up and left. But not Dad.

"Late in the day a news crew arrived and set up outside the polls, and our candidate drove up with his wife to cast their votes for the cameras. Dad called out, 'Paul, how're you doing? Gordon Alexander here!' And the guy looks over at us—we're standing there dripping wet, waving our soggy signs—and the guy gives us a thumbs-up and goes inside without a word.

"God," Doug said. "I can still feel how cold I was that day."

"Oh, sweetheart." A wave of love and tenderness swelled up in her. "Then this race—it's sort of a quest for justice for your father?"

"Huh?" He stirred, then shook his head. "No, the truth is that the Party was probably right. He wasn't really good enough. But see? That's the difference. I am."

She pulled her arms free and sat up.

"Cam, I can make people think about things in a way that they haven't done before. I can accomplish something real for the people, something that'll last long after whatever bones we throw them in the current year's budget. You see?" He put his hand on her chin and turned her face to his. "You see why I have to do this?"

"I guess," she said. "But could you do me one favor?"

"Of course. Anything."

"Give me a little more time? You know, to get used to the idea? Don't announce just yet."

"All right. If you'll do a favor for me."

"Anything."

He reached around her to sort through some papers on his desk. "Sign this voter registration form." He laughed. "Let me be sure of one vote at least."

She got to her feet and took the page from him. The spaces for her name and other personal data were all blank. The space for party affiliation was not.

"I've always been an Independent," she murmured.

He handed her a pen. "You can't straddle the fence forever."

She looked up at him and saw the edge of expectancy in his eyes. This was a test, and one she couldn't fail so soon after their first quarrel. She filled out the form and dashed off her signature at the bottom.

Doug had some phone calls to make, so Cam left him alone and finished cleaning up the kitchen, then dragged the garbage can out to the curb for the Wednesday morning pickup.

She looked up at the sky. It was sharp and clear tonight, almost impossibly clear this deep inside the urban skyglow of the Eastern Seaboard. She stood and watched the stars switch on one by one, pinpoints of light in the vast black night, and before she knew it, her mind was veering off into the questions that she usually shied from, the ones to which there were no answers—where does the universe go and how *can* it go on forever, and if it does, what does that make us, and if it doesn't, what else is there?—questions that led nowhere but to a terrifying void.

There was a time long ago when such questions didn't frighten her, back in the days when she thought she had a handle on all the great unknowns of the universe. In those days the sky was a two-dimensional map in her mind, and she could trace the landmarks like a veteran navigator. Until one clear night the dimensions warped and the landmarks eroded, and she was never sure of anything again.

She was ten years old that summer. *Harriet the Spy* was her favorite book, and she spent hours eavesdropping on grown-up conversations, recording the numbers off license plates and jotting encoded notes into composition books that became top-secret dossiers. She was a precocious show-off who memorized facts and regurgitated them to dazzle people the way other little girls tap-danced or recited poetry.

That night she and her sister, Charlene, were eating Fudgsicles on the porch steps in their nightgowns. Their house trailer sat on a cinder-block foundation on a hilltop surrounded by fields of knee-high grass and weeds. In the valley below were four lanes of interstate highway, but the headlights didn't penetrate up here and the diesel engine roar of the tractor-trailers was only a dull distant whine. Up here the crickets sang louder than the trucks, and the stars shone bright in the sky.

Cam pointed them out to Charlene and rattled off their names—Polaris of course, but also Erakis, Delta Cephei, Enif, Antares the Fire Star, Spica—she could name them by the dozens. But Charlene was a lumpish child with no interest in anything outside her sphere of tactile perception. She was concentrating hard on the shrinking contours of her Fudgsicle and wouldn't even turn her face up to the sky to look where Cam was pointing.

It was many years before Cam came to understand how few pleasures Charlene had in her life and what a torture it must have been, to be the slowest pupil in school, tormented by her teachers and sniggered at by her classmates, forced every day to go to a place where every day she would fail, and to come home every night to a bright sassy sister who might help her with her homework but not without declaring, "See? It's so easy!"

But Cam didn't understand that then. She only understood that her audience was ignoring her, and she let loose a tirade of insults: Charlene was too fat and stupid to see past her own fat nose and she'd probably spend the rest of her life in a dark smelly room doing nothing but getting fatter just like a pig on a farm.

Tears wobbled precariously on the edge of Charlene's lower lids, and she ran inside spewing tears and flecks of icy chocolate. Through the window screen Cam listened to Charlene's grievance and their father's vague murmurs to pay no attention to

Cammy, advice that he always followed pretty well himself. But a moment later the door groaned on its hinges and their mother came outside.

She rarely did. She was the bookkeeper for the service station and did all of her work at the kitchen table under the harsh rainbow glare of a fake Tiffany lamp. After her work was done and she put away the books for the night, she'd sit at the table in the dark, her presence marked only by the glowing tip of the cigarette that was always in her hand or mouth. One night she accidentally burned a hole in the sleeve of Cam's best white blouse when Cam bent to kiss her good night. For two more years she had to wear that blouse with its telltale burn mark. It was like the stigmata of a chain-smoker's daughter.

Her mother carried a cigarette with her now and lit it as she lowered herself to the stoop. She was heavy with pregnancy that summer, and bitter with it, too. Cam braced herself for the same weary scolding she always got when she picked on Charlene. But instead her mother said, "You're wrong, you know. Three of those you picked out aren't stars at all. They're satellites."

She proceeded to point them out and name them: Landsat 1, Explorer 12, Soyuz 7. Cam stared with her mouth open as her mother talked about the government's "spy-in-the-sky"photo-reconnaissance program in the Sixties, about KEYHOLE satellites and launchers and capsule ejection and recovery, and night vision Starlight scopes and thermal imaging devices, and how the resolution had become so advanced that not only could you tell the make and model of a car, you could read the numbers on its license plate.

"How do you know all this stuff?" Cam finally managed to sputter.

Her mother flicked the cigarette out into the darkness, and it streaked in a red glow like a meteor before it hit the gravel and sizzled into nothingness. "I wasn't always like this, you know," she said, heaving to her feet. "There used to be more to me than this." She turned her face up to the sky, and for one brief moment it glowed in the starlight before she turned and went back inside.

That was the night Cam lost her bearings in the sky.

She lay awake and listened to the grandfather's clock downstairs as it chimed off the balance of her life in fifteen-minute increments. Doug slept soundly beside her, the deep sleep of the well-contented. Owen and Webb were reassuring when he talked to them; commitment was just around the corner, they told him. And despite his promise to give her more time, she knew the subject of his candidacy was a closed door. Her signature on the registration form had sealed it. Tomorrow Maggie Heller would file it, and her name would be one more added to the voter rolls of New Castle County.

Suddenly her eyes flashed open in the dark. She darted a glance at Doug, then slipped out of bed and tiptoed out of the room and down the stairs to the study. On the blotter where she'd left it on Sunday was Maggie Heller's computer diskette, the one listing all the registered voters in Delaware.

Cam switched on the computer, loaded the diskette, and pulled the document up on the screen. It was a list of names, addresses, and party affiliations in alphabetized chunks. Apparently Maggie had scanned the voter rolls from each of the state's districts in no particular order. Cam was momentarily daunted by the prospect of scrolling through four hundred thousand names, but then remembered Maggie's boast: the format was fully searchable.

She executed a search command, and in a matter of seconds Steve Patterson's name was on the screen in front of her. Her hunch was right. He was living in Delaware during the last presidential election, and if ever he were inclined to vote, it would have been then. And sure enough, he'd registered. But only two other pieces of data appeared with his name: his Lake Drive address, which she already knew; and his party affiliation, which was None.

She returned to the start of the list and executed a second search command, this one by address. The computer zipped ahead to where she'd been before, at the entry for Steven A. Patterson. No good, and she was already more than halfway through that alphabetized chunk. She hit the Search key again, then sat back and gazed at the screen.

Elizabeth Logan Whiteside, the next listing read, 132 Lake Drive, Rehoboth Beach, Delaware.

11

It was her own credo: go after the woman. The next morning, she did.

Elizabeth Logan Whiteside was born on September 12, 1967, and until June 1996 was employed as a teacher by a public school district in New London, Connecticut. There was no record of any employment since then, or of a current bank account. But she continued to maintain several charge accounts, and one of them was a bank-issued credit card.

Cam's call to the bankcard center was answered by a computer that prompted her to key in the card number, then offered a menu of options. She opted to speak to a customer service representative.

"Can you help me?" she blurted when a human came on the line. "I can't find my card, and I don't know if I just misplaced it or if somebody stole it."

"Name?" the human intoned.

"Oh—sorry. This is Elizabeth Whiteside."

"For security purposes, can you tell me your mother's maiden name?"

Cam took a breath and a guess. "Logan."

"One moment."

She waited, wondering if her gamble would backfire and the next human voice would be a security representative.

But it was the service representative again. "The last transaction on this account was in the amount of nineteen dollars and ninety-five cents. Vendor AOL."

Cam recognized that as the monthly fee for the online service provider, and she recalled the computer desk left behind in the house on Lake Drive. "No, that's automatic. What was the last charge before that?"

"Two hundred and sixty-five dollars and seventy-nine cents. Vendor Eddie Bauer."

Cam pounced. "Where?"

"Rehoboth Beach, Delaware."

Nowhere. "Hmm," she said, stalling. "I'm not sure. What about the one before that?"

"One thousand eight hundred ninety-nine dollars. Jim's Wide World of Computers. Wilmington, Delaware."

She hesitated again, wondering how to explain that she didn't recall a two thousand dollar purchase, and finally decided she couldn't. "Oh, sure, I remember now. They're all mine. I guess I just misplaced the card. Thanks anyway."

She hung up and cupped her chin in her hands while she thought. There was nothing in Beth Whiteside's recent charges to point out a destination. Eddie Bauer might mean camping gear, but it might also mean sweaters and blue jeans. And a computer and an online account could be used anywhere.

But Beth already had a computer and an online account before she left town. Which made Cam wonder: Did Beth buy an extra computer at Jim's Wide World? Or did she buy a replacement? And if it was a replacement, what happened to the one that got replaced?

She wheeled back to her own computer and pulled up a credit report on Jim's Wide World. As the name suggested, it was a sole proprietorship owned and operated by a man named James Rice. He was an authorized dealer for all the big names, but not surprisingly in a market dominated by national retailing chains, Jim had a hook. He took trade-ins.

"Hello," Cam said when Jim himself answered her call. "This is Elizabeth Whiteside. I bought some equipment from you last week?"

"Sure. I remember. You traded your PC for a laptop. How's that working out for you?"

"Terrific," Cam said, smiling. "I love it. But you know what? I forgot to write down the model number of my old PC, and I'm going to need it for the depreciation schedule on my taxes. By any chance—"

"Hold on a sec." She heard the sound of paper rustling. "Here you go. It's the HP Pavilion 7090."

"Right. Oh, and I'll need the serial number, too, I think."

"Okay," he said, and read off the digits.

"Thanks so much," Cam said. "I'm sure glad you keep records of this stuff. I bet somebody snapped that unit up the day after I left it."

He gave a groaning laugh. "Don't I wish. No, I'm afraid it's still here on the floor."

"Oh, really?" Cam sat up on the edge of her seat. "You know, I was just telling a friend how I traded it in, and she said she wished she could've bought it."

"Heck, send her over. I'll give her a real good price."

Ninety minutes later Cam drove away from his shop with Beth Whiteside's old computer crated up in her trunk. It wasn't the first time she'd seized a target's computer equipment, though it was the first time she'd done it without a court order and a team of deputies. When the sheriff knocked on a defendant's door with a writ of execution, the defendant's first step was to stuff all the cash on hand into his shorts; his second step was to delete all the financial records on his computer. What the typical defendant failed to realize was that deleting a file only removed its name from the directory; the actual data still remained on the hard drive.

Cam had inspected Beth Whiteside's unit long enough to confirm that all the files had been deleted, but she was gambling, five hundred dollars on her credit card, that Beth knew no more about computers than the typical defendant.

She drove north on Route 202 to the western suburbs of Philadelphia, where she followed a circuitous route under railroad bridges and over looping roads until she arrived at a complex of flat-roofed brick buildings. She cruised the student parking lot until she spotted the vehicle she was looking for: a conversion van equipped with outsized antennae and painted with a Grateful Dead logo on one side and a full-scale rendering of Jerry Garcia on the other.

She parked beside it and crossed the street to the high school's main entrance and through the lobby to the office, where a woman rose from behind the counter. "Can I help you?"

"I need to see Joe Healy, right away."

"And you are?"

"His mom." When the woman gave her a doubtful look, Cam raised her chin a notch. "I'm his stepmom, and we have a family emergency. I need to take him home right now."

"What's the emergency?"

"His grandmother passed away this morning." So there would be no question, she added, "His *real* grandmother."

Ten minutes later she had a pass that entitled her to get one boy out of school free. She made her way through the corridors amid boys and girls who were indeterminately dressed in baggy blue jeans and plaid shirts, and from fifty feet away she heard the shouts and whistles and rubber squeaking against wood that marked the gymnasium. She pushed through the double doors and found a dozen basketballs in play, half of them being dribbled in a staccato rhythm down the floor and the other half in flight across the court. A whistle blew shrilly and the play ceased, and suddenly all the boys were turning and staring at her. The whistle blew again, and Cam followed it to a squat man in a sweat suit.

"Excuse me," she called, and held out the office note like an FBI shield. "I've come for Joe Healy?"

A volley of catcalls erupted among the boys and one shouted, "Yo, Healy. Nice going, man."

The teacher barked, "Healy, front and center. The rest of you—shut up!"

A lank boy with long dirty-blond hair slouched his way through the crowd. His face registered only mild curiosity when he saw Cam. "What's up?"

"Oh, Joe, I'm afraid there's bad news," Cam said, trying to signal him with her eyes. "Hurry up and get your stuff. Dad's waiting in the car."

"Oh, no, Mom," he cried, striking his chest and overacting atrociously. "What bad news? What now?"

"It's Grandma, I'm afraid. Hurry up now."

"Oh, no!" he wailed, tearing at his hair. "Not Grandma!"

"Joe," she snapped. "We don't have all day."

Five minutes later he came out of the locker room dressed in jeans and a Grateful Dead T-shirt. "What's up?" he asked again.

"Data recovery. PC hard drive."

They left the building and crossed the street to the parking lot, Cam striding briskly to her Honda and Joe barely strolling after her to his van. She opened her trunk and he unlocked the rear doors of the van and together they hoisted Beth Whiteside's computer inside through a cloud of stale marijuana smoke.

Joe Healy was seventeen, a slacker, a Deadhead—and apparently also a pothead. He was also a genius at computer memory restoration. The interior of his van was lined with two walls of shelves packed with custom-built disk drive controllers, processors, monitors, modems, switches, and cables. At the front was a worktable, and it was here that he set Beth's computer. He plugged it into a battery pack, then hooked it up to a monitor and keyboard.

"Whatcha looking for?" he asked as the CPU hummed itself awake.

"Everything the user saved to the hard drive and an inventory of all the installed software. Oh, and she may have been a Net surfer, so try to get at the cache."

This was something Cam had learned from Joe during a custody case the year before. She represented a woman against an ex-husband who'd defaulted on the property settlement agreement. In hopes of gaining a little leverage in the custody battle, Cam sent the sheriff out to seize some of his assets in satisfaction of the arrearage, and one of the assets the sheriff brought back was the husband's computer. Cam enlisted Joe, who came up dry on any financial records but struck oil on the Internet cache.

As Joe explained it to Cam, a Net surfer didn't just peek at data as it drifted through cyberspace. Rather, each Web site file was automatically downloaded to the user's hard drive and saved there, whether he wanted it to be or not. When the cache of downloaded Web sites reached full capacity, the data was automatically deleted on a first in, first out basis, but until then, every file viewed remained in memory.

Joe had recovered twenty files from the husband's Internet cache, each one a hard-core pornography site. In short order, the husband paid off his arrearage and ceded full custody of the children to Cam's client.

"Looks like a snap," Joe said now as he worked his magic on the keyboard. "When do you need this by?"

Cam gave him a pained look. "I thought that was obvious. I need it right now."

"No way."

"But you said it was a snap."

"Yeah, but I got a calculus exam next period." He switched off the CPU and it died with a burbling sigh.

"Come on." She looked despairingly at the disempowered computer. "You can make the test up later. You have an excuse."

"Yeah, but not a very good one."

"Why not?"

"My grandmother already died three times this year."

She haggled with him in the parking lot, and as a cold wind gusted, they finally reached agreement. He'd work on it right after school and transmit whatever he found to her office computer that night.

Helen was away from her desk when Cam returned to the office. She leaned around the cubicle looking for her mail, and was surprised to see a clutter of cardboard boxes and old files on the floor. This was unusual by Helen's tidy standards. Cam bent over, pried back one flap of a box, and was startled to see Gloria Lipton's face looking up at her.

"Can I help you?" Helen said behind her.

"Oh—hi." Cam straightened and let the lid fall closed. "What is all this stuff?"

"It's Gloria's," Helen said, sinking sadly into her seat. "Mr. Austin asked me to go through it and see if I can find anything. Her computer, too," she added, and pointed at a CPU parked on the floor beside the bank of filing cabinets.

"Why? What are you looking for?"

"Friends, long-lost relatives. Somebody to ship all this to."

"She didn't have a family?"

"Not a soul, poor thing. Oh, that reminds me." Helen sorted through some papers on her desk. "You got a letter in the late delivery. Something I think you'll be interested in." She found it and held the page out to Cam. "From the Harriet M. Welsch Foundation?"

The name struck a faint chord in Cam as she took the letter from Helen. It was addressed to Campbell Alexander, Esquire—she was surprised that her married name had caught up with her so soon—and it stated that in recognition of her outstanding work in the field of family law, the foundation would be honored to have her join its board of directors.

Her eyes narrowed suspiciously. Since the only work she did in the field of family law involved money, either collecting it or avoiding payment of it, she expected that what the foundation would really be honored to have was her money.

Helen was waiting with a happy expectant smile when she looked up.

"Why would I be interested in this?" Cam asked.

"Why, I thought—because it's for—see? It says so here on the letterhead. 'For the support and guidance of motherless girls.' I thought since you lost your own mother so young, you might be—"

Cam folded the letter into two tight creases and handed it back. "I never knew my mother, Helen. You can't lose something you never had."

"Yes, but I thought—"

"I don't think so. Any other mail today?"

A moment's hurt flickered across the secretary's fleshy, good-natured face. "Yes," she said, lowering her eyes. "I'll have it sorted in just a moment."

Cam went into her office and powered up her computer, and after a few minutes Helen came in and placed a stack of mail in the In box. "And don't forget," she said as she left, "I still need your time sheet from Saturday."

"Oh, right. Thanks."

Saturday was the day she'd spent doing online searching for Steve Patterson. Doug was supposed to give her a client-matter number to log her time against. She picked up her extension and dialed his in Wilmington.

"Doug Alexander's office."

The voice that answered was neither Doug's nor his secretary's. "Nathan?" Cam said after a bewildered moment.

"Hey, babe. We were just about to call you."

"Who's *we*?"

"Doug. Listen, big doings down here. Jonathan Fletcher's throwing a dinner party tonight."

Cam cringed. Another evening with the Party people.

"You know what that means," Nathan went on. "Fletcher's going to announce how much he'll contribute. So you need to get yourself home and change, pronto."

"Where is Doug?"

"Out in the hall. I ducked in when I heard the phone ring. So, I'll see you at Fletcher's, okay? Dress up, but don't overdo it."

"I don't think I can make it."

Nathan was silent a moment, and she could hear Doug laughing in the background.

"You're making a mistake," Nathan said.

"Let me talk to my husband," she said tightly.

He put her on hold, and it was almost five minutes later before Doug took her off.

"Campbell? You sure you can't make it tonight?"

"Sorry, but I finally got a lead on Steve Patterson, and I need to chase it down tonight."

"Great. That's good news."

"Speaking of which, did you open a new file?"

"Damn. I forgot. Tell you what: here's a number you can use until I do the paperwork for a new one." He riffled through some papers, then read, "It's 893420–004."

"Okay, got it," she said, jotting it down.

"I'll miss you tonight," he said softly.

"Me, too. I love you."

"Me, too."

She reached for her time sheet and completed the entry for Saturday. But after she filled in the number, she stopped and looked at it. The first six digits identified the client; the last three identified the specific matter being handled for that client. The number 004 meant that there were at least three other matters for the same client. Which had to mean that Ash Ramsay was more than Doug's friend and mentor; he was also a client.

She shouldn't have been surprised. She'd heard Ramsay extol Doug's firm as the best in town, and if he was willing to raise two million dollars for his campaign, he'd certainly be willing to throw him a legal bone now and then.

But she couldn't help wondering what those bones were.

She turned to her computer and pulled up the firm's most valuable asset: its client list. She entered the numbers *893420*, and the program zipped through the data and landed on the name *Ramsay, James Ashton, Jr.* Beneath it was the name of the client manager, Douglas J. Alexander, then a listing of four matters: a real estate partnership; a tax advice matter; a piece of litigation that ended five years before; and finally the one she somehow knew she'd find: *Adoption Proceedings*.

The file was opened more than thirteen years ago, before Doug was even out of law school, but when he took over as client manager for Ramsay, all existing files would have been transferred to his name. This explained why it was no surprise to him that Trey was adopted; he'd had the adoption file all along.

But it didn't explain why he lied to her about it. *They can't find the adoption file,* he'd said. *Leave it alone.*

The code on the screen showed that the file was in off-site archives. Cam pulled up the firm's administrative forms file and scanned the list until she spotted the one she wanted: *Archive Retrieval Request.* She filled in the name and client-matter number for the Ramsay adoption file. When she came to the line for *Send to*, she stopped and thought a minute, then typed: *Send to: Jackson, Rieders & Clark, 1821 Market Street, Philadelphia, Pennsylvania 19103. Attn: Alexander.* The file clerk would see the name Alexander for both client manager and file recipient and send it without question, while her own mail room would see the name Alexander and automatically forward it to her.

She hit another key and instantly transmitted the request to the file department.

Almost as instantly she regretted it. Here she was, only three weeks married, and already going behind Doug's back and sneaking into his files.

But it wasn't *his* file; it was the firm's file, and she was the lawyer in the firm who'd been retained by the client to handle a closely related matter. Doug should have sent her the adoption file at the outset.

Still she worried. What if he found out she'd retrieved the file? How would he feel?

Probably the same way she felt when she realized he'd withheld it from her.

And she felt awful.

She was still at her desk when the phone rang at seven o'clock that night.

"Incoming," a voice said.

"Joe?"

"Open your e-mail and download the text attachments."

She clamped the phone to her shoulder and spun around to the computer. "What did you find? Anything promising?"

"Depends on what you're looking for," he said with a chortle. "If you're going for an insanity defense, I think you got a good shot."

"What's that supposed to mean?" His e-mail message appeared on her screen, and she clicked on the icon to begin downloading.

"I mean this chick's a major head case." He added, "Don't forget to download my invoice, too."

Cam got up for a cup of coffee while the download was in process, then settled in at her terminal and began to scroll through Joe's transmission. The only installed software programs on Beth Whiteside's computer were a screen saver, a word processor, and America Online. The only pages Joe recovered were those Beth had saved to her hard drive as word processing documents and those that had been automatically saved to the Internet cache. Cam began with the word processing documents, and it took her only a minute or two to understand Joe's crack about the insanity defense. The first several pages looked to be research notes about recycling programs, landfill regulations, and nonbiodegradable waste. But these were followed by pages of incoherent fragments of text that made strange references to a bunny and a rat.

Laboriously she worked through the fragments, and thirty minutes later an astonished laugh burst out of her. Beth Whiteside had written a children's book about a young rabbit named Bunny who refused to clean her room and hid under her bed so her mother wouldn't find her. The floor was covered with dust bunnies, which very nicely camouflaged Bunny. Mrs. Rabbit, after searching for Bunny in vain, took it upon herself to sweep the floor, and Bunny got swept up with the dust bunnies and put out with the trash. From there she had an adventure in the trash truck and a perilous slide into the landfill, where she was befriended by a street-tough rat who taught her all about the waste disposal crisis in America and the urgent need to keep our planet clean, starting with our very own rooms. At the end Bunny made her way home and promised her mother never to mess up her room again.

"Oh, God," Cam muttered aloud, irritated at how much time she'd spent to retrieve something so useless to her.

She moved on to the next set of documents. The first several looked like proposals to publishing companies. Several pages of personal letters followed. A number were to *Dear Mom and Dad,* with no name or address shown—breezy little notes full of weather updates and news of friends and relatives. A few mentioned Steve and how busy he'd been. All of them ended with *Love you a bunch,* and one of them ended with a P.S.: *Steve finished the house, and it's gorgeous! (As you can see from the en-*

closed photo). He's got another one lined up, and we'll be moving there in a week or two. I'm not sure of the address, but I'll be in touch soon. The letter was undated.

Cam plodded on. There were more letters to book publishers, apparently follow-ups to the previously unanswered letters, and then another personal letter.

Dear Carol and Elliott,

It was such a pleasure meeting you last week and staying in your beautiful little inn. I really appreciated your hospitality and good company while Steve was busy on the island.

We'll be back again next Tuesday, but staying just the one night until we get the boat squared away. Steve says to tell you how much he appreciates your help there, and also about the car.

Thanks again. Look forward to seeing you!

Cam felt a little pulse of excitement begin to beat. Steve and Beth had stayed in an inn somewhere, somewhere near an island, and they'd planned a return trip. She knew from the letter to Mom and Dad that Steve had lined up a new job, and now she knew from this letter that he was somehow busy on an island. Could it be the new job? But the letter was undated: this could have happened months ago. And even after she read the letter again, she couldn't find any clue to where the inn might be.

She scrolled back and forth in search of a file that might contain the addresses for the letters, but there was nothing, and she'd reached the end of the word processing documents.

She switched to the file Joe had named *Surf and Save*, containing the material he'd recovered from the Internet cache. Here she found proprietary Web pages for some of the publishing houses Beth had written to, and for a society of children's authors. There were entertainment guides and retailers' sites, and a big cache of travel and tourism sites, with pages for spas and ski resorts, maps of state parks and hiking trails, and guides to dozens of hotels, restaurants, and camping sites. If there were any road signs in there, they were buried under a landslide of data. It was like going through the phone book line by line in hopes of stumbling over the name of a long-lost friend.

It was another dead end.

* * *

Doug's spirits were as low as Cam's that night. Jonathan Fletcher's dinner party wasn't what he'd hoped for. Its only apparent purpose was to afford Fletcher yet another opportunity to scrutinize Doug. He still wouldn't make a commitment, either of his vote or his checkbook.

"God," Doug said bitterly as he trudged up the stairs to bed. "I'd rather deal with a PAC or a corporate board any day. At least there it's all out in the open. You know exactly what they want, and you know how much they're willing to pay for it. But with Fletcher . . . ? He doesn't need anything from anybody. You know what he says he's looking for in a candidate? Good character and strong leadership. Jesus."

The rest of the bad news came out as they undressed for bed. An assistant of Meredith Winters had called that day to request some more biographical data. Meredith was unavailable when Doug asked to speak to her directly; according to the assistant, she was still undecided.

"This thing's just not coming together for me."

He was sitting on the edge of the bed with his back to Cam and his shoulders in a weary slump. This was the second night in a row that he'd come home disheartened about the campaign, and it made her tender toward him. She rose up on her knees behind him and began to knead the knotted muscles in his neck.

He hadn't really lied to her, she decided. *They can't find their copies of the adoption records,* was all he'd said. Maybe he'd forgotten that the firm had its own set. Maybe he'd never even known. She spread her hands out to massage his shoulders, and he sighed and let his head roll back on his neck. The worst he might have done was to obscure a few facts, and she of all people was in no position to complain about that. She stroked her fingertips against his temples, then leaned forward and nuzzled his ear.

"Speaking of coming together . . ." she whispered.

He turned around with a slow awakening smile.

She went to sleep rich in love that night, and floated to work the next morning on that same blissful cloud. The screen saver was glowing on her computer, a soothing scene of orange fish swimming dreamily in a blue sea. The image matched her mood, and she smiled across the office at Doug's photo as she sat down behind her desk. But as soon as she touched the keyboard, the fish disappeared, only to be replaced by the impenetrable depths of Beth Whiteside's computer memory.

Her happy mood evaporated and she stared at the screen in hopeless frustration. The data was dense and unfathomable and almost certainly pointless. Beth Whiteside had probably surfed the Internet randomly, out of boredom. Her visits to the travel and tourism sites were probably nothing more than flights of fantasy, escapes from Steve's neglect and the loneliness she'd felt at the house in Rehoboth Beach.

Cam scrolled through some pages of text and landed again on Beth's letter to the innkeepers, Carol and Elliott. It seemed her best and only lead, and even though it meant scrolling through the data line by line, that was what she would have to do.

But her head was pounding before fifteen minutes had passed, and she knew she couldn't do it. It was too great a morass, as overwhelming as the list of the 400,000 registered voters in Delaware—

An image of Maggie Heller suddenly flashed in her mind, brandishing a diskette and boasting, "Fully searchable."

"Idiot!" Cam hissed at herself as her fingers flew over the keys. She converted Joe's entire *Surf and Save* file to a word processing document, then typed in a search command: *Carol and Elliott.*

The results came back: *Not Found.*

She took a breath and tried again. *Elliott and Carol.*

This time the computer buzzed and bleeped through millions of bytes of data and landed on a page entitled *Coastal Maine Guide to Bed and Breakfast Establishments*. In the middle of the screen was an entry for *Breakwater Breakfasts and Beds, Too, Baxter Bay, Maine*.

The cursor was blinking at the line directly below that, the one that read *Elliott and Carol Rubin, Proprietors*.

12

Cam flew to Portland that afternoon and rented a car at the airport. By the time she turned off the highway and descended into the village of Baxter Bay, dusk was falling along with a light snow. She switched on the headlights, and the snowflakes refracted strangely in their glow, dancing and shimmering like a swarm of crystal mosquitoes in a suspension of liquid and light.

Baxter Bay was a summer tourist spot, but it was also a working fishing village, and unlike Rehoboth Beach, it was not a town in hibernation. There were men on the wharves and women on the streets, and lights were glowing in shops and houses along the way. A restaurant sign flashed on as she drove by: BAXTER BAY CHOWDER HOUSE.

She followed the road along the seawall a few blocks away from the harbor until she saw a spotlight shining on a sign that swung from a wooden post: BREAKWATER BREAKFASTS AND BEDS, TOO. Behind it a three-story house rose up, and an arrow pointed to parking in the back. Cam followed it and pulled into an empty space between two cars.

Darkness fell as she switched off the ignition. She got out of the car and felt her way around to open the trunk for her bag.

"Miss Smith?" called a man's voice.

"Yes, it's me," she answered.

Suddenly the parking lot was flooded with light. "I'll be right out for your bags," he yelled.

"Please don't bother. I only have one small one."

She slammed the trunk shut, and as she turned toward the house, she found herself standing behind the front grill of a Ford Explorer.

"Watch your step on the walk," the man called again. "I salted it, but there might be an icy patch or two."

"I will, thanks." She ducked her head down and crept between the cars to the rear of the Explorer. It was backed in tight against a retaining wall, and a blanket of snow lay over the bumper. She squeezed her arm through the opening and felt for the license plate. She couldn't find it, so she pulled her arm free and took off her glove and reached in again. This time her fingers traced over the empty bracket.

"Is anything wrong?" the man said behind her.

"Oh—hi." She withdrew her arm and turned with a little laugh. "No, I just had an earring pop off. I thought I heard it land back here. But I guess I'll have better luck finding it in the morning."

"I'll look for it myself, first thing." He held out his hand. "I'm Elliott Rubin."

"How do you do? Camille Smith."

He took her bag and guided her over the treacherous walk to the house. "My wife, Carol," he said, pointing to the woman who stood waiting at the top of the stairs.

"Welcome to Breakwater Breakfasts," she said.

They ushered Cam through the door and into a center hall that ran the depth of the house, past a kitchen of pine-board cabinets, a dining room with a big farmhouse table, and a pair of sitting rooms with fires burning on each hearth.

"It's rare for us to have guests this time of year," Carol said as she led Cam toward the stairs.

"I'm afraid this is business, not pleasure."

"Yes, so you mentioned on the phone."

Elliott was bringing up the rear with her bag. "What is it that you do?"

"I'm an editor. Children's book publishing."

"Isn't that interesting!" Carol said. "We know someone who's been trying to publish a children's book."

"Well, good luck to him," Cam said grimly. "It's a hard market to crack into. It breaks my heart sometimes, the wonderful stories I have to turn away. But we can only publish so many, you know."

"Oh. I didn't realize."

They reached the second-floor landing, and Elliott opened a door and ushered Cam into her room. It had a needlepoint rug, a four-poster bed dressed in Laura Ashley linens, and a window seat overlooking the bay.

"Would you care to join us for dinner?" Carol asked. "I'm afraid it's nothing fancy, but we'd be happy for the company."

"Thank you, but I have a dinner meeting at the Baxter Bay Chowder House. Do you know it?"

"Oh, sure. It's right down the street."

"Hey, wait a minute." Elliott jabbed a finger at Cam so suddenly that she almost backed away from him. "You sure you lost an earring out back? Because you have two of them now."

"Oh." Cam's hands flew up to her earlobes and she gave an embarrassed laugh. "I must have been hearing things. Sorry."

"No problem. I'm just glad we don't have to do any searching tomorrow."

"Me, too."

The Rubins took their leave, and Cam closed the door and crossed the room to kneel on the window seat. The snow was still swirling softly outside, and behind the iridescent flakes was a sky as black as the water. No light penetrated, not even the faint pinpricks of the stars. An Explorer without tags, a friend trying to publish a children's book—it had to be more than a coincidence. She was close, she knew it. Steve Patterson was somewhere across that black water, and she watched the snow fall in a shimmering curtain of white until it was time to leave for dinner.

At 7:45 she returned on foot to the inn and let herself in through the back door as she'd been instructed. The snow had stopped, and she was warmed by a dinner-sized bowl of fish chowder, though wearied by the ninety-minute charade of sitting at the table alone while glancing frequently at her watch. Her hosts were in the south sitting room, in wing chairs on either side of the fireplace. They looked up with bright smiles when she appeared in the doorway.

"Could I make a call on my calling card?" Cam's voice was tired and disgusted. "I need to reach my office."

"Sure. There's a phone in your room—"

"Is there one here? I have to catch my assistant before she leaves for the night." She looked at her watch. "It's almost eight. She'll be leaving any minute."

"Sure, right there in the hall—"

"Thanks."

Cam dialed her own number in Philadelphia and charged it to her long distance calling card. "Mary," she said sharply as the unanswered call went into her voice mail. "Thank God I got through before you left. Look, we must have gotten our wires crossed." She raised her voice a few decibels. "The author was a no-show. I waited for her for more than an hour. Well, double-check, would you? I'll die if she's waiting for me at some other restaurant. What? You're sure about that? Do we have any way to reach her? No, the Delaware address is no good. She left there weeks ago. But she must have given us some kind of contact number up here."

Cam paused long enough to hear the Rubins hissing whispers to each other in the sitting room.

"Oh, shit," she groaned. "You know what this means? We only have a one-day shot at the illustrator. If I don't get both him and the author signed up by tomorrow, this book is no-go." She stopped and heaved a sigh. "Ah, well. I guess there's nothing I can do about it. Book an early flight home for me, would you? Yeah, right. I'll see you then."

By the time she hung up, Carol and Elliott were standing beside her with shining eyes.

"Oh, my God, I can't believe it!" Carol burst out. "I think we know the author you're looking for!"

"No," Cam scoffed.

"Beth Whiteside?"

"Yes!" Cam cried.

Beth Whiteside had stayed right there at Breakwater Breakfasts—in Cam's own room, as a matter of fact—about a month ago when her boyfriend was scoping out a new job. They were there now, just the two of them, twelve miles out to sea on a privately owned bump of land called Maristella Island. Deserted for years, the island had recently been purchased, and Beth's boyfriend was remodeling the house for the new owners. There was no phone service there, but Elliott made a few calls and lined up a man named Al who was willing to ferry Cam out to the island in the morning.

It was a happy coincidence for everyone.

The temperature rose thirty degrees during the night, and when the sun came up the next morning, it showed only as a pale glow behind a viscous wall of thick white fog. Elliott kept getting up from breakfast to check out the window again. "Pea soup," he declared for the third time.

The phone rang, and he answered it in the hall. "Yeah, hold on." He leaned his head around the door to address Cam. "It's Al. He's wondering if you still want to go."

"Now or never," she said.

Carol lifted her mug and arched an eyebrow at Elliott, warning him not to interfere.

After breakfast Cam went to the same phone and called her office while she waited for Al to arrive.

"Morning, Helen, it's me," she said when her secretary answered. "Any messages?"

"Oh, yes." There was the sound of paper rustling. "Your husband called late yesterday. He said to tell you he had to go to Washington. He'll be at the Hay-Adams Hotel, and you should join him there if you can."

Cam fell silent.

"Hello?" Helen said after a moment. "Dear, are you all right?"

"Is there anything else?"

"Let me see. Oh, an old file arrived for you from archives. Ramsay Adoption, the label says."

Voices sounded behind her, and Cam looked back to see Carol opening the door for a burly man with a grizzled salt-and-pepper beard. She turned and hunched over the phone.

"Take a quick look inside, would you, Helen?"

"Hmm. Well, here's a pleading. The caption says 'Family Court of New Castle County, Delaware. Petition for adoption.' The petitioners are James Ashton Ramsay, Jr., and Margo Vaughn Ramsay, his wife. Wait a minute—isn't that the—"

"Yes. What else does it say?"

" 'Hereby petition the court,' et cetera, 'for a decree of adoption of a male infant born on September sixteen, 1984, in Geneva, Switzerland, consent of the birth parents attached—' "

"Take a look at the attachments."

Pages were audibly flipped. "The first one's called Waiver of Notice, Consent to Termination of Parental Rights and Consent to Adoption. 'The undersigned, Steven A. Patterson, birth father of a male infant born in Geneva—' "

"Camille?" Carol called down the hallway. "Al's here to take you to the boat."

"I'll be right there." To Helen she said, "Is there a second consent form attached?"

"Let me see." More pages were flipped. "Yes, here we go. Waiver of Notice, Consent to Termination of Parental Rights and Consent to Adoption. 'The undersigned, Cynthia Vaughn Ramsay, birth mother of a male infant born—' "

"Cynthia?"

"We best be going now."

The man named Al was at Cam's elbow, but she couldn't think of anything to say, to him or to Helen. She hung up without a word to either.

The trip out of the harbor was a slow and perilous one. Al hung his head over the gunwale and navigated from one channel marker to the next, and Cam sat beside him listening to the pings of the sonar and the gentle rhythmic lapping of the water against the hull. The sharp cry of a gull sounded nearby, but she couldn't see it or anything else through the impenetrable white wall of the fog. A fine mist settled over the skin of her face; it tasted of salt, like tears.

They cleared the channel, and as they headed out to sea, the sun rose in a dull glare and shone behind the white wall of the fog. It was like a backlit screen, and the images that were whirling through Cam's mind seemed to project themselves onto it. She could see the portrait of Cynthia over the mantel and the photograph of Trey over the sofa—not the sister and brother she'd thought they were, but mother and son. She could see the photograph of Steve Patterson in his football jersey, and that morphed into an image of Steve and Cynthia together, teenage sweethearts, in love and in trouble. Then it all faded back into Ramsay's campaign poster, into the triad of Ash, Margo, and Trey, and the lie of two happy generations where in truth there stood three.

This, then, was what had happened to scuttle the perfect order of a marriage between Doug and Cynthia. This was what kept Doug a bachelor for another thirteen years, and made Cynthia load up on drugs and wrap her car around a telephone pole one cold dark night. She'd fallen in love with the wrong man, then compounded her error by getting pregnant.

The news leak the Ramsays were so afraid of wasn't the fact that Trey was adopted, but the fact that he was Cynthia's illegitimate son. Yet it was a tale as old as time, parents taking their daughter's child and raising it as their own, and it was usually done openly, with no bones about it. The mystery here was the secrecy. The question was why the Ramsays were willing to give up Trey before they'd give up the truth.

I'm not the one who lied to him for thirteen years, Steve Patterson said. But he'd been willing to give up Trey, too. He'd signed the papers and walked away, when he could have done what young men had done since time immemorial—married the girl and made the best of it. Either that, or pay for the abortion. The point was, there were other options.

Cam huddled deeper inside her coat, for that question led to another. Why didn't Doug marry Cynthia and raise the boy as his own? In one fell swoop he could have had the wife he was meant to have and earned the Ramsays' eternal gratitude. Cynthia would be alive today and standing proudly by his side, and Trey would be the little scamp in Doug's campaign posters.

Al turned toward her. His lips were moving, but no sound came out.

"What?" she shouted.

"I said"—he cupped one hand around his mouth—"it's not too far now."

He pointed ahead off the bow. The fog was lifting like a gauzy curtain rising up into the sky, and suddenly a shaft of sunlight shot down and shone on a tiny island. Al cut the throttle back until the engine sounded in a throaty rumble, then lifted a pair of binoculars to his eyes. "There she is," he said, nodding. "Maristella Island."

Star of the Sea. "Can I look?" Cam asked.

He handed her the binoculars, and she brought them up and scanned the island. A deepwater dock, a dense stand of evergreens, and a wide snow-covered meadow rising up to the rocky headland where a ramshackle mansion clung to the top of the cliff.

There was a flicker of movement in the corner of the binoculars, and she swung them back and zoomed in on a pair of figures standing in a pool of clear light at one end of the house. She fiddled with the focus dial until the image went sharper. Her pulse quickened. One of the figures was tall with dark hair, and the other was shorter and slighter with long sandy hair blowing loose in the wind. They were working together, dismantling a lean-to addition that sagged against that end of the house. Patterson was tearing the boards loose with a crowbar, and Trey was picking them up and stacking them in a pile.

As Cam watched, Patterson put down the crowbar and called to Trey, and when Trey loped over to him, his father tousled his hair, then flipped up his hood and chucked him under the chin. Trey stalked away, and as Steve grinned and watched him go, the wind gusted and caught his hair in a wild dark flurry around his face.

When at last it stilled, so did he. He turned suddenly and scanned the ocean. He said something to Trey, then said it again, sharper, and Trey dropped the board he was holding and ran inside.

Cam's view was lost behind the forest as Al steered for the dock, past a rocky beach, then into a cove. Another boat was anchored at the dock, but she didn't even think to jot down the identification number stenciled on its transom. Steve Patterson was striding down the path to meet them.

Al cut the engine, and a vast silence rose up as he slipped the boat sideways toward the dock. Patterson caught the mooring line and looped it over a piling.

"Morning," he said. "What brings you folks out in weather like this?"

Al jerked his thumb. "Lady here needed to see you."

Patterson turned to Cam, and she watched the edge come into his eyes. She could see his suspicion of who she was and his dread of what she might do. But she could also see his determination, to resist, to fight if he had to. Yes, she thought, he gave up Trey thirteen years ago. But he'd reclaimed him now, with a vengeance.

"Do I know you?" he asked her.

"No." The word came out in a croak, and she cleared her throat to speak again. "No. I'm afraid I've made a mistake. This isn't where I wanted to go."

Al turned to her. "But you said Maristella—"

"It was my mistake," she said to Al, then looked up at Patterson where he stood coiled with tension on the end of the dock. "I'm very sorry to have bothered you."

He stared at her a moment, then bent over and threw the line free.

Al turned the boat westward and opened up the throttle, and as they picked up speed, the wind tore Cam's hair out from under her collar and sent it flying like a banner behind her. A distant foghorn gave a mournful blast, and when she couldn't hold her eyes forward any longer, she turned and looked back.

He was still at the end of the dock, watching her go until the fog descended and cloaked her again.

By five o'clock she was on a plane back to Philadelphia, and she used the Airfone at her seat to place yet another call to Doug's room at the Hay-Adams Hotel. This time there was finally an answer. But it was a strange man's voice, and she could hear the voices of other men behind it.

"Is Doug there?"

"Yeah, who's this?"

"His wife."

She waited through a round of laughter in the room until Doug came on the line. "Campbell? Where are you?"

"On my way home. Who's there? What's going on?"

"We're celebrating. Webb's here, of course, and Nathan came down, and there's a couple of terrific guys from the national committee here. Can't wait for you to meet them."

"What are you celebrating?"

"First and foremost, campaign finance reform got buried today." He laughed as a raucous cheer rose up behind him.

"Oh?"

"And we've got great news, honey! Meredith Winters just signed on to the campaign."

A second ticked past. "Oh. That's wonderful. But you won't forget? You promised we could talk . . . ?"

"Sure, of course. Nothing's going to happen without you, Campbell. We're in this one hundred percent together."

"Great," she said faintly.

"Hey, what about you? Did that lead pan out?"

"Hmm?" She stared blindly at the seat back in front of her. "Oh, no," she said at last. "No, I didn't have any luck at all."

13

"Tell me about your wife."

Doug's eyes darted from his own reflection in the mirror to Meredith's beside it, then to the tailor who was packing up his tape and chalk across the room.

It was the end of a long morning for him, and the end of an arduous effort for Meredith, but here stood the results: Doug Alexander, not only a new voice for the people, but a new man entirely. He was now the satisfied owner of a dozen new suits, expertly cut and padded to straighten and broaden his stooped shoulders; the still slightly self-conscious possessor of a full head of newly styled, blow-dried hair; and soon, she hoped, if he did his exercises, the relaxed speaker of an ever-so-slight southern dialect.

This last was the hardest to accomplish. "My God," he'd muttered after listening to the tape of his own electronically altered voice. "You gave me a southern accent."

"Only a trace. And only because eighty percent of your state—the whole area south of the Chesapeake and Delaware Canal—is demographically as southern as Tidewater Virginia."

"Sure, but the whole area north of the canal is about as northern as New York, and that happens to be the area I'm from. Along with the majority of our population, I might add."

"You're right, of course, but tell me—where do you expect your greatest opposition?"

He'd conceded with a sigh, "South of the canal," and took the tapes from the dialect coach and packed them in his briefcase.

"Sure," he said now as the tailor took his leave with an obsequious bow. "What do you want to know?"

"I heard that her parents died when she was quite small?"

"That's right." He turned to the side to assess his new profile in the mirror. "They went to the Philippines as missionaries when she was a baby. Her grandmother kept her for what was only supposed to be a year or so. But there was a Muslim uprising in 1968, and something like a hundred Westerners were massacred, her parents among them."

"How awful," Meredith said, wide-eyed, then, "What kind of missionaries?"

"Hmm?" He looked up. "To tell the truth, I'm not sure."

She raised a quick hand. "Word of advice. Never use the phrase 'To tell the truth.' It implies that nothing you said before was."

He stepped away from the mirror with a self-deprecating chuckle. "I see your point."

"What was her grandmother's name?"

"Let me think." He pulled off the new suit coat and hung it on the rack with the others. "Was she a Smith? Yes, that's right. She was Cam's father's mother."

"When did she die?"

"When Cam was only seventeen or eighteen. Oh, and here's something interesting," he added, pulling on the coat he came in. "Cam never went to school. Her grandmother home-schooled her. She had to do some scrambling to get herself into college without a high school transcript."

"How'd she pay for college?"

"She had a tiny inheritance from her grandmother, and the rest was all loans and scholarships and work-study jobs. It's a real Horatio Alger story, don't you think? Orphan girl struggling to make good on her own?"

"I do," Meredith agreed.

The conference room door opened, and she gave an irritated glance at the old man who wandered in. It was Richard Portwell, the semiretired founder of the firm, who was still nominally her boss.

"Hello, there, Meredith," he said absently, in the professorial muddle that was his favorite affectation. He was all tweeds and elbow patches, and he held the bowl of an unlit pipe in his hand. "Just thought I'd pop in and say hello to our newest candidate."

Meredith locked her jaw. "Richard Portwell, Doug Alexander."

"Glad to know you," Doug said, smile on, hand out.

She tried to signal him not to waste his charm. Portwell might still be a substantial equity owner in the firm, but he hadn't had a major candidate since 1976, which was, not coincidentally, the last time he had an original idea. His only function seemed to be to fret publicly about the ethics of modern-day electioneering while privately funneling off the lion's share of the profits they earned from it.

"Heard good things," Portwell said, waving the pipe in the direction of his mouth. "Good things."

"Yes, and he's in good hands, too, Richard," she said pointedly.

"She's the best, you know," he said to Doug, this time waving the pipe in her direction.

"I do know."

"Actually Doug was just leaving, Richard. He has a lunch date with Senator Ramsay."

"Ash? Oh, do give him my regards."

"I will."

"A pleasure meeting you—"

Portwell hesitated, and Meredith had two horrible thoughts: one, that he'd forgotten Doug's name; or two, that he was actually going to say *my good man*.

"—I wish you a good fight," he said instead. " 'Once more unto the breach,' eh?"

Meredith shuddered. Even worse than she'd feared.

"Where were we?" she said when he finally left. "Oh, yes, Campbell. Tell me—are you two thinking about children?"

Doug reared back and sputtered a laugh. "We only got married last month. It's a little soon to be talking about children, don't you think?"

Meredith made a sound of agreement as she crossed the room to the telephone. "Although," she said, dialing the extension. "Some people think it's also a little soon for you to be in national politics. And it's our job to do everything we can to change their minds—Hello, Webb? If you're done going over the budget, we're all through up here."

She hung up and turned back to Doug in time to see the understanding dawn in his eyes.

Webb Black arrived promptly to collect Doug for their lunch meeting. His promptness was one of the many things that disturbed Meredith about him. He had a rigid little mind and a passive, diffident manner, when what she wanted in a campaign chairman was a creative thinker with a full-steam-ahead mentality. The fact that he knew everyone of consequence in Delaware was of no consequence to her; contacts counted for nothing if you lacked the ability to exploit them. She knew that Norman Finn handpicked Black for the job, and she knew why—because he could be controlled. But she was the one controlling this campaign now, and Black didn't suit her at all.

"I'm so glad you were able to come down with Doug this time, Webb," she said as she led them both to the elevator. "I know our finance people were anxious to meet you."

"They didn't really have much for me," he mumbled.

"So I'll be talking to you soon." The elevator doors opened, and she steered them on. "Have a lovely lunch, gentlemen. Oh, and Doug," she added with a hand on the edge of the door. "Get your office to fax me Campbell's résumé and personnel file, would you? Today. We need to put together an official bio for her, too."

The doors snapped shut as he called, "No problem."

The office of Portwell & Associates occupied two floors of the K Street building, the fourth and fifth, and it was decorated like the exclusive men's club that politics used to be, in Oriental rugs and distressed leather and humidors and even a brass spittoon to which Meredith always gave wide berth as she passed. Someday, soon she hoped, when this was all hers, she'd have it gutted and redone. No more mahogany and wainscoting. It would be something forward-looking, appropriate for the new millennium, like the inside of a spaceship or a biodome.

She did the laps until she reached her office, where her assistant Marcy was waiting to hand her the videocassette. "Lunch?" Meredith asked as she strode past her.

"On its way."

The screening room was the smallest of the firm's many conference rooms. It held a few chairs lined up on one side of a table opposite a wall of electronics and TV monitors. Meredith closed the door, kicked off her shoes, and wiggled her toes blissfully in the deep pile carpeting. This was becoming her favorite power lunch—an hour alone with a sandwich and her legs propped up on the table. She loaded the cassette and hit the lights, then settled back as Phil Sutherland's face filled the screen in the first of the rough-cut TV spots.

He appeared in every frame of every thirty- and sixty-second ad they'd put together. Not the customary format, but Meredith understood the thinking: Sutherland was his own best advertisement. He looked great—there were no special pads required in his shoulders—and he sounded great, too, despite his refusal to undergo her consultant's accent-training program. Meredith didn't try to change his mind on that point; his voice was already too well-known to tamper with now.

But Doug Alexander was an unknown commodity, and whatever points he lost in name recognition, he gained in malleability. More and more she was convinced that it was Alexander who was going to make her reputation this year.

A knock sounded on the door. Lunch, at last. "Come in!"

A white-coated waiter backed into the room with a dinner cart. She pressed the Pause button and swung her feet to the floor. "What's all this?" She was expecting only a delivery boy with a grease-stained paper bag.

"Lunch for Señorita Meredith Winters?" the waiter said in an accent that turned *Winters* to *Weenters*.

"Yes . . . ?"

"Also for Señor Bret Sutherland," he said, turning around with a grin and a flourish.

"You clown." She leaned back with a smirk and held it while he ducked to kiss her.

"I think we're being watched," he murmured.

Sutherland was pointing a finger at them from the screen.

Meredith scooted her chair back and positioned the dinner cart between them. It held a bottle of French wine, a bowl of apricot-colored roses, and two tuna sandwiches. "You've gone all out, haven't you?" she said dryly.

He pulled up a chair across from her. "I'm saving the good stuff for the day you finally give in."

"Not in your refrigerator, I hope. It'll go rotten and stink up your whole house."

"Ha. You're a lot closer than you think."

"Give it up, Bret."

But even as she said it, she knew that he wouldn't. Ever since she spurned him—who knew? maybe she was the first—he'd become obsessive in his pursuit of her. He popped up at every meeting she was billed to attend; he found excuses to deliver things to her; he even sent her flowers—she hated to think what budget *that* was coming out of. She'd done all she could to discourage him—withering glances, disconnected phone calls, threats to tell his father—but everything she did seemed to egg him on more.

He opened the wine and filled their glasses. "To victory," he said, clinking his glass to hers.

"The only victory I'm drinking to is Phil Sutherland's." She winced at the way that came out and hurried to sip her wine. "But as long as you're here"—she hit the Play button again—"you might as well take a look at this, too."

The tape began to roll again, and Bret turned obediently to watch. But even sitting quietly as he was now, she felt him drawing her to him. It was the forbidden candy phenomenon, she knew that. No, the bag of coke. No, not even coke. He'd be like heroin in her bloodstream. A few injections of Bret, and before she knew it, she'd be strung out and destitute in a back alley somewhere.

Another thirty-second spot came on the monitor. This one was an attack on the incumbent's opposition to defense spending, with a subtle dig at his lack of military service. Meredith jotted down an approving note.

The next words Sutherland uttered were "threat to our national security."

"Shit," she hissed and pushed the Pause button.

"What?" Bret looked over at her.

She ran a distracted hand through her hair. "I've got this opponent up in Delaware—you know, Hadley Hayes—and that's his favorite refrain: 'This threat to our national security.' We've been planning to turn it against him. Our whole negative campaign has been designed around that idea, showing what a tired old war-horse he is. And here I've got Phil Sutherland singing the same goddamn refrain."

She took a gulp of wine and scribbled on her notepad for a moment, wondering how to homogenize the Sutherland attack on his incumbent with the Alexander attack on his.

"Wait a minute," Bret said.

She flapped an irritable hand at him and kept writing.

"Wait," he said again, his voice tense. "He's not singing any refrain."

"I didn't mean—"

He jumped up and started to pace the room. "It's not like he's just paying lip service to the idea, and it's not like he's owned by the defense industry, either. He really means it. Fuck, he really *lived* it."

She leaned back in her chair and gazed at him. It never failed to confound her, Bret's unswerving hero worship of his father. It was a mystery to her how he could grow up witnessing all of Sutherland's schemes and machinations and still remain so unsullied by it all. It took only a year of political reporting for Meredith to lose her innocence, but Bret's was still utterly intact. For him there were no shades of gray, only black and white, and his father was most assuredly on the white side. God, Meredith thought, marveling at him—what she'd give for just one hour of Bret's simple-minded naïveté.

"You know, you're right." She sat up straight and crossed out all of the half-formed ideas on her notepad. "We won't change a word."

He gave a slow happy smile and ducked to kiss her again.

"Come on," she said, pushing him away. "I have to finish these spots and get them back to editing by three."

He staggered back, clutching his heart in a tragicomic burlesque of a wounded man, then dropped to his knees and inched up to the side of her chair. "Have dinner with me tonight? Please, merry Meredith?"

"All right, all right!"

What was she thinking? she screamed inside her head after she saw him to the elevator and headed back to her own corner office. There wasn't a restaurant in town where they could eat without one or both being recognized. Which meant dinner at her house. Which almost certainly meant dessert in her bed. She might as well find an alley and open her veins right now.

Marcy was on the phone, and she called out, "Mr. Pfeiffer on line one."

"*Gary* Pfeiffer?" At once Bret was forgotten. "Put him through," she said.

She hurried to her computer and brought up Pfeiffer's profile before she picked up the phone. "Gary—how are you?" she purred. Her eyes skimmed down the screen until she found the entry for *Spouse*. "And how's Eileen? I haven't seen you two for ages."

"We're both fine. Busy. Like yourself, I'm sure."

Pfeiffer's voice flowed like molten silver over the line. That was the word that always came to mind when she thought of him. Silver. He had a handsome head of hair silvering at the temples and sharp silver-gray eyes, and he even drove a silver Mercedes. But mostly he reminded her of the monetary aspects of silver. He represented ALJA—the American Lawyers for Justice Association—which made millions of dollars in campaign donations. In 1996, ALJA contributed $2.5 million to the President alone, which was more than all of the retirees, doctors, teachers, civil servants, and media and entertainment people combined. *Including* Geffen and Spielberg. Little wonder people called the ALJA America's third political party.

"Shaping up to be quite a midterm election, isn't it?" Pfeiffer said.

Her eyes began to dance. She'd had her fingers crossed for a call from Pfeiffer ever since Phil Sutherland announced his Senate bid. "I can't speak for the rest of this town," she said, "but we've got some pretty strong candidates in our office."

"So I heard. In fact, that's why I called. I hear you got yourself a new dark horse out of Delaware. Alexander, is it?"

The light went out of her eyes. She'd been counting on Doug to remain anonymous until it was time for him to announce. "Where'd you hear that?"

"Meredith, I have fifty-six thousand members. You have to figure one or two of those are from Wilmington."

She was mollified by that—at least the leak was on Doug's end and not hers. And she was also assuaged by the thought of 56,000 multiplied by two thousand dollars, the maximum for hard money contributions by individuals. A hundred and twelve million dollars! It made her dizzy to think of it. And the amazing thing was that Pfeiffer could deliver a good chunk of that if he ever set his mind to it, because his members really had that kind of money. No union could ever match that kind of power.

"Delaware's kind of a small potatoes race by your standards, isn't it, Gary? You have 434 other House races to be watching. Not to mention thirty-odd Senate races?"

"Don't you worry about me. I'm watching every last one of them. But your boy Alexander interests me. A few of my members might be interested in supporting him."

Her pulse quickened. "Do I hear an *if* at the end of that sentence?"

"Well, of course we'd like to see him take a stand against this latest attempt at so-called tort reform."

She kneaded her forehead. Her lunch with Bret must have addled her brain, because she wasn't following this at all. "But that bill's coming up for vote this term. It'll either be law or dead in the water by the time Alexander's sworn in."

"Dead in the water is what we're aiming for. And of course one of the people who could help us sink it is Ash Ramsay."

"Oh," she said as the light dawned. "You think Doug has that kind of influence over Ramsay?"

"I don't know. Be nice for him if he did, though."

"I'm not even sure where Doug stands on that issue himself," she hedged as she scrolled through her notes.

"Oh, the race is still young, and so is he. He's got plenty of time to form a well-considered position. After he weighs all the pros and cons."

She found it. Doug was in favor of the tort reform legislation. She should have known. He thought the products liability laws were crippling U.S. manufacturers and putting them at a disadvantage with their foreign competitors.

"Exactly how much weight are we talking about in pros?" she asked.

He made a happy little humming sound on his end of the line. "Hmmm. I think five hundred thousand has a nice ring to it."

Five hundred thousand! It was a quarter of their total fundraising goal. But getting it meant not only convincing Doug to change his position, but also convincing Ramsay, who'd already voted for tort reform once before. But now that she thought about it, didn't Ramsay make a point of saying that his vote was still in play?

"I don't know, Gary. If you've got that kind of money to throw around, I wonder why you don't throw it at the people who are actually voting on the bill. Ramsay himself, for instance."

"That would be rather obvious now, wouldn't it?" he said with a chuckle. "We'd see a *Wall Street Journal* story in a matter of days, with a table in sidebar listing the contributions received by every legislator to vote down the bill."

"Ahh. Whereas no one will make the connection to Doug." She really was too slow today. "You're a shrewd operator, Gary."

"I have to be, Meredith," he said lightly. "Or people like *you* would be running this town."

* * *

After the call ended, Meredith leaned back in her chair and mused. If she could frame the issue a little differently, turn it on its head a few times, Doug might come to see tort reform as pro-corporate management and anti-working man, in which case he should be happy to oppose it. Especially with a half-million-dollar incentive.

"This fax just arrived for you," Marcy said, coming into the office with a thick sheaf of papers. "Material regarding somebody named Campbell Smith?"

Meredith put her hand out for the papers. It was the personnel file Doug had promised her. "Get Bill Schecter up here, would you?"

Schecter appeared in her doorway five minutes later and waited expectantly on his feet until she finished dictating some notes. He was a fifty-year-old man with the well-scrubbed look of a Boy Scout leader. He'd spent most of his career in the FBI's Applicant Program, doing background investigations and security clearances for judicial and Cabinet appointees. It was Schecter, rumor had it, who found Anita Hill during the Clarence Thomas hearings; and he was also said to have uncovered Zoe Baird's nanny and houseboy. He took retirement after his twenty years were in, and now he worked for Portwell & Associates. His title was director of research, but his duties were the same as they'd been at the Bureau: he vetted the firm's candidates and their opponents and the families and associates of all of them.

"I have a new assignment for you, Bill." Meredith handed him the fax. "I need a full field investigation on this one—Pennsylvania and Michigan and whatever else comes up."

"What account do I charge this to?"

"Split it between the Sutherland and Alexander campaigns."

"Who's Alexander?"

"Our newest hero, Bill," she said. "Try to keep up."

14

Cam parked in the lot behind the Holiday Inn in downtown Wilmington and climbed uncertainly out of her car. It was seven o'clock and dark as deep night. Only a few days before there'd been a warm promise of spring in the air, but tonight an icy snow was falling. Sugar snow, old Mrs. Smith used to call it, the last snow in March that signaled the start of the maple syrup run. The old woman lived on the same forty acres all her life, and there was nothing about that farm she didn't know, including the weather that came down on it. Even at the end when her mind went cloudy and time lost all its linearity, she still remained a farmer's almanac of information about her apportioned parcel of earth.

It was almost twelve years since she'd died, but Cam still remembered everything she learned from her. She could look at a jar of honey and tell whether the fields near the beehives were planted in buckwheat or clover; she could look at a tree laden with pinecones and predict that a cold winter was on its way. Her stay with Mrs. Smith was a sort of intermission in the story of her life, a time of quiet isolation when she could catch her breath and think about where her life could go from there. It was nine months of hard work and simple pleasures where everything was exactly what it seemed to be.

Whereas nothing was today. Her very identity was a lie, and she had to spin thread after thread of new lies just to hold the eye of that web intact. But lately the threads were stretching too thin. Any more and the whole web would collapse.

She'd been feeling that strain ever since she told Al to turn the boat around at Maristella Island. When she returned to the Breakwater Inn, she'd blurted an explanation to the Rubins: her headquarters had called; her budget was being slashed, so there was no longer enough money to publish Beth's book; and it would be too cruel for Beth to find out she'd come this close only to be disappointed. The Rubins were all solemn nods and sympathy. They couldn't bear to tell Beth either.

It was more of the same the next day when she broke the news to the Ramsays. Patterson had covered his tracks completely. Although she'd followed a lead up to New England, the trail went cold in Portland. She was terribly sorry, but there was nothing more she could do.

"It's no worse than we expected," the Senator said.

Margo wept softly into the sleeve of her kimono, and Cam felt a lump grow in her throat. They'd already lost one child, and now, thanks to her, they were losing another. For a moment Cam wavered, teetering on the indeterminate edge between right and wrong, and truth and falsehood. For a moment she was ready to speak up and reveal everything. Until Doug spoke up first.

"What are you telling Trey's school? And his friends?"

Margo looked up with eyes that were surprisingly dry. "That he's transferred to a school in Switzerland. My friend Liesl wrote them a letter. It's all very official-sounding."

Switzerland, Cam had thought, *Trey's birthplace,* and said nothing more.

The next day she'd stopped by the Senator's local office and asked for copies of his old press kits, explaining that she was looking for ideas on how to put together her own biographical profile. The secretary dug out a folder, and in fifteen minutes Cam found what she was looking for.

In 1985, soon after Ramsay was sworn in for his first term in the Senate, a local magazine ran a feature story on his home and family, complete with photos of Margo holding their midlife miracle baby in her arms. The article explained her absence from the campaign trail the previous year: because of the high-risk nature of her pregnancy, she'd been under the care of a specialist in Geneva, an internationally renowned obstetrician named Liesl Dorfmann, who also happened to be a good friend.

A very good friend, Cam thought. One who was still supplying the Ramsays with cover stories today.

Cam climbed up the hill to Market Street. Wilmington was a different town at night, after all the power-suited bankers and lawyers departed for their suburban homes. After dark it took on a bluesy, waterfront feel, full of mumbled laughter and shuffling feet, a wino in a doorway, a gang of teens scoring drugs on the corner. This section of downtown had been blocked off for a pedestrian mall, an urban renewal project gone bad. A few of the restaurants here did a decent lunchtime trade, but they closed at three, and all the remaining shops were either closed for the night or for good.

She stopped under a streetlight and gave another doubtful look at the slip of paper in her hand. Doug had omitted the name of the restaurant in the message he left with Helen; all he'd said was for her to meet him at this address at eight. They'd never eaten in this neighborhood before, but lately Doug was full of surprises. She patted her purse nervously. Tonight she had a surprise for him, too.

She scanned the street numbers above the doors, and her heart sank when she finally arrived at the address. Either Doug gave the wrong address or Helen took it down wrong, because this wasn't a restaurant. It was an abandoned storefront with murky plate-glass windows, without even a fading sign to mark what it used to be. Her shoulders sagged and she turned to trudge back to her car.

"Cam, wait!"

Doug was sprinting down the block, and she turned back with an overjoyed smile.

"I'm so glad you realized the mistake," she said, running to him. "I didn't know how I was going to reach you, and I didn't want you to be sitting at the restaurant waiting for me."

"Mistake? There's no mistake."

She gave him a puzzled look as he steered her back to the abandoned store and opened the door.

"Surprise!"

The space suddenly flooded with light, and dozens of people were springing up and pressing in all around them. Cam blinked and tried to back away, but Doug's arm was behind her, nudging her forward. She sent a dazed look through the crowd. They were all grinning maniacally at her.

"You did it, Doug!" called a voice. "You really surprised her!"

Cam knew that voice, and she traced it to Maggie Heller, wearing a pointed hat and blowing on a paper noisemaker that unfurled like a lizard's tongue. Beside Maggie was Nathan Vance, and behind him was Webb Black.

"Doug, what's going on?" she whispered.

"She wants to know what's going on!" he said with a hoot of laughter as he pulled off her coat.

"Jeez, Cam," Nathan said. "Don't tell me it's so traumatic for you to turn thirty that you completely blocked it out of your mind."

Turning thirty, she registered slowly, then remembered the date. March 13. Friday the thirteenth to be exact.

Doug smiled and bent to kiss her. "Happy birthday, Campbell."

There was a burst of applause, then Maggie Heller led a hearty refrain of "Happy Birthday." At the end of it, Gillian appeared, the pretty little coed who'd helped at the brunch a few weeks ago. She looked like Alice in Wonderland tonight, in a blue jumper and a matching velvet headband, and she was wheeling out a cake ablaze with candles.

"Make a wish!" someone cried.

Doug held Cam's hair back, and she closed her eyes and leaned over and blew out all thirty candles.

Another cheer rose up, and someone else shouted, "All right! Now we know for sure Doug's going to win!"

Cam's smile shook as the crowd applauded.

As Maggie went at the cake with a carving knife, Cam looked around the room. It was an old storefront, as she'd guessed, but it wasn't abandoned after all. There were two neat rows of desks leading from the front door to a room in the back, and there were file cabinets still in their cardboard packing and phone sets wrapped in plastic on the desktops.

"What is this place?" she finally whispered to Doug.

Gillian appeared before him offering a slice of cake and a shy smile. He passed the plate to Cam and held out his hand for another.

"That's the second part of the surprise. Cam, you're standing in the Alexander for Congress campaign headquarters!"

Another cheer went up, and suddenly Cam felt as if she were the one who'd slipped down the rabbit hole.

"Great location, isn't it? Nathan found it for us."

Nathan stepped up with a smug look on his face. "And I got a surprise for *you*, Doug," he said. "Marge Kenneally signed on today."

"All *right*, my man!" Doug crowed, and reached up to slap a high five with him. "Great work!"

"Who's Marge Kenneally?" Cam asked.

"A state senator down in Milford," Nathan said. "She's agreed to run against Doug in the primary."

She looked up at Doug. "You're happy that somebody's opposing you?"

He shook his head fondly at her, a patient and patronizing prelude to his explanation. "She's doing it as a personal favor to me. If there's no contest, there's no primary. I have to have a straw man to run against."

"Why?"

"Because," he said, a little less patiently, "individual contributors are capped at a thousand dollars per election. If I don't run in the primary, my contributors are limited to a thousand a head. With Marge on the ballot, they're all good for two thousand a head."

"And don't forget the free publicity," Nathan said. "You get ninety-five percent of the primary vote, the press'll call it a landslide and never bother to mention that Marge was only doing her duty for the Party."

Doug nodded. "We'll have to be sure to show her our appreciation. Remind me after the election, would you, Nathan?"

"You bet."

Cam put her plate down on one of the empty, expectant desktops and touched Doug's elbow. "Honey? Could I talk to you for a minute?"

"Now?"

"Please."

He gave a perturbed nod toward the back and followed after her with his plate in hand. "Excuse me, everybody," he called over his shoulder. "My bride wants to thank me in private!"

She cringed at the laughter that followed them.

He hit a light switch in the back room, illuminating a conference table with a dozen chairs around it still in their plastic wrappers. She closed the door.

"What's up?" Doug said. "We need to get back to our—"

"You shouldn't have done this."

His eyes went soft and he came up and took her face in his hands. "Why not? You deserve a party more than anyone."

"That's not what I mean." She shook her head free and stepped back. "You shouldn't have rented this space. You shouldn't have bought all this equipment. You shouldn't have recruited Marge what's-her-name. You promised—"

His face went tight. "I've kept that promise. I said I wouldn't announce, and I haven't. But there're things that have to be done in the meantime. You can't expect me to be sitting on my hands—"

"Yes, I can! If you really meant what you said, that you wouldn't run if I didn't want—"

"I never said that."

Her face froze, and slowly the color bled from her cheeks.

"God, what is your problem?" he whispered harshly. "Most wives would be thrilled. They wouldn't be dragging me down every chance they got."

She turned her back to him and took a breath, then reached into her bag and pulled out the envelope.

"Here's my problem."

He looked at it blankly, then opened the clasp and slid out the picture. It was a color photograph—of her, nude, lying provocatively in a tangle of black satin sheets.

His face showed a flicker of astonished delight. "Cam—wow," he said before he caught himself. "But—do you think this was wise? I mean, where'd you have this done?"

He thought she'd done it as a gift for him. "Ann Arbor, Michigan," she said tightly. "In 1991."

He pulled his eyes from the photo to stare at her. "What did you say?"

"Doug, I was broke. I needed money to buy books and a meal ticket. This guy was advertising on campus bulletin boards. He paid five hundred dollars, and that was a fortune to me then. So I posed for him. He took about a dozen shots like this one."

"Where . . . ?" He lowered himself into a chair, and the plastic wrap crackled under the dead weight of his body. "What did he do with them?"

"I don't know. I assume he peddled them to one of those magazines."

"You never tried to find out?"

"I just wanted to forget about it. And I did, too, until—this."

He slid the photograph back into the envelope and folded down the brass clasp with abundant care.

"Doug, I'm so sorry." She dropped to her knees beside his chair. "If I'd known about your political ambitions, I would have told you this before we were married, I swear. But I never guessed—you never mentioned—"

"You had your secret, I had mine." He let out a hollow laugh. "They just happened to be incompatible. Porno model and politician—it's like some sick version of 'Gift of the Magi.' "

She picked up his hand, and it lay stiff and lifeless in hers. "I'm sorry."

"Who knows about this? Nathan?"

"No—God, no. I never told anyone."

"How'd he pay you, this—photographer?"

"Cash."

"Did you give him your name?"

"Not my real one."

He rose abruptly. "Then what ties you to the pictures? Nothing."

"*Doug!* It's *me* in the pictures. Anyone can see it. You saw it yourself."

"Who can prove that's you? The world's full of look-alikes. If anyone brings this up, we'll just deny it." He turned and paced the length of the conference table. "It probably never will come up. For all we know, this guy never sold the pictures to anybody. And what are the odds that some two-bit pornographer in Michigan is going to follow a congressional race in Delaware?"

"Whatever the odds—" Cam looked up at him, her eyes gone wide. "You're willing to take that chance? And expose me to that?"

"Hey—you're the one who exposed yourself."

She stared at him.

A new burst of cheers sounded outside, and he went to the door. "Put that away," he said, pointing at the envelope on the table. "Ash!" he exclaimed before the door slammed behind him. "Thanks for coming!"

They drove home in their separate cars and climbed upstairs and undressed in silence.

Doug doused the lights and stretched out on his back a foot away from Cam. She waited a few minutes, then inched across the mattress and ran her fingertips across his chest and up to his jaw. The muscles in his neck and shoulders went tight, and he made no move toward her. She squeezed back the tears, then slowly moved her hand downward and inside the waistband of his boxers. Softly she stroked, and slowly the stiffness went out of his neck and into his groin, and when at last she heard him groan, she lifted her face for a kiss.

But he didn't kiss her. He grabbed her head and pushed it down and held it there.

She understood. She'd cheapened herself in his eyes tonight. He'd never look at her, never touch her, with the same worshipful reverence again. She knew this was the price she might have to pay, but what she hadn't considered was that she'd pay that price whether she got what she wanted or not.

Then she understood something else. All deals were off now. He wouldn't feel any obligation to discuss anything again. The burden of her secret had freed him to act only for himself. Tonight she'd fired the final weapon in her arsenal, but somehow he'd defused it and left her with nothing. There were no more practical objections to raise, no more political analyses to overwhelm him with, and no more sweet talk to cajole him to her way of thinking.

He reached a quick and joyless orgasm and rolled away from her with a shudder.

There wasn't even sex anymore.

When at last she slept that night, she had a dream that she was underwater, swimming with sluggish limbs through a dark and heavy sea. She was stroking hard, pulling till her arms ached, but it was all blackness around her, and she didn't know where she was going or whether she was making any progress, or even why she was trying so hard. Then slowly, dimly, a shaft of light opened up, and slowly, faintly, she could see that there was a shoreline ahead. Far, far ahead. She was out of breath, and she opened her mouth and flooded her lungs with a rush of cold black water, then put her head down and continued swimming toward the light.

She was drowning, but she kept on swimming.

Doris Palumbo heaved a sigh as the telephone rang and the baby began to wail again. Forty-five minutes she'd walked the floor with that child and now she'd have to start all over again. She scooped the baby out of the Portacrib and clamped her to her shoulder with one hand while she reached for the phone with the other.

"Hello?" she shouted.

"Could I speak with Doris Palumbo, please?"

She massaged the baby's tiny back until her cries began to subside into sobbing hiccoughs. "Yes, what is it?"

"Mrs. Palumbo, my name is Helen Nagy. I'm an employee of the firm of Jackson, Rieders and Clark, in Philadelphia?"

The boys were watching cartoons downstairs, and Doris paused to listen as a squabble threatened to erupt between them. "Yes, what's this about?"

"I understand you were acquainted with Gloria Lipton?"

"Gloria?" Doris was so surprised that her hand stopped stroking the baby's back, and Megan let out a sudden screech of protest. "Why, yes," she said, massaging again. "She's one of my oldest friends." The boys' quarrel escalated, and she moved to the top of the stairs and shouted down, "You kids be quiet now. Grandmom's on the telephone." She jiggled the baby again. "Why?" she asked the caller. "Is something wrong with Gloria?"

"I'm very sorry, Mrs. Palumbo. She's passed away."

The edge of the bed met the backs of her knees, and Doris sat down so suddenly that it startled the baby into silence. "Oh," she gasped. "Oh, my." She took a long, ragged breath. "I'm sorry, it's just that she was so young—What was it? Had she been ill very long?"

"I'm sorry to have to tell you this, but she was murdered."

"Oh!" Her arms squeezed together in a reflex and the baby let out a piercing shriek. "Oh! Poor little Megan," she cried and jounced her again until she was quiet. "Who did it?" she asked. "What was it all about?"

"Apparently it was just a random street crime. The police have no leads."

"Oh, my God, I can't believe it. Poor Gloria. For somebody to come out of nowhere—" There was an outburst downstairs, and Doris clamped her hand over the phone and shouted, "Be quiet! I'm trying to talk here!"

"Mrs. Palumbo, the reason I called is that we've been trying to locate any relatives Gloria might have, or friends who ought to be notified. I found your name in her address book, and I wondered if you might know anyone—"

"Gloria didn't have any family left. As for friends, well, it was always the four of us—Gloria, me, and Abby Zodtner, and Joan Landis. But, Lord, it must be ten or fifteen years since we lost track of Abby, and I don't keep in touch with Joan anymore. Oh, dear—what does that mean? Does that mean there's nobody to bury Gloria? What's going to happen to her?"

"Gloria left her affairs in very good order," the woman said. "She had a prearranged funeral already paid for."

"Oh, that's just like her. She was always so organized."

"Do you have addresses for Mrs. Zodtner and Mrs. Landis?"

"Oh, it's not Mrs., I mean, their married names. Let's see. Abby married a fellow named Johnson. And Joan's husband had one of those funny English names, like Trueblue or Trueblood or something. I don't know where they ended up—he was posted pretty much around the world. But Abby now, she lived up there in Pennsylvania. Near Altoona maybe? But like I said, this was a long time ago."

"Thank you for your time, Mrs. Palumbo."

"Thank you for letting me know."

Doris hung up and sat in a daze for a moment until she realized that by some miracle the baby had gone to sleep on her shoulder. She rose carefully and eased her down softly in the crib.

Downstairs, Dylan and Joshua were brawling over the single flesh-colored crayon in the box. They were only cousins, but they spent so much time together that they fought like brothers. Doris came down and caught Joshua's fist before he could slam it against Dylan. "That's enough now," she said, and took all the crayons and put them out of reach. "Time for a snack."

The boys settled down at the kitchen table with apple juice and equal counts of pretzel sticks, and Doris watched them with her chin in her hands and her thoughts drifting back in time. It was so long ago, and they'd grown so far apart since then, but back in the Sixties they were inseparable. The four Secreteers, Abby used to joke. Abby was the pretty one, Joan the sweet one, Gloria the ambitious one, and Doris the bighearted mother hen of the bunch. Though in truth they were all pretty and sweet and ambitious, and they'd all come to Washington with their hearts wide open. They arrived in town the same month—July 1966—and went through training together and ended up rooming together, too, which was a blessing in an agency so top-secret they weren't even allowed to say its name. They had everything in common, four girls from four different pockets of rural America, each one fresh out of high school and the smartest girl in her class. They were all clear-eyed and professional and ready to do their duty for America, but they had their own agendas, too. At a time when the rest of the country was wearing long hair and blue jeans and protesting the war in Vietnam, they wore girdles and bouffant hairdos and dated military attachés. They always kept one eye on the steno pad and the other eye peeled for the perfect man.

None of them succeeded. Abby had the best prospects—she'd dated a congressman, for heaven's sake—but one day out of the blue she packed her bags and went home to marry her high school sweetheart. Joan married a terribly sophisticated Englishman she thought was a senior attaché for the embassy; later she learned he was a junior clerk. As for Doris, she met a Marine guard one morning while she was delivering a message to the White House, and he looked so dreamy in his dress uniform that three weeks later she eloped with him to Elkton. He looked less dreamy in his civvies after he mustered out, and anyway, after a few years, he mustered out of the marriage. Finally there was Gloria, who never married at all. She said she never met anyone who could measure up to her standards. Now, Doris thought mournfully, she never would.

Six o'clock came and went, and when the girls still hadn't arrived to pick up the kids, Doris heated up a can of SpaghettiOs for the boys. At seven o'clock she gave all three their baths and dressed them in the pajamas she kept on hand for times like this. At eight, Chrissie called. She'd had to work late, and one of the guys from accounting just asked her out to dinner, and would her mother mind keeping Dylan and Megan overnight? Of course, Doris didn't mind. She knew better than anyone that a divorcée with two kids had to grab every chance she could. Dawn called five minutes later. She'd worked late, too, and she was too exhausted to drive the ten miles to pick up Josh. Would her mother mind bringing him home?

She pulled snowsuits on over the pajamas and loaded the children into the car, and they set out just as the snow was beginning to fall. Doris started the song the boys loved best: *Said a flea to a fly in a flue / Said the flea, What shall we do?*

"Again, Grandmom," Joshua cried when she reached the end of the song. "Sing it again!"

She was starting all over, *Said a flea to a fly,* when something danced in the corner of her eye. She looked up at the rearview mirror and saw a blue light flashing behind her. Had she been speeding? She didn't think so. But hers was the only other car on the road—those lights had to be for her.

A truck weigh station was ahead on the right, and the unmarked car passed her and signaled her to follow. The sign said the station was closed, but the gate was open, and Doris drove through behind him. She was relieved to have a safe place to pull off. She'd only been pulled over once before in her life, and that was on a busy highway during rush hour; she'd been so worried that the young officer would be sideswiped by the traffic that she barely heard a word he said. This was a much better place.

When the policeman stopped, she pulled up behind him.

"Where are we?" Dylan asked, sitting up straight. "This isn't Josh's house."

"That policeman wants to talk to me," Doris said.

Behind her, Joshua unbuckled his seat belt and scrambled between the seats to see. "Is he gonna arrest you, Grandmom?"

"Of course not, sweetie."

The officer stepped out of the car and adjusted his hat before he strode back toward Doris. She wound down her window. "Hello? Is anything wrong?"

"Please step out of the car, ma'am."

"Oh." She hadn't realized she'd have to do that. Maybe there was a bad brake light he wanted to show her. She wound up the window again so the children wouldn't catch their death and tried to remember if her inspection sticker was current. "What is it, officer?" she asked, climbing out of the car.

Something swept out of the dark and slammed against the side of her face; the air left her lungs in a burst of surprise. It struck again, harder, and she felt bones cracking and blood vessels exploding in her face. She lurched to her knees. Another blow landed and spun her halfway around. She clutched at the fender of the car and tried to claw herself to her feet, but he wrenched her back by the arm and threw her down on the icy gravel.

A muffled wail came from inside the car.

"Not here, please," she gasped as he pushed her legs apart. "Not in front of the children!"

He cut off her protests with an arm pressed hard across her throat. "Lie still," he whispered softly. "And be real quiet."

The night closed in around her in a great silent swell of darkness until the only sounds she could hear were the faint screams of her grandchildren and the pounding of their tiny fists against the glass.

It sounded, she thought faintly as her blood poured out into the gravel, like the wings of moths battering against a window to reach the light.

15

Nothing had changed. It was still the same four-lane highway through the valley, the same exit number off the interstate, and the same GAS, FOOD, LODGING marker that persuaded the motorists to turn off and fuel up. That marker was all that kept Johnson's Sunoco in business, a lesson Cam learned one day when she was eight or nine and not a single car pulled up to the pumps. All day her father kept walking out to the access road and looking up and down in search of the cars that weren't coming. That night after dark he climbed in his truck with Cam beside him and they drove to the next exit fifteen miles east and got on the interstate there. He slowed down as their own exit approached. Skid marks streaked the roadway, and they ended where the marker should have been. He pulled over to the shoulder, and Cam watched from the cab window as he studied the mangled signpost on the ground. He could have called the highway department; in a week or two they would have sent out a crew. Instead he loaded the sign into the truck and drove back to the garage. Cam stayed out of his way and watched him weld and hammer it back into shape. She was in bed by the time he loaded it into the truck and took off again, and she woke the next morning to the familiar hydraulic hiss of the tractor-trailers as they slowed down and turned into the station.

Now, twenty years later, she was the one slowing down and turning into the station. It was her third approach today, and when no one followed her off the exit ramp this time, she pulled into the station and up to the pumps. A cold March wind howled through the valley and battered against her as she climbed out. She hooked the nozzle in the tank, then hunched her back to the wind and let her hair whip wildly over her face.

Everything was the same: the office and the twin bays of the garage; the rest rooms on either side, ladies to the right, gents to the left; the house trailer on the hill behind it; and the faded sign over the door that still read: JOHNSON'S SUNOCO, CHARLES JOHNSON, PROP. It was so much the same that she almost expected Darryl to saunter out and prop an elbow against the roof and say: "What can I do ya for, dollface?"

But Darryl had been fired thirteen years ago, and the pumps were all self-service now.

The valve shut off; the tank was full. It was time at last to go inside.

A plump young woman with bright blond hair was behind the counter, and she looked up and took a drag on her cigarette as Cam came in. Through the shop door behind her came the sounds of tools clanging and country-western music on the radio. Cam went to scan the selection of road maps on the wall rack, and she pulled out a map and pretended to study it. The stench of tobacco mingled with the smells of petroleum and axle grease, and she had to breathe through her mouth to keep the nausea from crashing over her.

Cam ducked her head and stole a glance at the young woman behind the counter. She used to sit on that same stool and do her homework while she tended the cash register after school. Darryl handled the cash sales outside, but he had to bring the credit cards in to her. Her stomach used to churn as he approached her with that indolent hip-rolling gait of his, and her fingers used to fumble as he stood there watching her run the card through for approval. He was twenty and she was fourteen and his eyes were all over her. By the time she was fifteen, his hands were all over her, too.

This young woman sat comfortably behind the counter and showed none of the agitation Cam used to in the same job. She looked happy, Cam thought. There was nothing here to overwhelm or baffle her, nothing to force her to the tears of frustration she shed so often as a child. She rotated on her stool. "Can I give you directions someplace?" she called.

Cam glanced out at the empty pumps. "Yes, thanks." She came over and spread the map open on the counter, and the woman propped her cigarette on the edge of an ashtray and bent over it. "Where ya trying to get?"

Their heads were close, their eyes were down, and Cam said softly, "Charlene, it's me."

Slowly her sister's head came up and she gasped in three separate puffs of breath. "Oh. My. God."

"Please don't say my name."

Her eyes opened wide.

"Who's back there?" Cam lifted her chin at the door.

"Nobody. Just Dad. Hold on a minute." Charlene edged off the stool and shuffled sideways to the shop door. "Hey, Dad," she called in a tight voice. "Wanna come here a minute?"

Cam looked outside again. Her rented Nissan was still the only car at the pumps.

A man came to the doorway with an expectant half grin on his face, waiting to see who wanted him for what. His belly jutted over the belt of his grease-stained work pants, but all the flesh seemed to have gone from his face, leaving flaps of skin hanging loose and empty under his chin. His smile faded as Cam straightened, and suddenly he looked like a man grown old on worry. "Well, I'll be," he said. "Look at you, Cammy. All grown up."

"Don't say her name," Charlene hissed.

"All right," he said mildly.

"How have you been?" Cam asked with a trembling smile.

"Good, good. No complaints. Hey, you girls want to go up to the house? I'll watch the pumps, Charlene. You go on up, have a bite to eat."

He was already moving behind the counter and Charlene was already starting for the door, both of them behaving as if Cam were only a long-lost daughter come home and this was just some happy family reunion.

"I can't do that," she said sharply.

They looked at each other, then at Cam.

"I came to tell you something. I wish I could stay and visit, too, but I don't want anybody to know—" She stopped.

"That you're related to us." Charlene reached for her cigarette, and a half inch of gray ash dropped off as she put it to her mouth again.

"Don't worry," their father said. "No one's gonna find out anything from us. No one ever has."

"Does anyone come around anymore? That you know of?"

"Oh, sure. Somebody pays us a visit every year or so, just to let us know they're still watching."

Thirteen years, Cam thought. Jackson, Rieders & Clark had a

vault full of files that old and older; it was probably nothing for the FBI to keep a case open this long.

Charlene was staring at her, and suddenly she blurted, "Do you highlight your hair?"

"Do I what?" Cam lifted a hand to her hair. "Oh, no—I don't. I love the color of yours, though. You look great. Both of you," she said, and turned to her father's sagging face.

"You, too," he said. "Just like your mother."

Cam's gaze dropped to the map while the word hung untouched there between them. It was like roadkill—something to skirt around and try to get past without getting blood on the wheels.

"Oh, my God!" Charlene suddenly squealed. She was staring at Cam's hand. "You're married!"

"That's what I came to talk to you about."

"What d'you know?" her father said, beaming. "That's great. Just great. What's this fella's name?"

"It's better if you don't know."

A whine of brakes sounded outside, and they all went tense. It was a familiar sound to each of them; it meant there wasn't much time left. Cam spoke rapidly with her head down: "Here's the thing. He's going into politics, and some people might start looking into my background. Somebody might come here—"

"He's rich?" Charlene exclaimed.

"No, not at all—"

"Don't worry about it," her father said. "Anybody comes around, we'll tell them the same as always. You ran off when you were fifteen and we haven't seen you since. Or heard from you."

Cam nodded. The first two parts of that were true, and the third was nearly so; at any rate, it was what they'd agreed upon long ago. "But they might show you a picture," she said. "Of what I look like today."

Charlene ground out her cigarette in the ashtray. "You want us to say we don't recognize you?"

"Yes, but that's not really enough—"

"Oh," her father guessed. "You want me to come right out and say 'That's not my daughter.' "

She looked up at him. It was exactly what she wanted, and he said it without rancor or resentment. He said it without *any* expression, and it made her wonder—could he have denied Charlene so easily? He'd been a kind father, a benign presence in

Cam's childhood, but it was always Charlene who'd held his heart.

He's afraid of you, her mother used to say. *He doesn't know what to make of a girl as smart as you.*

But you're smart, too, Cam once pointed out.

Yeah, that's right.

It was all meant to even out: Charlene could be his little pumpkin, because Cam was so clearly her mother's special child. But that was a relationship freighted with burdens and bewilderments. There were a hundred times when Cam would have traded it for this simpler love.

"Yes. Thank you," she said.

An eighteen-wheeler was pulling up to the diesel pump at the far end of the lot. Cam refolded the map and dug in her purse for her wallet, and as she handed Charlene a twenty, some conceit seized hold of her, or perhaps some urge to tie herself to these people who were too willing to let her go. "You've been getting the money I send?" she said. "The money orders?"

Charlene's eyes bugged out. "That was from you? We thought it was from Mom!"

The air went suddenly cold and still inside the station. Cam stared at her sister, then at her father, but no one spoke, and the only sound in the room was the rushing in her ears. Outside the driver of the truck was vaulting out of his cab.

"What—What would make you think that?" she whispered.

"I don't know," Charlene said. "The postmarks were from all over the place, so we just assumed, you know. . . And my birthday presents—the cards were always signed Mary Mack, so we thought it had to be Mom."

Cam stared at her. *Miss Merri-mac-mac-mac,* their mother used to sing, *All dressed in black-black-black.* There was something in the repetitiveness of the song that delighted Charlene as a little girl. *Again, sing again!* she used to cry.

"I never sent you any presents," Cam said numbly. "Only money orders."

"Oh. Then I guess the other *was* from Mom. But anyway, thanks for the money. That was awful nice of you."

"Real sweet," their father agreed.

A gust of cold wind shot through the room as the door opened behind Cam. "So I just keep on going west on Interstate 80?" she said. "And that brings me to Du Bois?"

"Yes, that's right," her father said after a beat. "Another twenty miles or so."

"Thanks very much."

She turned and stepped around the truck driver.

"You take care now," Charlene called.

"Thanks." Cam's voice cracked as she opened the door. "You two do the same."

She drove west on the interstate until she was sure the eighteen-wheeler wasn't following her, then exited and doubled back and picked up a state road that wound its way south toward Altoona. Her mind swam in a whirl of awakened memories. Five minutes inside the filling station had erased all of the thirteen years away from it. She was a teenage girl again, on the brink of a new life then as surely as she'd been last month when she'd married Doug.

That was the trouble with brinks, she thought. You might launch yourself off from them and soar exhilaratingly through the air. But you might just as easily stumble and plummet headlong over the edge.

Darryl Pollack was no good; everybody knew that even without Cam's mother constantly harping on the subject. It was the reason Cam had to check his cash receipts against the meters every day; it was why her father never left the garage to run errands until Cam got home from school and took over the office. She knew it so well that she never once let her guard down where the money was concerned.

He had narrow hips and heavy-lidded eyes and dirty blond hair in a ponytail down his back. He was supposed to keep busy in the shop between gas customers, but whenever her father wasn't around, he'd sneak up behind Cam and lean against the doorjamb, watching her. "Hey, J.B.," he'd say, and she'd spin around and say, "What?" He never answered, only moved his eyes slowly and deliberately to the breasts that were still so new and strange to her.

It took two or three weeks before she worked up her nerve to ask what J.B. meant.

"Jailbait," he said with a grin.

She didn't know what that meant either, but was too proud to ask again.

One day he interrupted his leering to say, "Bet they're not real."

She knew what that meant, but she was too young to know how to wither a man with a look and a scathing remark. Indignantly she replied, "Are, too."

"Prove it," he said.

She'd flushed so hot she thought her head would ignite, but she couldn't turn around, she couldn't look away, and it was finally Darryl who left, with a swagger in his hips that made her burn even hotter to watch it.

He came closer after that, sometimes nuzzling the back of her neck, sometimes thrusting his tongue in her ear, always staring fixedly at her chest. She started to think about his stare when she dressed in the morning and when she went to bed at night. It thrilled her to think that he could be so obsessed with her body. It made her feel that she had some magical power over him.

The next time he said "Prove it," she swallowed hard and said, "Prove it yourself."

He didn't hesitate. He thrust his hands under her shirt and fondled her so long and hard that her nipples were still tingling when she sat down to dinner that night.

"What's the matter with you?" her mother asked.

"Nothing."

"You're awful quiet."

"Is that a crime?"

"It's not that boy Larry, is it? The one who keeps calling here?"

"You mean the one you keep hanging up on?"

"You've got no time to be wasting on boys."

Cam shrugged and scraped her peas into a little heap. This was a familiar refrain. Boys were a silly distraction, a waste of time that would be far better spent studying. And that was at their best. At their worst, like Darryl, they were the path to degradation and ruin.

Her mother's eyes were still on her. "Is it that hoodlum Darryl?" she demanded. "Has he been bothering you?"

Cam put on a bored expression. Keeping secrets was already an old habit for her. Since she was little she'd kept a private place in her mind where she could hide all the ideas that were too precious to share with these people. Now she realized that she could have private places in her body, too, also precious, that she'd share only with Darryl. "I barely even notice him," she said.

"I don't like you working down there with him. He's no good. Besides"—she turned to Cam's father—"her schoolwork needs to come first."

He chewed a minute, then said, "The girl already gets straight A's. I don't see how she could do any better."

"I mean for her to do a lot better than this. The more time she gets to spend on her homework, the better her chances of getting into a good college."

"And the worse our chances of being able to pay for it. Unless *you* want to go down and cover the office in the afternoon."

It was an old battle, though the wounds were still raw. Cam's mother drew her mouth into a tight line and didn't speak again.

That night Cam undressed in the bathroom and looked at herself in the mirror. Darryl had left fingerprints in axle grease over all the places he'd been. Her stomach and breasts were covered with smudges; her nipples were black. It was as if she'd been branded. She decided she must be his now.

He seemed to think so, too. He'd come in with a credit card and grope under her blouse while the customer was still waiting at the pumps. He'd sit her on the stool with her legs spread wide and stand close enough to rub his crotch against her while they kissed. He stroked her thighs, and every day he reached a little higher. Every night she'd undress in front of the mirror and see his marks moving closer and closer to the target.

"I can make you come," he said one day, and she was so naive that she asked, "Where?"

She found out a few days later, when a customer came in and asked for a fan belt. Her father wasn't there to help—he'd gone to Johnstown to pick up a fuel pump—but the customer decided to look for himself. He was across the room scanning the shelves when she felt Darryl's hand dart up under her skirt. Her eyes opened wide, but she couldn't speak or shake him off, not with the customer standing there. His fingers crept inside the elastic leg of her panties.

"What time you expecting Bud back?" the customer asked.

Darryl slid his fingers into her crotch and moved them over the tender flesh inside.

"Oh, about five, I guess," she said shakily.

He nodded and squatted to look at the bottom shelf. Darryl began to stroke her, and she had to grip the edge of the counter with both hands to hold herself straight. Imperceptibly she began to rock against his hand.

"Here we go." The man straightened with a loop of rubber in his hand.

Darryl jerked his hand out and went back to the shop as the customer came over to the counter.

Cam thought she was going to die. She rang up the sale with her heart pounding and the flesh quivering between her legs. The customer wanted to make small talk; his daughter Linda was in her class, wasn't she? They see much of each other? Cam could barely give him an answer as she handed him his change. A pack of gum caught his eye, and she had to ring up a second sale and give him a second handful of change before he finally said goodbye and left.

"Liked it, didn't you?" Darryl jeered behind her.

"Oh, God!" she gasped.

He watched her face as he finished her, and when her breath stopped with the first real orgasm of her life, he flashed a grin of pure triumph.

She had to do it for him then; she understood that even before he started to pester her about it. But he stopped her when she tried to reach into his coveralls. He wasn't a kid, he wasn't going to settle for kid stuff like that. He was a man, and he needed it like a man. Did she understand? Or did she want to stop this right here and now?

She couldn't have stopped to save her soul; he had her in a frenzy by then. She couldn't eat or sleep, school went by in a fog, and some days she was so aroused by the anticipation that she came as soon as he touched her. "I always knew you'd be easy," he said. She thought it was a compliment.

He picked her up one night at the library where she'd told her mother she'd be studying. It was a starry autumn evening, and she ran out to his car like she was running headlong into the arms of romance and adventure.

They rode out of town to an old lumber road that led deep into the woods. He parked and jerked his head at the backseat, and she stepped out into a dreamlike forest of trees stretching their arms to brush against the sky. The woods were alive with the sounds of the night, and she breathed in a deep fragrance of pine needles and leaf mold.

She slid into the backseat and waited for him to kiss her, but he said, "Hurry up. Get your clothes off."

She was willing; after all his lavish attentions, she'd grown proud of her body and wanted to unwrap it like a gift she'd brought for him. But he was busy with his own clothes tonight and didn't even watch as she undressed. He ran his hands down her body, once over lightly, then pushed her back on the seat and spread her legs apart.

"Wait," Cam said. Already it wasn't what she'd expected. She had a hundred questions, but she could only put one in words: "Don't you have to put something on?"

"Kid stuff," he muttered. "I know what to do."

He was in, and a minute later he was out. "Oh, baby," he moaned and squirted all over her stomach.

She lay there, part of her burning with the force of his entry, another part burning with frustration, and all of her confused.

It was no different the next time, nor any of the times that followed. For weeks he'd been obsessed with bringing her to orgasm behind the cash register, but as soon as he had his own orgasms to think of, he lost all interest in hers. She still went with him when he wanted her—he'd branded her, she was still his, she guessed—but the fever was fading, and a great uncertainty was creeping in to fill the empty space it left behind. She started to feel irritated at him sometimes; she noticed his bad grammar and dirty fingernails; she started to worry about his so-called self-control. And she was beginning to feel the first stirrings of shame when a carload of his friends pulled into the station one day.

They were four guys loud and drunk at five o'clock in the afternoon, and they whistled and hooted when Darryl went out to pump their gas. One of them craned his neck to look into the office. "Hey, is that her? That cute little number in there?"

"Who?" another said. "The one Darryl's been banging?"

Cam went very still, waiting for his answer.

"Yep. What'd I tell you? Is she hot or what?"

She didn't wait for him to come in with the cash. She locked up the register and walked out of the station and up the path to the trailer. The door was wrenched open as she approached, and her mother's shadowy face appeared behind the mesh screen. "What's wrong? You look like you've seen a ghost."

Cam stopped with one hand gripping the porch railing. "No, I—I—" she began, but the gorge rose in her throat, and she bent over and vomited a stream of bile into the gravel.

Her mother held her afterward and bathed her face with cool washcloths and accepted the explanation without question: Cam had developed a sudden allergy to gasoline. It made her sick to her stomach just to breathe the fumes.

Telling lies was already an old habit, too, and she was already good at it. She never had to work in the station again.

In Altoona, Cam stopped at the rental agency to turn in the Nissan, then walked a few blocks down the street and rented a Ford from a different agency. She drove south again on Route 220, heading for the turnpike.

It was close to the same route she'd taken thirteen years ago, though that time it took her a week to get this far since she was traveling on foot and hiding in the woods from every police car she spotted. Her plan had been to hitchhike south to a place warm enough to winter, but already she was waking every morning with a layer of frost over her coat, and she knew she'd never make it far enough fast enough. She decided instead to head for a city where the radiant heat of the concrete might keep her warm at night. There was Pittsburgh to the west, and Philadelphia to the east, and the first car to pick her up at the toll plaza was heading east. Philadelphia it was.

She rode with him only as far as Harrisburg, which was the point at which he pulled over to a roadside rest and demanded payment in the form of a blow job. In the panicked struggle that followed, her elbow cracked into his nose and caused a fountain of blood to spray out of it. He grabbed it and screamed, and she shot out of the car and slid down the embankment and didn't stop running until she reached another highway a mile away.

Today, driving the same turnpike east, she scanned every roadside rest but couldn't pick out which one it was. Her memory was too murky of that day, those months. Her brain was so numbed by hunger and cold and so overloaded with fear and guilt that it couldn't absorb anything more. All she had left were dim impressions, faint and shadowy, like underexposed film.

It was six-thirty by the time she reached Lancaster, and already past visiting hours. She checked in at a motel on Route 30 and walked next door to an Amish restaurant where the guests sat together at long tables and heaping bowls and platters were passed family-style. She entered reluctantly, afraid she might be required to converse, but eating was serious business here, and everyone did it with silent concentration.

After dinner she returned to her motel room and tried to call Doug. There were three numbers to try now—home, office, and campaign headquarters—but the machine answered at home, the voice mail at the office, and Gillian at headquarters. All three were unable to tell her where Doug might be. She left the same message three times: she had an unexpected deposition in New York and wouldn't be home until tomorrow.

She didn't bother to check her own voice mail, which would only be full of screeching demands and missed deadlines. She'd been neglecting her work for weeks, and now the neglect was reaching malpractice level. She had a Superior Court brief due three hours ago: she'd intended to spend the day in the office finalizing it and having it filed and served. But on the way to work that morning she drove straight through Philadelphia and came out on the other side without a word to anyone.

She sat in the tiny motel room and wondered what her defense could be if—when—she was brought up on charges of malfeasance. She didn't have the usual excuse of too little time. With Doug away so much, all she had these days was time. Too little interest? The disciplinary board might be sympathetic to a plea of emotional distress, but what could she claim as the trigger? She'd already lost one family. How many more relatives could she kill off for the sake of covering her tracks?

By nine o'clock the walls were closing in on her, and she grabbed her coat and went outside. The night air was cold and damp, and a sheen of heavy dew already covered the cars in the parking lot and the aluminum chairs by the door of each motel unit.

She got into the Ford and drove the same route that she'd first taken on foot. It was a week after she'd fled from the driver in Harrisburg, but she'd made it only as far as Elizabethtown, eighty miles short of Philadelphia and far too small a town to get lost in. After only a few days she started getting suspicious looks from the local merchants whose doorways she slept in at night, and already the police cruisers were slowing down to look her over when she walked down the street. It was time to move on, but she was afraid to stick her thumb out on the highway again, and too cold and hungry to strike out on foot across the countryside.

A week before Thanksgiving she weakened and called home. She was prepared to do her penance, she'd confess everything and stay in her room forever, anything to be warm and well-fed again. But Charlene answered, and the little she knew and could articulate was enough to convince Cam that she could never go home again.

The next day she was foraging in a Dumpster behind a restaurant when she found the help wanted ads of the local newspaper. She sat down in the alley and gnawed on stale rolls while she scanned them, then wandered from one pay phone to another until she found one with a quarter in the change slot. She placed the call and pretended to write down the directions, but she didn't have a pencil and had to repeat them twice to be sure. She followed them eight miles out of town and arrived two hours late on the front porch of Hazel Smith.

"I'm Cammy Johnson," she said, too exhausted to remember to lie by the time the old woman opened the door. "I called about the job?"

Hazel Smith leaned heavily on the aluminum frame of her walker and squinted at Cam through the falling dusk. The smell of wood smoke rose up from the chimney, and the bleat of a goat came from the barn behind the house. Cam's feet were frozen inside her canvas sneakers, and she itched to move them and shake out the cold. But she stood still, and as tall and straight as she could. The job included farm chores along with the cooking and cleaning; she had to look strong.

The old woman opened the screen door and gave a slow, appraising nod. "I got some ham," she said at last. "And some boiled potatoes." She turned the walker and started back into the house. "Wipe your feet," she said.

The farm appeared ahead on the right, and Cam pulled over and stopped on the shoulder of the road in front of it. The old house was set back a hundred feet, and only one faint light glowed from a downstairs window. The place had been sold to an Amish man after Mrs. Smith died—the Amish were quick to snap up all the properties they could; they had plenty of money, but good farmland was a diminishing commodity in Lancaster County—

and he'd removed the electricity and phone lines before he moved his family in. Cam was the one who did the final sweep on settlement day, and she was the one who waited on the front porch to hand over the keys. The Amish man didn't know what to make of her—a girl without a family who wore tight T-shirts and loose hair and was going off to college in another state. He only knew he wanted her gone before the buggy with his wife and children arrived. He took the keys without looking at her, without even letting his hand brush against hers.

She got out of the car and gazed at the house as the kerosene glow in the window traveled slowly upstairs and disappeared. Bedtime came early for farm folk; Cam had to adjust fast. For two days Mrs. Smith allowed her to do little but eat and sleep, but after that the chores were all hers. Right after dawn the livestock had to be fed and watered, the goats milked and the eggs gathered, the milk separated to make the cheese and butter, then the kettle on for tea, and the oatmeal stirred and strained for breakfast. Cleaning took up the rest of the morning, for Mrs. Smith was like her Mennonite neighbors in ranking cleanliness right up there with godliness. The afternoon was spent chopping firewood in the winter, tending the vegetable garden in the spring, gathering the honey in the summer, and then it was time to start supper. Cam used to fall into bed exhausted at the end of the day.

Only three months before, Mrs. Smith had been doing all these tasks herself. "The end of your life is just like the beginning," the old woman used to say. "Almost overnight you go from a helpless lump to a walking, talking, self-reliant human being. Then, darned if the same thing don't happen in reverse at the end." In November she was cooking for herself and getting around reasonably well on her walker. By January she was bedridden, and the walker was stowed out of sight, never to be used again. By March she was incontinent and required diapering, and by May she was introducing Cam as her granddaughter to everyone who stopped by.

Cam was never sure whether Mrs. Smith really believed it, or if she simply found the fiction easier to live with than the fact that the only grandchild she ever had was slaughtered on the other side of the world. Either way, it seemed to give Mrs. Smith some comfort to wave at her when she carried in the tea tray, and to say: "You've met my granddaughter Cammy, haven't you? Bless her heart, I don't know what I'd do without her." It gave comfort to Cam, too; it was a better cover story than anything she could have invented for herself.

The next morning she checked out of the motel and drove across town to the nursing home. It was a complex of low brick buildings perched on top of a hill at the end of a long, curving driveway. Inside the lobby a receptionist sat behind a desk with a brass plate that read CONCIERGE.

"Just let me check," the woman said, and hummed as she worked the keys on her terminal. "Here we go. Oh, yes, you can see him. The family hasn't placed any restrictions at all." She buzzed an attendant to escort Cam to the day room.

It smelled strongly of disinfectant and faintly of urine, and it was furnished in vinyl and populated by old men in bathrobes and wheelchairs. A few of them were struggling with the morning newspaper, but most were slumped in front of a big-screen TV tuned to *Regis & Kathie Lee*. Two nurses were in the room with them, and they were the ones watching the show.

"Hey, Harold," the attendant called. "This pretty young lady's come to see you."

A few of the men turned to look at her, but not the old man in the wheelchair at the edge of the TV circle. He was carrying on a conversation, either with Regis and Kathie Lee or with some invisible companion, and he didn't interrupt himself to look her way.

"Harold," the attendant repeated, testily. "Didn't you hear me? I said you got company."

"No, you did not," the old man retorted. "Don't you try and fool me. You said, 'This pretty young lady's come to see you.' "

The attendant rolled his eyes. "Harold, you—"

"Thanks," Cam said. "I'll take it from here."

She pulled up a chair beside the old man. The nurses were engrossed in the TV show and paid her no attention, and while a couple of men across the room were staring, she counted on old-age hearing loss to cover her words.

"Good morning, Mr. Detweiler. Do you remember me?"

"Fool thinks he can trick me," the old man mumbled. "Have to get up pretty early in the morning, let me tell you. Made it my business for sixty years to remember exactly what people said. Every word."

"I'm Cam Smith. You knew my grandmother, Hazel Smith?"

He turned toward her, but his eyes were clouded with cataracts and his focus landed short of her face. "Was she a client?"

"Yes, sir." Lawyer Detweiler, Mrs. Smith always called him, as if it were a couple centuries ago and people still said Parson Brown and Farmer Jones. "Yes, she was. You were a big help to her."

"Guess how many clients I had over the life of my practice?" he said. "Go on, guess."

"A thousand?"

"Bah!" Spittle launched from his lips with the sound. "More like fifty thousand."

"So you're saying you don't remember her?"

"Nothing of the kind," he declared. "I remember every last one of 'em. Have to get up pretty early in the morning . . ."

His eyes drifted away and his voice trailed off into a mumble. Cam leaned forward to catch a phrase: ". . . free and clear of all liens and encumbrances."

Ten feet away another old man turned a page of his newspaper and sighed.

"Hazel Smith," Cam repeated. "She died twelve years ago, when I was a teenager. You were such a help to me, Mr. Detweiler. You took care of my grandmother's probate. Remember?"

He should have. He'd taken almost as much in executor's fees as she received as the beneficiary of the estate, then he set himself up as her trustee and managed to bleed out another ten percent in management fees before the money was finally hers.

"I had the best practice in the county," he said. "Everybody came to me. I did their wills, I did their real estate, I even did their criminal work when they got in a fix."

"Yes, you helped me sell my grandmother's farm. Estate of Hazel Smith to Abraham Mueller? And after the closing, you even drove me to the airport."

That was the part she remembered best. "Well, my girl, you're on the brink of a new life," Detweiler had said as Cam climbed out of the car with one battered suitcase and a ticket to Detroit. And she'd nodded eagerly, her eyes aglow. She still hadn't learned about brinks.

He was mumbling again, and she leaned closer to hear. ". . . do hereby bequeath, devise, and bestow . . ."

Cam gazed around the room and tried to think of some other way to test his recollection without going too far to refresh it. The TV program went to a commercial, and one of the nurses looked over and caught Cam's expression. "Don't take it too hard," she said sympathetically. "He has his good days, too."

Cam smiled. That was exactly what she was afraid of.

But a man with fifty thousand clients and advanced Alzheimer's wouldn't be expected to remember much. It was unlikely that anyone would bother to pay him a call.

The problem was that anyone could; there were no restrictions on visitors. Anyone might walk in tomorrow and find Harold Detweiler alert and lucid and ready to reminisce.

"My parents were killed in the Philippines," she said in a low voice as soon as the commercial ended. "My grandmother raised me. And after she died, you went through her papers, and you found my birth certificate. Campbell Smith, remember? You helped me get a Social Security number, and you arranged for me to take the high school equivalency exam so I could get my diploma."

"Philippines," he mumbled. "Hazel Smith." Suddenly his head swung up. "You don't look much like her."

"No, I look like my mother," Cam said. "Her name was Alice Campbell. She married Hazel Smith's son, Matthew. I'm their daughter, Campbell. Remember?"

He began to nod, and Cam held her breath, waiting for the memory to flow back and wondering how it would level out in his mind, whether it would corroborate her story or destroy it.

"Oh, sure—I remember now," he said. "You were in a car wreck on 322. Broke your clavicle, didn't you? I handled the insurance claim. Got you eighteen thousand dollars. Isn't that right?"

Her breath expelled in a light laugh. "Yes. Yes, that's right. And I just wanted to drop by to say thank you."

"You're welcome, young lady."

She got to her feet and picked up his hand to shake it. " 'Bye now," she said, and headed for the door.

"Give my regards to Hazel," he called after her.

* * *

She left Lancaster heading east and stopped near Downingtown to turn in the Ford and pick up her own Honda before going on to Philadelphia. It was Tuesday afternoon. She'd missed a day and a half of work without explanation, and the filing deadline for her brief had come and gone.

But as she drove into the city, an inexplicable calm settled over her. She'd swept her trail as clean as it ever could be. It was out of her hands now. And who knew? Maybe all her efforts would prove to be needless. Meredith Winters and a campaign office didn't commit Doug to anything. He could still back out of this race, and maybe he still would. He wasn't looking to be a place holder for Governor Davis—he said he was running to win—yet so far Davis had warded off his overtures with platitudes and double-talk. Doug could wake up to political reality any day now.

And once that happened, Cam knew she could make everything right between them. She'd tell him the truth about the nude photo and the studio in Philadelphia where she'd posed for it last week. And he'd understand. He'd have to.

Her office was exactly as she expected. Piles of work were teetering on her desktop, the message light was flashing frantically on her phone, and her chair was plastered with yellow Post-its screeching for her immediate attention. But she was resigned to this, too. She would beg for an extension on the brief, she'd recite a thousand mea culpas to the client, and she'd pitch herself into the backlog of work until she could see the surface of her desk again.

But first—first there was one other thing she had to do.

She turned to the computer and launched the old familiar search: *Abigail Zodtner, Abby Zodtner, Abby Johnson, Abigail Zodtner Johnson,* and this time even *Mary Mack.*

Where are you? her fingers whispered, a forlorn little voice calling out into cyberspace. *Are you there?*

Mom? Can you hear me?

16

On Wednesday, March 18, the management of Meyerwood Machine Parts announced that it was closing its plant in Middletown, Delaware, and moving its manufacturing operations to Hermosillo, Mexico.

On Thursday, March 19, Doug Alexander mounted a dais outside the Meyerwood factory gates and announced his candidacy for the United States Congress.

Before him stood a five-piece brass band; three news cams and a cadre of print reporters; a flock of Party people and local dignitaries; a brigade of volunteer leafleteers; and an audience of five hundred disgruntled workers who were shuffling through the gates for the first shift of the last weeks of their employment. Above him flapped a banner that proclaimed: DOUG ALEXANDER. HE'LL GET AMERICA TO WORK AGAIN.

The slogan was Meredith Winters's brainchild, as was the venue. Warm bodies were always required to launch a campaign, and if those bodies also happened to be hot with anger at U.S. trade policy, so much the better.

Behind him on the dais stood Cam, wearing a pink knit suit and a mask of terror clamped tight to her face.

As the crowd drew near, Doug lifted both arms to quiet the band. A moment of wondering silence passed, and then he spoke.

"I see the look on your faces," he said. "It's a look I've seen, we've all seen, all too often lately in this country. And I think I know what it means. You're wondering how this could have happened to you. You did good work here, you made money for this company—how could this happen? And what's going to happen now? You're wondering if you'll be able to find another job and how you're going to provide for your families. You're wondering if you've let them down. Some of you may even be wondering if you've failed.

"I can't answer all of those questions, but I can sure answer the last one. You haven't failed. Not one of you. It's Meyerwood Machine Parts that's failed *you*!"

He had their attention. They shifted their lunch boxes and braced their feet to stand and listen.

"But it's not only Meyerwood that's failed you. The government of the United States has failed you, too. For the last thirty years that government—your government—has been sending our jobs overseas. And they've been doing it deliberately."

It was a speech he'd made before, in one form or another, but today he had the audience, he had the issue and the venue, and the fire of his convictions was burning strong.

He talked about billions spent on meaningless retraining programs that could have gone to keep factories open. He talked about rich corporations looking to get richer and hundreds of foreign lobbyists wining and dining members of Congress.

"Let's call this what it really is," he said. "It's not the new global economy—it's war. A trade war, an economic war, but a war that threatens our way of life as surely as Nazi Germany ever did.

"It's time you had somebody fighting that war for you. It's time the working people of America had the ear of Congress.

"Well, you've got both of mine, and you've got my heart, too. This November send me to Congress, and let me fight for you. Help me get America to work again!"

Behind him Cam seemed to recoil as the crowd exploded into cheers and a volley of balloons shot into the air.

The band started up again, and Doug climbed down from the dais and started shaking all the hands that were thrust at him. Cam trailed uncertainly after him until Nathan Vance stepped up behind her and took her by the arm. "You're with me," he said, and pulled her toward his car.

"I don't have to go with Doug?" she asked as she climbed in beside him. It was a physical relief just to sink back and close the door on the crowd.

"He doesn't need you now. Smile and wave."

He pressed a button to lower her window, and a camera flashed in her face as she turned to obey.

Nathan pulled out onto the highway, and once they were clear of the crowd, he raised her window again. "And frankly," he said, "we don't need anybody studying you too much more today. Your face freezes up any harder and we'll be able to chip it apart and sell ice cubes."

"I did my best," she said tightly.

"I know you did, babe. But we have to work on making your best better."

He reached over to pat her knee. The dark skin of his hand looked strange against her pink skirt, but it was the pink that was out of place. The suit was delivered to the house the night before, courtesy of Meredith Winters. It was a color she never wore, but she'd worn it today, without complaint, and her only thought as she dressed was, *They already know my size.*

"That's why I volunteered to drive you back," he said. "I got some things we need to go over. First off, your car."

One day on the campaign trail and already she was suffering from noise-induced hearing loss. "My what?" she repeated.

"Your Honda. It looks bad—the candidate spouting off about trade imbalances and the decline of U.S. manufacturing while his wife tools around in a little Japanese car. You know Tom Biscardo? He has the Ford dealership on Concord Pike? He's meeting us there this morning. Good Party man, Tom. He'll give you a deal."

"Wait a minute. My Honda was manufactured in Marysville, Ohio. It's an American-made car, for God's sake. Meanwhile this—this truck of yours"—she spread her hands at the dashboard of the Chevy Tahoe—"was built in Mexico, if I recall. And what about Doug? His Ford was built in Ontario."

"Hey, if it looks like a duck and walks like a duck and says Honda on the back, it must be a Japanese car. As for Chevy and Ford"—he laughed—"hell, you can't get much more American than that."

"But Nathan, that's a phony distinction."

He gave her a look. "You just don't get it, do you, Cam? Image is reality, at least when it comes to politics. The only thing that matters is that the voters *think* you're driving a Japanese import. So we have to get you into something else before somebody snaps your picture in it."

Cam fell silent, thinking of all the people who already had snapped her picture today.

"Next item," he said. "There's some thinking that you should get a new haircut."

She wasn't surprised at that. Doug had already undergone a complete makeover, and after the pink suit arrived last night, she figured it was just a matter of time before somebody started in on her, too. But she was surprised that it turned out to be Nathan. She turned and looked at him.

"Okay, I'm just the messenger here," he said, holding up a hand. "Don't bite my head off."

She turned to her window. Maybe a new look was exactly what she needed. She'd cut her hair short and dye it black. Maybe even have complete reconstructive facial surgery.

"Item three," he went on. "How'd you like to work out of the Wilmington office?"

"Why?"

"Because a man who wants to be Delaware's only congressman can't have a wife who barely visits the state, that's why. Looks better if you work in Wilmington."

"At Jackson, Rieders and Clark?"

"Of course, where else?"

"Wherever else I can find work after I'm fired."

"Say what?"

Nathan's attempts at blackspeak always fell laughably short of the mark, but Cam didn't crack a smile this time. "I'm supposed to be gone already. The Malloy antinepotism rule, remember? Besides, I haven't billed a full day since this whole thing started. The other day I missed a court filing deadline. I filed a *nunc pro tunc* request, but my opponent's crying foul and the judge may just play tough and deny it. I'll be lucky if the client doesn't sue us."

Nathan only laughed.

"I mean it. It's just a matter of time before they fire me. I'll probably get disbarred, too."

He reached over and tapped her on the shoulder. "Hel-looo. Memo to Campbell Smith. Your husband happens to be running for Congress. As in U.S. Congress? You read me? Pay attention now, Cam. You're married to a man everybody wants to know. Which means everybody'll be lining up to keep you happy. I've already spoken to Cliff Austin, and he's bending over backward to accommodate you. You get a cushy new office in Wilmington, and you also get to keep your cubicle in Philly, for whatever that's worth. And by the way, you can forget the Malloy rule, because they sure as hell have."

It was more than she could absorb, particularly when it came from Nathan Vance, who was only an associate like herself. "Why are you the one talking to Austin about me?"

"That's tonight's announcement, but I'll give you a preview." He grinned at her. "You're looking at the new chairman of the Alexander for Congress committee."

She stared at him. "Webb Black . . . ?"

"Didn't quite have the stomach for the job."

"But you do."

He acknowledged it with a shrug.

"And obviously so does Doug," she said. "Or he couldn't cut off a twenty-year friend like that."

"Watch yourself, Cam," Nathan said.

"Oh, but you see, I don't have to. Everybody else is watching me now."

"Would you just get with the program here?"

"I don't *get* the program. I don't get any of it. I mean, God, Nathan, why are you doing this? What's in it for you? Or for Doug, for that matter."

"Same thing for both of us. Power."

"Power? Doug's a partner in a major law firm. What more does he need? And you're on the fast track to partnership yourself. Another few years and you'll be pulling in a couple hundred grand a year. What does power get you that money won't get you just as well? And without all the aggravation?"

He took his time answering, long enough for a glance up at the rearview mirror and a long silent gaze out over the passing countryside.

"I could give you a real good speech about having a voice and making a difference," he said at last. "But since I'm the only real friend you have in this state, I'll tell you the truth instead. You say I'm on the fast track to partnership? Maybe I am, maybe I'm not. It all turns on what a bunch of white men around a table have to say about it when the time comes. And even if I make partner, I still have to bring in clients, and that turns on a bunch of other white men sitting around a bunch of other tables. You see what I'm saying? No matter how well I do, there's always gonna be a bunch of white men who can cast me out."

"Oh, Nathan," she groaned. "The race card, from you? You're

the son of an accountant, a third-generation suburbanite, and a Yalie who knows how to sail. You had ten times more advantages than the average white kid. You never suffered a moment of discrimination in your life."

"You don't know what I've suffered," he said coldly.

She glanced at him and wondered if it were possible that she knew as little about him as he knew about her. "All right, I'm sorry," she said. "But even so, what's the Party but another bunch of white men?"

"A bunch of white men with the power to control high-level appointments, that's what. I scratch their backs, maybe I get a nice slot at the Justice Department. I scratch a little harder, maybe I get to put on the black robes."

"You're doing this to get a *job*?"

"Hey, babe, a federal judgeship with lifetime tenure is a little more than a job."

They rode in silence for a time, until Cam said, "I think I would have rather heard the speech about having a voice and making a difference."

"Listen," he snapped, "you and I both went after Doug. We both wanted something from him. And I'm no more ashamed of it than you are."

Cam said nothing, but as she turned and watched the roadside blur past her window, she realized that was her whole problem. She *was* ashamed of it.

He didn't speak again until they turned into her driveway. "You want to go in and change before we head to the dealership?"

She looked at the house and wasn't sure she ever wanted to go in it again. She shook her head.

"Okay then, why don't you get in your car and follow me?"

She looked at her car and shook her head again.

"Cam," he said, grinding out her name, "what is the fucking big deal about this car?"

"Nothing. I just don't feel like going. Here"—she reached in her purse and handed him her car keys—"you take it."

"You have to pick out a new car, too."

"You do it. I'll sure you'll find something appropriate."

"Cam," he said heavily, "I'm your friend, remember?"

"Yes, I know." She opened the door and slid down to the ground. "The only one I've got."

She climbed the stairs to the back porch, and a moment later she heard the Honda start behind her and drive away.

She came down off the porch and drifted past the garage and the dilapidated outbuildings and into the ruins of the garden. An old stone bench sat amid the weeds and bramble, and she cleared away a tangle of vines and sank down. A chill wind blew through the garden, and it stirred the dried brown leaves on a dead bush and made her shiver inside her suit jacket.

It was the middle of March, and the month didn't know which way to go between winter and spring. Yesterday the sun shone bright, but tomorrow it could snow. A thousand miles south it was spring already. Three thousand miles west it was perpetual summer, and she could be in a place she'd never been before, without family or friends or personal history.

She wondered if she could do it, get up and walk out of this life and into a new one somewhere else. She'd done it before, and she was only fifteen years old at the time—it had to be easier now. This time she'd have some cash, a few thousand dollars anyway, enough to take a plane or train, enough for a few weeks in an out-of-the-way motel until she could get a job and find an apartment. And now she knew all about personal documentation; she could adopt a new name and cover story without having to rely on a sweet old woman with a jumbled memory.

She looked back at Nathan's car in the driveway and thought *Tahoe*. She could go to Tahoe. Beautiful mountains, she'd heard, and lots of transients to lose herself among. She'd take Nathan's car—he wouldn't report it, not while she was still married to Doug—and she'd drive it to an airport, Pittsburgh maybe, and leave it in a towaway zone where it wouldn't take too long to be found and returned. And then she'd pay cash for a plane ticket and strap herself into a window seat and watch the ground fall off below her and fade away into nothing.

She hugged her arms against the chill and stayed where she was on the cold stone bench. Her life was easier to walk away from when she was only fifteen, because it never really seemed to be hers. But here and now—this was the life she'd been striving for for the past thirteen years. Campbell Smith of Greenville, wife of Douglas Alexander, and member of the bars of Pennsylvania and Delaware. She was vested in this life. She had ties—to Doug by vows of marriage, to her career by oaths to the court, even to this real estate by her name on the deed. At least the name she was using now.

She lifted her eyes from the ground at her feet and looked around her. For the first time it struck her that it was hers. These weed-choked acres belonged to her. It was like Mrs. Smith's farm, a piece of land to care for, a place to call her own.

A patch of yellow caught her eye on the other side of the garden, and she rose from the bench and went closer. It was a yellow crocus peeking out from under a mat of fallen leaves. She dropped to her knees and pushed away the moldy leaves to reveal a dozen more crocuses—yellows and purples and whites—all in full bloom despite the blanket of deadfall and years of neglect. She crawled on her hands and knees and rooted further until she found the vibrant green tips of daffodils pushing themselves up through the cracks in the frozen ground. Suddenly they were everywhere, hundreds of daffodils fighting their way out of the cold earth into the spring.

She ran to the toolshed and rummaged through the junk there until she found a rusty scythe, then went back into the garden and began to hack away at the weeds and brush. The bones of the old garden started to take shape in her mind, and she could picture how it used to be: an undulating mass of giant rhododendrons, a serpentine border of shrubs and flowering perennials, an island bed of roses, and a wisteria arbor opening onto a rectangular lawn that led to the octagonal folly at the far end of the garden. Cam swung the scythe and years of weeds and unchecked growth fell at her feet. She raked up the debris until blisters formed on her palms, and slowly she was able to see how the garden could look again. How she could make it look again.

It was mid-afternoon and she was piling the branches and brush into a heap when Nathan Vance pulled into the driveway and climbed out of a strange car.

"Cam," he called, approaching warily. "You okay?"

"Fine." With a muddy hand, she pushed the hair from her face.

His eyes moved over her soiled jacket and torn skirt. "Well, I got you that Ford Contour. Pretty nice, huh?"

She gave it a brief glance. "Great. Thanks."

"Well . . ." He shifted his weight. "A bunch of us are getting together down at headquarters. Want to change clothes and come with me?"

She shook her head and turned back to the heap of brush. "I

decided to restore this old garden. It could be beautiful again, don't you think?"

"I guess." He looked around doubtfully. "But you know, you could hire somebody to do this for you."

"I want to do it myself."

She struck a match and tossed it onto the pile of brush. The dried leaves caught the flame, and she leaned on the rake handle to watch as the fire crackled to life.

Nathan was watching her with a look of horror on his face, and she smiled to think how she must look to him—like Rochester's insane wife in the attic, dancing and cackling as she burned down Thornfield.

She stared into the flames as an idea came to her. Insanity could be another kind of escape route. Her body could stay here while her mind flew away. She'd become the Madwoman of Greenville, and no one would ever ask her to stand on a dais again.

It was an appealing prospect, but in her heart she knew it wouldn't work. Insanity wasn't something she could choose, not until it first chose her, and she also knew that it was the final refuge, and that she wasn't there yet.

It would be a massive undertaking to renovate four acres that had been neglected for twenty-five years, but she could do it. She was staying, and she could do it, even if it took her months, all spring through summer and into fall. All the way to November.

17

Trey scooped up a handful of pebbles from the beach and let them fly one by one across the water as he aimed for that perfect three-bounce skip. Beth was in the boat with her life jacket buckled and her eyes red and swollen. Steve came down to the dock with the last of her bags and a tight expression on his face. He called to Trey, "Come help me cast off."

Trey let the rest of the pebbles fly, and they hit the water like a fireworks starburst. He vaulted up on the dock and took the line. "Get up to the house," Steve shouted over the engine roar, "and stay there till I get back."

"Okay!" Trey shouted as he threw him the line. "Have a great trip!"

Beth turned away and set her face to the wind.

Trey stood on the dock and watched them go. They set off like this every Saturday morning, and they came back every Saturday afternoon with books and videos and a week's worth of groceries. The difference today was that Steve would be coming back alone.

Trey jogged up the path through the woods. His life had been pretty cool for the last ten weeks, but now it was going to be perfect. Now they could do everything they'd only talked about, like kayaking up the coastline or rappeling down the sea cliff—all the things that made Beth squeal, "Oh, Steve, no! You'll kill yourself!" Steve was too nice a guy to tell her to butt out, so she always ended up getting her way. She was like an evil force field: one electric whine from her and the field was activated to pen them in.

He ran across the meadow and all the way to the cove at the northern tip of the island where the seals liked to sun. Three young cows were hauling themselves up, wriggling and hunching laboriously to reach the big flat rock. He cupped his hands around his mouth and sent them a honking bark. He thought it was a pretty good imitation of seal talk, but two of the cows ignored him, and the third gave him a withering look that seemed to say he'd better try harder.

Which was Beth's line. "Try a little harder, Jamie," she chirped every time he blew off an assignment or wrote a half-assed essay. She was too dense to figure out that it had nothing to do with effort and everything to do with attitude. Steve said she was a teacher and she knew what she was doing, but it turned out to be *kindergarten* she'd taught, and she tried to use the same curriculum with him, almost down to fingerpainting and nap time. Her idea of an English class was making him read *The Call of the Wild*, then giving him a quiz that asked what the name of the dog was.

Trey was bored out of his mind for the two hours that he had to spend with her each day, and he complained loud and long during his sessions with Steve. "Don't you think you're exaggerating a little?" Steve finally asked, hiding a smile as Trey did a dead-on impression of Beth in her singsong voice saying, "And we know what the answer is to *that* one now, *don't* we?"

"Hey, you don't believe it, come see for yourself."

The next morning Steve took him up on it and slipped into the dining room while Beth was droning on about checks and balances among the three branches of government. "Don't let me interrupt," he said as he took a seat at the end of the table. "Pretend I'm invisible down here."

Trey sat up straight and put on an expression of polite interest, but Beth lost her place in her notes, said a senator's term lasted four years instead of six, and ended up filling the hour by having Trey read the rest of the chapter out loud.

That night he lurked in the hall outside their room and picked up most of their argument about it. "This is never going to work if you're going to second-guess me all the time," Beth sputtered, and Steve replied, "Beth—honey—it isn't working *now*."

Over breakfast the next morning, Steve announced that Beth needed to spend more time on her writing, and that he'd be taking over English and history for a while.

"All *right*!" Trey crowed.

Beth picked up her coffee mug and left the table.

* * *

The first book Steve assigned was *Alive*, the true story of a soccer team who survived a plane crash in the Andes by eating their dead. It was the coolest thing Trey had ever read. Steve told him another true story, about a wagon train party that turned cannibal when they got marooned in a mountain pass. That led to a history lesson on manifest destiny and westward expansion, then to a biology lesson on survival instincts, and then to a free-ranging philosophical discussion of how far people might go to save themselves.

They were walking on the beach for that last part—another improvement in Trey's life, the outdoor classroom—and Steve asked, "Ever read *1984*?"

Trey shook his head and hoped he wouldn't have to. It sounded like one of those year-in-review studies the old man brought home. But Steve said it wasn't about the past at all; it was written in 1949 and was about the future. It imagined a world in which people were brainwashed and reduced to automatons, and all their longings for freedom or individual expression were stamped out by the Thought Police. A guy named Winston tried to rebel, and he was captured and tortured until there was no degradation left that he hadn't suffered. With one exception: he never betrayed his girlfriend Julia. But the Thought Police knew he had an uncontrollable fear of rats. They took a cage full of starving rats and as they began to fit it over his head, Winston finally broke down. He screamed, *No! Do it to Julia! Not me! Do it to Julia!*

Chills skittered up and down Trey's spine when he heard that line. Steve brought the book back from his next trip to the mainland, and Trey started reading it at the dock, held it up in front of his plate at the dinner table, and didn't put it down until he finished it after midnight.

The seals lifted their heads as the sky turned gray, and they arched their shapeless necks and launched themselves in an ungainly slide down the rocks and back into the water. The wind started to whip whitecaps in the sea, and Trey pulled out a pencil and paper and tried to capture the sting of the wind and the spray of the water in a five-minute sketch. Not bad, he thought, holding it up for appraisal; it didn't totally suck.

He went into the house and fixed himself a snack in the

kitchen, a plate of tortilla chips smothered in salsa and melted cheese. He was used to fending for himself in the kitchen at home—half the time nobody was home for meals but him and Jesse—and he found that he preferred his own cooking to Beth's. Steve must have, too, because pretty soon he and Trey were cooking all the meals.

Beth started to make little snipes. If she came into the living room and found them playing a board game, she'd say with exaggerated casualness: "So—how are the house plans coming, Steve?" And no matter what he answered, she'd say, "That's all? You were so much farther along on the Rehoboth house by this time."

Trey finally figured out that she was jealous of him, and it made his mild dislike of her shoot up to active hatred. For the past few weeks it had been open warfare between the two of them, shouting matches when Steve was out of earshot and simmering hostility when he wasn't. But finally, last night, they went at it right in front of him.

Beth started it. He sat down for dinner in a dirty shirt, and she stared pointedly at the food stains down the front.

"I don't have anything else to wear," he said. "You haven't done my laundry all week."

"You haven't brought it down all week!"

"You never told me to."

"I have to tell you?"

"Would you get off my case?"

"What?" she shrieked.

Quietly Steve said, "Beth—"

"You're always on my back about something!"

"Me! You're the one who's always—"

"Beth!" Steve said sharply, and when her eyes turned wildly in his direction, he said, "Lighten up, would you?"

She stared at him, then threw down her napkin and left the room.

The best part was that Steve didn't follow her.

In the morning, Steve broke the news to him. Beth just couldn't adjust to the isolation of island life. She was going home to Connecticut.

Trey finished his nachos and looked for something to do. It was easy to fill the day when Steve was around, but today he drifted from room to room, feeling almost as bored as he would on a day in Delaware. But then he thought of something he'd been wanting to do ever since he got here, and it was the one thing he couldn't do when Steve was around.

He took the stairs two at a time to his tower bedroom, then jumped up on the bed and reached up for the trapdoor in the ceiling. His fingertips barely grazed the hooks of the latch, so he pulled a drawer out of the chest and dumped it upside down on the bed and stood on top of it. This added six inches to his reach, and it was all he needed. He unhooked the latch and pushed up on one side of the door until it fell over its hinges and a blast of cold wind rushed down. He grabbed onto the platform, balanced there a second, then gave another heave and pulled himself through.

The wood groaned loudly as he jumped to his feet, and he looked down at the pockets of rot Steve had mentioned. But they were easy to spot and easy to step clear of, and meanwhile—his jaw dropped as he slowly rotated around the widow's walk—the view was awesome. He could see all the way from the seal cove on the north down to the dock on the south. He went to the seaward side and leaned over the half wall. It was a sheer drop, straight down the three stories of the house, then two or three times that distance down the cliff.

It was totally amazing. The surf crashed in huge white breakers against the rocks, and the gulls soared below him, so that he could see their backs and the spread of their wings as they angled them into the air currents. The wind was whipping his hair and slapping his cheeks, but he barely noticed. He hung over the side of the widow's walk and watched the gulls swoop down to the sea. Their cries floated up to him through the wind, a sharp, mournful sound like the music of the shoreline.

Then another sound came through the wind, and Trey lurched up and wheeled around. "Oh, shit," he said out loud. Steve was back, too soon, and he was heading for the house at a full-out run.

Trey scrambled back inside and latched the door behind him. The contents of the dresser drawer were all over his bed, and he was still trying to stuff things back into place when Steve burst into the room.

"Jamie!" He grabbed him and held him by both arms. "Jesus

Christ! Are you all right? What the hell were you doing up there?"

Trey shook him loose. "I just went up for a look. It's no big deal."

"No big deal? The wood's all rotted! I told you not to go up there!"

The look on his face was almost funny, as if it was unfathomable to Steve that he would ever dream of doing something he'd been told not to do.

"It's not all that bad," he said. "A few holes here and there. That's all."

"That's not all! And I told you to stay away from there."

"All right, already." He turned away with a sullen mouth and went back to stuffing things in the drawer. He slid the drawer in the dresser, and when he turned around, Steve was still watching him.

"What did the Ramsays do when you disobeyed them?"

"Nothing."

"Yeah," he said, disgusted. "That's pretty obvious."

Trey glared at him.

"We'll let it slide this time," Steve said. "But listen up, Jamie. There's new house rules. You disobey *me*, you pay the price."

"You can't tell me what to do."

"Oh, yes, I can." He grabbed his chin and turned his face up to meet his eyes. "I'm not your pal, and I'm sure as hell not your staffer. I'm your father. Don't you forget that."

He released him with a light slap on the cheek and headed for the stairs. "Come on. Let's go get some lunch."

"I'm not hungry," Trey said tightly.

"Suit yourself."

Trey flopped on his bed and spent an hour staring at the trapdoor in seething resentment. Who did this guy think he was, coming out of nowhere and telling him what he could do? *I'm not your pal,* he said, but he'd been doing a pretty good imitation of it for the past ten weeks. Now suddenly he wanted to play strict father. If Steve thought he was going to roll over and play obedient son, he could forget it. He had another think coming.

That was one of Jesse's expressions—*he's got another think coming*—and Trey felt a wave of wistfulness for his old companion. He'd always been a good friend, and for sure he was a better one than Steve, because he knew his place and kept to it.

He was a man who'd taken orders all his life, first in the Navy, then in the state police, and now for the old man. Jesse never once tried to tell him what to do. Jesse was always waiting to see what he wanted *him* to do.

Time stretched into the second hour, and Trey started to notice how quiet the house was with Beth gone. He'd never realized how much noise she made, whether it was her off-key singing in the shower or the clatter of keys at her computer or her saccharine voice calling into the study, "Steve, honey, have a minute?" It used to set his teeth on edge. He wasn't going to miss a bit of it.

But for the first time it occurred to him that maybe Steve would. In fact, maybe that was what made him act like such a jerk—he'd just broken up with his girlfriend. Come to think of it, Steve did it for him. Trey wasn't sure he'd ever be willing to make that big a sacrifice himself, for anybody.

He got up and went downstairs and found Steve setting up the chessboard in the library.

"Feel like a game?" Steve asked.

"I guess." Trey sat down at the table.

"I made that sandwich for you." Steve pointed to the plate at Trey's elbow.

"Thanks." He picked it up and took a bite—meat loaf and mustard, his favorite—then made his opening move.

On May seventh a memorial service for Gloria Lipton was held in the ceremonial conference room on the fiftieth floor of the offices of Jackson, Rieders & Clark. It was a remarkable event in two respects: the firm had never before held such a service for anyone who wasn't a lawyer, and a nationally prominent one at that; and Gloria had been dead and buried for more than two months. It was arranged at the behest of the consulting grief counselor retained by the firm; it would, she thought, provide the sense of closure that the unsolved murder was denying them.

Clifford Austin was already speaking at the front of the room when Cam arrived. She slipped through the rear door and tried to take an unobtrusive seat in the audience. Something was on the chair under her, and she tugged out a little booklet. *Gloria Lipton, In Memoriam.*

A hand tapped on her shoulder, and Cam looked back at a trio of other lawyers, all beaming at her. "Hey, Cam," one whispered. "Good to see you again."

"How are you?" another said. "We never see you anymore!"

She smiled and faced forward again. It was true that they seldom saw her; she spent only Tuesdays and Thursdays in the Philadelphia office now. But it was also true that everyone had been making an inordinate fuss over her ever since Doug launched his candidacy.

It wasn't supposed to be this way: Tuesdays and Thursdays were supposed to be her days of anonymity, while Mondays, Wednesdays, and Fridays were the days she lived her public life. On those days she worked out of the Wilmington office in between coffee klatches and civic meetings, cocktail receptions and Party assemblies. On those days she dressed in low heels and conservative suits and wore her hair pulled back in a chignon. (After much experimentation and a conference call to Washington, it had been decided that she not cut her hair after all. The chignon, Meredith's people decreed, was a demure yet sophisticated look that added a good five years to her appearance.) On Tuesdays and Thursdays she worked out of the Philadelphia office, and she dressed in short skirts and high heels, with her hair long and loose, the way it used to be.

She let it fall forward now to hide her face from the curious eyes around her while she pretended to study Gloria's memorial program. It was a slick little brochure, like a theater playbill without the advertisements, and it recounted the life of Gloria Lipton in words and pictures.

Up at the podium, Cliff Austin was speaking dolorously about his long and productive partnership with Gloria, and about her steadfast devotion to the firm in general and to him in particular. He was followed by some of Gloria's friends among the secretarial ranks. Cam's own secretary Helen Nagy told a sweet and funny story about the time when Gloria wouldn't allow Mr. Rieders to leave for his Court of Appeals argument because his shoes weren't shined. He said there was no time, but she held his argument notes hostage until he agreed to let the shoeshine man into his office. He ultimately won the appeal, and Gloria took full credit for it.

Another gray-haired secretary talked about Gloria's attention to current events and how she never flinched from controversy, but was always willing to share her experience and wisdom with others. She'd become famous for her letters to the editor, as well as to the President, the Cabinet, and various members of Congress, as the situation demanded.

"And if Gloria were still with us today," the woman said coyly, "I have no doubt that a certain partner in our Wilmington office would have the benefit of daily bulletins from Gloria."

Laughter broke out, and all eyes turned to Cam. There wasn't any choice: she lifted her head and sent a hundred-watt smile through the crowd.

After the service, she returned to her office and sorted through the mail that still lay unopened on Helen's desk. Twelve pieces for Grant Peyton, one for her. Only two months ago it would have been the other way around. She had so little work these days that she might as well have been on formal leave of absence, as Doug and Nathan were.

She took the envelope into her office and opened it. Not even work-related, it was another fund-raising appeal disguised as an invitation to join the board of the Harriet M. Welsch Foundation. *Dear Mrs. Alexander,* it read. *In recognition of your outstanding work in the field of family law, we would be honored . . .*

Mrs. Alexander—it still sounded foreign to her. She remembered that the first letter from this foundation was addressed the same way, when she was only two weeks married and nobody was using her married name yet.

Now she understood their dogged interest in her. It wasn't her money they were after, it was her husband. They'd known from the start who she was married to and what his political plans were, and they saw some advantage in connecting themselves to him through her.

She crumpled the letter and lobbed it into the trash can.

There were still a few rays of daylight left when got she home that night, and she went straight to the garden.

Her cleanup detail in March had revealed the original architecture of the garden, and once March passed into April, the colors and textures started to reveal themselves, too. Every morning before she got in her car, and again every evening when she got home, she took a stroll through the garden. Every day there was something new for her to see, a new vista for her to gasp over, or a new flower for her to wonder about. It was like a gift the garden labored over while she was away, as if to surprise and delight her when she returned. Tonight she spotted something new by the edge of a curving path. Thick green spikes of fibrous growth were protruding an inch above the earth. It was amazing—an inch of growth that wasn't there that morning. The foliage had a bulblike texture. A late-emerging hosta? she wondered. She got up and started for the house to check her reference books.

"There you are!" Doug called from the driveway. "I was wondering where you got to." He was wearing a knit shirt and khakis, a casual look she seldom saw him in these days.

Her steps slowed. "Doug—you're home early."

"I've been home for hours."

"Why? Is something wrong?"

He was regarding her with a strange look. "Did you forget what day it is?"

Her hand flew to her mouth. "Oh, God." Her mind raced through the calendar. "Was I supposed to be somewhere?"

"Yes," he said gravely. "Right here. With me." He folded his arms around her and pulled her close. "It's our anniversary," he whispered. "Three months today." His eyes were twinkling when he leaned back. "You know, it's only when you've been married forever that you measure it in years. For us it's still months."

That was her cue: *And sometimes still days.* She let out a shaky laugh.

"Come on in." He hooked his arm around her waist and moved her toward the house. "I'm fixing a special dinner. I thought we'd spend a quiet night at home."

She looked up at him, surprised and touched as they climbed the stairs together and went into the kitchen.

"Hi, Mrs. Alexander," the college girl, Gillian, sang out sweetly as she turned from the stove.

"Hi," Cam said, bewildered.

"Gillian came over to help me out with the cooking," Doug explained as the girl lowered her eyes demurely under her black velvet headband.

"Oh. You shouldn't have."

"Oh, but I wanted to! I want to do everything I can to help Doug's campaign."

He took Cam's briefcase from her. "Why don't you go upstairs and freshen up?" he suggested. "We'll finish up here."

* * *

Twenty minutes later Gillian was gone and Doug was in the dining room, pouring the wine. The table was spread with his grandmother's best linens, candles were burning, and something lush and classical was playing on the stereo. He pulled Cam's chair out and kissed her cheek as he seated her. "I'll be right back."

Cam gazed around the room. It was a replay of the anniversary dinner she'd staged for him in February. She was certain that Gillian had misspoken—tonight's dinner had nothing to do with the campaign—but she remembered that she had a hidden agenda that night in February, and she couldn't help wondering if Doug had one, too, tonight.

He came through the swinging kitchen door with the plates, set them down, and took the chair across from her. "Did you hear the news?" he said, shaking out his napkin. "About Hadley Hayes?"

"No, what?"

"You remember the representative from Texas who died last month? Vasquez?"

"Yes?"

"He left a vacancy on the House Committee on Military Research and Development. And guess who just filled it? Hadley Hayes."

Cam studied him warily across the table, trying to gauge which direction his mood was going. "Oh," she said. "I'm sorry."

"Sorry? This is great for us! Don't you see?"

"No, I— Why?"

"This gives Hayes the perfect launchpad for all his outdated bullshit about military preparedness. Before long he'll be proposing the Star Wars missile defense system all over again."

"And that's good."

"Sure. One, he'll be like a kid with a new toy. He'll be so preoccupied with it that he probably won't remember that he's up for reelection until October. And two, he plays right into my hands on the issues. We'll be able to paint him like the dinosaur he is, while we hammer away at the real-life issues."

"That's wonderful."

He settled back in his seat with a satisfied smile. "And there's more good news, too. Jonathan Fletcher finally got off the fence and announced his contribution today. Guess how much?"

Cam shook her head; she didn't know how to play these games.

"Two hundred thousand dollars!"

"Great. I'm so glad."

He beamed at her and picked up his fork.

Cam looked down at her plate. "What do we have here?"

"Veal marsala."

Her head came up and her eyes suddenly flooded with tears. It was the same dish he brought her the night they met, in a container from the Green Room. The same night he stayed at the office until two A.M. to walk her safely to her hotel. The same night she fell in love with him.

"I love you," she said now in a voice thick with grief.

"I love you, too. I've missed you these past few weeks."

"Yes, it's been so hectic lately—"

"But not tonight. Tonight it's just you and me."

He made love to her tenderly that night, with soft sighs and gentle strokes and fervent whispers of how he adored her. It was, she knew, a reward for her good behavior these last several weeks, for dressing as she was told, for going where she was steered and standing where she was positioned. She felt no resentment. After all, if she believed she'd married a stranger, then surely so must he. She lay with her arms wrapped tight around him and her cheek pressed close to his, and she timed her hips to his as they moved against each other in a slow and sensuous climb to climax. They came together, one of only a few times since they'd been lovers, and it left them gasping with surprise and wonder.

Afterward Cam lay with her head on his chest and her eyes open in the dark. His fingers were weaving through the strands of her hair, which told her that he was awake, too.

"Let's have a baby," he said.

"Hmm, I can't wait."

"Then let's not." He rose up on one elbow. "Let's start now. Tomorrow. As soon as possible."

She smiled. "Where's all this eagerness coming from?"

"From you! From us. I love you, Cam, and I can't wait to see you pregnant." He smoothed his hand over her stomach. "I can't wait to see our baby in your arms."

"Wouldn't it be better to wait until after the election?"

"No. Not at all. It's not like it would hurt my chances. To tell the truth, it would only improve them."

"How?"

"You know—the family-man image, all of that. A lot of voters still can't accept a nontraditional wife. If you're pregnant on the campaign trail, it'll counterbalance that."

"I see."

"What do you say?" He bent to kiss her, then raised up over her with a grin. "I'm ready to do my part."

She could feel the edge of his expectancy as he hovered over her, waiting for her answer.

"I don't know, honey—" she began.

"And let's not forget about the pictures."

"What?"

"Your nudie pictures. Say somebody does come forward. It'll make it that much harder to believe it's you if you're looking like a young madonna. So, you see, sweetheart, this works to your advantage, too."

Their bodies were still sweaty from sex, yet Cam went suddenly so cold she couldn't feel her toes.

"Yes, I see."

"We'll do it, then?"

She nodded.

He fell asleep soon after, so deeply he didn't even stir when she swung her legs to the floor. She went into the bathroom and opened the medicine cabinet and took out her packet of birth control pills. Only three months ago she'd stood at another bathroom sink and deliberated over the same pills. It was their first morning in St. Bart's, and she'd wanted his baby so badly she almost flushed the pills down the toilet. All that stopped her were the state of their finances and Doug's vague references to *someday*.

She looked up at her hollow-eyed reflection in the mirror, then lifted the lid on a canister of cotton balls and hid the packet deep inside.

18

Meredith's brain screamed awake at the insistent chirp of an electronic beeper beside her head. An arm reached over to grab it from the nightstand, and she opened her eyes furiously as the bedside lamp switched on.

"What are you doing here?" she ground out. Her voice sounded like an old woman's this early in the morning, and she flopped over and pulled the pillow over her head before he could notice that her face was like an old woman's, too.

He laughed. "Don't you remember?"

"What are you *still* doing here? I said you couldn't stay the night."

From under the pillow she heard him pick up the phone and punch in the touch-tone beeps of a ten-digit number.

"Morning, Dad. What's up?"

She cringed. Sutherland was in western Maryland this week—the only reason she'd allowed Bret to stay—but if he happened to be at a phone with a Caller ID display, and if he happened to glance at the number, he'd have to recognize it as hers. She'd warned Bret not to use this line, but he was like a kid on a motorcycle: the danger was half the pleasure.

Though, of course, she was the only one who knew how deep that danger was. For the hundredth time she told herself: this was insane. She had to end it now.

"Don't worry," he was saying. "I'm going out there tonight. I'll talk some sense into him."

She rolled over and lifted one corner of the pillow to peer at him. His hair was tousled from sleep, but his black eyes were alert and shining.

"Hey, did you catch that spot last night? I thought it was dynamite. Yep—" Bret cocked his head and grinned at her. "That Meredith's really something. Okay. Yes, sir, I'll call you then."

He hung up and dropped out of sight over the side of the bed. She crawled to the edge and looked down. He was doing push-ups, nude, and the sight of it made her insides burn.

"You're suicidal, you know that?" she said.

He bent one arm behind his back and held it there for a count of ten push-ups, then switched arms in midair and repeated the count on the other side.

"Who are you going to talk some sense into?"

He rolled to his back and started doing crunches with his fists at his ears. "There's some crank out in West Virginia. A reservist who was called up for Desert Storm, and now he thinks the country owes him an income for the rest of his life. He tried Gulf War Syndrome for a while, but that didn't pan out, so now he's trying to blackmail Dad."

"Blackmail? Over what?"

"Who knows?" He came to his feet in one fluid motion.

"If you don't know"—she sat up and reached for her robe—"what makes you think you can just go out there and stop—"

Bret flipped himself across the bed, grabbed her, and ground his mouth against hers until she was gasping for air.

He grinned. "Stopped *you*, didn't I?"

"So that's your plan?" she said dryly when she could speak again. "You're going to kiss him into silence?"

"I'll improvise."

She headed for the shower, halfway hoping he'd join her there, but when she was still alone ten minutes later, she turned off the taps and came out in a towel.

Bret was already dressed and grabbing for his coat on a whirlwind path out the door.

"Well," she said, stung. "I never drove a man out this fast before."

"I'll meet you up in Baltimore."

"Baltimore?"

He tossed the morning *Post* at her and took off at a gallop down the stairs.

Thirty minutes later she was on her way to Baltimore.

Rain sluiced down in sheets over the car windows, and she stared at it in simmering silence. The Beltway traffic was backed up for two miles before the I-95 junction, her cell phone reception was shot to hell, and there was nothing but the swish of the windshield wipers and the driver's banalities to distract her from the horror of today's headlines.

The *Post* lay folded on the seat beside her like a mutant cast-off child she refused to look at. But she didn't need to look at it. Bad news tended to acid-etch itself into her brain the moment she read it. And there was no question this news was bad. As bad as it got.

SUTHERLAND SAID TO BE SOURCE BEHIND 1968
PENTAGON LEAKS

There was an adage to the effect that there were only two scandals that could ruin a popular politician: being caught in bed with a dead girl, or a live boy. But the joke missed an important third: betraying your country. For a candidate like Phil Sutherland, who put love of country on a higher pedestal than anything else, it would be fatal.

Nineteen sixty-eight. How was she supposed to control events that happened thirty years ago? She could barely remember Lyndon Johnson's presidency, let alone the events that led to its collapse. And neither could Tim Robson, the staff reporter who committed this atrocity, and who was at least ten years younger than she. But the source for most of his material was Dean McIverson, age seventy-one, a former *Post* reporter himself. Meredith hadn't heard of McIverson for so long that she'd assumed he was dead.

Just like her cell phone. She flipped it open and tried again, and by some miracle the call went through this time, although on a line crackling with static.

"Marcy, thank God," she shouted when her assistant answered. "Any word from the General?"

"He's still en route from Cumberland. He'll meet you at the office in Baltimore. Hopefully by ten."

"Ten?" Meredith looked at her watch and groaned. That meant another ninety minutes of tortured speculation. There was no way Sutherland would discuss this on his own cell phone. Even on a good news day, he suspected his enemies were listening in. After developments like this, she could almost believe him.

"Transfer me to Brian."

"You mean Ryan?"

"Yeah, whatever. Oh, and Marcy—"

"Yes?"

"I want every phone in the office set to speed-dial Tim Robson's number at the *Post*, continuously. I want his phones jammed. Nobody gets through to him this morning."

"I'll get right on it."

A minute later Meredith's young intern came on the line.

"Brian, what d'you got?"

"I found the clippings. I'm faxing them up to Baltimore."

"So what's the story?"

"I don't quite have it pieced together—"

"Oh, never mind." What was she thinking? If she couldn't remember the machinations behind the Vietnam War, how would this twenty-two-year-old boy have any clue? "Transfer me to Richard Portwell," she said with a sigh. He might be a pompous old fool and a major thorn in her side, but he was the quickest source of political history she had.

"Hello, Richard. How are you?" she sang out when he came to the phone. "I'm so glad I found you in. This is one of those many occasions when I need the benefit of your wisdom and experience."

"Yes, I saw the story. Takes me back, I must say."

"I'm a little confused. Is this the old Pentagon Papers business?"

"Good heavens, no. This episode predates Daniel Ellsberg, and it involves a different issue altogether. The papers Ellsberg stole pointed to a Pentagon cover-up of the scope of the war. McIverson's story suggested something far worse."

"Can you fill me in?"

"Certainly," Portwell said with a lingering enunciation that made her grit her teeth with frustration. "Context first. Go back to 1968—we'd been in Vietnam since 'sixty-one, and the body count was something like fifteen thousand. Enormous antiwar sentiment was building—you remember that, I'm sure. But what you may not remember is that there was substantial discord in the military over what they saw as Johnson's failure to fight the war like a war. Particularly when he started scaling it back in an effort to defuse Gene McCarthy. With me so far?"

"I'll try to keep up." Irritably she pictured Portwell in his tweeds and flannels, leaning back in his chair and drawing ruminatively on his pipe.

"In the early part of 1968, rumors started to surface that the Pentagon was totally at odds with the White House over this. There was even a rumor that a group of high-ranking officers was developing scenarios of a takeover of the war policy."

She let out an astonished laugh. "Are you talking military junta?"

"Of course, it never came to that," he said with a sniff. "I'm trying to convey the enormity of the stakes involved."

"So where does McIverson come in?"

"He was one of the *Post*'s star reporters back in the Sixties. Back when Woodward and Bernstein were still fetching coffee and covering zoning hearings. In March of 1968 he wrote a series about the dissent building in the Pentagon. And he backed it up with quotes lifted from classified documents."

"Which he's claiming he got from Phil Sutherland."

"Just so. The Pentagon denied everything, including the authenticity of the documents, but the story grew legs anyway, and basically eroded Johnson's final base of support. Within a matter of days his presidency was dead, and on March thirty-first he made his famous speech declining to seek reelection. But he had the last laugh, you might say. In that same speech he declared a halt to all bombing above the twentieth parallel."

"His way of giving the finger to the Pentagon."

"Rather. Which of course drove the military boys wild. McIverson takes credit for all of this, you know. Though, now that I think of it, I never once heard him take credit for Richard Nixon."

Portwell was still chuckling at his own joke when Meredith asked: "Where's McIverson now? What's he been up to?"

"He's been out of the business for years. Ill health, I think."

"Hmm." She turned her face to the rain-streaked window as the wheels started to turn in her mind. Age seventy-one, poor health—dementia? "Well, thanks so much. I knew I could count on you. Could you transfer me to Bill Schecter?"

"Certainly. Wait—he's that FBI fellow?"

"He works for us now, Richard."

"Oh, Meredith," he said with distaste. "I see what you're up to. You're going to shoot the messenger because you don't like the message he brought you. But that never accomplishes anything."

"It does if the messenger made up the message."

"You mean, if you can make it look like he did."

"Either way, Richard."

After a minute the line buzzed against her ear. Portwell had hung up on her, or more likely, fumbled the call transfer. She dialed Schecter's number herself and gave him the assignment. There was no time for a field investigation on this one, only for a quick and dirty file search. The dirtier the better.

The car splashed to a stop in front of the Sutherland for Senate office, where one of the young staffers was watching for her. He opened an umbrella and ran out as she stepped from the car.

"Any sign of Bret?" she asked, striding for the door.

He gave a guarded nod.

"What?"

The young man's Adam's apple bobbed in a hard gulp. "He's out of control, Miss Winters. He's been ranting and raving—"

She could hear it for herself the moment she stepped inside. "Who the fuck is this asshole?" Bret was screaming. "Who does he think he is? Somebody get him on the phone. You! I'm talking to you! Call him up. Well, find out!"

Meredith tossed her coat at the staffer and followed Bret's voice to the conference room at the back.

"He can't get away with this!" he was bellowing behind the door. "Who does he think he is, coming out of nowhere thirty years later? I mean, fucking Jesus—"

She opened the door, and something whizzed past her head and smashed against the wall. She looked down at the china shards at her feet, then up at Bret where he stood with his throwing arm still extended. Half a dozen other people were seated at the conference table, and they were all watching him in helpless embarrassment.

"Okay, that's enough," Meredith said. "Throwing tantrums won't do your father a bit of good."

She stepped over the crockery and took her place at the table with a nod at the staffers seated around it. Bret flung himself into a chair and slouched down low with a look of pure anguish on his face.

"But it's not right," he said. "I mean, isn't there some kind of rule that says journalists don't reveal their sources?" He turned to Meredith. "You were a journalist. Isn't there a rule?"

She felt a strange sinking sensation as she gazed at him, one she might have called tenderness if its real name weren't weakness. She had a growing soft spot for Bret, and not only for his good looks and sexual prowess, but for all his youthful exuberance and naïveté. People said *soft spot* like it was a good thing, when what it really was was a vulnerability, like the fontanel of an infant, a place where grievous harm could occur.

"You bet," she said coldly. "We don't reveal our sources to the police or prosecutors or grand juries, not even if they jail us for contempt. Because as long as we're still reporting, we want our sources to know they can trust us. But if we're out of the business and never hope to talk to another source for the rest of our lives? Hey, it's 'Extra, extra, read all about it.' "

Bret flushed hot.

A secretary came in with a stack of papers. "That fax came for you, Miss Winters. The McIverson articles? I made copies."

Meredith took one copy and passed the rest. "Clean that up, would you?" she said with a vague gesture at the broken coffee cup on the floor.

The group around the table read through the stories while the secretary swept up the pieces of china. The moment she left the room, Bret threw down his pages.

"What if it's true? So what? He was right! The Gulf War proved he was right! There's no point in fighting a half-assed war. If anybody'd listened to him back in the Sixties, think of all the lives that might have been saved!" He picked up the pages again and swatted them through the air. "Dad was a hero to do this!"

"You think that's how we should spin it?" Meredith said.

"Damn right I do! Why not, if it's the truth?"

She shrugged. "People have this funny idea about heroes. They don't think sneaks and snitches qualify."

His eyes bulged out, and quickly Meredith laid her hand over his. "Bret," she said softly, "there's a lot of secret heroism that won't survive the light of day. That doesn't make it any less heroic. It just means it has to stay secret."

He stared uncomprehendingly at her, his face full of pain and stubbornness. He was like a wild animal caught in a trap, too crazed by fear and suffering to accept any help to get free. But she held his gaze and squeezed his hand, and slowly understanding seemed to settle into his eyes.

Meanwhile, the others around the table were exchanging a meaningful look themselves. Abruptly Meredith withdrew her hand from Bret's. "Somebody remind me," she said briskly. "Where was Phil posted in 1968?"

"He was just back from a two-year tour," a man spoke up. "He was a captain by then, and he was assigned to the Pentagon as an aide to General Hutchins."

"Hold on." Meredith reached for the speakerphone. "Brian," she said when she got through to the intern. "What was the official Pentagon response to the McIverson series?"

"Denial. They claimed the documents were all forgeries. But here's a funny thing—McIverson challenged them to have a typewriter expert examine their equipment and compare it to the type on the documents, and they refused. Security concerns, they said, plus there were too many typewriters in the Pentagon anyway, and it would be a ridiculous waste of time."

Meredith pushed a button and ended the call. "Okay, I see three possible scenarios. One, the documents were genuine, and somebody leaked them to McIverson. Two, McIverson fabricated them. Or three, somebody else fabricated them and leaked them to McIverson. Of course, with either one or three, we run the risk that the somebody was Phil."

"I vote for two," a horrified staffer said.

"Bill Schecter on line four," the secretary called.

Meredith punched the button on the speakerphone. "Bill, tell us what you got on McIverson."

"He had a distinguished career at the *Post*," he said. "Pulitzer prize, national acclaim, the whole nine yards. In 1971 he left to pursue a lifelong dream of sailing the South Pacific in a one-man boat. Posed for pictures in San Diego when he took off and three months later when he arrived in Tahiti. Took a job with the *Cleveland Plain Dealer* in 1972, and in 1974 announced his retirement."

"That's it?"

"That's it," Schecter said. "Except, during those three months he was alone sailing the South Pacific . . . ?"

"Yeah?"

"Somehow he was also a patient at an alcohol rehab center in Richmond."

"Son of a bitch!" Bret hollered.

"Thanks, Bill," Meredith said. "Fax me the backup."

"You got it."

She looked down the table at the staff. "Okay, McIverson's a drunk and a first-class fabricator. Let's get our hands on those South Seas photos, and send somebody down to take a picture of the rehab clinic in Richmond. Tell them to get a shot of some old drunk in a hospital gown, just so nobody misses our point. And Ann . . ." She turned to the campaign press secretary. "Put together a list of our best friends in the media, and we'll decide who to feed this to."

"But"—the woman chewed on her lip—"can we really use this? McIverson wrote the Pentagon story in 1968. This is three years later."

"So?" Bret stared furiously at her. "This is thirty years later, and he's using it against us!"

"That just proves my point—"

A commotion sounded in the outer office, and a look of relief flooded over Bret's face. "Here he is now," he said, and got up to throw the door open.

General Sutherland strode into the conference room with his jaw clenched tight and a dripping raincoat draped over his shoulders. Behind him trailed the young staffer who'd accompanied him to the western corner of the state yesterday. Meredith felt a moment's amused sympathy for the young man. The last three hours of his life must have been a living hell.

Sutherland threw off his coat and sat down stony-faced at the head of the table. "Where are we?"

Meredith summed it up in five minutes, then said, "Fill us in, General. You were at the Pentagon in 1968. There must have been some kind of flap over these stories."

"You better believe it. There was a full-scale internal investigation. I was interrogated, along with a hundred other people. We were all cleared. There was no plot, there was no leak. And by the way, we had our own experts check the type, and there was no match."

"Why didn't they put out a news release to that effect?"

"Because McIverson would have demanded the right to send in an outside expert, and we never could have allowed that."

"Then that's it," Bret said, on his feet again. "We deny it, and we smear this son of a bitch McIverson, just like Meredith said."

"But wait," the press secretary said. "Let's assume that McIverson did fabricate the whole thing. What's his motive for dredging it up thirty years later?"

Bret wheeled on her. "He's trying to sink this campaign. What d'you think?"

"But why?"

"Who the fuck cares?" he screamed.

Sutherland spoke a single sharp word: *"Bret."*

Silence fell like a shroud over the room.

He pointed a finger at his son. "Calm down, sit down, and watch your mouth around the ladies."

"Yes, sir," Bret mumbled and took his seat.

"In answer to your question, Ann," the General said, "McIverson's a print reporter, and I'm a radio host. Radio talk shows are the bane of the media establishment. They don't like people forming opinions without the so-called cognitive filter of the press. By sourcing this story, McIverson kills two birds: he gets another fifteen minutes of fame, along with the respect of his colleagues for undermining the fastest-growing public forum today."

Meredith sat back with a dazed smile. Sometimes Sutherland could still impress her.

The group began to buzz over the mechanics of the thing, when and where to hold the press conference, who to pass the McIverson material to, how hard to hit. The faxes kept pouring in from Meredith's office, and the phone calls were coming in hot and heavy as one reporter after another angled for an immediate reaction from the Sutherland campaign.

At eleven o'clock the call they'd been waiting for came through. "Ann?" the secretary called from the door. "It's Tim Robson, for you."

The press secretary looked uncertainly at Meredith.

"Go ahead, take it," Meredith said. "But tell him you haven't read the *Post* today. Tell him you usually save your recreational reading for the weekend."

Ann nodded and left the room.

Meredith felt Sutherland's eyes on her. He knew she was stalling, and he knew what it meant.

"Hey, everybody," she spoke up over the clamor, "could you give us a minute here?"

There was momentary chaos as the room cleared, but at last Meredith was alone at the table with Sutherland.

"I have to ask you one question," she said.

"The answer's no."

"No, I'm not asking that question, Phil. All I want to know is this: if we deny McIverson's allegations, is there anything out there other than his word to contradict us?"

Sutherland gave her one of his rare smiles and rose to his feet. "Meredith," he said as he threw the door open, "that's the question I thought you were asking the first time."

The story played itself out through the next two news cycles. Sunday morning Dean McIverson was back in the drunk tank, and Monday morning the *Post* ran a retraction of the Robson article. A flurry of reports and analyses covered that notable event, but by Monday night the story had burned itself out.

Meredith threw a little celebration at her offices as soon as the eleven o'clock news was over. She'd been running for five days with little sleep and not much food, and the champagne went instantly to her head. She turned from giddy to tearful, and by twelve-thirty was making a sloppy speech about her first-class support staff that she knew she was going to regret in the morning.

By then Sutherland had disappeared from the party. She went in search of him through the darkened corridors of the offices and finally found him in the screening room with a remote control in his hand and the video footage from Doug Alexander's announcement on the monitor.

"Phil." She pouted in a way she hoped was still pretty on a forty-two-year-old face deeply etched with fatigue. "It's your party, and you're missing it."

"Let's not fool ourselves, Meredith." His eyes were glued to the screen. "It's *your* party."

"Well, then. All the more reason." She stopped, unable to recall where she'd meant to go with that thought. Though it hardly mattered. Sutherland was transfixed by the screen, and specifically by the big-eyed young woman in the pink knit suit.

"Phil." Meredith pulled a chair close to his. "Bill checked her out. She's all clear. You saw the file. Everything's there all the way down to her birth certificate. There's no way your paths ever crossed."

"I know it." He hit the Rewind button, and the tape blipped in reverse. "But there's something about her—" He stopped and pushed Play, and again Campbell Smith's face filled the screen.

"Phil." She twined her arm around his neck and gave his shoulder a rub. "You just dodged a cannonball. Could you please relax and enjoy it for a minute?"

He cracked a smile and turned to smack her on the lips. "Why don't you go on home?" he said. "I'll join you there in say—forty minutes."

"I'll be waiting." She got up and swayed briefly on her feet, then pulled herself steady and marched out of the office.

She called for her car, said her good nights, and rode the elevator down to the dimly lit lobby. The car hadn't arrived yet, and she took a moment to pull out her compact and study her face in the mirror. God, she was a ruin. Red eyes, smeared lipstick, and only forty minutes to make herself look ravishing. *A woman's work was never done,* her mother would have said, or maybe, *No rest for the weary.* Though, Jesus, in her wildest dreams her mother never could have guessed how hard she had to work. Meredith puckered up her lips, cringing at the deep lines that radiated out from them, then screamed out loud as another face crowded into the mirror beside hers.

She turned with her hand over her heart. "Bret—would you *please* stop sneaking up on me like that?"

"You sneaked up on me," he whispered, stepping close. "And stole my heart while I wasn't watching."

"Oh, God," she muttered. "What country-western song did you lift that out of?"

He grinned, and Meredith was afraid her heart would melt. She turned away as her car pulled up outside. "Oh, there's my ride."

"I'll meet you at your house."

"No!" she almost shrieked, and when his eyes clouded, she reached out and touched his cheek. "Not tonight, baby. I'm just all done in."

She ran out of the building and into the car. As the driver pulled away from the curb, she looked back to see Bret standing on the sidewalk like a woebegone child. The makings of a sob swelled up in her throat, and she sank into the seat and squeezed her eyes shut. It was only the champagne, she told herself, and five days of round-the-clock spinning. She wasn't really falling in love with him. She wasn't that foolish.

She couldn't be.

19

May passed into June, but there were different markers in time these days, and they were all laid out on a giant melamine board on the wall of campaign headquarters: it was eleven weeks since Doug announced his candidacy; three months until the primary; five months until the general election. The first Saturday in June was outlined in red. It would be Doug's biggest fund-raising event so far, a five-hundred-dollar-a-plate dinner featuring appearances not only by Senator Ash Ramsay but also by Senator John DeMedici of Ohio, the Party's front-runner for the presidential nomination in 2000.

Cam was reading in bed Thursday night when she heard Doug's footsteps on the stairs. It was almost midnight; the fund-raiser was only two days away, and he'd been working late every night that week in a frenzy of anticipation. She hurried to switch off the lamp and flopped over under the covers.

But feigning sleep did no more good tonight than it had for the past month. He rolled into bed and reached for her. He was too tired for this, she could feel it in his back and shoulders, but she could also feel his determination. He wanted a baby, or at least a pregnant wife, and if that meant nightly sex, that was what he was going to do. It was a ritual now, just like the pill Cam continued to gulp down every morning.

He finished quickly—this was goal-directed sex—and kissed her on the cheek as he withdrew. "What's this?" he said, his fingers touching where his lips had been.

She swiped at the tears with the back of her hand. "I don't know."

"I know," he said heavily as he rolled off her. "I'm disappointed, too." He scrunched up his pillow and burrowed in to sleep. "But don't worry. We'll hit it this month."

* * *

As soon as he was asleep, she got up and went downstairs.

Starlight shone through the undraped windows and fell in dull gleaming circles on the bare wood floors. She wandered the rooms in the dark, navigating from one patch of starlight to the next, and staring out through one black pane of glass after the other. For a long time she stood at the rear window and looked out over the garden that had sustained her these last months. But everything was black in the night. She couldn't distinguish the flowers from the weeds.

She switched on a lamp in the living room and sat down with the gardening encyclopedia. She started with the A's, and over the next hour read through each entry, trying to memorize the Latin names for every tree, shrub, and flower grown in North America—the sunlight and soil requirements, where to plant, how much to water, when to divide. She numbed her mind with the minutiae of it all.

It was one-thirty when the phone rang on the table beside her. She grabbed it before it could ring again and wake Doug.

"Campbell? Is that you?" a woman's voice said.

"Yes?"

"Please, is Douglas there?"

"Mrs. Ramsay?"

"Oh, God, what time is it? He's asleep, isn't he? I'm sorry, I don't know what I was thinking—"

"Is something wrong?"

"You'll never guess. It's Trey—he's been found!"

Cam's feet hit the floor. "What? How?"

"He called the police himself. He reported his own kidnapping, whether Ash wanted it so or not. I had a call from the FBI in Maine asking if we'd misplaced any of our children. I didn't know what to say. I mean, the official story is that Trey's at school abroad."

"What *did* you say?"

"Nothing—I hung up! Jesse's out of town, and I've been trying to reach Ash, but there's no answer at his apartment, or at his office. I don't know where he could be—there wasn't anything on his calendar tonight—Oh, God, I don't know what to do."

"It's all right, Mrs. Ramsay. Try to calm down—"

"Is that Margo?" Doug loomed suddenly behind her and

grabbed the phone. "Margo? What's wrong?" He listened, then said: "Don't worry, I'll track him down. Is Jesse there? Right, I forgot. Listen, I'll be right over. Don't do anything, don't talk to anybody until I get there."

He hung up, and Cam followed him across the hall to the study. He flipped through the pages of his address book and dialed a number. "Hello, Kitty? It's Doug Alexander. Sorry to be calling so late, but I need to speak with Ash. It's urgent."

He sat down at the desk to wait, then said: "Ash, there's trouble. Margo had a call from the FBI up in Maine. Apparently the locals got a call from Trey, and they called Margo to verify . . . Nothing. She says she hung up on them. I figure we can probably spin that out as shock. Yeah. How soon can you . . . ? All right, I'm on my way over there now."

He hung up and got to his feet.

"I don't understand," Cam said from the doorway. "This is good news, right?"

"As long as it doesn't get leaked out the wrong way." He started to skirt past her.

"Who's Kitty?" she asked, blocking his way.

He took her by the shoulders and kissed her. "Better keep that to yourself," he said, and moved her aside.

It was another middle-of-the-night mission, but this time the Ramsay house stood in darkness. There was no moon, only a faint speckled glow of starlight, and they had to stumble their way up the steps to the front door. Doug groped for the bell and pressed it, and they could hear its echo rolling inside. When no one answered, he rang again, then pounded on the door. Finally he reached up and ran his fingers along the lintel until he found the key.

"Margo?" he called, swinging the door in. He hit a switch and the lights came on in a pair of iron sconces on either side of the hall. They stood a moment, straining to listen through the silence, but there was still no answer.

"I'll check upstairs," he said, and took off.

Cam groped her way down the hall and through the kitchen. A dim pool of light spilled out of the sitting room, and she traced it to a small lamp on the table beside the old sofa. Margo sat in the middle of it, in a silver brocade kimono with her gray hair hanging long and loose over her shoulders. A book was open on her lap, but her gaze was fixed on the wall over the fireplace.

"Mrs. Ramsay?"

"Oh." She stirred as if a breeze had touched her, but her eyes didn't move. "Campbell. You're here."

"Yes, and Doug, too."

"It's not from life, did you know that?"

"What?"

"Cynthia's portrait. It wasn't painted from life. Because of course she wasn't alive. The painter had to work from a photograph. Here it is. See?"

She pointed to the book on her lap. It was a photo album turned to an eight-by-ten glossy of Cynthia Ramsay.

"Still, he did a wonderful job," Margo said. "He captured her perfectly, don't you agree? Her purity."

"Doug spoke to the Senator, Mrs. Ramsay. He's on his way home right now. Everything's going to be all right."

"Oh, I don't think so," she said hoarsely, and closed the album with a heavy thud. "They called back, you see. The FBI in Maine—they called back. Not their fault, of course. They didn't know the protocol. No one told them that I'm not permitted to speak for myself."

Her eyes shifted at the sound of footsteps on the stairs, and a moment later Doug came into the room.

"Ah, there you are." He knelt beside Margo and took her hands in his. "Ash is on his way home right now. He'll get this all straightened out."

Margo shook her head with a hollow laugh.

"What?" he said, glancing back at Cam.

"Mrs. Ramsay had a second conversation with the FBI."

"Oh, God." There was a brief, furious flare in his eyes before he turned back to her. "Margo, what did you say to them? Think carefully now."

"Because I didn't before?" She pulled her hands free. "Is that what you're implying, Douglas?"

"No, we just need to know—"

"I told them everything. All right? I forgot to wait for the press release to learn what my reaction was. I told them that my son had been kidnapped. I told them that Steve Patterson grabbed him off a dark street almost four months ago, and that we didn't know where he was, or how he was—"

She broke off and covered her face with her hands.

Doug spiraled to his feet. "I better get Ash on his car phone."

Ten minutes later he hung up with a list of additional calls to make. Margo went upstairs to lie down, Cam made a pot of coffee, and Doug worked the phone until the doorbell started to ring. The aide in charge of Ramsay's local office arrived first, followed by U.S. Attorney Ronald March, and finally two men flashing FBI shields.

Doug ushered them all into the library and sat down behind the Senator's desk. "Okay," he said, clasping his hands on the blotter before him. "Where are we?"

Cam took an inconspicuous seat in the corner as one of the agents stood to make his report.

"The local police in the town of Baxter Bay monitor an emergency band on the radio. They intercepted a message—" The agent flipped a page on his notepad. "—at 7:38 P.M. from a male identifying himself as James Ashton Ramsay the Third. He gave his location as Maristella Island and stated he'd been held hostage there since February by a man named Steve Patterson. He stated that Patterson abducted him from Greenville, Delaware, on February twentieth. He furnished a home address and telephone number in Greenville, which matches this residence here." The agent flipped another page. "The locals reported the call to the Bureau's resident agency in Portland. They called this number. There was a disconnect. They called again, spoke to a woman identifying herself as Mrs. Ramsay, who confirmed the report.

"At 2:45 A.M. today, a Coast Guard cutter was dispatched to Maristella Island with two special agents aboard. They took into custody a white male who identified himself as Steven A. Patterson, age thirty-four. Taken into protective custody was a young white male who refused to identify himself, but is presumed to be James Ashton Ramsay the Third."

"Refused to identify himself?" Doug cut in. "What the hell does that mean?"

Ronald March held up an appeasing hand at Doug. The dome of his head shone in the harsh lamplight, and his hair stuck out around it like a monk's fringe. "Did the boy confirm that he'd made the radio call?" he asked the agent.

"No, sir. He was reportedly in an emotional state. But the suspect was overheard saying to him, quote, 'Calm down, Jamie, it's all right, it's going to be all right.' "

"Oh, God," Doug muttered and spun a quarter turn in Ramsay's chair.

"Where was the boy found?" March asked.

"In a bedroom on an upper-level floor."

"Any locks on the door? Or restraints of any kind?"

"The door was locked from the inside. When he refused the agents' requests to open it, they had to kick it in."

March ran a palm over his scalp. "He's not sounding a whole lot like a victim."

Doug snorted. "This is a kid who's made an art form out of being difficult. Believe me, this is par for the course."

"That'll be all for now," March said to the agents. "But stick around outside in case anything comes up."

They nodded and left, and soon another voice sounded in the hallway, a booming one, and Doug jumped up and opened the library door on Ash Ramsay.

"You reach everybody?" he demanded, striding past him to assume the seat Doug had been warming only a second before.

"Your press secretary's en route; everyone else is here."

Ramsay moved his eyes over the occupants of the room. "Campbell," he said, lighting on her in the corner. "Would you mind keeping an eye on the door?"

There were already two FBI agents stationed at the door.

She got up and left the room.

The long night grew longer. Cam sat on the stairs, elbows on her knees and her chin in her hands, dozing briefly, then startling awake as the doorbell or telephone rang again. Ramsay's press secretary arrived from Washington and was swiftly admitted to the inner sanctum, and later one of Ronald March's assistants arrived to join the deliberations, and the FBI agents were summoned in for a second briefing.

Nothing stirred until almost dawn, when a light step sounded from upstairs and a throat cleared. Cam looked up to see Margo on the landing. She was dressed now, in a black suit and heels, and her hair was pinned up.

"Can I get you anything, Mrs. Ramsay?" Cam asked, rising from the staircase.

"My husband, if you don't mind, dear." Margo descended the

stairs. "Tell him I'd like to see him in the sitting room. Now." She glided toward it without a backward glance.

Cam crossed the hall and tapped on the library door. "Senator?" She cracked the door open, and the conversation inside screeched to a halt. "Mrs. Ramsay would like to speak with you."

A brief spark of irritation lit his eyes before he smiled at her. "Tell her I'll be with her shortly."

"Excuse me, Senator. She asked to see you now."

The smile disappeared, and a tight hard line took its place as he stood.

"She's back here," Cam said, and walked ahead of him before he could dismiss her again.

Margo was on her feet just inside the sitting room. Ramsay came in and took her by the shoulders, and she flinched as he bent to kiss her on the cheek.

"Well, Margo, looks like we're getting our boy back."

"Back from where? Boarding school in Switzerland?"

"You didn't leave me much wiggle room there, did you?"

"I'm sorry. I didn't know what to say."

"No, I suppose not." He raked his hand through his hair until it stood out in a white mane around his head. "I guess none of us saw this coming."

"Which means everybody was wrong, and Trey hasn't been all right at all! Something made him call for help."

"Maybe. I don't know. I've given up trying to figure out that boy." His hand dropped from his hair to the back of his neck, and he gave it a weary massage as he wandered past his wife to the window.

"Well?" Margo folded her arms over her chest. "What have your advisers advised? What are we supposed to say about all this?"

"Like I said, we don't have much choice." He stared out into the murky gray light of the backyard. "It's too late now to try and arrange anyone's cooperation or silence. You said he'd been kidnapped, so now he's been kidnapped. We have to go public with the whole damn story."

"All of it?" she said shrilly.

Ramsay turned with a retort forming on his lips, but he cut himself off when he saw Cam still in the doorway.

"Don't worry, Senator," she said mildly. "If you're referring to

Cynthia"—she gave a nod at the portrait over the mantel—"I pieced that together months ago."

Margo sank into a chair as if she were suddenly ill. But Ramsay gave Cam a look of curious appraisal.

"I'm not surprised that you figured it out," he said, "but only that you kept it to yourself all this time. I must say, young lady, I admire your discretion."

She shook her head, refusing the compliment, if that was what it was.

"See there, Margo?" he said. "You might as well resign yourself to it. One way or the other, the truth will out."

At seven o'clock Ramsay's press secretary placed the call to the *News Journal*'s managing editor, who arrived within the hour and was ushered into the living room along with a staff writer and photographer. Margo and Ash sat side by side on a Chesterfield sofa under a Japanese silk screen and announced the joyous news that their son had been rescued and his abductor arrested.

Now that Trey was safe, they could tell the world of their ordeal. Their daughter Cynthia, who died so tragically in an automobile accident ten years ago, had suffered another tragedy earlier in her life. She'd become pregnant by a man who deserted her. Cynthia couldn't bear to part with her child, but she was so young and still had her education to complete. And so the Ramsays themselves adopted her infant son and raised him as their own. It was the best thing they'd ever done. Not only did the boy grow up with two loving parents in a stable household, but every day of his life had enriched theirs. Without him they would have been inconsolable after they lost their daughter.

Recently they'd experienced every parent's worst nightmare, one that far too many adoptive parents are forced to suffer. The man who'd abandoned their daughter resurfaced last year and made threats against the Senator and his family. When they refused to negotiate with him, he snatched their son off the street and took him into hiding. The FBI search proved fruitless, and there was nothing the Senator and his wife could do but hope and pray.

Now, nearly four harrowing months later, they'd learned that Trey had broken free long enough to contact the authorities. He'd been recovered and would soon be safely home.

Grimly, U.S. Attorney Ronald March announced that the

boy's abductor, identified as Steven A. Patterson, was in custody and would be charged under the federal kidnapping statute.

An air of self-congratulatory giddiness infused the house the moment the press departed. One of Ramsay's aides began scrambling eggs for a celebratory breakfast, and the whole group squeezed in around the table on chairs borrowed from other rooms. The Senator raised a glass of orange juice in a toast to his "kitchen cabinet," then extended his hand around the table to personally thank all of them for their friendship.

He lingered especially long over his handshake with Ronald March. "I owe you one for this, Ron," he said warmly.

"I've owed you for years, Senator. About time I got a chance to return the favor."

Ramsay went upstairs to shower and change for his return trip to Washington, but everyone else remained at the table. A mood of hilarity seemed to seize them, of danger averted and tension released. It was as if they'd successfully defused a bomb.

Ronald March's office called, and while he was still on the phone, the Senator returned in a fresh white shirt with a tie hanging loose around his neck.

"Okay, thanks." March hung up. "Senator, that was Portland. They're putting Trey on an eleven o'clock flight. He'll be in Philadelphia at 3:05."

A sudden pall fell over the room. Margo put her glass down with a rattling clink, and for a moment no one spoke.

"Good," Ramsay said finally. He went down the hall and stood in front of the mirror to knot his tie.

"Oh, Ash." Margo, stricken, rose from her chair to follow him. "You can't leave now."

"I've got Judiciary hearings all day. We've got a full roster of witnesses. But I'll be home tonight. We'll have the whole weekend to spend with the boy."

"But you should be there when we pick him up—"

"And attract the attention of the press? You want flashbulbs popping in his face the minute he steps off the plane?"

"No," she said, stung. "But I do want someone beside me when he steps off the plane."

Ramsay looked over at Doug.

"I'd be happy to go," Doug said, taking a thoughtful sip of

coffee. "But I might attract attention, too. And frankly, it's not the kind of publicity I need heading into an election."

Cam bit her lip, shocked and shamed.

"No, you're right," Ramsay agreed. He slid the knot of his tie up to his throat and reached for his suit coat.

"I could send a couple agents along," March offered. "We're going to need to take the boy's statement anyway."

Margo turned plaintively to her husband. "Is that how we want our son brought home? By FBI agents?"

Ramsay pulled on his coat, Doug took another sip from his mug, March loitered nearby, and Margo stood in the midst of them staring at her husband with a look that was furious and frustrated and helpless.

Cam was hovering on the edge of the group, and every instinct she possessed was screaming at her to hold her tongue and keep her head down.

"I'll go," she said.

Everyone looked at her in surprise.

"Well, Margo," the Senator said. "There you go."

Cam went home and tried to get some sleep before it was time to go to the airport. But she couldn't sleep through all the sights and sounds that kept looping through her mind: a dark-edged face turning away from the glare of her lights; a husky voice sifting into her sleep; a body coiled tight with tension on the end of a dock five hundred miles away; a shaft of sunlight opening up through the fog to reveal a man and boy, laughing together.

Margo was right: something happened up there, something made Trey place that call. Which meant that she must have been wrong about what she thought she saw between them on Maristella Island. She was wrong about what she did that day—or rather, what she failed to do. Twice she'd withheld information she shouldn't have, information that would have protected Trey if only she'd let it go.

No matter what happened on Maristella Island, she was as guilty as Steve Patterson.

The flight was delayed at JFK, they were told at the gate, and the arrival was now scheduled for three-thirty. Cam sat beside Margo, and they waited together in silence. Margo clenched a

Chanel bag on her lap, and the quilted leather turned dappled and shiny from the perspiration of her kneading fingers.

At last the jetway opened, and they stood behind the ropes and watched the passengers stream off the plane and pour into the terminal. It was a small commuter jet that emptied in only a few minutes. They scanned the faces of businessmen passing by with garment bags hoisted on their backs, the families swept up in swift happy reunions, and finally the crew in their crisp uniforms with their luggage rolling behind them. They stood together at the gate, neither speaking the obvious to the other, until a woman's voice came over the P.A. system: "Would the party meeting arriving passenger Thomas Belber please report to the ticketing counter?"

Margo gasped. It was the name Trey was traveling under.

"I'm sure it's nothing," Cam said. "Probably just a security precaution." She went to the counter. "That's us. Meeting Thomas Belber?"

The flight attendant gave her a harried look. "I hope *you* can do something with him."

"Excuse me?"

"The plane has to be cleaned and in Pittsburgh in three hours. I'm sorry, I don't want to have to call security."

"For what?"

The woman gave Cam an exasperated glare. "He won't get off the plane!"

Margo's hand fluttered to her mouth as she sank into the nearest chair.

Cam followed the flight attendant aboard and scanned all the empty rows of empty seats until she spotted him, slouched low in a window seat near the back. "Let me talk to him alone," she said to the attendant.

She went down the aisle and stopped beside his row. He was scowling furiously at his reflection in the tiny square of Plexiglas. "Hi, Trey. Remember me?" He didn't turn, but his shoulders stiffened as her reflection floated like a ghost image over his. "I'm Cam Alexander. Doug's wife?"

He gave a sullen shrug and didn't move. The bill of his cap was pulled low over his face, and his hair hung long and uncombed over his shoulders.

"Shall we go? Your grandmother's waiting for you inside."

A beat, then his head spun her way. "Grandmother?" he burst out. "Everybody knows? I'm the only one in the world who wasn't clued in?"

"No—" She gave a quick shake of her head. "No, I didn't get clued in until after you were gone. Doug knows, too, but that's all." Until now, she thought.

He set his jaw and looked away.

She perched on the arm of the seat across the aisle from him. A moment passed, and he still made no move to stand.

"I guess I owe you an apology," she said.

"What for?" he muttered.

"Can you keep a secret?"

He lifted a shoulder.

"This is a big one," she warned.

"Yeah, whatever."

"Well. After you disappeared back in February, your grandparents hired me to find you—"

"I already knew *that*."

"And I did."

He looked at her and blinked. "Nah," he said, his voice up an octave.

She nodded. "I tracked you up to Baxter Bay. Or, I should say, I tracked Beth Whiteside. To an inn called Breakwater Breakfasts. I found the Explorer parked in the lot behind it. And from there I hired a boat out to Maristella. It was a foggy day, and very cold, but you were working outside. It looked like you were taking apart a shed on the side of the house—"

"I remember!" he blurted, wide-eyed. "A lady came. But then she said she made a mistake and left."

"That was me. And I guess that was the real mistake I made. Leaving without you. It's just—I thought you seemed happy."

A red heat flushed up his neck.

"I'm sorry." She came across the aisle and sat down in the seat beside him. "It's all my fault."

He turned his face away, and in the glass she saw him squeeze his eyes shut.

Hydraulic rumblings came from the belly of the plane, and a fierce buzzing of whispers from the front, but Cam sat still and silent beside him and let the minutes tick by. The only thing that stirred was the soft down on his arm where the air vent hit it, until at last he took a breath and spoke again.

"You're a lawyer, right?"

"Yes," she said, startled.

"Can I ask you something?"

"Shoot."

"How can they call it kidnapping? I mean—does that mean he's not my father?"

A burst of laughter sounded at the front of the plane as a cleaning crew came aboard with vacuums and squirt bottles.

"No," she said. "He is your biological father. But his parental rights were terminated. That's when the law steps in and says it's not going to recognize a parent-child relationship anymore. Technically—*legally*—the parent is no longer your parent. He becomes like a stranger to you. That's what happened here. And that's why I should have called the cops that day in the fog." She lifted her hand from the armrest between them and laid it on his knee. "I never should have left you there."

He stared at her hand and didn't speak.

"You know what? I take it back. I shouldn't have told you to keep that a secret. Tell anyone you want. It's up to you."

He looked up and finally let his eyes meet hers. "No," he said. "I'm not telling anybody."

Voices were rising in an agitated conversation up front; she couldn't hold them off any longer.

"Come on, let's blow this joint," she said, and got to her feet.

She resolved not to look back as she headed up the aisle, even though she could tell by the look on the attendant's face that Trey wasn't following her. She gave the woman a quick, sharp look as she passed her, a warning not to interfere.

She was halfway through the jetway when she heard the sound of pounding feet behind her.

"Hey, wait up," he called.

She slowed, and he fell into step beside her.

20

They were the sounds that Trey had heard every Friday night of his life, and that he'd associate with Friday nights forever: the front door bursting open, the feet stamping in the hall and the bags thudding heavily to the floor, the five-day quiet broken by the old man's booming shouts.

Tonight the booming was followed by the hissing of whispers, and he knew it was all about him.

Leave me alone, he wanted to scream. Nobody would leave him alone. From the time they kicked in his door last night until he slammed this one shut this afternoon, he hadn't been alone for a single minute. FBI agents, flight attendants, airline security guards—they'd all been hovering over him constantly. He couldn't drop his guard for a second. That had to be why he felt so exhausted now. That plus the fact that he'd gone about thirty hours without sleep.

It must have been exhaustion that made him almost lose it on the plane with Campbell Alexander, that awful minute when everything he'd dammed out of his mind started to flood back in, so hard and fast it was like it had a blast of hydrostatic pressure behind it. Everything came rushing back—the rotten wood crumbling under his feet, the collapse of the railing, the dizzying slide down the steep-pitched roof, dangling over a fifty-foot sheer drop to the ocean with the wind howling and his own voice screaming where no one could ever hear—

No! He gritted his teeth and shoved it away. He couldn't let himself remember—he'd been fighting for five hundred miles not to remember.

Terminated. That was the word Campbell had used, and he grabbed it now and turned it over a few times in his brain. It had a final sound to it, a firm, solid sound, like *determined*. It was a sound like a door closing, or a book falling shut at the end. It meant it was something he never had to think about again.

"Trey, darling?" The old lady's voice trembled up the staircase. "Your father's home."

Your father.

He stayed where he was, flat on his back across the bed. For the last two hours he'd sat, lain, and sprawled here, tossing and shifting and moving around to try to make it fit again. It was the same bed he'd had before, nothing had changed about it, and nothing had changed about the room, either. But something had changed, something didn't fit right, and he knew it had to be him.

More whispers, this time from the other side of his door. He rolled up and sat cross-legged on the bed, and after a brisk knock, the door swung open and they stood on the threshold.

"So," the old man said. "Here you are, home safe."

Trey looked up at him. He'd always had the oldest parents in school and never thought much about it, but suddenly the old man looked ancient. The corners of his eyes drooped, and his skin hung in deep folds over his jawline. He looked like a wax figure of himself left out too long in the sun.

The old lady stood at his elbow with a strained smile. Her aging had gone the other way: her skin shrank and her bones grew until she was all sharp and angular, with cheekbones that cast shadows on her face and collarbones that jutted out so far you could have poured soup into the hollows they formed.

Together they stood and beamed at him from ten feet away, and through their broad smiles and bright eyes, he could see their fear. It was like he was some wild animal who might spook and run if they got too close. Or maybe even turn and charge.

"I think he's grown—don't you, Ash?"

"Well, for sure, his hair has. What d'you say, m'boy? Any chance of a haircut in the near future?"

He didn't answer.

The old lady's hands wrung together. A panicked look was creeping into her eyes, the one that meant, *Oh, God, not a scene, please.* "Trey, darling—"

"Don't call me that," he said.

"What?" She turned a flustered look up at the old man.

"Trey." He rolled again and landed on his feet on the far side of the bed. "Because you know what it means? The third. As in the third generation of Ramsays. But guess what, Grandma? It turns out I'm not the third—I'm the fourth. The whole thing's been nothing but a big fucking lie."

The word hummed like a tuning fork in the room as the old man scowled and the old lady's hand fluttered to her mouth. It was a word he'd always been careful not to use in front of them, but now there it hung, still vibrating in the dead air between them.

"So what are we supposed to call you?" the old man asked finally. "James, Jim, Jimbo? You tell us."

Trey blinked in astonishment. That was it? They weren't going to say anything? But then he realized: they were afraid to say anything, because now they were afraid of what he might say back. That was the reason the truth couldn't be spoken between them for thirteen years. It gave him this power over them.

"Jim," he said.

"Jim it is, then."

They left, and as he flopped back on the bed, an idea crept into the back of his mind and started skulking around the edges of his thoughts: *Steve would have said something.*

No. He squeezed his eyes shut. *Terminated,* he remembered, and he spoke it aloud, like an incantation.

The doorbell rang at eight-thirty, and he lurked at the top of the stairs as Jesse limped through the hall to answer it. A bald guy with a briefcase came in, and the old man emerged from his library to greet him. "Thanks for handling this yourself, Ron," he said. "I appreciate it."

"Don't mention it, Senator. It's good practice for me to keep my hand in now and then."

The old man ushered him into the library, and then, without even turning around or looking up, said, "Come on down here. We need to talk."

After a minute, Trey trudged downstairs. The bald guy was sitting with his legs crossed in one of the wing chairs in front of the desk. The old lady sat in a distant corner of the room.

"You remember Mr. March," the old man said.

"Hello, Jim," the bald guy said, smiling. "Good to see you again."

Jim. Quick study, this guy.

"Sit." The old man pointed a finger at the other wing chair as he settled behind his desk. "Ron has a few things to go over with you."

Trey sat down. "What about?"

"About what happened to you, Jim," March said. "Now, believe me, nobody wants you to suffer any more than you already have. No one wants to put you through any unpleasantness at all. But we do need to know what happened. And we will need you to testify if and when the case goes to trial."

"You need me to testify," he repeated.

Across the room the old lady breathed a heavy sigh.

March raised a conciliatory hand. "All you have to do is answer a few questions, Jim. It won't take long. We'll have you on and off the stand in no time. Then we can all put this behind us. You'd like that, wouldn't you?"

Trey nodded and shifted in his seat. The leather surface felt slippery beneath him.

"Well, that's fine." March opened his briefcase and took out a legal pad. "Now, let's go over a few points. Let's go back to that night in February—"

"Are you recording this?"

The old man snorted.

"No," March said, with a surprised laugh. "There's no need. This is just so I'm clear on what happened, so I'll know the best way to put the questions to you when you're on the witness stand. All right?"

Trey shrugged and slid to the other side of the chair.

"Tell us exactly what happened that night in February. Everything you can remember."

Trey cast his mind back to that night. He remembered the mailbox-bashing and the pilfered joint, and it suddenly occurred to him that they might be laying a trap. The old man settled deep into his chair and watched him through the slits of his drooping eyelids. March waited with his pen poised over the pad.

"Well, I was walking home," Trey said, treading carefully. "From my friend Jason's house? And then this van rolled up, and the driver was like, 'Need a lift?' And I was like, 'Sure.' So I hopped in the back."

He flicked his eyes at the old man. No reaction, only deep fatigue.

"And the driver was Steven Patterson?"

"Yeah. And then he locked the doors and headed in the wrong direction."

"He offered you a lift home, and after you were inside, he locked the doors. Is that right?"

"Well, it wouldn't make a lot of sense to lock the doors *before* I was inside."

"Trey," the old man said wearily.

"Yeah, that's right."

"Then what happened?"

"I went totally postal, you know? I tried all the doors, and I yelled and banged on the windows—"

The old lady kneaded her forehead. "Oh, Ash, is this really necessary?"

"Skip on ahead, Ron."

"All right," he said doubtfully. "He took you up to Maine, is that right, Jim?"

"Yeah."

"Were you ever out of his sight for any length of time during that trip?"

"No."

"Until you arrived on that island?"

"No, he never left me."

"And once you arrived, was there any way off the island?"

"There was a boat."

"Did you have access to it?"

Trey squinted at him. "What d'you mean?"

"Was there any way you could have gotten to that boat and sailed off by yourself?"

"Nah. He would've killed me if I tried."

March gave him a quick, sharp look. "You don't mean . . . ?"

"No," Trey said, pained. "I mean, I didn't have access."

"All right. From February twenty-first to June fourth, did he ever let you off that island?"

Trey shook his head.

"Okay, in court, now, you'll have to give a verbal answer. That means—"

"No, I never left the island."

"Were there any visitors while you were there?"

He thought of Cam Alexander and shook his head.

"Remember a verbal—"

"No."

"Was there a telephone?"

"No."

"But there was a shortwave radio, correct?"

Easy question, simple answer. *Yes.* Trey took a breath to say it, but the word caught somewhere in his throat.

"Is that right, Jim?"

He couldn't say it. His head started to pound, until it felt like the plates of his skull were closing in and tightening around his brain. *Terminated,* he said to himself, but it didn't work this time. How could it, as long as they were *making* him remember? He shook his head.

"No, now, you have to give a verbal—"

"Oh, Ash!" the old lady cried. "Does he have to talk about this? You can see for yourself he's—"

"But I do need—" March said at the same time.

"All right. Hold on, the both of you." The old man came up straight in his chair and fixed a steely gaze on Trey. "You know you're going to have to talk about this eventually, don't you?"

He nodded.

"And Ron—you have the report of what he said over the radio up there in Maine?"

"Yes, but—"

"All right, then. Listen up, Trey. You'll be under oath. That means you tell the truth and no fun and games about it. You understand?"

"Yeah."

"That's all you have to do. Listen to Ron's questions carefully, be sure you understand them, then tell the truth. Can you do that?"

"Sure."

The old man folded his hands in front of him. "Then we're all squared away here."

Ronald March sat uneasily in his chair, a dissatisfied look in his eyes, but after a minute he put his pad away.

Trey got to his feet. "Can I go?"

"Run along," the old man said, and waved a hand of dismissal.

He went upstairs to the room that no longer fit and stood a long time in front of his bathroom mirror. His face should have changed, but it hadn't, not in any way anyone could see. He found a pair of scissors and came back to the bathroom and cut his hair with dull crunching slices. He started at chin level, then brought it up to his ears. No change. He cut it closer, an inch or two from his scalp. The sink and floor were covered with his hair, but his face still looked the same.

He went down the hall and got the old man's razor, then lathered up his scalp and shaved off the stubble until there was nothing left but skin, white and tender and raw.

He looked in the mirror. Now he was changed. Totally.

His dream started that night with an exhilarating rush. He was back with his friends, and they were pumped and running wild through the roads of Greenville. Jon Shippen pulled alongside in his brother's car, and they all piled in and took off for a body piercing parlor in Wilmington. But when the car pulled up to the place, it was a van, and Trey was the only one in it. He went inside. Ronald March was behind the counter, and when Trey asked him for an eyebrow ring, he led him to an airplane seat and strapped him into it. "So you'll hold still," he explained. Then he opened the overhead luggage compartment and took out a metal cage and fitted it like a helmet over Trey's head. "How's that work?" Trey asked. March laughed and slid open a little door on one side of the helmet. Trey heard a skittering sound, and when he shifted his eyes he saw a big black rat coming through the gate with one long fang protruding like a piercing needle. "No!" Trey screamed, but the rat kept on coming and the tooth kept on flashing until he screamed again, "No! Do it to Steve! Not me! Do it to Steve!"

He bolted up with the scream strangling in his throat.

A dream. Only a dream.

His heart was jumping like a wild animal in his chest. He sucked in a long ragged breath and held it while he strained to listen for noises outside his room. Nothing. They hadn't heard.

He threw back the tangled knot of his sheet and rooted through the pockets of all the shirts in his closet until he found a loose cigarette. He lit it and took a deep drag, then choked and sputtered when the stale smoke hit his lungs.

He held his breath to listen again, but again they hadn't heard. Their bedroom was at the far end of the hall; they never heard him, even when he was little. Cynth's room used to be right next door, but she never seemed to hear him either.

Steve would have heard.

The cigarette trembled like a seismograph in his hand. He sat down and tried to steady his arms on his desk, but it was all coming at him again, crashing over him like a giant swell of ocean, and all his incantations of *terminated* couldn't keep it from swamping him.

Something blew in the boat engine, and Steve spent the afternoon down at the dock working on it, leaving Trey alone in the house to cram for finals. It was something he'd bargained for—if he passed the exams, he could take the summer off like a normal kid. But as exam day loomed closer, Trey was starting to regret it. He was tired of sitting at his desk, and equally tired of pacing back and forth to the window to watch for Steve's return. He wasn't coming back, not soon enough to dispel this boredom.

Maybe that was good. For three months the trapdoor to the widow's walk had been looming over him, tantalizing him with what little he remembered from his brief foray up there. Three months later Steve was no closer to rebuilding the widow's walk, and, it seemed plain to Trey, the widow's walk was no closer to collapsing.

An invigorating blast of wind hit him as he came up through the trapdoor. He threw his head back and let it whip his hair and sting his cheeks until all his senses came awake and his body was alive again. He could see for miles, for hundreds of miles, and he spun around in a whirl to take it all in. He felt a squishy sensation under his feet, barely noticeable, like he was standing on soggy grass, but the next instant the soggy grass turned to quicksand and he was falling.

The railing collapsed as he grabbed for it and pitched him down over the slope of the roof until his foot rammed against the gutter and stopped him at the edge. He screamed, but the wind was howling and the surf was crashing and Steve was half a mile away. He pressed his belly to the shingles and tried to claw himself up, but the shingles were too slick, and he slid back down with a terrifying lurch. He clung on until his fingers went numb, until all he could feel was the salty taste of sea spray on his face.

But then he felt the tight grip of hands over his wrists, and the solid weight of arms holding him safe. He was in his room again, on solid ground, and in that single moment he felt safer than he'd ever felt in all his life.

A sob ripped out of him now, and he threw his arms around his newly bald head as everything he'd been fighting back finally broke through and five hundred miles of tears streamed down his face.

21

Saturday night at the Delaware Art Museum.

Meredith Winters stood at the entrance in a black cocktail dress with a cell phone to her ear. It was a balmy June evening, twilight was falling, and the air was tingling with the anticipation of a major event. A steady line of cars was turning off the parkway and looping around to the museum entrance, and it was here that Meredith stood watch over the arrivals. Everything was falling nicely into place. Inside, the tables were arranged in the upper atrium lobby—twenty round tables covered with stiff white cloths, and one long head table draped with the obligatory red, white, and blue bunting. The caterers were at work in the pantry kitchen, and the cash bar was already open for business. On the lower level behind her, a three-piece combo was tuning up for a little light music to greet the guests as they came in.

Senator DeMedici's advance team had just arrived and gone upstairs, and his security team was up there, too, with handheld detectors and a bomb-sniffing Labrador. DeMedici was almost as security conscious as Phil Sutherland—it seemed to go with the turf of presidential aspirations. But Meredith was more than happy to indulge his paranoia, because DeMedici's appearance here tonight not only sold a good third of the dinner tickets, it guaranteed a heavy media turnout. Even now, the TV news vans were beginning to circle—CNN plus the networks—while a dozen print journalists were flashing their press cards at the door.

Though it also might have been Ash Ramsay's little family crisis that was drawing them. Meredith had arrived in town that morning to a headline that screeched, SEN. RAMSAY'S SON RESCUED FROM KIDNAPPER. She read the story with all her alarm bells poised to ring, but amazingly enough, it had a positive slant.

There was a photo of a freckle-faced boy and another photo of the grave-faced Ramsays, and it took two column inches of text before there was any mention of the fact that the kidnapper was the boy's own biological father. There followed a poignant account of the Ramsays' anguish and heartache these last few months as they awaited some news of their son, and their relief and joy at his safe return. In order to be with her son tonight, Mrs. Ramsay would not be attending the dinner in honor of U.S. Congressional candidate Doug Alexander. Senator Ramsay, however, would be appearing as scheduled.

Meredith was pleased at the plug for tonight's event, but the best part was the closing sentence of the article: "Both Senator and Mrs. Ramsay stated that Mr. Alexander had been an abiding comfort and support to them during their ordeal."

Perfect. A well-slanted story that would reach voters who rarely read substantive political news but who devoured all the tabloid scandals they could find.

But what wasn't so perfect was the runaround she was getting from Norman Finn on the other end of the cell phone.

"We need a little more time here, Meredith."

"Time? It's been almost three months since Doug announced. It's been almost four months since the Party—your party, remember, Finn?—selected him. How much time does the governor need before he can decide whether he supports his own party's candidate or not?"

"It's a little more complicated than that."

"No, it's not. It's this simple: is he coming tonight or isn't he? If he is, fine, we'll be delighted to see him, we'll have some very kind words to say about him. But if he's not—then it's over, Finn. We'll run against him the same as we're running against Hadley Hayes."

"Sam doesn't take well to ultimatums."

"No, and he hasn't taken well to reason, flattery, or begging, either. Look, if he's got his eye on Hayes's seat for himself in two years, just say so."

Finn chuckled. "He's got his eye on Hayes's seat for himself in two years. Surprise, surprise."

She flushed hot. She'd known this from the start—everyone had—but the longer Davis kept stringing them along, the more she'd let herself hope. Well, no more.

"Tell the governor I hope he has a relaxing night at home. But not to expect too many more of them. Things are about to get unpleasant for him."

"Hey, you better check it out with your boy before you go making threats like that."

"Hey, yourself. I've had to rein him in these last few weeks. But now I'll go ahead and turn him loose."

"Meredith—"

She disconnected.

"Meredith!" Maggie Heller cried as she came charging across the entrance plaza. "How wonderful to see you! Isn't this weather great? Didn't we pick the best night for this?"

A remark that presumed that Maggie had any involvement at all in selecting the date. "Yes, it's lovely," Meredith said as she slipped the phone into her bag.

"Did you hear the final count on ticket sales?"

This *was* something Maggie was involved in, and Meredith looked up with sharp interest. "No, what?"

"Two hundred and ten!" she crowed.

Over a hundred thousand dollars—almost enough to pay her own past due bills.

Another car pulled up to the entrance, and Maggie squealed like a bobby-soxer spying Frank Sinatra. "It's Doug!"

He gave them a wave from one side of the car as his wife stepped out from the other. As instructed, she had her hair pinned up and was wearing a shapeless navy-blue dress.

"Doesn't Campbell look wonderful?"

"Yes," Meredith said. "She's positively glowing."

Maggie's head swiveled. "Are you trying to tell me—"

"Oh, I'd never be so presumptuous." Meredith smiled coyly. "A young couple has a right to their privacy, not to mention the right to make personal announcements in their own good time."

Maggie's eyes opened wide with the thrill of secret knowledge. By the time the evening was over, Meredith expected that at least fifty people would have heard the rumor of Campbell's pregnancy. Although Doug insisted they were working on it, they were working a little slow to do the campaign any good; Meredith had decided that this was one of those occasions when it was necessary to get the story out early and let the truth catch up with it later. And if the worst happened and no pregnancy developed—then a well-placed rumor of a tragic miscarriage would accomplish almost as much.

Doug made his way past a line of well-wishers and up to the museum door. "Any word on Davis?" he mumbled to Meredith.

"Sorry, Doug. He's taking a pass."

"God*damn* it." He smiled and waved to the crowd. "But you left the door open, right?"

"Doug, we agreed. You said it yourself—it's shit-or-get-off-the-pot time."

He wheeled on her. "So you let him shit on me? Is that it? Is that what I'm paying you for? To let people shit on me?"

Behind him his wife blanched at the outburst, but it was all old news to Meredith. Every candidate she'd ever known revealed a ferocious temper sooner or later. The conventional wisdom put it down to strain and public scrutiny and all that, but she didn't buy it. She believed it was something they brought with them from the start, part and parcel of the congenital arrogance they had to possess simply to be able to see themselves as leaders.

"Doug, this works out perfectly for you," she said. "After you serve your two years in the House, the field will be wide open for you to go after Tauscher's seat yourself. Sam Davis won't be around to stop you. We'll make sure of that."

He stopped, considered briefly, and turned back to the crowd with a smile.

Meredith led them to the lower-level lobby and positioned them midway between the door and the staircase, the most strategic spot for greeting the guests as they arrived. The upper atrium was ringed by a glass-walled balcony, and a dozen early-comers were already pressing to the edge to gaze down at their candidate.

"Where the hell's Nathan?" Doug grumbled.

"I'll find him."

The cloakroom was at the foot of the staircase twenty feet away, and Meredith ducked inside and pulled out her phone.

"Alexander for Congress," a voice chirped.

"Who's this?"

"This is Gillian," the girl replied in a singsong.

Ah, yes, one of Maggie's crew, the little ingenue with the big crush on Doug.

"Where's Nathan?"

"Oh, hello! Is that you, Miss Winters? Nathan's on his way to the dinner, but he had to stop at Mr. Fletcher's house."

"Jonathan Fletcher? What for?"

"I don't know. He got a call a little bit ago—"

With a jolt, Meredith realized that he must have gone to pick up the old man's check, probably with the idea of staging a dramatic presentation of it here tonight. She smiled as she disconnected. Nathan was developing quite a flair for this business. So—once he arrived with the check, who was the best man to present it to Doug? Not the keynote speaker, John DeMedici. He was an outsider, and this was very much an insider donation. Of course—Ash Ramsay, the stalwart victim of the hour. He could deliver the check with a speech that would wring tears from the ladies, and before the night was done, their husbands would be pulling out their checkbooks all over again.

When she came out of the cloakroom, a long line of guests were waiting to shake Doug's hand. One of them was a distinguished-looking man with silvering hair and a well-tailored suit. He was looking around the atrium with a careful eye, and when he spotted Meredith, he immediately peeled off in her direction.

"Well, I'll be," she said. "If it isn't Gary Pfeiffer."

"I was hoping to see you here, Meredith." He pulled a drab, thick-waisted woman up beside him. "You remember Eileen."

"Of course I do!" she said, though the woman was so nondescript Meredith was afraid she might forget her again before the evening was over.

Pfeiffer nodded toward the candidate. "Care to give me a personal introduction?"

Meredith deliberated whether he was worth squandering her currency this way, but finally decided he was, if not for this candidate in this race, certainly for another one in some other race.

"I'd be delighted." She linked her arms through the lobbyist's and his wife's and marched them over to Doug.

"Doug, I'd like you to meet some old friends of mine from Washington. Gary Pfeiffer and his wife, Eileen."

"Good to see you, thanks for your support," Doug said, still on autopilot. "Please meet my wife, Campbell."

"How do you do?" she said, extending her hand beside him.

"Hello." Pfeiffer paused with an awkward little hitch in his handshake. His smooth body language seemed suddenly tongue-tied. "Excuse me," he said, peering down at her. "Have we met?"

"I'm sorry, I can't quite place—"

"Gary's up from Washington," Meredith said, but not for Campbell's sake. It was Doug's recollection she wanted to jar.

"Oh, of course," he said. "Lawyers for Justice?"

"That's right," Pfeiffer said, pulling his eyes from Campbell. "I've been looking forward to meeting you. When you get a quiet moment, I'd enjoy talking with you."

Doug gave a noncommittal nod and turned to the guests behind them.

When Pfeiffer pulled Meredith aside, she knew what was coming: *Can you get me five minutes alone with him tonight?* In view of Doug's reaction, she started to prepare her own noncommittal nod.

Instead he said, "That's his wife?"

"Yes. Campbell Smith. Why?"

"I don't know." He glanced back. "She looks familiar."

Strange, Meredith thought. That was the same thing Phil Sutherland said. But an iron-jawed general and a silver-tongued lobbyist—there was no way the girl could have gotten around *that* much.

She saw the Pfeiffers to the staircase, then drifted back to the candidate.

"What's *he* doing here?" he whispered. "Didn't you tell him where I stand on his bill?"

"Of course. He's here to scout out the opposition."

His eyes narrowed.

"You should be flattered, Doug. He paid a thousand dollars just to look you over."

"Thanks for your support," Doug said, reaching out to shake the next hand.

There was a sudden flurry of activity outside, and Meredith looked out to see a dozen photographers scrambling into position on the steps. She made a beeline back to the candidate. "It's Ramsay," she said. "Better get out there and greet him."

Doug strode forward at once and was waiting as the battered blue station wagon pulled up and Ash Ramsay stepped out. It was one of those perfect images, Doug grasping Ramsay's hand and gripping his elbow, Ramsay taking Doug's hand in both of his and giving one slow meaningful nod before they fell into silent step together into the museum. The video crews captured the entire thing on film, and so did the cameras of a dozen newspapers.

It was a Kodak moment for Meredith, too.

* * *

Norman Finn arrived soon after, with a cigarette in his mouth and his little wrenlike wife in tow. He snubbed out the cigarette in the saucer of sand by the door and abandoned his wife six feet later to zoom in on Doug. They greeted each other loudly and warmly, as if they were old allies and not new enemies. Meredith expected nothing less from a pro like Finn, but she was impressed at how far Doug had come.

The next arrival was the one she was really looking forward to. Nathan Vance came through the doors and gave an agitated look around as Meredith sidled up behind him. "I understand you have a surprise for us," she purred.

He turned warily. "How'd you hear?"

"Ve haff our vays. So, what's your plan? I thought we'd recruit Ramsay."

"I guess we'll need him. Does Doug know yet?"

"No. I thought I'd leave that honor to you."

"Thanks a lot," he muttered. "Remind me to return the favor sometime."

She gave him a sharp look. "Wait a minute. Am I missing something?"

"We're all missing something," he bit out. "About two hundred thousand dollars."

"What?"

Doug was crossing the lobby toward them. Nathan gave an edgy glance around him. "Is there someplace we can talk?"

"In here," she said, and led them both into the cloakroom.

"What's up?" Doug asked.

"Jonathan Fletcher died this afternoon."

"Oh, God." Meredith's eyes fell shut. "He never wrote the check."

"He never wrote any of them. I spent the last two hours going through his papers. He never made any of the payments, and he never made any written record of the pledge, either."

"But he still made it," she said. "We've got witnesses to that."

"An oral pledge to make a campaign contribution can't be enforced against his estate."

Doug didn't say anything. Meredith looked over and saw more than disappointment in his expression. There was a major storm brewing.

"Get Willoughby in here," he said. "He did Fletcher's will. And John Simon. He's his banker. And Ash—get Ash."

Nathan ducked gratefully out of the room. Meredith braced herself, and she didn't have to wait long.

"This is all your fault." Suddenly Doug's face was mottled red and twisted with rage. "You and all your stalling and pussyfooting around. You cost me weeks in this campaign, and now you cost me two hundred thousand dollars, too. So what am I going to do? Huh? You tell me, Meredith. What the hell am I going to do?"

She thought fast. The blame could be dodged easily enough: fund-raising wasn't her responsibility, at least not precisely; she'd had little to do with the courting of Jonathan Fletcher; in any event, the old coot always meant to donate in his own good time, and nothing she did would have altered his timetable. But blame wasn't really the issue now. Money was.

"I'll tell you what you do now," she said. "Gary Pfeiffer's offering you more than twice what Fletcher was."

"Pfeiffer?" He spat out the name. "He represents a bunch of ambulance chasers who've done more harm to the U.S. economy—"

"Spare me the stump speech, would you, please? Pfeiffer can get you two hundred and fifty individual contributors who'll each kick in the maximum. We're talking five hundred thousand dollars, Doug. And this is hard money, direct to your campaign. This is better than the money Fletcher was offering, because it doesn't go through the Party. Finn and Davis never get their greasy little fingers on it. You can spend it the way you want to, and you don't have to sell your soul to Norman Finn to do it, either."

The flush slowly receded from his complexion and the muscles slowly relaxed in his face. "Hard money?" he repeated.

"And not only that," she said, the adrenaline kicking in now that she had him hooked. "This is your chance to give the finger to all those corporate bigwigs who've been bleeding out multimillion-dollar salaries while they close down their factories and lay off their work force. If tort reform fails, it's a victory for the little guy. And that's who you really care about."

The cloakroom door opened and Nathan came in with Owen Willoughby and John Simon, who together explained that under Fletcher's will, the entire estate poured into a trust from which a few nephews and a dozen charities would receive periodic payments over the next twenty years.

"Okay," Nathan said tensely. "Then we'll find out who the trustees are and get them to write the check."

Simon glanced at Willoughby and cleared his throat. "Well, you're looking at one of them."

Nathan let out an astonished laugh. "Why didn't you say so?"

The banker looked away.

"Nathan, you know he can't help," Willoughby said. "None of the trustees can. The charities would cry foul if the trust made any political contributions, and they'd get the Attorney General to sue on their behalf. The trustees can't risk that."

"Are you a trustee too, Owen?" Nathan said, fuming. "Or are you just angling for the legal work?"

Willoughby's eyes flared. "Why, you—"

"Hey, Nathan, Owen," Doug cut in. "It's all right. We'll manage without Fletcher's money. We'll manage just fine."

Nathan shot him a look of utter bafflement, but before he could say anything, there was a knock on the door and Ash Ramsay and Norman Finn were squeezing into the already crowded room.

All they brought to the huddle was commiseration. Ramsay seemed not only sorry, but deeply embarrassed.

"I'm sorry, Doug," he said, squeezing his shoulder. "Jon didn't have a lot of pleasures left in his life. About the only one was having folks like us dance attendance on him. Making you wait and wonder was half the fun for him. But I never should've let it go on so long. If I'd known—"

"If you'd known, you'd be the most powerful man in the world, Ash. Instead of only the fourth or fifth most powerful."

Ramsay guffawed, the rest of the men cackled, and on that happy note they exited the cloakroom.

"You want to tell me how you did that?" Nathan whispered to Meredith. "When I left, he was biting your head off. And five minutes later—"

"Watch and learn, Nathan," she said, gliding away. "Watch and learn."

Two hours later the dessert plates were cleared, the speeches were over, and the final round of applause was starting to fade. Cam knew what that meant: time to go to work again. She had the drill down. In the receiving line: smile of greeting, quick handshake, *how nice to see you, thanks so much, I was hoping you'd make it, how have you been?* During the dinner: tiny bites, small sips, two minutes of conversation to the right, two minutes to the left. During the speeches: polite, attentive listening while Ramsay and DeMedici spoke, and a rapt, adoring gaze while Doug did. After the dinner: *thanks so much for coming, I do hope we'll see you again,* then a thoughtful pause, leading to a big bright smile, *Yes, we're all very proud.* After the last eleven weeks, she could do it in her sleep.

Though tonight was not her best performance. Her attention had wandered a little—her eyes kept drifting to the table where the silver-haired man was seated. She couldn't think where she'd met him before. Pfeiffer, Meredith said, but the name didn't ring a bell. Lawyers for Justice, Doug said, which probably meant they'd met at some bar function. Funny, she was usually so good with names and faces—she had to be, with her history—but too many had been thrust at her these last few months; she must be on overload.

As the applause ended, Cam rose from the table to receive Doug's perfunctory kiss, then they both turned, arms around each other's waists to wave to the audience before Doug peeled off in one direction and she in the other.

Maggie Heller was looming in her face before she'd gone ten feet. "Oh, Campbell," she whispered loudly. "I can't tell you how happy I am for you. No, thrilled!"

"Thank you."

"Don't you worry. Your secret's safe with me!"

"What?"

Maggie's eye landed on someone else and she darted away.

A moment later Ash Ramsay was bearing down on Cam. "There you are," he said, taking her by the arm. "I haven't had a chance to visit with you all night."

"Thanks for coming, Senator."

"Have you toured the exhibits yet?" He steered her toward the gallery wing of the museum. "We have the best collection of English pre-Raphaelites in the country. You know the pre-Raphaelites? Rosetti, Holman Hunt?"

She shook her head.

He led her out of the atrium lobby and into a smaller room where the walls were covered in deep shades of rose and green, and the paintings shimmered like jewels against the rich luster of the background. A trickle of guests came in behind them, and before Cam could view any of the paintings, Ramsay abruptly turned her in another direction. "But you really ought to see our Howard Pyle collection. Here it is, right next door."

The next room was empty. The exhibit was called "High Seas Adventures" and consisted of vibrant, colorful scenes like the ones that used to appear on slick paper in old Robert Louis Stevenson novels.

"The father of American illustration, they call him," Ramsay said. "Founder of the Brandywine school of painting, and the major influence of N. C. Wyeth and Maxfield Parrish and the rest."

"I don't really know much about art," Cam murmured.

He looked back. No one was coming after them. "Campbell, I wanted to thank you personally for the way you helped us out yesterday. Margo couldn't have managed without you."

"How is Trey?"

"You mean Jim?" he said, rolling his eyes. "Seems we're not allowed to call him Trey anymore. He shaved his head last night, the damn fool boy."

"What?" Cam cried. "Why?"

"God knows. Makes me wonder why he even wanted to come home if this is the way he's going to behave."

They stopped before a painting called *The Buccaneer Was a Picturesque Fellow*. A dashing pirate in a long red cloak was striking a jaunty pose while he stood guard over his booty.

"But Margo says he'll talk to you," Ramsay said, moving on, "and for that I'm grateful."

The next painting was *The Flying Dutchman*. A man stood braced on the storm-swept deck of his ship, scowling out from under the brim of his hat with demonic, haunted eyes.

"Senator, I know it's none of my business—"

"It is now. Speak your mind, young lady."

"It's just that—" She held her gaze on the desolate shipboard figure. "I wonder if things would be easier for him if the criminal prosecution weren't going forward."

"I'm sure it would."

"Then why . . . ?"

"Well, for one, I don't trust Patterson not to pull the same thing again."

"You could get a restraining order."

"Already have. Lawyers took care of it yesterday. But look here, Campbell, there're some political realities we have to live with. We have to see this thing to the end. Or it looks as if we acquiesced in the whole business."

"But if Patterson goes to prison, I'm afraid Trey might feel responsible—"

"He is responsible. He made the call."

"But he probably didn't appreciate the consequences—"

"High time he learned, then."

The next painting, *The Mermaid,* was a dreamy moonlit fantasy in deep blues and gleaming phosphorescent whites. A mermaid was rising up out of a foaming sea to the rocks where her mortal lover was bending down to embrace her.

"Ash, got a minute?" sounded a voice from the hall.

"Excuse me, Campbell," Ramsay said. "Looks like my party chairman needs me."

He strode off toward Finn, and Cam drifted along to the next painting, *Marooned.* It was a bleak expanse of yellow sky and sand, vast and empty. In the midst of it a pirate sat alone with his fingers laced together and his head slumped over his knees. The ocean appeared as a tiny sliver of blue in the distance. There was no rescue in sight.

"Figured it out yet?"

She turned as Gary Pfeiffer came up behind her.

"Because I just did this minute," he said.

In the next second so did she. The image clicked into place, Gary and Derek, the two men sharing a Mediterranean-style house on the ocean. "Rehoboth Beach?"

He nodded.

She remembered how kind he was to her that day, inviting her in out of the rain, giving her a cup of tea by the fireside. There was nothing kind in his expression now. His eyes were hard and his features taut.

"I have a proposition for you," he said.

"What?"

"I won't tell your secret if you won't tell mine."

"I don't have any secrets, Mr. Pfeiffer."

"Oh? Three months ago your name was Cammy Johnson, if I recall, and you were suffering from man trouble. Now it seems your name is Campbell Alexander and your man happens to be running for Congress."

"Let me explain," she said, keeping her voice calm. "I'm a lawyer, and I was there that day on client business. I wasn't doing anything illegal, and I don't have any secrets. Except, of course, for my client's confidences. Sorry," she added with a light laugh.

"I'm sorry, too. You see, if you don't have a secret and I do, then we've got a serious imbalance between us."

She went pale. "Mr. Pfeiffer, as far as I'm concerned, you don't have any secrets, either."

With a grimace, he gestured back toward the atrium lobby. "Have you met my wife?"

She thought of Derek's sleek young body and the way the two men leaned so comfortably into each other on their suede-covered sofa.

"Or have you met any of the fifty-six thousand members of the organization that employs me? Not to mention the thousands of state and federal legislators my business depends upon?"

Cam swallowed and lifted her chin. "I don't know why any of those people would have any interest in your private life," she said. "I only know that I don't. Would you excuse me, please?"

She walked away from him so rapidly her heels clicked like Morse code against the floor.

Meredith was at the bar ordering a vodka and tonic. It was almost ten o'clock; she could start drinking for real.

"Bourbon, neat," said a voice beside her, and she looked up at Gary Pfeiffer.

"Good speech your boy gave," he remarked.

"Why, thank you, sir," she said, toasting him.

"I'm thinking we could do some business."

"Maybe so." She took a sip from her drink.

"Why don't you send me your press kit on him? Give me some paper to send to my board members."

"All right."

"Position papers, complete bio, the works."

"Sure thing."

The bartender handed him his drink, and Pfeiffer started back into the crowd. "Oh, and Meredith," he said, an afterthought over his shoulder. "Complete bio on his wife, too."

"You got it," she said happily.

22

The line extended through the courthouse doors and all the way up King Street to the corner of Fourth. Cam took her place at the end of it and kept her head down as the news cameras shot their obligatory front-of-the-courthouse footage. The Ramsays would not be attending, the newspapers had assured her of that much, but there was a risk that one of the reporters might recognize her. That was why she dressed in her Philadelphia clothes today. With her hair down and a pair of oversized sunglasses covering much of her face, she prayed she'd be anonymous.

Two U.S. marshals were operating the metal detector at the door. Cell phones and tape recorders were being confiscated, and receipts written and signed. Cam looked again at her watch. The arraignment was at ten, only ten minutes away.

She reached the front of the line, placed her briefcase down on the X-ray conveyor and walked through the metal detector without setting off any alarms. "Fourth floor, Courtroom B," the guard recited without asking where she was bound. He didn't need to. Everyone was bound for the same place.

She squeezed in the elevator with the rest of them. Senator Ramsay had an office on the third floor of this building, and she held her breath as the number 3 illuminated and the elevator lurched to a stop. But when the doors opened, no one from Ramsay's staff was standing there. No one was standing there at all. Someone grumbled and hit the button to close the doors.

They arrived on the fourth floor, and Cam followed the crowd into the courtroom and ducked into the last row of seats. The bench was still empty at the front of the courtroom, and so was the prosecution table. But on the other side of the aisle, a swarm of reporters was buzzing around the defense table. A man stood in their midst with his eyeglasses in his hand. He was holding forth in a voice full of emotion and jabbing the air with his glasses to punctuate his words.

This was Cam's first sighting of Bruce Benjamin, the Wilmington lawyer now representing Steve Patterson. He was a tall man, tan and gray in a well-cut suit, and she could see why people said what they did about him. From fifty feet away he gave off an aura of power and aggression so strong it was almost an aroma. She read once that male trial lawyers had testosterone levels thirty percent higher than the general population. If so, Benjamin had to be a textbook example. He was a combative grandstander, a notorious scorched-earth practitioner, but the kind with substance behind his show. The kind that other lawyers dreaded.

Cam strained to hear what he was saying to the reporters, but there were too many people milling around the courtroom and too many buzzing voices, and she didn't dare get up and draw attention by drawing closer.

She shouldn't be here. She was supposed to be in her office in Philadelphia today, not attending a hearing that had nothing to do with her and hers. No one had asked her to come, and no one would welcome the news that she'd come on her own. If her photograph were to appear in tomorrow's *Journal* with a caption that read, *Wife of congressional candidate Doug Alexander leaving the courthouse after Steven Patterson's arraignment*—well, that was precisely the kind of publicity Doug had warned her to steer away from. Anything that raised more questions than it answered was to be avoided at all costs.

Especially when the questions were ones she couldn't even answer herself. She didn't understand what her interest was in a boy she barely knew and a man she never met. But ever since Margo's call Thursday night, Cam couldn't shake them out of her mind. She kept seeing them as she first saw them together, captured in a shaft of sunlight as it opened through the fog. She didn't understand how the boy she saw grinning up at his father that day could be the same boy who called the cops and had him arrested Thursday night.

But maybe she did understand. Maybe that was the source of her obsession. She saw something in Trey's eyes when she sat down beside him on the plane. Anger, dread, memories too raw to touch—they were all there, but there was something else, too, and it struck a chord deep within her. All week long it had resonated, like a hollow, aching echo in her chest.

A door opened at the front of the courtroom, and a deputy bustled out of chambers and deposited the file on the bench. The court reporter came out and settled in at his machine, and then the rear doors banged opened and Ronald March entered the courtroom.

Cam slid lower in her seat. She'd assumed some low-level assistant would handle today's arraignment, not the U.S. Attorney himself. The reporters spotted him in the aisle, and they spun away from Bruce Benjamin to swarm around him.

"No interviews in the courtroom," March said loudly, brushing them off to take his seat at the prosecution table. "You know better than that."

Benjamin gave him a look of amused disdain.

Another door opened and Steve Patterson came into the courtroom with his hands cuffed behind his back and a marshal holding his elbow. He had a week's growth of black beard; it gave him a wild outlaw look. The marshal steered him to his place beside Benjamin and unlocked the manacles. He shook out his arms and sent a quick sharp look through the spectators. Cam barely ducked her head in time.

Leave, she told herself fiercely. *Now, before the judge comes out.* But it was already too late. The chambers door opened and the deputy called, "All rise. Court is now in session. The Honorable Nora Breitman presiding."

She was a woman in her fifties with a head of flaming red hair and a pair of blue half-frame glasses pinching the end of her nose. "Good morning. In the matter of United States versus Steven A. Patterson?"

March and Benjamin were on their feet, making their appearances for the record.

"Mr. March, your office has filed a criminal information charging the defendant with violation of 28 USC Section 1201?"

"That's correct, Your Honor."

"When will you present this matter to the grand jury?"

"Defendant waives indictment," Benjamin called out. "He also waives preliminary hearing. Along with objections to venue."

The judge gave him a sickly smile. "You're being awfully

accommodating to the government this morning, Mr. Benjamin. That *is* you, Mr. Benjamin?"

When the mandatory laugh period expired, he said: "Those are my client's wishes, Your Honor."

"Is that so?" She pursed her lips. "Mr. Patterson?"

He got to his feet. He was wearing khaki pants and a button-down shirt. From the back, he looked less like an accused felon than an office worker on a casual Friday.

"Has Mr. Benjamin explained that you have the right to have a grand jury review the evidence against you and decide whether they think charges should be brought?"

"Yes. He has." His voice sounded young and husky, tense.

"Has he explained that you have the right to a preliminary hearing? Where you would hear the government's evidence against you? And where I would have to decide if there was sufficient evidence to go forward? Has he explained all that?"

"Yes."

"Do you understand that you're waiving that hearing?"

"I do."

"And you're doing it of your own free will?"

In a low voice he said: "I'm doing it because I don't want my son to have to testify."

"Your Honor!" March thundered. "I object to him characterizing the boy as his son. He signed away his parental rights to this child fourteen years ago. It's a little late in the game for him to be claiming—"

"He's the boy's natural father," Benjamin said. "What's he supposed to call him? Cousin?"

"How about victim?" March retorted.

"Enough, both of you," Breitman snapped. "Mr. March, you are out of order. I'm trying to engage in a colloquy with the defendant here. There's no occasion for you to object. Understood?"

"Yes, Your Honor."

"And Mr. Benjamin," she said, turning her scowl in his direction. "How long have you been trying cases in this court?"

"Twenty-five years," he said in a tone that recognized the setup but refused to show contrition.

"Long enough to know that you address your comments to the court and not to opposing counsel. Do that again and I'll cite you for it. Understood?"

"Perfectly."

"All right, then." She twisted her shoulders irritably and settled back in her chair. "Mr. Patterson. You want to spare the boy from having to testify. But you are aware that you're the one facing charges, not him? And that you could be convicted and sentenced to—" She turned to the prosecution table. "What do the guidelines say on this one, Mr. March?"

"Sixty-three to seventy-eight months."

"Mr. Patterson?" The judge squinted hard at him. "You understand that you could be convicted and go to prison for more than five years?"

"Yes."

"All right," she said incredulously. "The defendant waives indictment and preliminary hearing. Also objections to venue, which I expect would be meritless anyway. Let's have the charges read, shall we?"

She handed a paper down to the deputy below her, who stood up and read the criminal information in a monotone.

"How pleads the defendant?"

"Not guilty," he said.

She studied him. "Mr. Patterson, you realize that if there's a trial, the child will probably have to testify then?"

He stood silent a moment, and the judge's gaze sharpened, but before she could say more, he answered in a low voice: "Yes."

"Nevertheless that's your plea?"

"Yes."

"Any other business to attend to, counsel?"

"Defendant renews his motion for release on bond," Benjamin said. "He has no prior record, he's a licensed professional architect, with twelve years' steady employment, good credit, and a long list of satisfied clients."

"Your Honor," March said, "the defendant has no ties to this community and is a demonstrated risk for flight."

"No ties?" Benjamin scoffed. "His only blood relative in the world lives here."

"Judge!"

Benjamin threw up his hands. "I didn't say *son*!"

"Whatever," Breitman said, glaring down at him. "That blood tie wasn't enough to keep him in the district last February, now was it? Why should we expect it to be enough now?"

"He's not going to leave without the boy."

She gave Benjamin a pained look. "That puts the rabbit in the hat, doesn't it? Isn't that the real concern here? That if he's free on bond, he'll take the boy out of state again?"

"Exactly." March folded his arms over his chest.

"Not at all," Benjamin said. "Because now there's a restraining order in place. He's in violation of that if he gets within five hundred feet of the boy."

She rolled her eyes. "There was also a kidnapping statute in place last February. If that didn't have any deterrent effect on Mr. Patterson, I wouldn't hold out a lot of hope for a restraining order. Your request is denied, Mr. Benjamin. Defendant will remain in custody pending trial. To commence—Got my book there?"

The deputy rose up from in front of the bench and opened the scheduling calendar on the desk, and the two of them murmured over it for a minute until Breitman gave a nod.

"Monday, July twenty-seventh."

Everyone lurched up from their seats as the judge stepped off the bench and disappeared through the rear door.

Laughter broke out when she was gone, as if the spectators were a class of squirming pupils whose teacher was called out of the room. The reporters made another feint toward March, but he waved them away, saying, "Outside, everybody. You know that."

Steve Patterson stood at the defense table and stared straight ahead at the vacated bench. The marshal came at him with the manacles, and from fifty feet away Cam could hear the sound of the locks snapping shut over his wrists. July 27, she thought. More than six weeks away. Six more weeks of locks. At least.

She stayed where she was as the crowd streamed past her to the rear doors. She didn't notice Ronald March packing up his briefcase and shaking hands across the aisle with Bruce Benjamin. She didn't notice him turning toward the back of the courtroom, and she didn't notice the sudden smile that lit his face. She only heard him call out, "Campbell? Campbell Alexander?"

Steve Patterson heard it, too, and his head whipped around. His eyes landed on her and opened wide.

"What brings you here today?" March asked.

"Just—" She cleared her throat. "Just passing by."

"How's that husband of yours doing?"

"Fine," she said, looking beyond him. "Busy."

The marshal had his hand on Steve's elbow and was nudging

him out of the courtroom, but he shook his head and stayed where he was. He stared at Cam the same way he did on the dock at Maristella Island last winter. His eyes were shadowed with the same suspicion, and his body coiled tight with the same tension. But now there was confusion there, too.

"Well, you tell him I was asking about him, you hear?"

"Yes, thanks, I'll do that."

The marshal shoved Steve toward the door, and he threw one last bewildered look at her before he disappeared.

She retrieved her car from the municipal lot two blocks away and headed north to Philadelphia. The sun was in her face, and her eyes watered as if they'd been scorched, so much that when she crossed the city limits, the billboard's eternal question swam in her vision. DO YOU HAVE A WOUND THAT WON'T HEAL? The same old question, every day.

Today it made her think of Trey. She knew now what it was she saw in his eyes last Friday, and she knew where it came from. Because whatever happened on that island, whatever Steve Patterson might have done, it was Trey who called the cops and had him arrested, and it was Trey's testimony that would send him to prison. That kind of guilt would be a burden for anyone, but for a troubled adolescent, it would be unbearable. It would be like a wound that wouldn't heal, the mark of a filial Cain.

She spent the afternoon in a windowless conference room staring down a witness who gave back little more than scowls and exasperated puffs of fetid-smelling breath. He was an ex-husband in default of a property settlement agreement that was signed so long ago Cam had never even met her client. The woman had long since moved on and remarried, and her ex-husband now vented all his hostility at Cam. So far she'd seized over a million dollars' worth of his assets, but there was still a deficiency of two hundred thousand, and he'd been fighting ferociously not to pay it. Cam knew that his attorneys' fees would soon exceed the amount he owed; she also knew that he'd rather pay his lawyer than his ex-wife.

After three hours she'd learned nothing she didn't already know, and she finally dismissed him with her customary proviso reserving the right to recall him upon the discovery of any additional information.

* * *

Helen was gone for the day, but she left a message slip taped to Cam's chair. *Mrs. Ramsay, at home, urgent.*

"Oh, Campbell—forgive me, but I didn't know what else to do, and Ash said you're the only one he'll talk to."

"The Senator?" Cam said, confused.

"Yes. I mean, no!—Trey."

"Trey? Why? Has something happened?"

"Oh, it's all so humiliating. He was arrested this afternoon. For shoplifting a twenty-dollar T-shirt at the mall. Twenty dollars! Can you imagine? As if he didn't have drawers full of them at home. I don't know what could have gotten into him."

Cam turned and gazed at the shaft of sunlight that streamed past her office window. "Steve Patterson was arraigned today, wasn't he?"

There was a chilly silence before Margo said, "That's got nothing to do with us."

"No, of course not. How can I help, Mrs. Ramsay? Do you need a lawyer recommendation?"

"No, thank God. Jesse spoke to some friends and worked it all out. But I don't know what to do about Trey. I want him to see a professional, but he won't hear of it. So, Ash thought, and I thought, too—maybe if you talked to him?"

Jesse Lombard was weeding the shrub beds by the front steps, and he rose and limped painfully to the driveway as Cam pulled up. He was wearing a short-sleeved shirt, and for the first time she noticed the Navy insignia tattooed over each of his triceps. What a cruel irony, she thought, for him to survive Vietnam only to be shot down on the streets of Wilmington. But that was the way of this world: danger came too often from unexpected sources.

"Is he here?" she asked him.

He kept his eyes on the ground and nodded. "In his room."

Margo opened the door and pointed her up the stairs, and a minute later there she stood, at the bedroom door of a thirteen-year-old boy she barely knew.

She knocked. "Hi. It's Cam Alexander."

There was no answer.

"I know—weird, huh? I'm embarrassed to even be here bothering you like this. I'll leave this minute if you tell me to."

The door was wrenched open, and she had a glimpse of Trey's scowling face before he turned and retreated to the other side of the room.

She took a step in. It was a large room furnished with dark wooden pieces that were probably a century old. The windows were draped with a rich tapestry print, and a matching spread lay in a heap at the foot of the four-poster bed. It was a handsome room, stately, with little trace of child in it. Ash and Margo could have slept here.

Trey was leaning against the far wall with his arms folded high and his hands tucked in his armpits. The brim of his cap was pulled low, concealing his face but exposing much of the ghostly pale skin of his scalp. There was an agitated twitch in his left knee.

"Want me to leave?"

He didn't answer.

"Bad scene at the mall today, huh?"

He shrugged.

"Want to talk about it?"

He made a snorting sound and shook his head.

Maybe Margo was right, Cam thought. Maybe today's escapade had nothing to do with his father. She thought back to that night in February when he was bashing mailboxes with the wolfpack of young vandals. Clearly he had behavior problems even before Steve Patterson came into his life.

"Your grandparents want you to see a therapist about it."

"What's the big deal?" he burst out. "One lousy T-shirt!"

"Maybe." She came in and sat down on the foot of his unmade bed. "I'd say it depends on why you took it. If it was just to impress your friends, or to give the finger to your grandparents, then you're probably right—it's no big deal."

He was staring hard at the floor while his knee bounced in an agitated spasm. "But . . . ?"

"I'm wondering if you did it because you wanted to be arrested."

"Why would I want that?"

"Because he was."

His head jerked up, and in that instant she saw that the grief in his eyes was boundless, and she knew that she wasn't wrong, about anything.

"If that's the case," she said, fighting to keep the choke out of her voice, "it might be good to talk to somebody about it.

Sometimes it helps you sort through your thoughts if you can bounce them off somebody else."

He gave a stubborn shake of his head and looked away.

"Well, here's the deal," she said, standing up. "Either you agree to see a counselor, or we have to come up with some kind of alternative plan."

He hesitated. "Like, what kind of plan?"

"I don't know. I just got here. Do you have any ideas?"

He shook his head again.

"Hmm. Let me think. Okay, here's a plan. I'll tell them your problem is you have too much time on your hands. So what you need is a job."

"They'd never let me. Besides, I don't want a job."

"Oh, too bad. I really could have used the help."

"Huh?"

"In my garden. There's some back-breaking work I have to do. Rototilling and transplanting and all kinds of chopping and pruning. I've been trying to do it all myself, but it's too much. I guess I have to hire a landscaping crew."

He didn't say anything.

"That garden used to be a showplace. But after so many years of neglect, it's nothing but a ruin. I have this dream, though, that I could restore it. I can see it in my mind, the way it could be. But—oh, never mind. It's probably a stupid dream anyway." She headed for the door. "Listen, why don't you come up with your own plan? I'll try to buy you a few more days."

She was across the threshold by the time he spoke. "When would you want me to start?"

"Saturday morning, eight o'clock."

"What's the pay?"

She turned around. "Five bucks an hour plus lunch and all the iced tea you can drink."

His left knee was still wildly uncertain, but he uncrossed his arms and said, "Okay."

She was making a mistake, she knew it before she reached the bottom of the stairs. There was danger here, everywhere. But Margo stood waiting with anxious eyes, and together they reached the Senator on the phone and put the proposition to him. "Hell of a good idea," he declared, and it was done.

* * *

That evening, Gary Pfeiffer was relaxing in his courtyard with a book and a glass of white wine when he heard the doorbell ring inside. He turned the book sideways to look at his watch. Ten minutes to ten. Too late for anyone but home invasion criminals.

"You getting that, Eileen?" he called into the house.

"Got it," she called back.

He took another sip of wine and turned another page. He was reclining on a teak chaise with cushions six inches thick and covered in pure white duck. A cast-iron reading lamp stood beside him, and glowing in amber pinpoints through the courtyard were low voltage landscape lights of hammered copper weathered to a verdigris patina. Six feet away a man-made waterfall gushed over imported river rocks, producing a musical white noise that muted all sounds of life in the nation's capital.

The house was a three-story brick Federal just off Embassy Row. Its rear wall was lined with French doors, and from the courtyard he could see through to the gleaming granite surfaces of the kitchen and the bleached oak bookcases of his library. A set of broad steps led from the house down to this courtyard, which was surrounded with ivy-covered brick walls six feet tall. It made for a private haven, a setting of unparalleled beauty and tranquillity, and he ached to be somewhere else.

Thanks to last weekend's fund-raiser in Wilmington, he hadn't been to the beach house for nearly two weeks, and it was still another two days before he could be there again. Rehoboth was beautiful this time of year, during the pristine weeks of early summer, before school let out and the hordes of kids invaded. Today's weather was perfect, Derek told him when they spoke that morning. The sky was blue and the ocean bluer, but words failed him after that: Gary needed to come and see for himself.

"I wish I could," he'd sighed.

"I know you do. That's all that matters."

It was a lonely life Derek had signed on for, but he rarely complained. It was Gary who complained, long and bitterly, while Derek gave him neck rubs and told him how much faith he had in him. Another two or three good years like this last one, Derek reminded him, and he'd be able to leave Washington forever.

"It's a hand-delivery," Eileen called. "At this hour, imagine that."

"Who's it from?"

"Let's see. Portwell and Associates? It's a K Street address."

Meredith Winters. Gary swung his feet to the bluestone slates. He'd been waiting for this delivery all week.

He took the package from Eileen and went into the library with the half-empty glass and sat down at his desk. Meredith's card was paper-clipped to the top of a four-inch stack of paper. He flipped through the materials: press clips, polling data, radio transcripts, and one position paper after another. He bypassed all of them. He didn't care what Alexander's positions were, and neither did the members of ALJA. The only thing that mattered was whether he could deliver Ramsay's vote this term.

At last he was looking at a photograph of Alexander's sparkling young wife.

What a twist of fate that turned out to be, that a stray he brought home one day would turn out to be the wife of a congressional candidate. A cruel fate. He and Derek were always so careful: in three years, they'd never gone out in public together. Not once. Rehoboth wasn't called the Summer Capital for nothing; the place was crawling with Beltway people. So they never went on the beach together, or to the bars, or on the streets, or anywhere.

But this girl wasn't on the street. She showed up on their doorstep, a rain-bedraggled waif with a broken heart, and like a fool, he'd invited her right in.

No, that wasn't right. She'd *sneaked* right in. The bitch had invaded their home, she'd used subterfuge to do it, and that meant anything was fair now.

He opened the file on Campbell Smith Alexander and flipped through the summary report by Meredith's investigator, who hadn't found anything—but Gary's resources were considerably greater. The 56,000 members of the American Lawyers for Justice Association included the most prominent and successful plaintiffs' attorneys in the country. Many employed their own teams of investigators, and all had connections and access to information they wouldn't hesitate to share with him if he asked. He was their chief lobbyist and spokesman, in Washington and every state capital across the country, and they'd give him whatever he needed, no questions asked. After all, he was Gary Pfeiffer, guardian of truth, justice, and the one-third contingency fee.

He spent the next hour scouring the file for some blemish, the smallest wrinkle, anything that might give him leverage over Campbell Alexander.

She was born on March 13, 1968, at Lancaster General Hospital, to Matthew Samuel Smith and Alice Campbell Smith; copy of birth certificate attached. Her paternal grandmother was Hazel Smith, record owner of forty acres, more or less, situated in Mount Joy Township; copy of deed attached. In June 1970, Matthew and Alice Smith traveled to the Philippines; visa and passport records attached. In August 1970 they were killed in a Muslim insurrection; consular report and contemporaneous Manila newspaper accounts attached.

The next record came fifteen years later, and consisted of a handwritten medical chart noting each office visit and house call for patient Hazel Smith. One entry had been circled in red by Meredith's investigator. *Pt. now completely incontinent, but granddaughter coping well.* The death certificate came next, then the probate papers. The girl's own records began after that, but they were the ordinary stuff of life: a driver's license; a GED certificate; a college financial aid application; semester-by-semester transcripts; and a Pennsylvania Bar application that included fingerprinting and an FBI computer run that came up empty.

Gary leaned back in his chair and reached for the forgotten wine. But it was room temperature by now, and he spat it back into the glass.

"Honey?"

Eileen stood in the doorway ready for bed in a pair of silk pajamas. Five years ago he'd made the mistake of admiring a pair of man-tailored pajamas she was wearing, and since then she'd worn nothing else. It still hadn't occurred to her that it was the pajamas he desired, not her in them.

"Coming to bed soon? It's awfully late."

"Is it?" He looked at his watch. "I had no idea. But listen, don't wait up. I'll be a while yet."

Her face sagged with an expression of disappointment she wore as regularly as the pajamas. " 'Night," she murmured.

He turned back to the file. If he couldn't get anything on the girl, then the only thing left was to get something on her parents. They were evangelical Christians—he'd have to tread carefully here—but who knew? Maybe they'd gone in for snake handling. He reached for his directory of ALJA members and flipped through the listings in search of a familiar name. Yes, here was one he recalled. Wilson Minchoff, a Lancaster lawyer with a high volume personal injury practice who almost got his ticket pulled a few years back for improper solicitation of accident victims. But ALJA had swooped in and bailed him out, and today he was alive and well and handing out his card at intersections everywhere.

Gary opened his laptop and entered a reminder to call Minchoff first thing in the morning and get him to recommend a good local investigator. He'd need to supply the parents' full names, and he flipped back to the birth certificate to find them. There: Matthew Samuel Smith and Alice Elizabeth Campbell.

As he turned back to the computer, a single word on the birth certificate seemed to jump out and follow him.

Male.

He spun back and looked again. It was only one typewritten word almost obscured against the printed background of the seal of Pennsylvania, but there it was. *Male.* On March 13, 1968, Alice Campbell Smith had given birth to a baby boy.

The call would no longer wait until morning. Gary picked up the phone and dialed Wilson Minchoff at home.

23

Doug had an important campaign appearance Friday night, the annual picnic and softball play-offs of the building trades union. Nathan drove them to the park in his Tahoe, and they went through a receiving line of union dignitaries, then posed with assorted union members for ten minutes of photo ops. A gulp of lemonade and a chicken drumstick, then it was off to the softball field for Doug's speech.

The sky was pale with twilight, and a tickle of a breeze was blowing as Nathan and Cam took their seats in the bleachers. The band played a rousing prelude, the union president gave a rousing introduction, and Doug came out to the pitcher's mound with a portable microphone in his hand.

Nathan had heard it all before, so his focus was on the audience, not the speaker. He kept up a running commentary as he pointed out people Cam knew or ought to know. Norman Finn was there, working the crowd in the VIP box; he'd been a no-show at most of the recent events, and Nathan wondered if his appearance tonight was a signal that he wanted back in. There on the other side of the field was Stan DiMineo; he ran the union PACs, and his reaction to Doug's speech was the one they should watch for. And look, there was Gillian. Did Cam know she was a paid staffer now? She was taking off the fall semester to see it through, and here she was showing up on her night off. You had to admire dedication like that.

Cam followed where he was pointing and found Gillian looking lovely and ethereal in a pale floral sundress. "Hey, Gillian!" Nathan yelled and shot up his arm in a big wave. She smiled, and for a second it looked like she was starting to wave back, but suddenly she checked herself and looked the other way; she must not have seen them after all.

Doug's speech ended to warm applause, and he left the pitcher's mound and went to the announcer's booth to join in the play-by-play during the game. Cam stayed in the bleachers with Nathan as the starting lineups were announced and the players from the two top locals jogged onto the diamond.

The breeze stirred again as the game got under way, and Cam's memories stirred, too, at the smell of the hot dogs and beer and the crack of the bat and the cheers of the crowd. Only last summer she'd played softball herself, in a coed league of the big Philadelphia law firms.

"Remember our last game against Morgan, Lewis?" Nathan said.

"Funny, I was just thinking about that."

"Remember you hit that double—"

"Yeah, at the start of the inning. Then nobody got a hit for *hours*, and I was alone out there trying to steal third—"

"In your little shorts and bikini top—"

"It was a jogbra."

"Whatever, there wasn't a batter on our team who could keep his eye on the ball."

"That's not true," she said, indignant. "You could. Remember? You hit the line drive that finally got me home."

"Sure, *I* could. But then, I always keep my eye on the ball."

He sat up as the batter hit a pop fly out to left field. The outfielder stumbled and missed the catch, and the batter rounded first and landed on second.

"Yes," Cam said after a moment. "I know."

She looked down at her hands in her lap and then at her legs stretched out on the empty bleacher in front of her. They ended in a pair of white canvas grasshoppers that were like no shoes she'd ever worn before. The same was true of the plaid cotton blouse and the knee-length skirt of stiff green poplin. She felt like a foreign body to herself.

"Hey," Nathan said softly, watching her. "Come on. It won't be long now."

She nodded. It was only four more months until the election, then a year before the campaign machinery would have to crank up again for the reelection. It was only every other year for the rest of her life.

She lifted her head and returned her attention to the field as the base runner was tagged out at third.

* * *

That night she had the dream again, the familiar one where she was swimming through a dense sea to reach a distant shore. She'd had the dream so often that it was becoming part of the rhythm of her sleep, an automatic reflex like breathing in and breathing out. But this time it was a little different. This time she breathed through a pair of gills and her legs flipped behind her in a ripple of iridescent blue and green. This time she rose up out of a foaming sea with bits of shell and strands of kelp tangled in her hair. And this time the figure on the shore was striding out of the moonlight to meet her at the water's edge.

Saturday morning the Ramsays' blue station wagon pulled into the driveway, and Cam put down her pruning shears and went to meet it. She was dressed for hard work today, in a baggy T-shirt and denim shorts, her hair tied back in a thick braid.

"Morning, Jesse," she said at the driver's window as Trey climbed out the other side. "Want to come back for him around four?"

"I'm supposed to wait."

"No need for that. I'll be here with him all day. Besides, I'm sure Mrs. Ramsay could use you at home today."

He pondered a long moment, but finally put the car in reverse and left.

She turned and eyed Trey. He was wearing layers of oversized shirts and heavy twill pants that bunched in deep folds around his ankles. He'd probably expire before noon.

"Ready to go to work?"

"I guess."

She pointed to her car. "Hop in."

She drove first to the machine rental shop and looked over the selection of rototillers until she found the one she wanted, then left a deposit and directions for delivery later that morning. From there it was on to the garden nursery, where she inspected a heap of steaming compost and ordered a truckload. She bought bags of peat moss and all-purpose fertilizer, and Trey shouldered them to the trunk of her car and packed them in tightly.

"Now the fun stuff," she said. "Want to grab that cart?"

He pulled it along after her as she wandered the aisles through a dazzling array of flowering annuals. The sun beat down and rose up hot and steamy from the ground, and before they were halfway through, Trey had to stop and peel off two layers of shirts until he was down to a plain white T-shirt. Cam made her selections and bought as many flats as they could squeeze across the rear seat of her car.

It was ten o'clock when they got back and unloaded the car. The rototiller hadn't arrived yet, so she took him on a tour of the garden, pointing out the existing borders and beds and the chalk lines in the grass where she wanted the new ones cut in. She showed him a dead dogwood that would have to come down, and she paced off the dimensions of the reflecting pool she hoped to install one day. She ended the tour with the folly.

Trey went inside and climbed up the spiral stairs to stick his head into the second story. "What is this thing?"

"They call it a folly. You know what that means? Something foolish or stupid."

He hopped down and followed her back outside. She tried to shut the door behind them, but the wood was warped and she couldn't force it back into the frame. "Have any ideas?" she asked, grappling with it.

"For what?"

She gave up on the door and turned around brushing her hands clean. "For how to get rid of it. Short of hiring a wrecking ball, that is."

"Get rid of it?" he exclaimed.

"Sure. Look at it—it's a wreck. And it's not like it serves a function."

"This is a garden," he said, pained. "None of it serves a function."

She laughed.

"Besides, it does serve a function." He stepped back a few yards. "It's a—what d'you call it? A focal point. See? You've got this long view-thing going here. There has to be something at the end of the view. Or else, what are you looking at?"

She came up beside him to look and nodded thoughtfully.

"And I mean, look." He went back to the folly and circled it. "See how it's an octagon? And how that shape is repeated in the little window upstairs? You gotta admit, that's majorly cool."

"Yes, but look at the way the stucco's pulling off. And the broken window panes. And how the door's all warped?"

"But that can be fixed."

"Maybe," she said doubtfully.

"At least think about it."

"All right," she said reluctantly. "If you'll think about what it might take to fix it up."

"Okay, I will."

She turned away before he could see her smile.

By the end of the day, they'd prepared a bed that measured five feet by fifty, amended the soil, and planted four flats of annuals that still left most of the bed empty but provided a sense of accomplishment. They sprawled in the shade of the big oak tree to polish off the last of the iced tea while they waited for Jesse to arrive. Trey drained his glass, then pulled off his cap and mopped the sweat off his forehead. Cam's eyes flitted toward his shaved head, and he quickly put the cap on and flopped back spread-eagled on the grass.

"Tired?" she asked.

He shrugged. "Maybe a little."

"Same here." She lay back with a loud, theatrical groan. "Just a little."

He laughed.

She sank into the grass with a deep contented ache in her bones. In one day with Trey she'd accomplished more than she could have in two, maybe three, days alone. Part of that was because he did most of the brute labor—bucking against the rototiller, hauling loads of compost—but it also might have been some multiplier effect that made a job shared go that much faster. It was a surprising thought for Cam, who'd always worked alone.

She folded her arms under her head and gazed up under the canopy of the old oak. From out in the garden, on her feet, the tree looked like a solid symmetrical mass of greenery on one sturdy trunk. But under here she could see the network of limbs and branches; she could trace the way the tree flowed, all the way from its roots to the highest tips of its leaves.

"Can I ask you something?" Trey said.

"Hmm?" She stirred lazily.

"This is another legal question."

"Okay."

"This kidnapping thing—it still doesn't make any sense to me. Okay, I get the parental rights stuff. But doesn't there have to be a ransom demand before it's kidnapping?"

She rolled her head on the grass to look at him. "That's a good question. You'd think so, but that's not the way Congress wrote the law. The statute makes it a crime to hold someone for ransom, reward, or otherwise. Which pretty much takes motive right out of the equation."

"But then anything could be kidnapping." He sat up. "Like—for instance, when you took me to the garden shop this morning. Why wasn't that kidnapping?"

"That's a *great* question," she said, smiling. "Have you been sneaking out to law school when no one was looking?"

He flushed and shook his head.

She sat up, too. Her braid had come loose, and she reached back to twist it tight again. "The answer is that kidnapping requires an unlawful seizure. There has to be some kind of force or deception. And the valid consent of the victim is a complete defense. So assuming we went to the nursery with your consent, I'm not guilty of kidnapping."

He hooked his arms around his legs and rested his chin on top of his knees. "What d'you mean by *valid*?"

"Informed, rational, no mental defect or infirmity—all that stuff."

He lapsed into silence, and after a moment she realized she had the perfect opening. *Now can I ask you a question?* she'd say. But she couldn't do it, and soon the moment passed.

"There's Jesse," Trey said, getting up at the sound of tires in the driveway. Cam groaned and held up her hand, and with a grin, he reached down and hauled her to her feet.

"What do you say?" she asked, brushing off the seat of her shorts. "Willing to wear yourself out again next week?"

"What happened to tomorrow?"

"Oh, I can't. We have some kind of luncheon to go to."

"I was thinking I could come over anyway. Maybe rake up all that junk behind the row of hollies we were talking about."

"Really? That would be great!"

He ducked his head with a quick, embarrassed smile.

24

Joan Truesdale removed her hat and fanned a breeze against her face until the glare of the sun became too much and she had to put it back on again. The Bermuda sun was always too much for her, even after twenty years. She still longed for the soft New England sun she'd grown up with, the one that filtered itself between mountains and through tall evergreens and felt clean and dry when it touched her. This sun was steamy and fetid and felt like a contagion on her skin. Her dress hung limply on her heavy frame and clung in clammy patches to her back and under her arms. Her hair frizzed up under her hat like cellophane crackling.

She squinted wearily down the South Shore Road for her connecting bus to Devonshire. Three-thirty already, and Desmond had to have his medicine before teatime. There was no help for it. She hefted her shopping bags and started the long walk home.

The road was narrow and winding, as all Bermuda roads were, built as they were for the occasional horse-drawn carriage but now carrying tens of thousands of buses, cars, and motorbikes. There was no sidewalk, nor even a shoulder to walk on, only a narrow strip of dirt between the roadway and the mass of tropical foliage that grew thick beside it.

The bus rumbled past her, too late and much too close, and behind it came a streaming line of tourists on mopeds, all having a raucous good time. They never realized their danger, and there was an unspoken agreement among Bermudians never to tell them of it. The cycle rental shops did a booming business, and so did the hospital, where the most frequent emergency room visitor was a tourist with his flesh scraped off. Road rash, they called it, as if it were only a local infection.

A few of the passing tourists were clutching little American flags in their hands, and with a jolt Joan recalled the date. July fourth. Very much a nonholiday here in the British colony of Bermuda, but one she always tried to observe in her heart. Every year for the past ten, she'd made herself a promise: next Independence Day, she'd be watching the fireworks on her native soil. It never happened, of course, but after thirty years of marriage she was so accustomed to broken promises that she thought little of it, even when the promise came from herself.

There was a rich man's house ahead on the right, and its entrance was marked by a Chinese moongate, the familiar circular stone archway that adorned hundreds of residential and commercial establishments on the island. Moongates were thought to bring luck, and superstition had it that if you made a wish while you passed through, it had to come true. Joan had dozens of ungranted wishes to refute the legend, but nonetheless, in honor of the holiday, she decided to try one more. She put her bags down and stepped through the moongate, whispering, "May I never spend another Fourth of July on this godforsaken island."

She retrieved her bags and walked on, past the cottage colonies where the poorer tourists rented housekeeping apartments. Down the lane and up the hill was their own cottage, a pale orange block with a blinding white roof of limestone stair steps to catch the rainwater and funnel it to the cistern underground. A single palm tree leaned desultorily over the side of the house, and a pair of wilting hibiscus bushes flanked the front door. They'd grown too big, and they clawed at her on her way inside.

"Where have you been?" came the bellow as soon as she crossed the threshold. "I've been needing you!"

"Only out to the market, Desmond," she called back to the bedroom. "But the bus never came, and I had to walk home."

"You missed my four o'clock!" he roared. All the strength that was gone from his body seemed now to reside in his voice. He rattled the windows sometimes.

"Only by five minutes, Des." She went into the tiny kitchen and put the kettle on to boil.

"Where are you, then? A man waits all afternoon for his wife to come home, and she can't be bothered to look in on him?"

She carried the tray into the bedroom and reluctantly sniffed the air. He'd messed himself again.

"Bath first, then tea?" she suggested.

He rolled his shrunken head on the drool-stained pillow. "Ha. You'd like that, wouldn't you? Keep me waiting even longer."

"Tea first, then."

She pulled up a chair beside him, and as she lined up his pills, his tongue rolled out to receive them. It was the same ashen gray as his complexion, and as flaccid as his arms and legs.

"Good," she crooned as he swallowed. She held the cup to his mouth while he sucked in a little slurp of tea.

"I suppose you were off with your fancy friends," he said. "Dancing, I don't doubt."

"Oh, Desmond." She sighed. "Apart from the fact that I don't have any friends, fancy or otherwise—I don't know a place on this earth, let alone this island, where you can go dancing in the middle of the afternoon."

"You're meeting somebody, I know you are."

"I thought we agreed a long time ago, Des. No one but you would give me a second look."

"That's right!" he shrieked. "I was the only one. And look where it got me. Shackled to you day in and day out. Always dragging me down. I would've risen if I'd married better! They would have promoted me! I had that from two senior officers!"

"So you've told me, dear, many times."

She coaxed him to finish his tea, then, while he lay stony-faced on the bed, she stripped him and washed him and carried away the soiled linens.

He was dozing by the time she returned, and she sank down in the chair beside him. He was eighty years old, and before long his weight would equal his age. He'd been dying of assorted maladies for the past ten years, and any one of them alone could have finished the job, but so far none had. Joan sometimes thought they'd been forgotten by God, misplaced in His mind as they moved from one Third World posting to another. Her greatest fear was that if God had forgotten them, He would forget to take Desmond when his time came. No, not true: her greatest fear was that He'd already forgotten.

She picked up their wedding photo from the bedside table. It was impossible to believe they were one and the same, this emaciated man in the bed and the elegant man in the photo. Laurence Olivier, the girls used to call him, and there *was* a resemblance. Joan had loved the crisp way he talked, the almost pompous way he carried himself, and when he'd declined to talk much about his background or circumstances, she'd chalked it up to British reserve and loved that about him, too.

But mostly she'd loved the fact that she *had* him—she, Joan Landis. The other three were her dearest friends. She loved them like sisters, but the truth was, they crowded her out, Abby with her looks, Gloria with her brains, Doris with her bubbly personality. Pretty young girls were invited everywhere in Washington those days, and those three fit in so easily. Joan could remember watching them at some party somewhere, probably a dozen parties: Abby laughing gaily, her head thrown back to expose her long, lovely throat; Gloria in a sharp and earnest policy discussion with some high-ranking official; Doris filling up plates of appetizers and carrying them to handsome young men who were trapped in conversations with their superiors. While Joan stood alone against a wall, staring at the floor, and wishing she were anywhere else.

It was against one of those walls that Desmond found her. She'd spoken to him warily, not only because she was shy, but because by that time the other three had all been Approached. It happened exactly the way they'd been warned during their security briefings: a handsome man, sometimes foreign, often not; a little wining and dining that spun rapidly into a whirlwind romance; then the Approach. It would be political if he sensed the slightest trace of antiwar sentiment, and who didn't have at least some of that in 1968? Financial, if the girl struck him as mercenary enough. And sentimental if she were the softhearted kind; he'd trot out the dying mother or the blackmailed father or whatever personal crisis forced him to this small act of treason.

Agency secretaries were the prime targets of these men, not only because they were gullible and underpaid, but because they were so invisible to their bosses. They were regarded as mere functionaries, easy on the eye perhaps, but never a brain or a pair of eyes they had to worry about. It didn't occur to them that their secretaries might understand any of the bits of information that passed through their manicured fingertips.

The other three girls all survived their Approaches, duly reported them, and were able to laugh about it later. But it hadn't yet happened to Joan, and when Desmond Truesdale spoke to her at the party, she hardly knew how to respond.

The next morning she submitted his name to Security, and the report came back in time for their first date the following Friday:

clean. It was the only question she'd asked, and she'd lived to regret it. If she'd asked, they could have told her his true age, for instance, and his exact rank; his history of making trouble in the office and being transferred out of it; the plans that were already being laid to force his early retirement.

He was in a deep sleep by now. Joan looked at her watch. It was only five. She could still make it to church.

She climbed on the bus with the brisk "Good afternoon, everyone" that Bermuda etiquette demanded. The seats were packed full with red-skinned tourists and black-skinned Bermudians. A small black child was in a seat near the front, and as soon as Joan stepped into the aisle, his mother's voice shot up from the back: "You get yourself out of that seat, and let this lady sit down!"

Another rule of Bermuda etiquette, to honor the elderly. The little boy scrambled to obey, and Joan sank down in his place, torn between gratitude and self-pity. She'd aged before her time, she knew that. She was only fifty-one, and every day she saw women older than she playing tennis and running on the beach in skimpy swimsuits. They weren't old women yet. But she was. When she was first married, she was embarrassed that people used to mistake her for Desmond's daughter. Today she was embarrassed that they didn't.

The bus traveled around Harrington Sound through Bailey's Bay, over the causeway, past the airport, and over Mullet Bay Road. It dropped passengers like bread crumbs along the way, and by the time it pulled into the narrow streets of St. George's, there were only a handful of people left on the bus with her.

She'd timed her visit well. There were only a few tourists in Duke of York Street, and she was happy to see that no one was climbing up the steps to St. Peter's. Her prayers required solitude.

The church was a simple whitewashed building three hundred years old. The plantation shutters at the two front windows were propped open, and so were the cedar doors at the narthex, but Joan was the only one who passed through them. She walked down the center aisle and turned to face the altar. The light was dim, and the street noise muted. A tranquil, blessed refuge. She genuflected at the end of a pew, then went in and lowered herself to her knees.

She began as always with the Confession. *Most merciful God,* she murmured aloud, *I confess that I have sinned against thee in thought, word, and deed, by what I have done, and by what I have left undone. I have not loved thee with my whole heart; I have not loved my neighbors as myself.*

They'd been married two months and were on their way to the Sudan by the time Desmond told her his age. She could hardly believe it: there wasn't a line on his face. He laughed and said there was a picture of him in an attic somewhere that had done all the aging for him. Wide-eyed, she'd declared, "I hope it stays there forever!" And he'd laughed again and told her what an adorable little puss she was.

She spent the first ten years of their marriage praying that he wouldn't die, and the last ten praying that he would.

I am truly sorry and I humbly repent. For the sake of thy Son Jesus Christ, have mercy on me and forgive me . . .

Footsteps sounded behind her, and she glanced back to see a couple wandering through. They seemed embarrassed to have interrupted her prayers and quickly stepped out the side door leading out to the cemetery.

. . . that I may delight in thy will and walk in thy ways, to the glory of thy Name.

The picture came out of the attic the year the government forced him to retire. Desmond had bought the cottage many years before with the idea of retiring there someday. But the someday was forced upon him too soon, and the cottage became a prison. He sat inside day after day, chewing over his circumstances like a bitter root. He aged ten years in one.

More footsteps sounded behind her, but when Joan looked back she saw at once that this man was no tourist. He fell to his knees on the other side of the aisle and clasped his hands before him in an attitude of fervent penitence. A man of God, she felt certain of it.

She clasped her own hands more fervently together as she moved on to the Prayers for the Sick. *Heavenly Father, giver of life and health: comfort and relieve your sick servant Desmond*—she left out the part about healing him and hoped He wouldn't notice—*that he may be strengthened in his weakness and have confidence in your loving care.*

She glanced again at the clergyman across the aisle. His face shone as he prayed, like the face of Moses when he came down from Mount Sinai. It meant he was talking to God; and it meant God was listening.

But was He listening to her? She bowed her head and began the Prayers for a Person Near Death. *Deliver thy servant Desmond from all evil,* she murmured, *and set him free from every bond; that he may rest with all your saints in the eternal habitations; where with the Father and the Holy Spirit you live and reign, one God, forever and ever—*

"Amen," whispered a voice in her ear.

Her eyes opened. The man was beside her, looking down at her with the face of an angel.

"Amen," she repeated, entranced.

The blow crushed the back of her skull, and she fell against the kneeler as he descended upon her, a terrible avenging angel, sent to punish her for her sinful thoughts and words. *Oh, Father, forgive me, for I knew not what I did.*

He opened her legs, and she saw a band of cherubs watching from the sky; he cut her throat, and she saw the face of God turning away from her.

At last the perpetual Bermuda heat was gone, and a miraculous cold began to spread from her feet up to her heart. The glaring Bermuda sun was gone, too, and in its place was a great black well of darkness rushing down to embrace her. But one little circle of light still glowed. It was a moongate, and suddenly she remembered the wish she'd made that day: *May I never spend another Fourth of July on this godforsaken island.*

She'd gotten her wish. After a lifetime of wishes, this was the one she'd finally been granted. It made her smile to think of it.

So very long since she'd smiled . . .

25

Trey woke with a lurch and sat up straight in the dark. If he'd been in a dream, he couldn't remember it now. All he could remember was that today was Thursday, and that it had to be today.

His school blazer and khakis had been hanging on the back of his closet door since Sunday night, but nothing happened Monday, and he later read in the paper that it took Monday and Tuesday just to pick the jury. He spent most of yesterday sitting in his room, waiting for the call, but it still didn't come. Finally, last night, he heard the familiar stomping in the hall, the Friday night sounds two days early. The old man was back from Washington, and that told Trey everything he needed to know. Thursday would be the day. Today.

It wasn't dawn yet, but he was so wired he couldn't go back to sleep. He couldn't even lie down. He threw himself out of bed and paced off the dimensions of his room. He felt brittle, like one touch would snap him into a thousand pieces. He needed to move, he needed to shake this feeling off before he exploded.

He pulled on a pair of gym shorts and laced up his shoes and crept down the stairs. A gray haze lay over the front lawn and as far down the road as he could see. He plunged into it, running flat-out, arms and legs pumping, until he felt the wind on his face and the sweat on his back. It was a hundred-yard dash stretched out for two miles, and it didn't end until he reached Cam's house.

It was too early, she wouldn't be awake yet, but he ran up the driveway and looped around to the backyard. The garden spread out in front of him, a thousand bursts of color blooming out of the mist. Six weeks of his life were invested here, but there was still a lot left to do. The reflecting pool was laid out but not yet dug up—they had to wait for the plumber on that—and there was still the folly to rebuild. He saw that another load of shredded hardwood had been delivered since he was last here, which meant his next job would be to mulch the rest of the beds. He wished he could start today.

He went into the folly. All eight walls of the lower level were covered with his drawings, pinned up there by Cam. She went through a little ritual every time he gave her another one: she'd unroll it, study it with a little smile catching on her lips, then look up solemnly and ask, "Can I keep this?" Like she didn't know he was only doing it for her.

He went up the narrow spiral stairs to the second story, the little room he'd made his secret hideaway, and he worked it all out in his mind, one more time until he was sure. By then the sun was shining through the cracked pane of the little octagonal window. He got up on his knees and looked out at the garden. The morning haze was burning off. It was time to go.

Jesse drove them downtown, the old man riding shotgun up front and the old lady in the back with Trey. One of the local staffers was waiting for them behind the courthouse, and he snapped to attention as they got out of the car and held the door open as they passed inside. They went down an empty corridor to a private elevator and up to the fourth floor.

Ron March was waiting when the doors slid open. "Good morning, all," he said, pasting on a smile.

He led the way across the elevator lobby and through a set of double doors and into the back of the courtroom.

Trey's feet seemed to falter. The rows were packed with people, to the left, to the right, ahead of him. A great hush fell over the room, and he felt the stubble of hair rise on the back of his head as they all turned to stare at him. His grandparents were taking seats in the first row, and March was on his feet in the aisle, beckoning to him. Trey moved forward with his heart hammering in his chest. A woman was peering down at him from an elevated seat in the middle, and it took him a dazed moment to realize she must be the judge. She had bright red hair, the kind of color that always made the old lady sniff and say, "Not found in nature."

"Right up there," March said, pointing to the witness stand.

Trey climbed the two steps up, but before he could sit down, another woman sprang in front of him brandishing a book.

"Raise your right hand and place your left hand on the Bible," she said. He had to think a second before he got it right. "Do you solemnly swear to tell the truth, the whole truth and nothing but the truth, so help you God?"

"Yeah," he said. "I mean, yes."

"Be seated."

He sat down and scanned the courtroom. The jury box was to his right, packed with strangers, all staring at him. March sat at a table in front of him, and behind him were the old man and the old lady. Across the aisle, a man with bronzed skin and silver hair sat at another table. Trey recognized him from the newspaper photos. *Defense counsel Bruce Benjamin,* the caption always read. Beside him was Steve.

It was the first time Trey had seen him since the night the boat pulled away from Maristella, the first time since then, and suddenly his throat burned and his eyes stung, and he clenched his teeth tight. *No, God, not now.*

March went to the lectern in the middle of the courtroom. "Good morning," he said heartily.

Trey cleared his throat. " 'Morning."

"Please tell the jury your name."

"James Ashton—"

"Move that a little closer," the judge interrupted.

Trey threw a startled look up at her. Her mouth was colored with a bright orange lipstick, and she stretched it wide to smile at him. "So we can all hear you," she said.

"Oh. Sorry." He pulled the microphone toward him. "James Ashton Ramsay." He jumped a little at the reverberation.

"And you go by Jim, don't you?"

"No. I go by Jamie."

March frowned and picked up his pen to scrawl something over his notes. Trey's gaze drifted away from March and across the aisle. Steve was wearing an unfamiliar suit along with an unfamiliar smile. It looked guarded and uncertain.

"All right, then. Jamie. Where do you live?"

"At 127 Martins Mill Road, Greenville, Delaware, 19807."

Somebody snickered at the back of the courtroom. Shit, he thought. Nobody asked for the zip code.

"Who do you live with?"

"Senator and Mrs. Ash Ramsay."

March grinned at the jury. "Your parents, right?"

"No. My grandparents."

"Who are your parents by adoption, correct?"

Out of the corner of his eye he could see defense counsel Bruce Benjamin lean over and whisper something to Steve. But Steve didn't whisper anything back. He just sat there, watching Trey.

"I'm not sure," Trey said. "I mean, they never said so."

March's eyes shifted in his skull, a quick little slide like rapid eye movements in sleep. "That's all right," he said amiably. "The jury's already heard all about that. Tell us how old you are."

"Fourteen in September."

"Where do you go to school?"

"Tower Hill."

"You went there last year, too?"

"Yeah. Well, up until last February."

"I'd like you to turn your attention back to last February. Friday, February twentieth. You remember that day, don't you?"

He licked his lips. "Umm, not really. I mean, I'm not sure of the date. Is that when Steve came for me?"

Murmurs rippled among the spectators, but March held tight to his smile. "Yes, Jamie. That was when you were kidnapped."

"Objection!" Benjamin called.

"Sustained. Mr. March, you know better than that."

"My apologies, Your Honor. Jamie," he said, the smile freezing up. "Tell the jury what happened that Friday night."

"Okay, well, I went over to my friend Jason's house and hung out there until like nine-thirty. And then I left and went down Sentry Bridge Road to the corner of Chaboullaird Road."

March nodded encouragement. "Yes, then what?"

"Then I stood there and waited for my dad to come."

March blinked as whispers began to scuttle through the crowd behind him. "Senator Ramsay?"

"No, my real dad. Steve Patterson."

The old lady's gasp was audible. March looked back at the old man as the whispers in the courtroom swelled to a buzz. When he turned back to Trey, his eyes were shifting wildly in his skull.

"You're not telling us that you knew he was coming?"

"Well, sure. I'm the one who asked him to."

Steve's eyes went dark and he leaned over and whispered something to his lawyer. This time it was Benjamin who shook his head and kept his eyes fixed on the witness stand.

"Your Honor . . ." March's voice rose over the hum of the spectators. "May I speak at sidebar?"

She rolled her chair to the far end of the bench, away from the witness stand and the jury box. March and Benjamin went up, and the court reporter lifted his machine and carried it down to join them.

Trey couldn't hear their words, but he could pick up the frantic whispers of Ronald March and the smooth, smug tones of Bruce Benjamin. Steve was watching him with an expression he couldn't read, but he had no trouble deciphering the reactions on the other side of the courtroom. The old lady was biting her lip to keep from crying, and the old man sat with his arms crossed high on his chest and an ominous frown on his face.

The lawyers came out of their huddle, and March strode back behind his table and ducked his head to speak to the old man. When he rose again, the top of his bald head was glistening with sweat. He returned to the lectern and spoke three words into the microphone: "No further questions."

Benjamin started to rise.

"By golly, I've got a few," the judge said.

Benjamin sat down again.

She leaned over and looked sharply at Trey. "What do you mean, you *asked* the defendant to come?"

His mouth was dry. A pitcher of water sat on the table in front of the witness stand, but he knew if he tried to pour himself a drink, he'd fumble it and spill water everywhere. He gulped air and said: "I wrote him a letter, a bunch of letters, and I asked him to come get me. I told him where to meet me and what time—"

"Whoa. Back up. You wrote letters to the defendant?"

"Wait," Trey said. "The *defendant*—is that my father?"

"Let's call him Mr. Patterson, shall we?" she said dryly. "Are you saying you wrote letters to Mr. Patterson?"

"Yeah. First he wrote some letters to my grandparents, but they threw them away. Except for the one that I found. I wasn't sure I understood what he was saying to them, so I wrote back. And he wrote back to me and explained the whole thing. Then I wrote back again, and so did he, and this went on for a couple of months until finally I asked if I could live with him and to please come get me."

The judge's eyebrows arched high over the blue frames of her glasses. "How did he respond?"

"He said no. He said it wasn't right, and it wasn't fair to my grandparents. He said he'd go to court and do it legally. But I knew he'd lose for sure against my grandfather. So I just begged him to come get me, and I kept on begging until he said okay."

"Uh-huh."

Her voice crackled with disbelief. Trey flicked his eyes to the other side of the courtroom. Steve was still staring at him with a tangle of emotions that he couldn't begin to unravel.

"Now, Jamie," the judge said, looking hard at him over her glasses. "We have to be very sure of this. Did Mr. Patterson force you to go with him?"

"No."

"Did he trick you or deceive you in any way?"

"No."

"You went with him of your own free will?"

"Like I said, it was my idea. I had to talk him into it."

She leaned back in her chair until the springs squawked. "Mr. March," she began slowly, "I'm afraid I—"

"Your Honor, if I might ask a few follow-up questions?"

She waved at Trey with a gesture like, *You see what you can do with him.*

"Trey." No more *Jim*, no more *Jamie*. "On the evening of June fourth, you made an emergency radio transmission from Maristella Island, you remember that?"

Trey's stomach lurched. No, he didn't remember that. He'd put it out of his mind, so far that he forgot to work out any way to explain it. "No," he said finally.

"No, you don't remember?"

"No, I never made any radio transmission."

"You radioed for rescue," March said, his voice rising. "You said Steve Patterson kidnapped you."

"Objection," Benjamin said. "Leading."

The judge looked over at him. "Mr. Benjamin, I think this record more than makes out a showing of surprise in connection with this witness. Objection overruled. The government may lead."

"Well?" March said. "Isn't it true that you radioed for help on the night of June fourth and reported that Steven Patterson had kidnapped you?"

"No, that's not true." Trey looked up at the judge. "What's he talking about?"

She raised a shushing hand at Trey followed by a warning finger at March. "If you're planning to impeach, I sure hope you have a witness in the wings."

His face froze, and Trey felt a hot rush of relief. There was no witness in the wings; there was nobody to testify to what he did and said in Maine. March hadn't bothered to bring an agent down from Maine, because March assumed he had him.

"Just a few more questions, Your Honor?"

"Don't go far," she warned.

He pinned Trey with his glare. "The night of June fourth, FBI agents came to Maristella Island, didn't they?"

"Yes."

"They arrested Steve Patterson and they arranged your return to Delaware, didn't they?"

"Yes."

March paused a deliberate beat. "So who called them?"

"I don't know."

"Move that microphone closer—"

"I don't know!" Trey yelled. "I was asleep, it was the middle of the night. I heard shouting and I woke up, and then I heard their boots on the stairs. I didn't know who they were, I jumped up and locked my door. And they pounded and pounded on it, and then they kicked it in, and it like exploded into my room—there were splinters of wood flying everywhere. And they grabbed me and hauled me downstairs, and there was my dad with his hands cuffed behind him, and I'm like 'What's going on?' And he's like, 'Calm down, it's okay.' "

His breath ran out, and he stopped and took another one, but before he could say more, he noticed how quiet the courtroom had become.

"If you didn't call them, who did?"

"Who else?" Trey cried. "Who else could make them do that to us? Senator Ash Ramsay, that's who!"

A clamor of voices rose up, sharp angry ones over excited buzzing ones, March bellowing "Your Honor!" while the judge hammered on her gavel and screeched for order. People were on their feet, marshals were bursting in the back, and underscoring it all was a low keening wail that could only have come from the old lady.

"Enough!" the judge roared, and pounded on her gavel for a full two minutes until at last the commotion died down.

She leaned over the side of the bench and stared at Trey. "You swore to tell the truth here today, you understand that?"

"Yes."

"And is that what you've done?"

"Yes."

She pursed her orange-colored lips at him, then sat back and swiveled to the other side of the courtroom. "I assume you have a motion, Mr. Benjamin?"

He stood up with a smirk. "I do indeed."

She sighed and swiveled her chair the other way. "Members of the jury, this is as good a time as any for your luncheon recess. We've got some legal issues to hash out while you're gone. We'll reconvene, say at two, and see where we all stand."

The jurors rose and filed out, and when the door banged shut behind them, Bruce Benjamin moved to the lectern.

"You're excused, too," the judge said absently to Trey.

He scrambled off the witness stand and walked stiff-legged down the aisle and out of the courtroom. He expected somebody's staffer to be there waiting for him, with instructions to stash him away somewhere, but the corridor was empty.

For a few minutes he stood and listened to what was going on inside. It was like a trio of three voices singing one discordant song, high and low, loud and not so loud, different verses that kept coming back to the same refrain: the government's burden of proof, no evidence of unlawful seizure, the absolute defense of consent.

Still no one came to spirit him away. He cracked the door, slipped inside, and sat down in the last row.

"Consent has to be decided by the jury," Ronald March was saying. "There are serious credibility issues here."

"But once again, Mr. March, do you have any witness to refute the boy's story?"

"Not at the moment, but—"

"His testimony is perfectly consistent with every other piece of evidence you've put on. Frankly, I don't see how the jury could disregard it."

"But we all know what happened here today!"

"Do we?" the judge said sharply. "I'm not sure I do."

"Your Honor," Benjamin said. "We have unrefuted evidence of consent. The only thing any of us could know is that this boy consented to go with his fa—" He stopped, rolled his eyes, then said in overenunciated tones, "With the defendant."

"But it has to be a valid consent," March put in. "An informed, rational, voluntary consent. Which this thirteen-year-old boy was obviously incapable of giving."

"Why?" the judge asked.

"Because he was only thirteen years old—"

"No. I'm not willing to charge incapacity on the basis of age alone. Give me another reason, Mr. March. Give me some evidence of impairment or disability, mental, emotional, anything. You have anything like that, I'll bring the jury back to hear it."

"A moment, please, Your Honor?"

March bent over for another huddle with the old man. Trey craned his neck to see. The old man's chin was on his chest, and he shook his head. March said something else, and the old man shook his head again.

March turned back to the bench. He stood a moment, gazing down at the table, shuffling papers around in the file. "We will present no such evidence," he said.

The judge flopped back in her chair. "That's it, then. Mr. Benjamin, your motion is granted. Mr. Patterson, it is the judgment of this Court that you are acquitted of all charges."

She banged her gavel desultorily, said, "We're adjourned," and spun her chair until she disappeared behind its high back. In a flap of black robes, she was gone.

Voices started to fire in ricochet shots through the courtroom, and people were jumping to their feet and climbing out into the aisle, some of them to mill around up front and others to crash through the rear doors and gallop to the phones outside. Bruce Benjamin turned from the lectern with a broad smile. Steve shook his hand with a smaller smile, the same edgy one he'd worn all morning, then he looked past him, searching the courtroom until he spotted Trey. He sidestepped his lawyer and headed for the clogged aisle.

Trey started for the aisle, too, but one of the old man's staffers finally appeared in front of him and blocked his path. "You have to come with me now," he said.

"Get lost."

Trey shoved past him, and the staffer grabbed him by the elbow, and another man materialized and grabbed the other one.

"Hey!" Trey yelled.

Up front a third man stepped into the aisle in front of Steve. "Hold it right there," he said.

"Get out of my way."

"There's a restraining order in effect," the third man said. "You take one more step, you're in violation of it."

"Get out of my way," Steve said again.

The man's hand shot up in a signal, and two marshals charged through the crowd and grabbed Steve by the arms.

"Hey!" Trey screamed.

The men holding Trey turned him around and shoved him back. He twisted and kicked at them, but he couldn't get loose. They dragged him out and down the hall to a tiny room, and they didn't let go until they had the door slammed behind them.

"What the fuck is this?" Trey shrieked, spinning wildly away from them. "What're you locking *me* up for? I didn't do anything!"

The two of them stood shoulder to shoulder, blocking the door, and said nothing.

The explosion he'd felt on the edge of at dawn finally came now, at 12:45 by the clock on the wall. He kicked a metal chair out of his way, and when it toppled over and fell to the floor, he kicked it again, and then again, until it crashed against the wall, and when that still wasn't enough, he knocked the other three chairs over, too. He stood a minute, panting hard, then grabbed the table and heaved it over. It landed with a resounding bang against the tile floor.

He felt something then, a change in the electrical charge of the air that made the hair rise again on the back of his neck. He turned around. The two staffers had stepped aside, and the old man filled the doorway between them. His expression sat like stone upon his face.

"I asked you to do one thing here today. What was it?"

"Ash, please, let's talk about this at home," the old lady said as she slipped in beside him.

"I guess he forgot," the old man said to the room. "He forgot the one and only thing I asked him to do. To tell the truth."

"I didn't forget anything," Trey said darkly.

"Oh? So you deliberately set out to make me look like a fool here today? To make me look like some goddamn laughingstock?"

Trey set his jaw.

"Or I suppose you think you've worked some kind of justice? Is that what you think, boy?"

Ronald March came in behind him. "Let's shut the door here, Senator," he said, and squeezed past him to close it.

"Well, it's a sorry kind of justice if it takes a lie to get you there! All you did today was perjure yourself. You lied, you violated your oath, and by God—you didn't learn those values in *my* house! Is this what you learned from him? Is this the kind of man you've set free today?"

"Ash, please," the old lady said, clutching at his arm.

He shook her off and fixed his granite eyes on Trey. "Let me tell you this, boy—it'll be a cold day in hell before you ever see him again!"

"Senator, let me call your driver—"

"Yes, why don't you do that, Ron? Let's see if you can accomplish that much, at least."

March flushed a mottled red from his neck all the way over the top of his hairless head.

"Call down to Jesse," the old man said, yanking the door open. "Tell him I want to go straight home." He strode down the corridor with his wingtips striking the floor like gunfire.

The old lady sagged against the doorjamb. "Would someone get a chair for me, please?" she asked shakily.

A staffer scrambled to pick one up off the floor.

"Shouldn't you catch up with the Senator, Mrs. Ramsay?" March asked. "So you can all go home together?"

She let out a tear-edged laugh. "He didn't mean home to Greenville, Ron." She sank down into the chair. "He meant home to Washington."

26

Cam kept herself away from the courtroom, but she couldn't keep herself away from the TV and newspaper accounts, and when she understood what Trey had done, she realized two things: that she was the one who planted the idea in his mind, which made her complicit in his perjury; and that she was glad of it.

He didn't come to work the next day. She waited until noon to call, and when the machine answered, she left a cheery, upbeat message, suitable for any member of the household who might hear it, reminding Trey of the work they'd planned, telling him how much she was counting on his good help. But no one picked up, and no one called her back.

The damage control appeared in the Sunday morning paper. According to a Washington source, reportedly "close" to the Ramsays, the Senator and his wife blamed themselves entirely for what took place in the courtroom. They hadn't realized the severity of their son's trauma after he was returned to them. He'd refused to see a counselor and they'd failed to insist upon it. Now, of course, they realized that no thirteen-year-old boy could have gone through such an ordeal without suffering enormous pain and confusion. What happened in the courtroom was clearly the result of that confusion. But now he was receiving the professional help he needed, and with all their love and God's help, they had every hope that he'd soon be himself again.

Meredith Winters read the same story at her desk Monday morning and recognized the hand of Nick Kosmidis at work. He was Ramsay's chief strategist and was big on mea culpas that sounded contrite but stopped short of any actual admission of wrongdoing.

She folded the paper and leaned back with her fingers steepled over the bridge of her nose. A bad run of luck for Ash Ramsay, all these revelations: a son who turned out to be a grandson, a daughter who turned out to be a slut, a trial that turned out to be a major embarrassment. He had to be hurting badly.

At last.

"Marcy," she yelled out into the hall. "Set up a conference call with Nick Kosmidis and Ramsay's legislative guy."

"Got it," Marcy said, dialing.

Meredith pulled up her calendar while she waited. She was booked solid for the next two weeks, but she'd make the time; nothing she had down was as important as this.

"Both holding, Miss Winters."

"Gentlemen," Meredith said, picking up. "When can we talk?"

The August heat descended, and when Cam left her office in Philadelphia Tuesday night, the pavement was so hot she could feel it through the soles of her shoes. She walked to the parking lot through waves of steamy heat that seemed to oscillate off the pavement and tighten around her throat. Her car came into view, and she picked up her pace as she rooted for her keys in her purse.

"Campbell?"

Her body jerked at the sound of his voice, then everything was spinning, whirling crazily around her head, until the heat swelled up and swallowed her into blackness.

"Campbell?"

Her eyes flashed open. She must have fainted, though she never had before. She was swaying on her feet and her head was still swimming, but she knew where she was, and even without looking, she knew whose arm was around her waist to hold her steady.

"I'm sorry. I didn't mean to startle you," he said.

"No, the heat—"

"Here." He pried the keys from her hand and unlocked her car door, then guided her sideways into the seat. "Lean over. Put your head between your knees."

She did, and it was a relief just to hide her face in her lap. The blood seeped back into her brain, and slowly the dizziness subsided.

"My name's Steve Patterson—"

"I know who you are." She sat up, though she kept her head down. "You shouldn't be here."

"Better here than Wilmington, I thought."

"Yes, but—"

"Look, I know who you are, too, okay? But no one's going to recognize me here, and I need to talk to you. Five minutes, that's all I ask."

She looked up, and there he was, not a dim, distant figure, but a flesh-and-blood man three feet away with a wilted collar and a little patch of beard on his chin he must have missed when he shaved that morning.

"Please."

He suggested a cold drink, and she suggested an out-of-the-way bar on Twenty-third Street. Inside it was cool and dark and the music was soft. They took an empty booth in the back, and as Cam slid across the smooth vinyl of the seat, she started to feel a little calmer. It was only the heat that made her faint, and it was only the unexpectedness of his approach that startled her.

"What would you like?" he asked as a server drifted their way.

"I don't care. Whatever you're having."

He asked what was on tap and ordered two, then leaned toward Cam. "I wanted to thank you for what you did last winter. Or I guess I should say, for what you didn't do. It meant a lot."

"For all the good it did."

"No—it did a lot of good. We had three months we wouldn't have had. If you'd blown the whistle on me back in February, he would have gone home and I would've just been a guy he hung out with for a week. Those months made all the difference. I don't understand *why* you did it . . . ."

He paused, waiting for her to offer an explanation, but she let the silence go unfilled. "Well, anyway," he said after a while, "thanks."

More customers were arriving and taking the seats around them, but it was a muted happy-hour crowd, the kind that sought gentle narcotics more than blasting stimulants. Their bodies blocked out the neon window lights as they arrived and cast a kaleidoscope of shadows through the bar.

The server returned and set their drinks on the table. Cam wrapped her hands around the frosty mug, and the chill seeped in through her fingertips and spread through her body. She lifted the mug and let the cold beer sluice down her throat.

"I guess I should say congratulations," she said.

A shadow fell over his face. He shook his head. "That's not the way I wanted it to go. I wanted to fight this thing head on. Did I have the right to do what I did or not? The last thing I wanted was my thirteen-year-old son taking the rap for me."

She shrugged. "His way won. Your way wouldn't have."

"Spoken like a lawyer," he said. "Spoken like *my* lawyer, as a matter of fact."

"Sorry." She looked away, trying to affect no more than a casual interest in what she was about to say. "You don't hold it against him? What he did that night?"

"Jeez—of course not. He's just a kid. More to the point, he's *my* kid."

"Oh," she said, bewildered.

"That's the other thing I wanted to talk to you about. I was wondering if you've seen him? If you know how he's doing?"

"No. He didn't come to work this weekend."

"Work?"

"Oh, sorry, you don't know. I hired him to work in my garden. He cuts the grass and helps out on the weekends."

"Hey, that's great—"

"But he didn't come this weekend. I tried calling him—"

He leaned forward, and his face loomed pale in the sudden light. "They have him locked up, don't they?"

"In seclusion, I guess."

"God."

Cam studied the patch of beard he'd missed on his chin. He had a deep cleft there; she wondered if he missed that spot every time he was distracted or in a hurry.

"It's probably for the best," she said, "if they really do have him seeing somebody. He should have gotten counseling after the shoplifting episode. It's my fault that he didn't—"

"Shoplifting?"

She winced at the look that came into his eyes. "Sorry. I guess you didn't know about that either."

He pressed his hands hard against his forehead as a hoot of laughter sounded from the booth behind them. Cam tightened her fingers around her mug. The frost had melted and was weeping down the sides of the glass.

"I have to see him," he said.

She felt panic rise like a gorge in her throat. "No—"

"He's like a powder keg. He could get into serious trouble. What if he's doing hard drugs? What if he snaps one day and mows down half his school with an automatic rifle?"

"I can't believe anything like that would happen—"

"Nobody *ever* believes anything like that would happen. Campbell, please, I have to see him. An hour, that's all I ask."

"I can't! There's a restraining order—"

"You think I don't know that?" he burst out.

A few people at the bar turned and looked at them.

"Sorry," he mumbled with an apologetic nod aimed vaguely toward the bar. He looked at her. "Do you have kids, Campbell?"

"No."

"Then I'm not sure I can explain." He took a gulp of his beer. "It's like the phantom limb phenomenon. You know what that is? Amputees who can still feel sensations from an arm or leg that's not there anymore? It's real. The pain receptors in the brain actually light up on an MRI. They say it's because the brain's still wired for the missing limb." He stared into his mug. "It's like that for me. Like I'm wired for Trey. I think I always have been. I wasn't sure what it was before, I only knew that something was missing, that I felt cut off somehow. But after we had these months together, and after he was taken away from me, I felt it again. Only this time I knew what it was."

She couldn't look at him. She watched the meltwater trickle onto her fingers on the sides of the glass.

"But I guess if you've never had kids of your own—"

"No." She gazed out into the bar, looking at nothing. "I wouldn't understand."

"Would you think about it at least? Here—" He pulled a pen from his pocket and jotted something on a slip of paper. "Here's my phone number. If you change your mind . . ."

She looked at the scrap of paper on the table between them. The number didn't have the Delaware area code. "Where is this?"

"West Chester. I rented an apartment there."

She looked up. "In Pennsylvania."

"Yeah, I thought I should stay off Ramsay turf. If that's even possible."

His face was in the light, and it glowed like the phosphorescent moon in her dream. But he wasn't only the man on the rocks, he was also the man on the roadside in her headlights, the one with the edgy, unsettling look, the one she knew from the start was a danger to her. Abruptly she slid to the end of the booth.

"I have to go."

He stared down at the table, his disappointment patent. "No, I got it," he mumbled as she stood and opened her purse.

But she wasn't reaching for her wallet. She was reaching for the scrap of paper, and as she took it, his eyes came up, wide and wondering, and followed her out into the street.

She had the dream again that night. Once more she was swimming for Maristella, stroking hard with her arms and flipping her heavy mermaid's tail behind her. But the sea was warm and viscous tonight, and she could barely move through the heavy water. Steve stood on the rocks ahead, and he was bending down through the mist to meet her. But she couldn't reach him. The heavy sea closed in around her and held her back.

She woke in the morning with a pool of sticky warmth under her hips and realized her period had come during the night. She got up and went into the bathroom, and when she came out Doug was on his feet and staring down at their bed. The evidence lay like a Rorschach inkblot on the sheet.

"So we missed it again," he said. "After what . . . ? Three months of trying."

She went around him to strip the sheets off the bed.

"Here it is August already. Even if you got pregnant tomorrow, it would be too late."

She bundled up the sheets and clutched them in front of her. "Yes, I know."

"So what's the point?"

Thursday morning the office mail brought the Superior Court decision in the appeal Cam nearly fumbled when she missed the deadline last March. The court had granted her application to file late, and now as she flipped through the pages of the decision, she saw that it had granted her the case as well. She'd won, whether she deserved to or not.

After a few clumsy attempts, she managed to draft an appropriately self-congratulatory transmittal letter to the client, and took it out to Helen to mail. She returned to her desk to log the seven-tenths of an hour that the client would have to pay for her self-congratulation. She opened a drawer to get a fresh pad of time sheets and was startled to see Gloria Lipton looking up at her.

It took her a second to recognize the brochure the firm had put together for the memorial service last May. She must have swept it into the drawer without realizing it that day. She hadn't looked at it then, but now she leaned back and flipped through the pages, past photos of Gloria as a child and then in her cap and gown. And then she turned the page and looked at a picture of her own mother.

Her breath stopped in her lungs, but her heart kept pounding, louder and louder until it was roaring in her ears. *Gloria's career began in 1966 with a top-secret job in Washington!* the caption read. *Here she is with three of her colleagues.*

It was a black-and-white photo of four young women with their arms around each other, stepping forward as if to meet the world. Gloria was recognizable on the left, with a sharp eye and a tight smile even then. Beside her was a round-faced girl with black hair, and next to her was a wan-looking blonde. And finally, on the right, was a girl with sparkling eyes and a luminous smile, one that Cam had seen too seldom in her life, but one that was unmistakably her mother's.

She lurched out from behind her desk and into the corridor with the memorial program in her hands. "Helen?" she asked her secretary with a tremor in her voice. "You helped put together this program for Gloria, didn't you?"

"Yes, why?"

"I was curious where you got these old photos."

"They were in Gloria's desk. You remember, I had a box full of her things down here for a few weeks."

"Oh, right. What happened to that box?"

"We threw it out, after we couldn't find anyone to claim Gloria's things. Why do you ask?"

"Oh—I don't know." Cam struggled to steady her voice. "See this woman here?" She pointed to the black-haired girl next to

Gloria. "She looks familiar for some reason. I thought if I went through that box, I might figure it out."

"Sorry." Brightly Helen added, "I did talk to her, though. Or one of them. I'm not sure which."

The brochure slipped out of Cam's fingers and fell to the floor. She stooped to retrieve it, and pulled a mask of composure over her face before she rose again. "Do you remember her name? Whichever one you talked to?"

"Oh, Lord, the older I get, the worse I get with names. Let me think. They were written on the back of the photo, and then I found one of them in her address book, and I gave her a call. And what a sad call to make! She hadn't heard the news, and she took it awfully hard." Helen heaved a sigh. "What a shame. Poor Gloria."

"What was the name of the government agency Gloria worked for? Did she ever tell you?"

Helen shook her head. "But you know what she did tell me? It was so secret even its *name* was classified. Can you imagine?"

"Wow."

Cam went back to her office. She stared at the vibrant young woman so full of life in the photo. Could Helen actually have spoken to her? No, it had to be one of the other two. If she couldn't find her mother after all these years and with all her resources, certainly Helen couldn't have done it with nothing but an old photograph.

But she did speak to somebody. Cam dialed the firm's telephone system administrator and ordered a printout of all the long distance calls made from Helen's extension since February.

She drove home in a fever that night, agonizing over what to do next and sick at heart because she knew there was nothing. Her hands on the wheel were clammy, and there was a creepy feeling on the back of her neck that made her keep glancing up at the rearview mirror. But there was nothing behind her but the thousands of cars of rush-hour commuters.

She spun a quick turn into a gas station and closed herself up in the phone booth at the edge of the lot.

"Johnson's Sunoco."

"Charlene, it's me."

"Oh, my God—"

"Don't say my—"

"No, I know, I won't."

"I can't talk, but I need to know—have you heard from Mary Mack lately?"

"Huh? Mary who? Oh! You mean—"

"Right, Mary Mack. Any letters or packages or anything?"

"No, I don't think so. My birthday's not till November."

"Do you remember her ever mentioning any of her old friends?"

The response was drowned out as a tractor-trailer roared past. Cam plugged her other ear. "What? I didn't hear you."

"I said, no. I didn't think she had any."

"The people she used to work with maybe?"

"Uh-uh. Dad might know better."

"Is he there?"

"No, this is his lodge night."

Cam turned with a start as bright lights hit her, but it was only a passing car turning on its headlights as the dusk deepened.

"Cammy," her sister said shyly. "I saw your picture in the paper. With your husband."

Cam's breath caught. Charlene said her name, she mentioned Doug, an FBI agent could be listening, he'd be sitting up straight and motioning to his partner at this very moment.

"He looks real sweet—"

She hung up and looked back desperately at the highway.

It was a different highway almost twenty years before, but it was August then, too—a hot, dusty day at the tail end of the summer when she held her little sister's hand and watched the truck go down the road until it disappeared from sight. Charlene was still crying—she'd been crying since their mother's groans woke them at dawn—and Cammy turned and put her arms around her.

"Don't cry, Charlene. I'll take care of you."

She took her back up to the trailer and tied on her mother's apron to cook breakfast, then parked Charlene in front of the TV while she did the dishes and made the beds and scoured the bathroom and vacuumed the rugs. Her mother would be so pleased when she got home. She'd say, "Oh, Cammy, what would I ever do without you?"

Late in the morning there was the sound of gravel crunching, and she and Charlene flew to the window, looking eagerly for their father's truck. But it wasn't a truck, it was a car, a shiny, black one they'd never seen before. The driver's door swung open, and Charlene started to cry again as a man in a dark suit and glasses stepped out.

"Go back to Mommy's room," Cammy told her. "I'll take care of this."

Charlene scurried to the back as the man climbed the steps to the trailer door. Cammy peered at him through the jalousie slats of the door window, and when he pulled off his sunglasses, she realized he wasn't a stranger at all. He'd been here once before, maybe twice, when she was little. She remembered that her mother gave him coffee, and that she'd been jumpy and nervous around him, like when the minister sometimes called.

Cammy opened the door, and the man leaned in and looked around. "Hello, little girl. Is your mommy at home?"

"No. She's at the hospital having a baby."

"A baby? Well, how about that? Congratulations!"

"May I tell her you stopped by?" she said, best manners forward.

"Is anyone else at home?"

She thought of her little sister cowering with terror in the bedroom and shook her head.

"I guess I'll leave your mommy a note. Got any paper?"

"Yes. Won't you please have a seat?"

He sat down at the table while she ran to the book bag she'd so carefully packed for the start of school next week. She brought out a brand new tablet and a glittery pink pencil and laid them carefully on the table in front of him.

"Would you like a glass of water?" she asked as he touched the pencil to his tongue and began to write.

"Why, thank you. Very nice of you to offer."

She hauled herself up on the counter to reach the top shelf where the real glass glasses were kept, and she pulled one out and filled it with iced water and set it down beside him.

"Have an envelope?" he asked, still writing.

She dove under the seat where her mother stashed her bookkeeping supplies and came out with a business envelope printed with Johnson's Sunoco in the upper corner. The man finished his note and ripped the page off the tablet and folded it into the envelope. Then he opened his wallet and pulled out five crisp hundred-dollar bills and added them to the envelope before he licked it shut.

"Give this to your mommy when she gets home from the hospital, would you, please, sweetheart?"

"Yes. Don't forget your water."

He smiled and drained the glass.

She stood on the stoop until his car disappeared, then dashed back inside to copy down his license number before she forgot it. Virginia, RYW-694. Then she took the side of her glittery pink pencil and rubbed it over the top sheet of the tablet until his writing was revealed in ghostly white impressions. Then she ran to the toy closet and dug out her Harriet the Spy secret code and fingerprinting kit.

"Cammy?" came a wavering voice from the bedroom. "Is it safe to come out now?"

"Not yet."

She sprinkled the magic fingerprint powder over the glass and wrapped the magic developing paper around it, then she dove under the seat again and came out with a jumbo-sized envelope. Into it she slid the rubbing of his note, the license plate number, and the fingerprint paper. Later she would puzzle over the contents of the note, and much later she would piece together what it all meant. For now she tucked the envelope under her mattress and called out, "All clear now, Charlene."

Their father came home at dinnertime with a bucket of chicken and some sad news to tell them. The baby wasn't put together quite right, and when God saw His mistake, He took him straight back up to heaven. Nobody really knew why it happened, but the important thing was to always remember it was a blessing.

But their mother didn't seem to feel blessed. When she came home the next day, she went to bed and turned her face to the wall. She didn't cry, but she didn't talk either, and when the girls tiptoed in to see her, she stared at them with sunken eyes.

Cammy thought she knew what might cheer her up. The next morning after her father went down to open the station and Charlene went out to play, she dug out the stranger's envelope and carried it to her mother's bed. "A man came and left this for you when you were in the hospital," she said.

Her mother's eyes wandered over it and away.

"It's a note and some money," Cammy said insistently.

She took it listlessly, but when she saw the cash inside, she sat up straight and read the note. She looked up frantically at Cammy. "Did he say anything to you?" she demanded.

"Yes," Cam said gravely. "He said, 'Congratulations.' "

Her mother's face collapsed, and she covered it with the cash and sobbed until the bills were drenched with her tears.

Doug didn't reach for her when he came to bed that night, just as he hadn't the night before. After he fell asleep, Cam pressed herself against his back and tried to time her breathing to his, in and out, slow and deep, hoping to hypnotize herself to sleep. The windows were open, and she could hear the crickets sing and the wind rustle in the treetops. It was a hot night, too hot to lie so close. A layer of clammy perspiration was growing between them.

The grandfather's clock downstairs measured off the hours through the night, and after it chimed twice, the wind began to moan. A rumble of thunder sounded, and Cam counted the seconds before a flash of lightning lit the sky. Five seconds, then four, then three. The spiderweb cracks in the ceiling began to tremble as the storm rolled closer and closer, and then at last the clouds burst open and the rain began to hammer on the roof.

She got out of bed and dragged a bucket under the leak in the back bedroom, then ran through the house to close the windows. By the time she reached the living room, the sills were wet and droplets of water were spreading like quicksilver on the hardwood floor. Another clap of thunder sounded, and for a second the yard lit up like klieg lights were shining on it. She leaned her forehead against the glass. The grass was bending like marsh reeds, and the trees tossed loose and wild in the wind.

Suddenly the air in the house was suffocating. She opened the front door and went out barefoot onto the porch. She stood a moment with the wind lifting her hair and whipping at her nightgown, then she plunged down off the porch and into the storm. The rain battered against her and soaked through her nightgown, and she spun around and around through the overgrown grass. Her toes dug into the sodden earth and she lifted her face to the rain, her mouth open, drowning in the downpour. Her nightgown melted into her skin, and the rain plastered her hair to her head and streamed down her back and over her hips to form a puddle of water at her feet. Another crash of thunder and the sky cracked open with a jagged streak of lightning, and she lifted her arms high and felt the wind tunnel through her and come out screaming on the other side.

The sky went dark, the storm rolled on, and there she stood, drenched and foolish and still alive.

She must have become the Madwoman of Greenville after all. She was so forsaken that she could even flirt with death and not get a second look.

27

"Welcome to your first power lunch," Meredith said.

Nathan Vance reached around her to open the door. "We got power lunches where I come from, too, you know."

"Ha," Meredith said, striding past him into the restaurant. "What kind of deals get cut over lunch in Wilmington? Bank loans for shopping centers? Amendments to the local land-use regulations? Compare that to what we're doing here today."

"What we *hope* to do here today."

"Please. A little optimism."

The hallway was lined with portraits of the Presidents on one side and of the First Ladies on the other, which made for a head-turning entrance for most of the visitors she brought here. But Nathan looked singularly unimpressed as he passed through. No country bumpkin, this one: she could smuggle him into a meeting of the Joint Chiefs of Staff and he'd still act as if it were business as usual.

The din of a hundred pulsating conversations assailed them as they arrived in the high-ceiling dining room. In a week's time the President would be testifying before a grand jury, and Washington had become a fever swamp of rumors and speculation. It was always a city of factions, but it was more polarized than ever, as charges and countercharges were levied, accusations made, exposures threatened.

It was all good for business, much of which was being done right here, today.

"Good afternoon, Miss Winters," the maître d' greeted her. "Table for two?"

"Three. We'll be joined."

He swept them to her favorite table, pulled out a chair for Meredith, then departed with a little bow.

She did a quick scan of the room. Lobbyists and legislators were the standard coupling, but this was the season of reporters and lawyers, and she observed several prominent pairings. "Oh, Nathan, look," she said. "There's Betsey Wright."

"Oh?" he said, studying his menu.

"Clinton's chief of staff back in Little Rock? Now has a nice lobbying practice here?"

"I know who she is," he said, smirking.

His aplomb was driving her crazy. "You know," she said as she snapped her menu open. "It's perfectly acceptable to engage in a little celebrity-gawking in a place like this."

"There's only one lobbyist I want to gawk at today."

"Well, gawk away," she said, waving an airy hand. " 'Cause here he comes."

Nathan got to his feet.

"Nathan Vance, Gary Pfeiffer." She pointed Pfeiffer to the seat beside Vance's, where she could keep an eye on them both.

"Glad to meet you," Nathan said.

"Same here." Gary took his assigned chair, but scraped it to the end of the table where he could see them both. His idea of triangulation, she supposed.

A waiter presented himself for their drink orders. The usual club soda for Meredith, the usual bourbon for Gary, an iced tea for Nathan.

"Just down for the day?" Gary asked.

"Overnight."

"Where are you staying?"

"Right here, at the Willard."

"Great place. Lots of history. You know it was the Willard Hotel that gave us the word *lobbyist*?"

"How's that?"

"They all used to hang out in the lobby of the Willard. One day President Grant referred to them as 'those damn lobbyists,' and the term stuck."

Their drinks arrived, and they ordered their meals—the signal to end the ritual small talk and get down to business. But Gary ignored protocol and launched a second round. "I understand you're a lawyer?"

"Yes. So's my candidate."

"And so's his wife?"

"Yes. In fact, Cam and I went to law school together."

"Where was that?"

"Michigan."

"Funny, two Michiganders ending up in Wilmington."

"Well, the first stop was Philadelphia. And that wasn't really so strange. Pennsylvania was home for each of us."

"Somebody told me she was orphaned at a young age?"

Meredith gave him a look. *Somebody told him?* She'd sent him her complete file.

"That's true."

"What an amazing young woman. To overcome something like that, then to put herself through school and pass the bar—"

"And don't forget, marry brilliantly," Nathan added.

"Maybe he's the one who married brilliantly."

Meredith all but rolled her eyes. Oh, God, is that what this was all about? Gary Pfeiffer, smitten with Cam Alexander? Though who could blame him with that deadly dull wife of his.

"Of course he did," she said. "Doug's never made a move that wasn't brilliant. Including bringing the three of us here together today."

It was about as subtle as a blowtorch, but it seemed to bring both men back on track.

"Yes, where do we stand on that?" Gary said, shaking out his napkin. "I think I can still put a package together, not as big as the one we were talking about back in June, of course. Maybe fifty? Assuming you've got the Senator on board."

"You know, Gary—" The waiter came out of the kitchen with their luncheon plates, and Meredith tracked his approach and timed her next remark accordingly. "Much as we'd love to take your money, I'm not sure we feel right about it. You'd be throwing it away, and who in good conscience can stand by and watch that?"

His eyes narrowed, and she let him stew as the waiter laid their plates and took their drink refill orders.

"My members don't feel it's a waste," he said as the waiter departed. "It's an investment in the machinery of democracy, as far as we're concerned."

She picked up her knife and fork and sawed off a tiny portion of the grilled swordfish. "But who'd want to invest in a machine that's about to be carted off to the junkyard?"

"I assume we're not talking about your candidate now?"

"Oh, you!" She slapped him on the elbow with a tinkling

laugh. "I'm talking about ALJA's opposition to the tort reform bill. You throw any more money that way, it's like investing in the Edsel. Or Betamax. Remember Betamax?"

"I don't know what you're talking about. We defeated that bill the last time around, remember."

"Yes, but the field's changed since then," Nathan spoke up. "More to the point, the field's changed since you and Meredith talked last spring."

"The President's not going to veto the bill this time, Gary," she said. "He doesn't need your money anymore."

"All you needed the last time was enough to stop an override," Nathan said. "But this time you need more than thirty-four percent of each chamber. You need fifty-one."

"And you don't have it," Meredith said.

"But you know all this." Nathan leaned closer. "It's why half a million last spring got whittled down to fifty today. You have to spread your money around a lot more than you'd planned. At the same time that your members are starting to lose heart and close their checkbooks."

Gary sliced his steak with the concentration of a surgeon, and he chewed slowly and methodically before he spoke again. "Hypothetically, let's say you're right. I don't see where your candidate benefits from turning me down. You're saying he'd rather refuse my money than back a losing horse?"

Meredith's eyes went wide. "Oh, he's not refusing it."

"He just wants a hell of a lot more," Nathan said.

Gary laughed uneasily. "You're going to have to walk me through that one, folks."

"Gary, you can't afford a vote on tort reform. Financially or otherwise."

"You need to stop this bill from ever coming up for vote," Nathan said.

Gary looked quizzically at Meredith.

"Anonymous hold," she explained.

He sat back abruptly.

"A century-old tradition," Nathan said, "whereby a single senator can indefinitely delay action on a bill."

"But that's only used when a member can't make it to the floor for the vote, or the debate preceding the vote. It's only a temporary set-aside."

"Usually," Meredith agreed.

"With many notable exceptions." Nathan laid a file on the table. "Which we have the records on right here. Full history of each bill. With one exception: the name of the senator requesting the hold."

Gary sat very still.

"Think how much better you'll do if you can put this off to the next Congress," Meredith said. "You don't even have to tell me what your polls say, because I know they say the same as mine. Next term you've got a shot at winning this war, veto or not."

"You think Ramsay'll go for it?" he asked finally.

"Let me put it this way: he'd rather stop tort reform with an anonymous hold than go against it with a public vote."

"But it's gotta be worth it to him," Nathan put in. "Which means it's gotta be worth it to us."

"And think what this would mean for your budget, Gary. You don't have to spread your money around to every two-bit member from Podunk. With us, you get one-stop shopping."

He eyed Nathan. "How much?"

"A million."

He swallowed, but he didn't flinch.

"That's five hundred of your members at two thousand a head. Doable, Gary. Very doable."

"We can make it even easier than that," Nathan said. "Give us seven fifty in hard money, and the rest can be soft money to the state Party."

Meredith flicked her eyes at Nathan, then busied herself with a dissection of her salad greens.

"Let me hear from Ramsay's people," Gary said finally. "Maybe we can do some business."

"What the hell was that?" Meredith demanded in the cab back to K Street. "Why would you funnel our money to the Party?"

"It's time to mend our fences, that's why," Nathan said. "I've been working on Norman Finn, and he's starting to see the light. A quarter of a million ought to make his eyes bug out."

"Why bother? We've already proved we don't need them."

"Doug may not need them. But what about you and me?"

She gaped at him.

"Watch and learn, Meredith," he said, laughing. "Watch and learn."

* * *

When Cam got home from the office Friday night, she was greeted by the scent of fresh-mown grass. Her eyes swept over the front lawn. After almost two weeks of neglect, the grass had finally been cut. She got out of the car and went through the wisteria arbor into the garden. It was freshly cut here, too.

She sat down on the stone bench with a sigh. She'd put off cutting the grass herself in hopes that Trey would be back, but Doug must have finally gotten disgusted with it and hired someone else. Or, rather, told Nathan to hire someone else. Whoever it was, he'd done a good job. The clippings were raked up, and the flower beds were edged the way she liked.

But something looked out of place, and she got up and walked down to the folly. That was strange. The door was tightly closed, despite the fact that it didn't fit into the frame. She turned the knob, and it swung easily on its hinges, and when she closed it again, it latched with a smooth click.

"I planed it, and installed a new knob set."

She turned around. Trey was behind her, and she was so happy to see him that she grabbed him in a quick, impulsive hug. To her surprise, he let her hold him for a moment, and he was still smiling when she stepped back.

"I missed you! I mean, the grass got so high."

"Yeah, it took me forever to cut it. I had to keep stopping to empty the bag."

"How'd you get the mower out? The shed was locked."

"Doug was home for a while this afternoon."

"Oh, good." She stopped and beamed at him. "I really did miss you, you know."

He thrust his hands in his pockets. "I got here as soon as I could."

"How'd you manage it?"

"I went on a hunger strike, and finally the shrink said I had too much time on my hands."

He was laughing, but as he spoke Cam realized what she'd felt as she hugged him. He was too thin.

"Come on." She took him by the hand and headed for her car. "Let's go get something to eat."

She made him call home on the car phone, then drove him to a pizza parlor and watched him polish off most of a large pizza with sausage and extra cheese. Then she took him to a Dairy

Queen and bought him a Blizzard, and when he still seemed hungry after thirty-two ounces of ice cream, she got him an order of french fries, too. She sat across from him with her chin on her knuckles and watched him eat. He was slowing down now and making a ritual out of it, dipping each fry into the ketchup and licking it dry before he popped it in his mouth and swallowed.

"I can't believe you cut the grass and still had time to fix the folly, too."

"Only the door. I still have to replace the broken windowpane. And I'm trying to figure out how to patch the stucco. But maybe that's not the way you do it. Maybe you're supposed to take it all off. I don't know, I wish—" He broke off.

"You wish you could ask Steve?"

He swallowed hard and turned his face away.

"Sorry," she whispered.

"Doesn't matter."

"Trey, how are things at home?"

He shrugged. "That doesn't matter either. He's leaving tomorrow for some tour of the Pacific. And I'm leaving soon, too."

"What?"

"I'm starting school in Connecticut next month. He had to pull all kinds of strings to get me in. The shrink says it's full of kids like me." He pushed the plate of fries away. "Must be some place, huh?"

"Oh, Trey."

He looked out the window at the cars whizzing by on the highway. His fingers crept into his shirt pocket and came out with a loose cigarette, and he stuck it between his lips and reached in another pocket for a match.

"No." Cam snatched the cigarette out of his mouth. "I love you too much to watch you kill yourself."

His eyes flashed in a burst of anger.

"I'm sorry," she said fiercely, dropping it in a puddle of ketchup. "But I mean it."

The anger was slowly replaced by a stunned embarrassment.

She'd startled herself with that outburst, and she hurried to change the subject. "I'd like to start work on the reflecting pool this weekend. Try to get the sod stripped off so we can lay it on that side of the garage where the grass won't grow."

He nodded.

"Then maybe we can actually start to excavate."

"Great."

"So what do you say?" She pushed up from the table. "Can you be there at eight o'clock tomorrow?"

"Okay." He got up and started to follow, then reached back to the plate.

"Hey—" she began hotly.

"What?" he said, all innocence as he popped one last fry into his mouth.

Doug was in the living room with a few of his campaign staffers when she got home, but he broke off in mid-sentence to get up and greet her with a hug and a kiss. "How was your day? Another hot one, wasn't it?"

"Hmm."

"Want to join us? We're trying to hammer out the schedule for the rest of August."

"Mind if I go shower first?"

"Go ahead. I'll fix you an iced tea," he said, and kissed her again.

She went upstairs and let the cold water cascade over her until it washed away the perspiration of the day, then wrapped a towel around her hair and came out into the bedroom. Doug had made the bed that morning, not very well, but at least he'd made the effort. He deserved some credit for that, just as he deserved some credit for the effort he made at showing affection in front of his guests just now. She stretched out on top of the bedspread. A minute's rest, and then she'd be able to go downstairs and make the effort that was required of her, too.

She shifted her weight a little. There was a lump under her shoulder, probably a wrinkle in the sheet. She ran her hand over it to smooth it, but the lump was hard. She reached under the covers and pulled it out. It was a headband. A white silk headband, as soft and pure as the girl who owned it.

"Honey?" Doug called up the stairs. "Your ice is melting."

"Be right down."

She slid the headband deep under the covers.

The heat should have kept people away from an outdoor display garden on an August afternoon, but on Sunday hordes of them were streaming through the visitors' center and fanning out over the thousand acres of Longwood Gardens. There were harried parents trying to keep their children tethered, elderly couples hobbling along side by side, younger couples pushing strollers, and finally, a thirty-year-old woman in shorts with an almost-fourteen-year-old boy dressed in layers of oversized shirts, low-slung baggy pants, and heavy boots. He looked so hot that Cam had to stop and buy him a drink before they'd gone a hundred yards.

Most of the visitors were headed up the main path to the conservatories at the top of the hill, but Cam veered off to the right and led Trey down a long brick walk bordered on both sides by exuberant color-themed annuals: pinks massed with purples, then reds, oranges, and yellows fading to whites. At the back of the beds were six-foot-tall clumps of the exotic, big-flowered cannas that Longwood was famous for. She dragged him over to admire them, but he only sucked on his soda straw and looked bored. "I thought we came to look at the fountains."

She studied her watch and after a moment nodded.

They took another path east through the woods and around the lake until the sound of rushing water could be heard ahead. Trey picked up the pace through the woods, and they came to the bridge overlooking the Italian water garden. Dozens of fountains were spraying arcs of water over a long, geometric arrangement of pools. They pulsed in a lush, rhythmic roar and released a cool mist into the air.

Trey leaned his elbows on the railing to take it all in. "Now, see, this is what you oughta do in your yard. Forget all those flowers and stuff. Dig up the whole place and put in something like this."

Cam gave a distracted nod.

"But make it deeper," he said, "so you can dive in when you get tired of just looking at it."

She didn't answer. She was looking past him, up the path that led to the arboretum.

"Cam?" Trey cocked his head to peer at her from under the brim of his baseball cap. "Hel-loo? Earth to Cam, come in, please."

She turned to him.

"What's wrong?" he said, sobering.

"I've done something, Trey. I hope you won't be mad."

The blood drained from his face, and he came up off his elbows with a look of dread in his eyes. Too many people had sprung too many surprises on him lately. She hated to be one of them.

"I've been in touch with Steve. He wants to see you, and I set it up so he could."

His eyes opened wide. "You talked to him? Where is he?"

"Yes, he's—" She had to stop and clear her throat. "He's right behind you, Trey."

He spun around, and for half a second they stood there, ten feet apart. Then Steve opened his arms and Trey went into them, and Cam had to turn away from the rush of emotion she felt.

She stared at the dapple of the sun on the surface of the water and the prisms of light that refracted from the fountain sprays. It was almost hypnotic, the pulsing of the water, the gentle murmur of their voices behind her, the soft rumble of their laughter. She didn't stir until their voices started to fade and she realized they were drifting away.

"Wait a minute," she called after them. "Promise you won't take off? I mean, if I don't get him home tonight—"

They looked back, and Steve's eyes crinkled with amusement. "I guess I can see where she'd be a little nervous," he said to Trey.

Trey laughed.

"No, I didn't mean—"

"Come with us."

"Yeah," Trey said. "We're just gonna walk around a while. Come along."

She backed away. "No, you go on. I'll meet you later."

Steve clapped his hand on Trey's shoulder and Trey leaned into him, loose and relaxed, and Cam stood and watched in bewilderment as they walked away. She didn't know who was forgiving whom, or for what, but whatever had happened between them, it was obviously forgiven. She'd never known that kind of forgiveness, and she hadn't realized its power. It was like the force of a million gallons of pulsing water; it washed everything away.

Two hours later Steve was standing at the appointed spot, but there was no sign of Trey. "He had to hit the bathroom," he explained as Cam hurried up.

"Oh."

He stood facing the men's room door, and she took up position beside him, but something felt awkward; the distance between them wasn't right. She shifted from one foot to the other and frowned at her watch. Now that it was over, she was anxious to leave this place, this man.

"He's been talking about you nonstop," Steve said. "I think he's got a little crush on you."

"No," she said, stunned.

He laughed. "Why should that be a surprise?"

She felt her skin flush.

"He tells me you have a garden folly."

"Well, the remains of one."

"So he said. I was thinking I could take a look at it, see what I can do."

Her eyes flashed. "No—for God's sake, it's in my *yard*."

"Yes, but—"

"Are you forgetting who I am? And who my husband is?"

"I get the picture. I just wanted some way to thank you for all you've done."

She turned away, her eyes stinging. "I can't get caught in this," she said tightly.

"You don't have to. If he's working in your yard and I stop by when nobody's home—"

"And what if somebody *comes* home? What if my husband shows up with half his campaign committee some afternoon?"

"It wouldn't have to get back to you—"

"It would."

He fell silent. Cam glanced at her watch again then back to the men's room door.

"I have to get him back," he said flatly.

"Yeah, well, do it legally the next time."

"You think I'm not trying? I've talked to almost every lawyer in Wilmington, and they all tell me the same thing. It doesn't matter whether I gave a valid consent to the adoption. It doesn't matter whether my parental rights were terminated legally or not. Because any irregularities in the adoption decree are deemed cured. Beyond attack."

"That's true."

"Make that *every* lawyer in Wilmington," he said bitterly.

"Not that it matters."

He looked at her sharply. "What?"

"What do you care whether the decree stands or not?"

"I have to get it overturned to get custody."

"No, you don't."

"Cam." He stepped in front of her and forced her to meet his eyes. "What are you saying?"

"Only that you don't need to undo the adoption to get custody. Anybody can sue for custody. The only thing that's relevant is the best interests of the child. If the court decides that it's not in Trey's best interests to live with the Ramsays, it doesn't matter what their legal status is. They could be his birth parents and you could still get custody."

"Jesus," he said after a moment, "why didn't any of the other lawyers tell me this?"

"You were probably asking the wrong question."

Her eyes moved past him as Trey came out of the men's room. His shoulders were hunched and the brim of his cap was pulled low over his face.

"He doesn't want to go back," Steve said. "I better see you to your car. Make sure he doesn't pull anything."

She nodded, but before they started for the parking lot, she touched her hand to his elbow. "Do me a favor?"

"Sure."

"If you talk to anybody about this—any other lawyers? You didn't hear it from me, okay? We never met."

"That's easy," he said, staring at her. "Because I don't even know who the hell you are."

28

A week after Cam requested it, the interoffice mail brought her a printout of Helen's long distance calls. It went on for fifteen pages, listing every number dialed from her extension over the last six months, but identifying it only by the city and state called. She wished she could ask Helen to pick out her call to Gloria's friend, but she couldn't think of a cover story that wouldn't arouse her suspicions.

Laboriously she went through each listing herself, extracting the names from the reverse directory then running a database search on each one. Some turned out to be clients, quickly eliminated, and others were court reporters and offset printers and messenger services, which she also crossed off. She hit on one likely prospect, a woman in Virginia named Doris Palumbo, but when she dialed the number, a recording announced that the number was no longer in service.

It was nearly noon by the time she finished. Half a day wasted in futile pursuit. She sank back in her chair and stared at her computer in glowering frustration. This was where her much-vaunted computer-tracking skills had brought her. Nowhere. What a useless piece of equipment. She'd like to call office services and have them cart it away to the scrap heap where it belonged. Except that they wouldn't. They'd assign it to one of the new lawyers arriving on board next month. Old computers never died in this law firm; they just got passed to someone lower in the pecking order.

Cam sat up straight. *Gloria's computer.* The computer that sat for weeks by Helen's desk. The one that Gloria must have used to compose all of her meticulous correspondence. The one with the hard disk she must have saved it to.

* * *

At ten o'clock that night Cam emerged from the stairwell on the fiftieth floor. Emergency lights marked the corners of the corridors, but everything else was in darkness. She stood and listened. The only sound was the hum of the computers, a whooshing sound like the ventilator on a coma patient. She crept along the row of offices and stopped beside each closed door and held her breath to listen for voices, snores, the rustle of turning pages. There was nothing.

She opened her briefcase at the secretarial station outside Clifford Austin's office. It had taken her two hours that afternoon, even with Joe Healy coaching her over the phone, but at last she'd hacked into the firm's equipment inventory files and traced Gloria Lipton's old computer to its new location—here, logically enough, at the desk of Austin's new secretary.

She took out a flashlight and switched it on. The CPU tower was on the floor under the desk, and she crawled behind it and shone the light on the rear panel until she found the serial number. Yes, a match. She rose up to the keyboard and switched on the monitor, and as the eerie green glow lit the darkness, she brought up the directory of the hard drive. None of the files showed a date of creation before February 20, which meant that all of Gloria's files had been deleted.

She shut down the computer and took out the list of instructions Joe had e-mailed her. First, disconnect the power cable. Done. She turned the CPU around and with the flashlight clamped under her chin and a Phillips screwdriver in her hand, she opened the PC case. She studied Joe's e-mail again, then disconnected the data and power cables, unscrewed the mounting brackets, and slid out the hard drive.

She put the CPU back into place and plugged in the power cable, although it was pointless. By nine o'clock the next morning, Austin's secretary would discover that her hard drive was missing, and everyone would assume the worst. Clifford Austin was not only a big-time trial lawyer, he was chairman of the firm. They'd suspect theft of the firm's financial information, or maybe his confidential client files or his litigation strategies. The police would be called; fingerprints would be lifted.

Cam put the hard drive into her briefcase, added the flashlight and screwdriver, then pulled off her surgical gloves and tossed them in, too.

* * *

She took the expressway north and west out of the city to the all-night Denny's that squatted beside the Valley Forge off-ramp. The Grateful Dead van was parked in the back, and Cam parked beside it and walked around to the front of the restaurant. Through the plate-glass window she spotted Joe at a booth with a few other kids hunched over their coffee and cigarettes. She tapped on the glass, and he looked up with a grin and came outside.

"Mission accomplished?"

"So far," she said.

He went to his van, and as he opened the rear doors, a car pulled into the lot and caught them with the full blast of its high beams. They both turned and ducked against the glare like a pair of escaping felons, a boy breaking curfew, a woman breaking a dozen other laws. But the headlights passed, darkness returned, and Cam handed over the hard drive.

"It'll be a while before I get to this," Joe said. "I got a shitload of backlog."

He watched her expectantly, waiting for her usual insistence on overnight turnaround, ready to do the little dance they always did until they reached some kind of terms. But he didn't know what she'd handed him tonight; he didn't realize this wasn't the usual assignment; he didn't understand that a week or two was nothing after almost fourteen years.

"Fine," she said.

The following Friday she was in her office in Wilmington writing thank-you notes on embossed correspondence cards to everyone who'd hosted a coffee or tea or cocktails for the campaign over the past few weeks. The rules were clear: no form letters allowed, and not even typewritten notes. Elegant handwritten cards were required, as if she were a well-bred woman of society and not an overeducated piece of trailer trash.

The phone rang, and she answered it before her nominal Wilmington secretary could preempt her.

"Campbell?" It was Cliff Austin's voice, and a jolt of guilty terror shot through her. "Could you join us for a short meeting?"

"Uh—okay. If I leave now, I should be there by—"

"Look at your phone display. I'm right down the hall."

She couldn't remember when Austin had last visited the Wilmington office. As she walked down the corridor to the large conference room, she wondered how she'd been found out. Not through fingerprints, and there wasn't enough time to have DNA results on any hair or skin cells she might have left behind, if they even did that for a property crime. What then? Were there hidden cameras somewhere? Or was it a simple matter of checking the sign-out logs at the security desk in the lobby? Could she have been the only employee on the premises at the time? Impossible—a major law firm never shut down; there was always somebody working somewhere.

She opened the conference room and was momentarily blinded by the sunlight streaming through the wall of glass overlooking Rodney Square. The conference rooms weren't windowless here the way they were in Philadelphia. Here she could see everything. The first thing she saw was Cliff Austin at the head of the table.

"Good morning, Campbell."

"Good morning," she said carefully.

" 'Morning, sweetheart."

Her head swiveled to Doug at the far end of the table, and beside him, Nathan Vance.

"What a surprise," she said, stunned.

Doug laughed.

No, this made no sense. No matter what the state of their marriage, he wouldn't laugh at a development like this. It would be devastating to the campaign for his wife to be arrested for industrial espionage or whatever it was that she'd done.

"Please have a seat," Austin said.

Cam circled the table to escape the glaring wall of light and took a chair midway down. This was the same conference room where she'd worked late one night last summer, the night that Doug brought her dinner and told her about Caesar Rodney's eighty mile ride through a thunderstorm to sign the Declaration of Independence. Recently she'd read that the legend wasn't quite true: Rodney actually traveled in a covered carriage.

"Doug's been filling us in on the assignment you handled for Senator Ramsay last winter," Austin said.

Cam looked at him in an uncomprehending daze.

"A representation which makes you uniquely qualified to take on the next phase."

"The next phase?"

He picked up a stapled sheaf of papers. "This is a petition for custody that was filed Wednesday in the Family Court of the State of Delaware for New Castle County, captioned 'Steven A. Patterson, Petitioner, versus James Ashton Ramsay, Jr., and wife, respondents.' We've been retained to represent the respondents in this matter. Or more to the point"—he looked up—"you have."

Cam stared at him. She'd come into this room expecting to be accused of a crime. This was worse.

"It's a great honor, as well as a great opportunity," Austin said. "For you and the firm. I'm very pleased, Campbell."

Any associate would kill to hear words like that from the head of the firm. "Who filed the petition?" Cam asked.

"Bruce Benjamin."

"Oh." She felt a spurt of relief. "Then I can't possibly handle this. Benjamin's way out of my league."

"Not true. He's not even a family law specialist, as you are. And you'll have all the resources of your department. There's no way Benjamin can outgun Jackson, Rieders."

"Yes, but when it comes down to the wire, it'll only be me and Benjamin. I can't do it. Not against Benjamin. And not with a U.S. senator for a client."

Austin frowned and looked to the foot of the table.

"Cam," Doug said.

After a beat, she turned toward him.

"Ash requested this as a personal favor."

She gazed at him and thought, *I don't know this man.* He wasn't the same man who brought her dinner that night and walked her to the hotel. That man no longer existed. Maybe he never existed. She saw in him what she wanted to see that night, and conjured up the rest.

"Cam," he said, waiting.

"Ramsay can have any lawyer he wants," she said. "What difference does it make whether it's me or not?"

"Come on." Doug's tone made an instant leap to impatience. "You're the only one Trey will have anything to do with. You know that. And that makes you the only one who can keep him under control. The last thing Ash wants is a replay of what happened in the criminal case last month."

The perfect sense of it took her breath away. She'd coached Trey on his testimony, and she'd coached Steve on his legal strategy, and now the two events had fused and backfired on her.

"But that's exactly why I can't get involved," she said. "Trey and I have become friends. I'd feel like I was double-crossing him if I took the other side."

"He's a kid," Doug said, disgusted. "A mixed-up punk kid who doesn't have a clue what's best for him. And neither do you, I might add."

"I don't agree," she said. "And I won't do it."

His eyes flickered over her with undisguised distaste. "Cliff? Would you mind giving us a minute?"

"Certainly."

Austin rose stiffly from the table. Cam glanced at Nathan, expecting him to get up and follow, but he stayed where he was. When the door closed, Doug tilted back in his chair and studied the ceiling. It was Nathan who leaned forward to speak.

"Here's the deal, Cam. For whatever reason, Ramsay's got himself in a stew over this thing. He wants you to handle it. And he wants it bad enough to do us a significant favor in return."

"What more could he possibly do?"

"He could help us out with a piece of legislation some of our potential contributors are interested in."

"Tort reform?" she guessed.

Nathan nodded. "Bottom line, Cam. You handle this case for Ramsay, he gives the contributors what they want, and they give us what we want."

"And what exactly is that?"

"A million dollars."

Her eyes flared wide before she laughed. "And here I was afraid I'd never amount to much as a lawyer. It turns out I'm worth a million dollars! Who'da thunk, huh, Nathan? I must be like the dream team all by myself."

"Cut it out," Doug said as he came up straight in his chair. "We're talking one case, Cam. A minor nuisance at most. Versus a million dollars. You hear me? A million dollars is riding on this. My whole future is riding on this. I don't think it's too much to ask you to do this one thing."

"But I do," she said quietly.

"Goddamn it." He slammed his hand on the table. "Do you know how little you've contributed to this campaign? Next to nothing, that's what. No wait—" He held up his hand. "I take that back. Thanks to you we get to live with the constant fear that your porno pics are going to show up in next month's *Penthouse*."

Cam glanced at Nathan, but when his expression didn't change, she turned accusingly to Doug. "You told him?"

"Hey," Nathan said lightly. "What kind of chairman would I be if I didn't know all the bad stuff? He had to tell me."

"Oh, of course." She nodded. "He had to. I wonder, though—has he told you all the bad stuff? For example, did he mention he's fucking Gillian?"

Nathan shot a look at Doug, whose face said everything until he buried it into his hands.

"Jesus!" Nathan moaned.

"It's her fault," Doug muttered from behind his hands. "If she gave me even an ounce of encouragement—God, Cam, sometimes you act like you don't even like me anymore."

"Oh, is that all you're looking for? Someone to like you? Here I thought it was someone to worship the ground you walk on."

Nathan reeled to his feet. "Okay, stop it right there, both of you, before you say something really awful."

But there was nothing left to say. Cam gazed around the room, at the windows looking out to the statue of Caesar Rodney, at the long oval table that was stacked that night with a thousand pages of paper and a hundred volumes of case reporters, at the light switch on the wall Doug hit by mistake to send her into darkness. The room was in the stark light of day now, and she knew that it was over, here in the same room where it began.

"Okay, listen to me." Nathan thrust his hands in his pockets and rocked on the balls of his feet. "We're going to chalk this all up to campaign stress. It's only thirty-two days to the primary, eighty to the general. We're getting down to the wire now, and we're all a little edgy. But we're going to pull together, and we're going to get through this."

"Not without the ALJA money, we're not," Doug said.

Cam stared at him. It was impossible to believe he was the same man she met that night. But she knew he had to be thinking the same of her, and she knew that he wasn't wrong, either.

"All right, I'll do it," she said, her voice as bitter as his. "I'll do this one thing. But that's all. And eighty days from now, it's over. We're over."

"Deal," Doug said.

"Wait. Stop it, both of you." Nathan locked his fingers over the top of his head. "You two are the most important people in the world to me, and I won't stand by and watch you drive yourselves apart in the heat of the moment like this. So you listen to me, 'cause here's how it's going down." He dropped his hands and pointed a finger at Cam. "You're going to handle this case and do your usual bang-up job. Hear me?" He turned and pointed at Doug. "And you're going to keep your eyes on the prize and your hands off the help. You got that?"

Doug stared at the table with his face burning hot.

"As for me," Nathan said, "I'll fix it so that you never see that girl again. Then after the election I'll book you two a nice little trip to the islands, and you can relax and take a long look at each other and see where you stand. But not before. Okay? Are we all on the same page here?"

Doug got to his feet looking humbled and chagrined. "Thanks, Nathan," he said thickly, and wrapped him in a bear hug. "You're a good friend."

They turned together and looked at Cam, and she looked back, but only at Nathan. He was her only friend, and she couldn't bear to lose him today, too. He held out his hand, and she rose from the table and went into his arms. After a moment he stepped back and pulled Doug into his place in the embrace.

"I'm sorry, Cam."

"Yeah," she said. "Me, too."

On the way home that night she stopped at the phone booth at the gas station and waited with her heart thudding in triple time to the rings of the telephone until he answered it.

"It's me," she said.

The line went silent, but not dead. She could picture him listening with his teeth clenched and his knuckles white where they gripped the phone.

"I guess Benjamin told you."

Still silence.

"Steve, I didn't have any choice."

She waited for him to argue with her about the choices she had, but he wasn't going to give her even that much.

"Trey's working tomorrow," she said, "and Doug's going out of town. If you park on Chaboullaird, you can cut through the woods and no one will see you."

She hung up.

* * *

A flurry of meetings, a two-hour conference call with Ramsay patched in from Bora Bora, a final handshake over dinner at Morton's, and the deal was done.

Meredith ordered extra print runs of campaign posters, bumper stickers, buttons, yard signs, and T-shirts. She doubled the size of the phone bank at campaign headquarters and added three more paid staffers. She paid the pollster the retainer he demanded before he'd schedule the first of his telephone surveys. She scheduled a sweep of border-to-border appearances, a factory opening in Milford, a rally at the university, a Hall and Oates concert at the stadium. She ordered final cuts of the radio and TV spots and bought air time in both the Philadelphia and Baltimore markets—an unprecedented move for a congressional campaign in Delaware, but no one ever had this kind of money to play with before. All of the ads ended with a sonorous voiceover by James Earl Jones: *Doug Alexander. He'll get America to work again.*

When the check arrived the last week of August—or rather, the checks; there was a nice thick packet of them—she paid all the bills and still had enough left over to give herself a raise.

29

Cam arrived at Family Court and presented her courthouse ID to the guard. "Conference with Judge Miller," she said, and he checked a list and waved her through. She rode up to the third floor and announced her name a second time, then took a seat in the waiting area.

A dozen other people were also waiting there. One or two were recognizable as lawyers, but the rest were mostly poor and mostly black and must have been parties or witnesses to some proceeding or another—divorce, neglect, nonsupport, abuse. A cross section of almost everything that could go wrong inside a family was presented here.

Bruce Benjamin stepped off the elevator and announced himself at the window, then swept the room with his eyes before he stationed himself against the wall. He must have recognized her, but ignored her anyway, because that was what big-time lawyers did to junior associates. It was **her** job to get up and approach him.

" 'Morning, Mr. Benjamin. Cam Alexander."

He extended his hand and nothing else.

She took up position beside him and wondered how much he knew. Did he know that she'd violated the rules of professional conduct and spoken to his client half a dozen times since the case began? That his client had been violating the restraining order and meeting his son once or twice a week for the past four weeks? And that she'd arranged it for him?

No, Benjamin didn't know anything, she could tell by his indifference to her. Besides, Steve was too much like her; he didn't know whom to trust, so he trusted nobody.

The judge's bailiff came out and called their names, and they followed him through the security door and down a corridor to chambers. Judge Miller rose from behind his desk and gave them each a handshake and nervous smile.

"Patterson versus Ramsay," he said, settling into his chair with a heavy sigh. He was a round-faced man with little round glasses and a big round body. Until recently he'd maintained a struggling private practice in Newark, but now, thanks to Governor Davis, he had a twelve-year appointment and a small but guaranteed salary. All of the Family Court judges had been named either by Davis or his opposition predecessor; there was no way to draw a politically neutral judge in this forum.

"I have to confess I've never had one of these," he said, fingering the case file. "A petition for custody filed by a nonparent against the parents. Then it turns out the nonparent is really the parent, and the parents are the nonparents. It's all out of order, isn't it?"

"Not in the eyes of the law," Cam said.

"No. Not there." He darted a hopeful look from one lawyer to the other. "I don't suppose there's any chance of working out an agreement? Joint custody or something?"

"None," Cam said at the same time that Benjamin did.

"Then I suppose we have some issues to address here—"

"Judge, before we begin . . ." Benjamin leaned forward in his chair. His muscles were tensed for attack, and his voice was pitched at courtroom volume. "There's a very serious matter I must bring to the Court's attention."

"What's that?"

"Upon the filing of the petition, an injunction automatically issued against both parties, forbidding"—Benjamin hit that word hard—"the removal of the minor from this jurisdiction."

"Yes?"

"We have information that the respondents are about to remove the child to the state of Connecticut. If they already haven't."

The judge looked at Cam.

She spread her hands. "I'm afraid I'm at a loss. Perhaps if Mr. Benjamin could elaborate . . . ?"

Tersely he said, "The Ramsays have enrolled the boy in boarding school in Connecticut. Judge, this is a clear violation of the automatic injunction, and I demand that sanctions be imposed and that the boy be returned to this jurisdiction immediately."

"I don't know where Mr. Benjamin could have gotten such an

idea," Cam said, eyes wide. "The child is enrolled in the Tower Hill School here in Wilmington, just as he has been every year since kindergarten. In fact"—she looked at her watch—"he should be in third period English right now."

Benjamin raised his chin and looked at her through narrowed eyes. Since he didn't know where his client's information came from, he couldn't know that it was half a week out of date.

"If you don't believe me, call the school and confirm," she said. "Please. I urge you to."

Benjamin pulled his lips tight as a couple of emotions battled in him. He'd come in here and fired his missile only to have it intercepted by hers. A defeat. But his client would be well pleased at the news. A victory. "Apparently my information was incorrect, Judge," he said finally. "I apologize."

"No harm," Cam said.

The judge paged through the file again. "I have here respondents' motion to dismiss the petition?"

Her turn to fire. "Your Honor, you said it yourself: this isn't the typical case. This isn't a dispute between divorcing parents who each have an equal claim to the child. This is a dispute between parents in an intact marriage on the one hand, and a complete stranger on the other."

"Stranger?" Benjamin said with a sneer.

"In the eyes of the law. Judge, imagine yourself and your wife being suddenly sued by an outsider demanding custody of your children." She'd done her homework here; Miller had three children at home. "Why should you have to defend yourselves against such an attack on the strength of nothing but a barefaced petition for custody?"

Benjamin countered: "The statute clearly permits the award of custody to a person other than a parent if it's not in the best interests of the child to remain with the parents. And in that regard—"

He'd done his homework, too. He handed over the transcript of Trey's testimony at the criminal trial; Senator Ramsay's calendar for the past year demonstrating how little time he'd spent at home; Trey's report card from last year, with comments suggesting academic underachievement and disciplinary problems; and an affidavit from the local manager of the Gap, attesting to his apprehension of Trey in the act of shoplifting last June. This information strongly suggested problems in the minor's adjustment to his home, school, and community within the meaning of the statute. At a minimum, it established grounds for a full evidentiary hearing at which the Court could determine where the minor's best interests lay.

"Any objection to my receipt and consideration of this information?" the judge asked Cam.

She was still puzzling over the store manager's affidavit. She was the one who'd blurted out the shoplifting episode to Steve, but the details of when and where it happened could only have come from Trey. The same was true of his report card.

"No objection," she said.

Miller looked relieved to avoid a skirmish on this issue, at least. Hesitantly he denied her motion, pending a home evaluation by a court-appointed expert to determine whether it was in the child's best interests to be removed from respondents' custody. If it was, he would proceed to hear Mr. Patterson's petition; if it was not, then the motion to dismiss would be granted.

The judge scribbled out his order: the home evaluation to be completed within the next twenty days; copies of the report to be furnished to the court and both parties; with a hearing to commence thereafter, beginning October 5.

At the end of the day Cam reached Ramsay in Washington and made her report. "That's fine, just fine," he said. "You've done good work, Campbell, like we knew you would."

He was just back from his month in the South Pacific, and his mood was mellow. It was very different from his mood last week during their transpacific argument about where Trey would start school. Ramsay didn't see the problem—parents sent their sons to prep school all the time—hell, he'd gone himself—and besides, the boy was out of control, and this school could deal with that sort of thing, certainly a lot better than Margo and Jesse could. But in the end Cam prevailed. Trey's name was withdrawn from the roster of the school in Connecticut, and this morning Jesse delivered both Trey and the tuition check to Tower Hill.

It was, Cam thought, the only real accomplishment of her entire career in antifamily law.

Gary Pfeiffer felt an enormous sense of accomplishment as he headed for the shore at the end of the week. Before the August recess, S.4 had been marching resolutely toward a Senate vote.

The committee reports were in: the bill was assigned a calendar number; floor action was scheduled. The next inexorable steps: debate, vote, and referral to the House. But this week the march of S.4 was inexplicably halted, a development explained only by a passing mention in the *Roll Call* that the bill was being held at the request of a member.

He'd worked feverishly for those few words. It took hundreds of phone calls, doling out favors here, exerting pressure there, striking deals and trade-offs so complex and attenuated he could have used a flow chart to map them all out. But at last it was done. The money was raised and delivered, and Ash Ramsay had so far kept his word.

That was the fly in the ointment, of course, the wriggling little worry that left him with a sense of unease even amid the sense of accomplishment. Meredith Winters was right: an anonymous hold was better than a public vote in most respects, the principal one being that anyone who tried to trace ALJA's trail of money would run smack into the Senate's wall of anonymity. But it was worse than a public vote in other respects, the principal one being that Ramsay could renege at any moment.

But Gary was determined not to worry about that this weekend. He crossed the Bay Bridge at Annapolis with the sun on his neck and the wind in his hair, and when he touched ground on the other side, he felt a happy little kick just to be on the same peninsula as Rehoboth Beach. September after Labor Day was his favorite time at the shore. The noisy, clamoring families were packed up and gone, but the water was still warm, the sun was still hot, and there was a rich mellow languor in the air. And always, best of all, there was Derek.

He was waiting inside the front door, and they caught each other and clung together in the hall, kissing hungrily and spewing out laughter at the pure ecstasy of being together again.

"Miss me?"

"A little," Gary said. "Been good?"

"Of course." Derek stepped back with a twinkle in his eye. "You know I save all my badness for you."

He turned and, with a fetching little wiggle of his hips, led the way upstairs.

After dark they sat out on the walled terrace and watched the stars light up over the ocean. Faint shadows moved on the other side of the dunes, and they could hear the occasional soft drift of laughter, but they felt alone here inside their walls. Safe. They held hands between the chaises, and a cool salt breeze blew up off the water, bracing and clean.

"The neighbors were down this week," Derek said, nodding at the Shingle Style house next door. "Remember? The Westovers?"

Gary nodded and thought what a funny circular world he moved in. Apparently the architect who transformed that place was the same man whose lawsuit against Ash Ramsay led to the deal with Doug Alexander. Which meant that the fellow not only improved their view, he gave ALJA its victory over tort reform. Gary reached for his wineglass and lifted it in a silent toast to the unknown architect.

But after a moment the wind shifted, and again he felt that damned uneasiness. What would happen when the lawsuit was over? What if Ramsay won? What leverage would he have over him then?

"What's the matter?" Derek asked softly, squeezing his hand.

Gary smiled over at him. "Here with you? Not a thing in the world."

The doorbell chimed, and Derek pulled on his robe and went inside to answer it. When he returned, he was holding a package out at arm's length and eyeing it with comic wariness.

"Courier delivery from Eileen," he yelped. "Think it might be a letter bomb?"

"Doubt it," Gary said, putting his glass down. "That would require too much imagination."

Derek laughed and handed it over, and Gary read the hastily scrawled note paper-clipped to another envelope inside. *Gary, This arrived after you left. Thought it might be important. Love, E.*

Inside was the long overdue report on Campbell Alexander. Sometime back—July?—the investigators had reported "unexpected leads" that required additional time, not to mention money, to track down. He'd paid them and let it go. It hardly seemed important anymore. It was three months since the girl saw him at the fund-raiser; if she had any inclination to expose him, she would have done it before now.

Still, the idea was tantalizing, a congressional candidate's wife leading a double life. "Sorry, babe," he said to Derek as he got to his feet. "I need an hour."

"No problem. Gives me time to whip up something wonderful for dinner."

Gary took the package to his study, put his bare feet up on the desk and leaned back to read the report on the mysterious Mrs. Alexander.

First was a vital records report out of Lancaster County, confirming that the child born to Matthew and Alice Smith on March 13, 1968, was indeed a boy. Field interviews with members of the Smiths' missionary society established that the child went to the Philippines with his parents, traveling on his mother's passport, and was presumed to have died with them.

From there the file was transferred to Philadelphia, and a surveillance team engaged to observe the subject in Philadelphia and Wilmington and points in between. They observed her continuously from June 22 to June 26 without results, and sporadically thereafter, until the evening of August 6, when surveillance was terminated. On that date she entered a telephone booth on the lot of a service station; the number she dialed was observed telescopically, and the call was traced to yet another service station—Johnson's Sunoco, in Shawville, Pennsylvania.

The file was then transferred to Pittsburgh, where another team conducted additional research that was now believed to have established the subject's identity as follows: *Camille Nicole Johnson, aka Cammy Johnson, aka Cammy Smith, aka Campbell Smith, aka Campbell Smith Alexander. Born June 8, 1969*. A year younger than her official biography, Gary noted. That was something one didn't encounter often, a woman lying about her age in that direction. *Parents: Charles A. Johnson and Abigail Zodtner Johnson, married January 15, 1969*. A little premarital hanky-panky there, but what the hell, it was 1969, the era of Make Love, Not War. *One sibling: Charlene, born 1971. Father's occupation: Proprietor of Johnson's Sunoco, Shawville, Pennsylvania. Mother's occupation: Housewife, previously employed July 1966–January 1969 as clerk/typist with National Reconnaissance Office, Washington, D.C.*

Gary's eyes opened wide. NRO? The NRO was a black agency, so top-secret that its very existence wasn't revealed until 1992. It was a joint venture of the CIA and the Air Force, he recalled, formed in the early Sixties to run CORONA, the spy-in-the-sky satellite program.

He flipped ahead. School records, a D&B on Johnson's Sunoco, tax records, police records—He stopped on the police records. *Missing persons report filed November 5, 1984, by Charles A. Johnson. Daughter Camille missing since November 3. Age 15, 5'5", 115 pounds. No disposition noted. A second missing persons report filed November 8, 1984, also by Charles A. Johnson. Wife Abigail missing since November 6. Age 36, 5'5", 140 pounds. Disposition: Jurisdiction surrendered to FBI, CI Unit.*

Gary's feet hit the floor. "Holy Christ!" he yelled. CI was Counterintelligence, the FBI unit of domestic spycatchers.

"You call me?" Derek shouted.

"No sorry. Talking to myself."

"Well, just don't start answering."

Finally the file was transferred to Washington. *According to sources*—here was the reason for the long delay; these were probably back alley exchanges—*on November 5, 1984, a federal warrant was issued for the arrest of Abigail Zodtner Johnson on charges of espionage and conspiracy to commit espionage.* The next day she went missing, and she'd been at large ever since.

Sources would not reveal the nature of the alleged espionage, but did not deny that it might have involved enemy interception of an ejected CORONA satellite capsule.

A footnote: on January 11, 1969, a flotilla of U.S. Navy river patrol boats was sailing up the Mekong River on a mission to cut off Vietcong supply lines when it was fired upon by a large enemy force. Massive casualties were suffered, and the incident prompted much speculation, for there seemed no way the VC could have known of the flotilla's movements short of satellite surveillance photographs. However, an official investigation of the NRO was terminated without conclusion.

Gary closed the file and sat a long time in an unfocused gaze at the wall. Campbell Alexander, daughter of a Mata Hari? If he'd had this information ten days ago, he could have saved himself a million dollars. But no, it was better this way. Cleaner. He'd stopped S.4 legally, the democratic way.

But this information did give him the peace of mind that had so far eluded him, because there was no way the Alexander people would dare to double-cross him when they had a skeleton this size in their closet.

He locked the file in a drawer, and when Derek called him to dinner, he went to the table without a trace of uneasiness to mar their time together.

30

Delaware held its primary on Saturday, September 12, and Maryland on the following Tuesday, which made for a hellish workweek for Meredith Winters. It was a ninety-minute drive between Baltimore and Wilmington, and on Saturday she made the trip four times. A quick send-off for Doug Alexander at the start of the day, then back to Baltimore for a rally at the Inner Harbor. She returned to Wilmington for Marge Kenneally's concession speech that evening, then it was back to Maryland to attend Sutherland's speech to the Urban League.

But there was a hidden boon in the timing of Delaware's primary. It was the first election held since the President admitted his affair with That Woman, and pols and pundits across the country were watching closely in an effort to augur the post-Lewinsky fallout. The results were inconclusive on that point, of course, but it was enough for Meredith that the world was watching. Only thirty thousand votes were cast on the Party's ballot, but Doug took ninety-five percent of them, and by the end of the night she'd persuaded three editors to report it as a major landslide.

Tuesday was another hellish day, but at least she was able to spend all of it in Baltimore. By nine o'clock that night Sutherland was the projected winner, but his opponent bore old grudges and refused to concede until midnight. At twelve-fifteen the General delivered his victory speech to roars of acclamation, then shook hands all around with the staff and told them to enjoy the party without him; he was taking his wife home for a long autumn's nap.

Meredith headed home in a weary slump in the backseat of the limo, deeply exhausted and strangely unsatisfied. Another day, another victory, but what did it all mean anyway? Only that the stakes were notched up that much higher for November; only that she'd have to work even harder in the next two months than she had for the last eight. She was one of the youngest strategists in the business, but already she was too old for this life.

She rolled her head back against the upholstery with a sigh. It was the adrenaline withdrawal, that was all. Or maybe hormones. It was getting to be that time of month. Or, God, that time of life.

But, no. She knew perfectly well where these black thoughts were coming from. From a news item in the metro section last week, a three-paragraph report that former *Washington Post* reporter Dean McIverson was found dead in his home in Annandale next to an empty gallon jug of rubbing alcohol. He'd been out of the drunk tank for only a week.

The political repercussions were all to the good. Most people had forgotten last spring's flap over the alleged Pentagon leaks, and for those few who remembered, the manner of McIverson's death only underscored the fact that he was an irresponsible drunk. Nonetheless, his death weighed heavily on Meredith's mind. One day McIverson was the toast of Washington; the next, its refuse. All right, those days were thirty years apart, but she took little comfort in the chronology, because today everything happened at hyperspeed. Today Washington could chew you up and spit you out in a single news cycle.

She did have one comfort, though. For the last ten miles, Bret had been tailing her in his Corvette. They'd barely exchanged a word all day, but at the end of the evening they'd exchanged a glance, and that was all it took these days. A knowing look and they knew everything. She'd take him home and bundle him into bed and not come out for a week.

She woke at seven the next morning and spent an hour in wide-eyed contemplation of the ceiling. Bret slept peacefully beside her, the sleep of the innocent. He looked like a little boy lying there, his hand tucked under his face, his long lashes sweeping down over the curve of his cheek. Only twenty-four years old—the worst of his life still lay ahead of him. She hated to think what this town would do to him before it was over, how cruel the Beltway gossip would be by the time he was forty or fifty and had failed to live up to his father's legacy. It was a curse to be born to a father like General Phil Sutherland, but the bigger curse was that Bret would never see it as anything but a blessing.

Her heart welled up inside her, and she bent and touched her lips softly to his face.

He stirred and snuggled closer. "What are you doing awake?" he mumbled. "I thought we were sleeping in today."

"Sorry," she whispered, stroking his hair back from his forehead. "Go back to sleep."

"Not without you." He propped up on an elbow. "What's the matter?"

"I can't stop thinking about Dean McIverson."

"Oh." His face went solemn. "Are you thinking what I am? That it wasn't an accident?"

She nodded. "I don't care how drunk he was. If he knew enough to open a bottle of rubbing alcohol, he knew enough to realize it was going to kill him."

Bret took her hand in his. "He was seventy-some years old. His career ended thirty years ago, and his health was shot to hell. He had a right to check out if he wanted to."

"But what made him want to? The same thing that put him back in the drunk tank after ten years on the wagon. Me."

"You weren't exactly working alone, you know."

"Ah, yes," she said. "Strength in numbers. The absolution of running with a pack. The entire foundation of party politics."

"Come here," he said, and pulled her out of bed. "Come look out the window."

He opened the drapes, revealing her courtyard garden, the rooftops of her neighbors' houses, the trees still wearing the dauntless green of summer. "What am I looking at?" she asked.

He stood behind her and touched his fingers to her lids. "Close your eyes. You know which way you're facing? West. This is the view west. Over the Potomac, beyond the Beltway, all the way across Virginia to the Blue Ridge Mountains."

"That far, huh? And here I thought I paid too much for this house."

"Sssh. Listen. We're standing here on the top of the Blue Ridge Mountains. It's like we've got an angel's-eye view of the world. It's all blue mountains and green valleys, and look, see that silver ribbon winding through it? The Shenandoah River."

"Shenandoah," she repeated. The syllables were like a caress in her mouth.

"Those mountains beyond are the Massanutten. And beyond those are the Allegheny."

"And beyond that?"

His lips touched her neck. "The rest of the world."

She swayed back against him and tried to see it, the view west, away from the crowded seaboard cities and all their schemes and machinations and gossip and intrigues, and suddenly there was nothing but an amazing open expanse of land and trees and birds and sky. She took a deep breath and imagined the scent of pine and leaf mold and clean open air.

"Can you see it? How beautiful and wild it is?"

"Mmm," she murmured with a little smile, so transfixed that it was a moment before she felt his hands on her. Her eyes flashed open. "What do you think you're doing?"

"I'm showing the view how beautiful and wild we are."

"Bret, not here. The neighbors—"

"But we're not here," he whispered. "We're far away, on the edge of the world."

Her eyes fell shut as he entered her. He moved in her with long, slow strokes, and she could see the play of the sun on the slope of the mountains and the shadows of the clouds as they scuttled across the valley floor. Wild and beautiful, she thought. Two creatures mating in the forest. That was all they were, and all they ever had to be.

She came with a cry, a primeval wail that echoed through the mountains of her mind.

"Marry me."

They were lying entwined on the bed, half asleep, and her voice startled her in the stillness; the words escaped as reflexively as her cry only moments before.

"In a heartbeat," Bret said.

She took his hand and held it between her breasts. "This heartbeat?"

"This very one," he said, and pressed his lips to the pulse. "Today, if you want. Whenever."

"November fourth?"

He grinned. "It's a date."

She pulled his head up and kissed him.

"Kids?" he said after a minute.

"Maybe. If we hurry."

He yawned. "A little boy and a little girl."

She smiled. She already had all the little boy she needed in Bret. But maybe a little girl; maybe it wasn't too late. "We'll go away somewhere," she said dreamily.

"Anywhere."

"West. Maybe Denver." She stroked his hair. "We could live in the mountains. You could snowboard all day. And I'll be a print reporter again."

"Huh?"

"After we're married. Our new life together, away from Washington. Far away."

"Meredith . . ." He raised up on his elbow and looked down at her, alarmed. "We can't leave."

"After the election, I said."

"But after the election, Dad'll be in the Senate. He'll need me more than ever."

She looked past him to the window. A cold wind was shivering the treetops outside. "Of course," she said. "What was I thinking?"

He smiled with relief and lay back down. "I guess now we can tell him, huh?"

"No, not yet. Let's wait till after the election."

"Okay." He yawned again and settled in against her. "Will he ever be surprised."

"Will he ever."

She cradled his head to her breast as he drifted back into his sleep of the innocent.

Cam drove home Wednesday night and went straight to the garden. Every day a new surprise awaited her, but unlike the springtime surprises, these didn't come out of the ground. Last week she'd come home to find the folly wearing a smooth new coat of creamy white stucco. A new door had been hung, and new windows installed, and inside, the stairs had been rebuilt and the floors sanded and varnished. Today she came through the wisteria arbor and saw that the reflecting pool had been excavated.

It must have been a massive job, digging a rectangle forty feet by ten and hauling all the dirt away. There was no way Trey could have done it alone, even if he wasn't in school all day. Still, he would maintain the charade, just as she would. She'd call him and thank him and discuss the next phase, and he'd pass along whatever Steve told him to tell her. Neither of them would mention Steve's name. They never had, not since Longwood Gardens.

It was much like the charade she and Doug had been maintaining. They passed in the hall, careful not to touch but not to shrink away either; they treated each other with polite consideration; and they retired to separate rooms at night.

She sat on the stone bench and gazed down the length of the garden, over the future reflecting pool and past the borders where the purple asters and pink sedums were starting to bloom. By the time the first killing frost came in November, her garden restoration project would be done. She might never see another season unfold in this garden, but it would be done.

Dusk began to seep into the shadows, and she went in the house and heated some leftovers for dinner. Doug wouldn't be home tonight; he was doing a victory sweep south through the state then continuing on to Washington. Tonight the U.S. Chamber of Commerce was holding a reception in his honor, and tomorrow he had sessions on the Hill with the Party leadership and a meeting at national Party headquarters. His victory in the primary was opening doors everywhere for him, no matter that it was over a nominal opponent who raised no money and made no campaign appearances.

After dinner Cam sat down at the computer and plodded away some more at Gloria Lipton's hard drive. Joe Healy had delivered a diskette containing everything he was able to recover from it, but it was badly fragmented. Bits and pieces of documents appeared in a chaotic jumble: a paragraph from a legal pleading, an address block from a letter, an excerpt from a billing summary. Joe couldn't begin to put the pieces together, but Cam had been trying to, every spare moment she could find since the disk arrived.

Tonight she was sifting through the correspondence. It was no easy task to isolate Cliff Austin's business letters and memos from Gloria's private correspondence, since her personal letters tended to be as formal as his letters to opposing counsel. And often more harsh. Tonight Cam stumbled over a piece of a letter that read, *It does you no credit to wallow in self-pity this way, Joan. You made your bed, you know*. And then there was Gloria's civic-minded correspondence: letters that scolded judges for their wrongheaded rulings, or questioned the motives behind legislators' votes, or criticized the mayor, the governor, even the President. *How dare you?* she'd written to one unidentified official. *Perhaps you've forgotten your own history, but others have not, and you can't expect us to remain silent forever.*

Cam remembered the joke someone made at Gloria's memorial service, about the advice she'd have for a certain congressional candidate if she were still alive. It made her wonder which way Gloria's scolding might have gone. *How dare you?* to Doug, or *You made your bed* to Cam?

She started again in the morning at her computer in Philadelphia. Slowly she scrolled through the diskette, past stern memos to partners about collecting their receivables and crisp thank-you notes for Christmas gifts. She came to an address block for Mrs. Joan Truesdale in Devonshire, Bermuda, and wondered if this might be the same Joan who was wallowing in self-pity. She ran a database search, then called directory assistance in Bermuda, but both attempts failed.

She opened her desk drawer and gazed down at the black-and-white photograph, Gloria on one end and her mother on the other and two unnamed women in between. It was a long shot that one might be Joan Truesdale, and even longer that she might know the whereabouts of her old friend Abby, but at the moment it was as close as Cam could get. She composed a letter to Joan Truesdale, asking her to call her to discuss matters pertaining to Gloria's death. She leaned back and studied the letter on screen for a moment, then sat up and inserted a line about unclaimed funds in Gloria's estate, just in case this was the same Joan who was wallowing in self-pity.

After the letter was stamped and in the mail, she went back to Joe's diskette and waded through one of Cliff Austin's long memos on productivity and inefficiency. It almost made her laugh as she sat there being unproductive in the most inefficient way possible. But then, in the middle of the memo, a block of text appeared that seemed once again to come from Gloria's personal correspondence. *After all, it's not like any of us has gotten the life we thought we would in those days. Look at poor Doris, having to raise her children alone, and now doing it all over again with her grandchildren. But you never hear a word of complaint from her.*

Doris. Cam opened another drawer and pulled out the listing of Helen's long distance calls. She'd written the names in the margins next to the numbers, and there it was—*Doris Palumbo*—with an exchange in Staunton, Virginia.

Another long shot, but she dialed the number anyway, and when a recording announced that it was no longer in service, she remembered that she'd tried it before and given up. This time she called the business office of the local telephone company.

"Hi, I've been trying to get through to this number, but they say it's no longer in service. Has she moved or changed her number or what?"

"That account has been closed."

"Really? I mean, why would Mrs. Palumbo do that? Go without phone service, I mean?"

"The account was closed by her executor."

"She's *dead*?"

"I really can't say."

Cam tried another computer search, but the probate records of Augusta County were not available online. She located the name and number of the local newspaper in Staunton, then called and asked for the morgue.

"Hi, I'm trying to find an obituary of someone who died recently in your town. Do you have that information in a searchable format?"

"Yeah," the woman said. "If you include hand-searching, 'cause that's what I have to do. But if you give me the date of death, I can probably find it for you in a day or two."

"I don't know the precise date. Sometime in the last"—Cam stopped and looked at the date of Helen's call—"six or seven months?" An incredulous laugh came over the line, but Cam went on: "Her name was Doris Palumbo. She resided at 3703 East—"

"Wait. Did you say Doris Palumbo?"

"Yes?"

"Hey, I don't even have to look that one up. I remember it clear as day. The poor woman was killed out on the interstate last winter."

"An auto accident?"

"No, she was raped on the roadside and her throat slit from ear to ear. It was the most awful thing you ever heard of. And they still haven't found out who did it."

A chill spread through Cam, from her hand on the phone down to her feet on the floor.

"Hello? You still there?"

"Yes."

"So you want me to pull that obit for you?"

"Yes, thanks. And could you also pull all the news stories about the murder? And could you fax it all to me?"

There was a delay while the cost was estimated and payment arranged, but by the end of the day Cam had a thick stack of articles reporting the heinous rape-murder of Doris Palumbo. The Weigh Station Murder, the newspaper dubbed it.

Late in the evening of March 13 a state trooper cruising the interstate noticed a car parked in a closed weigh station. He pulled over and discovered three small children inside the car, while on the ground outside lay the body of Doris Palumbo, age fifty-one. The cause of death was massive hemorrhage resulting from a single laceration of her neck. Seminal fluid was collected from the body, along with hair and fiber evidence. But without witnesses, fingerprints, or the murder weapon, the police had no suspects and no other leads to pursue.

The articles included a grainy photograph of a middle-aged woman with dark hair and full, fleshy cheeks. Cam slid the memorial program out of her desk and looked at the round-faced brunette standing next to Gloria. It was the same woman.

Two identical murders of two fifty-one-year-old women who both worked for the same agency thirty years ago. The same agency that her mother worked for.

No, don't panic, stay calm. Gloria and Doris had remained friends for thirty years. They must have had connections and experiences that had nothing to do with the NRO in the late Sixties. Maybe they'd dated the same psycho a while back, and he stalked and killed them both. Maybe one of them got tangled up in something and confided in the other, and the killer took them both out. There were dozens of possible links between the two women.

But at the moment, the only link was Cam.

She couldn't be that link.

That night, after the office was dark and quiet, she put on a pair of surgical gloves and addressed a manila envelope to the reporter at the *Philadelphia Inquirer* whose byline was on all the stories about the Center City Secretary case. She took the Virginia Weigh Station Murder stories, cut off the fax footprints from the top of each page, photocopied them and put the clean copies into the envelope, then slid the envelope into a file folder. She left the building with the folder at her side and paused briefly at the corner to deposit the envelope into the mailbox before she walked on.

It took a week for the story to break, but it made the headline: CENTER CITY SECRETARY CASE LINKED TO VIRGINIA MURDER.

The parallels between the two cases were laid out in a chart on page five. Gloria Lipton, single, age fifty-one, occupation secretary. Doris Palumbo, divorced, age fifty-one, occupation former secretary. Gloria Lipton died February 20. Doris Palumbo died March 13. Gloria Lipton's autopsy findings: blunt-force trauma to the rear of the cranium; forcible rape; and hemorrhage of the carotid artery resulting from a single laceration of the neck. Doris Palumbo's autopsy findings: the same. Presumed murder weapon in both cases: a carving knife. Status of both investigations: open.

But the biggest link wasn't listed in the chart; it appeared instead in the lead paragraph of the story. The two women whose lives and deaths were so similar had been friends for thirty years. In fact, according to the family of Doris Palumbo, they'd vacationed together in Reno, Nevada, only last July.

The same subject claimed Monday's headline, with a report that preliminary crime lab results suggested a match between the trace evidence found on both victims.

On Tuesday the story moved to the airwaves. In a televised news conference the mayor, flanked by the district attorney and the police commissioner, announced that the murder of Gloria Lipton was no longer considered to have been a random street crime. Rather, her killer was now believed to have come to Philadelphia in deliberate pursuit of Miss Lipton; he was probably known to her; and he was presumed to have left the jurisdiction after committing this crime. The subtext of the mayor's speech: ladies, it's once again safe to walk the streets of Center City.

On Wednesday the FBI announced the formation of a task force consisting of state and local law enforcement officers from both Pennsylvania and Virginia, to be coordinated by VICAP, the FBI's Violent Criminal Apprehension Program. On Thursday a twelve-man delegation of the task force boarded a plane to Reno, Nevada, on a mission to retrace the women's steps during their vacation last year. Meanwhile, VICAP was searching its database, looking for similar patterns in any other unsolved murders anywhere in the United States.

Trey was on the back porch when Cam arrived home on Friday, and he closed his sketchbook and came bounding down the steps to meet her. "Come on," he said, his cheeks flushed with excitement. "You gotta see this."

She put her briefcase down and followed him through the arbor and into the garden. He must have come straight from school, because he was still in his white shirt and khakis. His hair had grown out to a uniform two-inch length, and he almost looked the part of a conservative prep school boy, but for the gold stud winking in his earlobe. He'd shot up over the summer, and four months of hard physical labor in her garden had broadened his shoulders and corded his arms with muscles. His adolescent awkwardness was almost gone. It was as if he'd suddenly grown into his skin and everything was finally starting to fit right. He was fourteen now, Cam remembered, on the brink of manhood.

He turned around with a flourish when they reached the pool. Only yesterday its floor was covered with wooden two-by-fours and metal reinforcing rods. Today it was covered with a smooth, hard surface, tinted black to reflect the light.

"Oh," Cam said, stopping at the edge. "They poured the concrete."

"It's gunite," he said. "And it's sprayed, not poured."

"Oh, right."

"It needs to cure for a few days, but then we can fill it up, and all you have to do is flip a switch in the garage to turn the circulating pump on."

There was an October chill in the air tonight, and she hugged her elbows as she stood and gazed out over the length of the pool, then at the perennial borders that flanked it. Clumps of dead foliage were starting to spill over the edges, and the blooms that remained were fading fast. The season was almost over.

"Cam?" Trey was watching her with a shadow in his eyes. "Is something wrong?"

"No! It's beautiful. It's so beautiful I'm speechless."

They walked along the length of the pool while Trey pointed

out the features—the bluestone coping around the sides, the fill pipe on one side, the drain pipe on the bottom.

"C'mere. You gotta see this." He pulled her across the lawn to the folly and opened the door to usher her inside.

"Oh!" She clapped her hands to her face. The interior walls were freshly plastered and whitewashed, and standing by the window was a little round table with two bistro chairs tucked under it. It looked like a French café. She turned slowly in the tiny room. All of Trey's sketches and watercolors had been framed and rehung on the walls, but not, she was sure, by Trey.

"I hate to think I almost tore this place down."

"Good thing I talked you out of it."

"Good thing," she agreed. "How's it look upstairs?" She climbed up a few rungs on the spiral staircase and stuck her head through the opening. The walls were plastered and whitewashed here, too, and there was a futon mattress spread out on the floor.

"I hope you don't mind," Trey said. "I like to hang out here sometimes. You know, to read and stuff?"

"Of course I don't mind. It's a perfect hideout." She came down and went to the doorway to gaze out over the garden. "Everything's perfect. I can't believe it. I never thought this much would get done in one summer. Of course, it never would have—not without your help."

Trey pulled out a chair at the café table and flopped down in a contented sprawl.

"I'm so glad you stopped by today," she said. "This is a wonderful surprise."

He looked at her strangely. "But you asked me to come over today. Didn't you?"

"What?"

"You called? At least I got a message that you did. So you could talk to me about the case?"

"Oh." Her expression went flat. "Right."

It was the reason Ramsay had hired her. The boy would listen to her, he said, which meant it was her job to talk—specifically to talk up Ash and Margo and all the advantages of Trey's home life, to make sure he presented a good front to the evaluating psychologist and later to the judge if it came to that, to maintain the party line. It was the only reason Ramsay had hired her, and she'd taken a perverse, vengeful pleasure in not doing it. She'd done everything else necessary to prepare for the hearing: she studied the psychologists' reports and researched the case law; she subpoenaed witnesses; she prepared an accordion folder full of argument points and cross-examination outlines. But not once had she discussed the case with Trey.

She sat down across from him and after a moment said, "Can you keep a secret?"

He gave her a pained look.

"Sorry. We already established that, didn't we? Well, this one's about me. When I was fifteen, just a little older than you, I ran away from home."

"Oh?" He put on an expression of polite but mild interest. His idea of running away was storming out of the house, spending the night at a buddy's and coming home the next day in a sulk. He couldn't imagine the other kind, the kind where you ended up hustling on street corners and overdosing in alleys.

"I was at that crossroads age, you know?" she said. "That age when anything is possible, and you might go one way, but you might just as easily go the other? About the age you're at now."

Their eyes touched briefly before he glanced away.

"Bad things can happen at that age, and most of them you can't control. But the worst thing that can happen is if you make the wrong turn at that crossroads, and that part's all up to you. Something awful could happen in your life, but you're the one who decides where you go with it."

She picked up his hand where it lay on the table. "I don't know what's going to happen in this case, Trey. Maybe it'll end up the way you want, but maybe it won't. But whichever way it goes—" She felt a choke rising in her throat, and she squeezed his hand while she forced it down. "—it would break my heart to see you go hard and bitter over how this case turns out."

"You don't have to worry about me," he said, swallowing hard. "Because I don't care how it turns out."

"Trey, you don't have to pretend with—"

"No, I mean it. I don't care what that judge decides. Either way, I'm taking off with Steve when it's over. Legal or not, it's all the same to me."

Her eyes went wide. Was that Steve's plan? To do it legally until he lost and then do it anyway?

"No, don't tell me," she said sharply. "Don't say another word."

He sat back, startled by the harshness in her voice.

"Trey, I want us to be able to talk, but see, if I know certain things, I might have an obligation—"

"To tell them what I said."

"I'm sorry—"

"No, I understand."

"How?" she said sadly. "I barely get it myself."

"Hey—" He shrugged. "I grew up in the house of a U.S. senator. I know all about deals and compromises and what he calls temporary alliances. You know what one of his favorite lines is? You gotta dance with the devil if he's the one who hired the band. Believe me, this was all dinner table talk at my house."

He looked at his watch and suddenly scraped his chair back. "I better take off. But I'll see you tomorrow morning, okay?"

She nodded.

He hesitated at the door. "Cam, about whatever happened when you were fifteen? You shouldn't feel so bad about it. I mean, you were just a kid, right?"

He turned and took off across the garden.

How can you understand that? she thought, watching him go. *I don't even get it myself.*

After a few minutes she climbed the spiral stairs and lay down on the futon. It was the same futon she'd peered at through the windows of the house on Lake Drive last February. Steve must have reclaimed it from the Westovers, and he'd brought it here, to her folly.

She rolled over and pressed her cheek against the heavy cotton of the cover. It smelled of wood chips and pine needles and sea salt. It smelled like her dreams of Maristella Island.

Was that Steve's scent? she wondered. She couldn't know, but she turned her face into it and breathed it in until darkness fell.

31

She met the Ramsays at the rear entrance to the courthouse, where a bailiff was waiting to lead them to the judges' private elevators and down a private corridor to the courtroom. Dimly Cam registered that calls had been placed, strings pulled, arrangements made. This was the way it would be from now on, Doug said to her once on a winter morning long ago. No more standing in line or waiting on hold. If there was a brunch at their house, someone else would bring the food and cook it. If they made a mess, someone else would clean up after them.

They arrived first and took their seats. The courtroom was small, no more than fifteen by twenty feet, and there was no jury box or spectator gallery, only an elevated bench for the judge and two tables facing it for the parties and their lawyers. There was no court reporter, either, but only a tape deck set up on the bailiff's desk. The witness stand was at the back, between the two counsel tables, facing forward, while the lectern for examining counsel was up front, where the witness stand would have been in any other courtroom. There was a reason for it: the judge was the only fact-finder in these proceedings; his was the only view that mattered.

The door from the public corridor swung open and the bailiff came through, followed by Bruce Benjamin and Steve Patterson. They took their places, and Cam spoke a hushed greeting across the aisle to Benjamin, which he returned with a grunt. Steve sat in the seat farthest from her and kept his eyes straight ahead.

Judge Miller came through the door from the private corridor, and Benjamin remained on his feet after the judge took the bench.

"Good morning, Your Honor. We're here today on the petition of Steven A. Patterson—"

"I know why we're here."

"If I might make a brief opening statement—"

"You might sit down, Mr. Benjamin, and let me run my own courtroom my own way."

Cam exchanged a glance with her opposing counsel, both of them thinking the same thing: the little man who'd been so timid in his shirtsleeves in his office turned into a tyrant in his black robes on the bench.

"Certainly," Benjamin said stiffly.

Everyone waited in a numbing silence while the judge paged through the file. Cam stole a glance at the other table. Steve sat expressionless, staring at a spot above the judge's head.

"All right, then," he said. "Let's get started."

Benjamin rose again. "Petitioner's first witness—"

"The first witness *I* want to hear from," the judge cut him off, "is Barbara Lawson."

"But we all have copies of her home evaluation reports. There's no reason to consume the Court's time—"

"I'll consume my time however I choose. I don't choose to have you consume it with these constant interruptions."

Barbara Lawson was ushered in. She was a tall, angular, black woman with a master's degree in psychology and twelve years' experience conducting home evaluations, mostly of low income families in custody disputes and termination proceedings. She took the witness chair, raised her hand to swear the oath, then offered herself up for questioning by the judge.

What followed was an almost surreal examination, as the judge led the witness line by line through a report they all had open in front of them. To Cam it was like watching an English film with English subtitles. Laboriously, the judge walked the witness through her credentials and qualifications, then her review of various file materials. It was half an hour before he asked her to describe her visit to the home of Senator and Mrs. Ramsay.

Nothing in her experience in Wilmington's projects prepared Barbara Lawson for an afternoon call on Margo Vaughn Ramsay. Margo had greeted her at the door, swept her on a tour of the house, then put on a wide-brimmed hat and taken her on a stroll through the grounds. Later she drew her back inside, seated her on a brocade love seat, and served her tea and scones on a silver service that had been in the Vaughn family for four generations.

She showed her family pictures and needlepoint pillows; she showed her photos of Senator Ramsay posing with heads of state; and she showed her Cynthia's portrait and shed silent tears as she recounted her daughter's brief, tragic life.

Mrs. Lawson had inspected the boy's room and found it spacious and comfortable. He had adequate desk space for doing homework, and a large yard for outdoor activities. He had a bicycle in good condition that he rode on nearby roads. The neighborhood was quiet and entirely residential, and the volume of traffic was low. It was a very safe environment.

She conducted a brief interview of the child when he came home from school that afternoon. Her impression was of an alert, well-nourished young man. He was somewhat evasive and uncommunicative, but this was not unusual for a boy his age in his particular circumstances. She later met with his guidance counselor and reviewed his school records. Although there was a history of academic underachievement and disciplinary incidents, it appeared to be exactly that: history. Since he returned to the respondents in June, his grades had markedly improved and there had been no disciplinary issues. The Tower Hill School was not one she'd had occasion to visit before, but she was certainly aware of its reputation. Her impression was that it was well deserved.

Because Senator Ramsay was in Washington at the time of her visit, Mrs. Lawson interviewed him by telephone. He confirmed all of the above information and was cooperative and concerned.

She also conducted a brief telephone interview with the boy's treating psychiatrist, who stated that she'd been seeing him since July, and that he was making positive progress.

In Mrs. Lawson's opinion, the child was well provided for in terms of food, shelter, clothing, medical care; he was receiving a high-quality education; and the respondents were fostering continuity in his education, neighborhood life, and peer relationships, as, indeed, they had done for the preceding fourteen years of his life.

On the following day, Mrs. Lawson conducted a home evaluation of petitioner Steven A. Patterson at his furnished one-bedroom apartment in West Chester, Pennsylvania. He was cordial and cooperative and invited her to inspect the premises, although he stated that he had no plans for the child to reside there. When asked what his plans were, petitioner was vague. He did not and had never maintained a family home. He worked sporadically as an itinerant builder/architect, moving from one project to another, sometimes staying for a year, sometimes for no more than a season. At the present time, he was unemployed.

Petitioner's parents were deceased, and he had no siblings and reported no current romantic relationship, although he admitted short-term cohabitation with several women in the past. He acknowledged that one such woman was cohabitating with him during a portion of the time that the minor was also living with him. The child did not attend school during that period. Petitioner claimed to have home-schooled him, but there was no evidence to substantiate this.

Petitioner appeared to be in excellent physical and mental health. He professed a strong emotional tie to the minor, but there was no opportunity for Mrs. Lawson to observe their interaction, because petitioner was currently subject to a restraining order requiring him to maintain a distance of at least five hundred feet from the boy.

In Mrs. Lawson's opinion, petitioner could offer the child nothing by way of continuity in his education, neighborhood life, or peer relationships. And continuity, she believed, was the single most important factor at this stage of the child's life. He'd undergone a number of changes recently, puberty being the major one, and along with it, a move from middle school to the upper school. To also change his custodial situation could be quite damaging to him, particularly if his new situation were fraught with all the instability of the petitioner's lifestyle.

It was two hours before the judge allowed the witness to state the conclusion set out on the last page of her report: it was in the minor's best interests to remain in the custody of the respondents.

Another two hours for the lunch recess, and then Bruce Benjamin was up behind the podium to ask "just a few" follow-up questions.

He'd tried cases in this court before, Cam knew, but he was made for a different arena. His voice was too loud and his movements too large for the intimate scale of this courtroom.

"Mrs. Lawson, you've been conducting custody evaluations for twelve years, correct?"

"That's right."

"Your office has developed a written checklist of the matters to be observed?"

"Yes."

"You attempt to follow it?"

"As much as possible given the particular circumstances."

"The second item on the list says, 'The child should be observed and evaluated on how he or she acts around each parent individually and collectively'? Does that ring a bell?"

"Of course. It's the primary means of evaluating the child's attachment to the parent."

A dramatic pause, a leaning forward with an elbow on the podium, the question coming out in a sharp hiss: "Then why didn't you do it here?"

"I explained. There's a restraining order—"

A thundering interruption: "I'm not talking about Steve Patterson! I'm talking about the people who have the boy now. The ones you seem to think should retain custody."

"I explained that. Senator Ramsay was in Washington."

"So you made a custody recommendation in favor of a man you never met."

"No, I've met Senator Ramsay. Many times."

Another pause, a straightening up and stepping back, a baleful eye fixed on the witness. "Oh? How's that?"

"At events and functions. You know."

"Political functions."

"I suppose that's what they were."

"Did you form a favorable impression of Senator Ramsay at those functions?"

"Yes, I did."

"Favorable enough to vote for him the last time around."

Cam was rising even before Ramsay's elbow reached her ribs. "Objection. We still have the secret ballot in this country."

"We have secrecy in a lot of things," Benjamin said. "But it's forfeited when a witness offers an expert opinion and there's an appearance of bias."

"But unless the Court transfers venue to another state or country, there's no way to avoid this alleged bias," she said. "Everybody in Delaware either voted for Senator Ramsay or didn't vote for him."

Judge Miller looked momentarily tantalized by the idea of transferring venue to another court far, far away, but he shook it off and addressed himself to the witness. "Mrs. Lawson, did your political leanings influence you in any way in this case?"

"Of course not. I conducted my evaluation in this case the same as in any other."

"Objection sustained. Move on, Mr. Benjamin."

He did. What were the ages of respondents? Sixty-eight and fifty-nine. Did she take that into consideration? Yes, but they were healthy, active people; it did not weigh heavily against them. How often was the Senator in Washington? Typically from Monday morning through Friday evening, she was told. Did she do anything to confirm that? Did she call the Senator's office and request a copy of his calendar for the past year? Did she know that in fact the Senator remained in Washington for eighteen weekends over the past year? Did she know that the minor had never visited him in Washington, had never even seen his apartment there? Did she know that the Senator went on a mission to Asia and the South Pacific for four weeks this summer? Without his family?

"Would it surprise you to learn that in the past year, Senator Ramsay spent only forty nights in the same house as the boy?"

"Not at all," she answered, gathering herself up, "in view of the fact that the boy spent a third of the year at a location that was concealed from the Ramsays."

Ramsay chortled under his breath beside Cam.

"What about the interaction between the boy and Mrs. Ramsay?" Benjamin asked next. "What did you observe?"

"I observed typical adolescent behavior. He arrived home from school and came into the living room when Mrs. Ramsay called him. She introduced us and said I'd be wanting to talk to him alone in a few minutes, and that meanwhile there was a snack waiting for him in the kitchen. He nodded and left the room."

Benjamin stood and waited and let a long silence go by. "That's it? That's the extent of interaction you observed?"

"Yes, but let me explain. With a younger child, we'll observe playtime, or perhaps the bedtime ritual. But with an adolescent, it's not unusual for the interaction to consist only of greetings in passing."

"Greetings in passing," he repeated. "Well then—let's examine the quality of the greeting, shall we? Did they kiss?"

"No."

"Hug?"

"No."

"Pat shoulders, touch hands?"

"No."

"Did he speak any words to her at all?"

She looked at her notes again. "Nothing I can recall."

"Mrs. Lawson"—another pause, the elbow back on the podium—"did he even make eye contact with her?"

"I wasn't in a position to observe."

"But wasn't that the whole point of your visit? To observe? Or was it only to take tea with a senator's wife?"

Cam didn't need to object. The judge was turning on him with a fiery face. "That's out of line! Mrs. Lawson performs a valuable service and shouldn't be abused over it."

"My apologies," Benjamin said, undaunted. He shuffled his papers for a moment, then gave the witness a puzzled look. "I can't seem to find your comments about the minor's interaction with the other member of the Ramsay household."

Her face went blank. "There is no other member."

"No? What about Jesse Lombard?"

She started to shake her head, then caught herself. "Wait. Is that the Senator's driver?"

"Is that how he was described to you?"

"No one said anything about him. I just assumed."

"No one told you that he's the boy's primary caregiver?"

Cam was on her feet, objecting that there was no foundation for that question, and Benjamin countered that he would call Mr. Lombard to testify later in the proceeding, at which point the judge ruled that he was putting the cart before the horse.

"Then let me ask it this way," Benjamin said. "Did anyone tell you that Jesse Lombard spends more hours per day with the boy than either of the respondents?"

"No. I'm not aware of that at all."

"Would it have made any difference in your evaluation?"

"I'm not sure. Probably not. We're generally more interested in the quality of time than the quantity."

"Ah, yes. For example, the quality of that greeting you observed. The one without any talking, touching, or looking."

"Your Honor," Cam said in a pained voice.

"I'll withdraw that," Benjamin said. "Let's talk for a moment about another important element of the parent-child relationship. Communication. Would you agree with me, Mrs. Lawson, that good communication is important?"

"I would indeed."

"How then do you rank the respondents' failure to mention to the boy that he was adopted? You are aware of the fact that they never told him?"

"Yes, but Mrs. Ramsay explained that. They planned to tell him when he reached an age of comprehension. Four or five, they thought, which is generally in line with the age that most adoptive parents begin to discuss the subject. But Trey was only three when his birth mother died. He thought she was his sister. They were afraid it would devastate him to learn that his dead sister was actually his mother. So they decided to withhold the information."

"But isn't it a fact that virtually every expert in your field believes that it's a mistake to withhold this information?"

"Yes."

"And that if the child finds out on his own, *that's* what's devastating?"

"I'm not saying I endorse the Ramsays' decision. Only that I understand it."

Benjamin's next subject was her interview with the guidance counselor and the review of the school records. What were the minor's grades like in seventh grade? Mostly C's with occasional swings up or down, she answered. In eighth grade? The same. How many disciplinary incidents in seventh grade? Five. In eighth? Also five, although that was over a shorter time period, since he did not attend school from February to June.

"So of course he's repeating the eighth grade this year?"

"No. He's in ninth grade now."

"Wait." Benjamin stopped and pretended to be confused. "He missed almost half of eighth grade and was still permitted to move on with his class to ninth?"

"Yes."

"And he's maintaining an A average so far this year?"

"That's right."

"And still you say there's no evidence that Steve Patterson home-schooled the boy?"

"Well—no clear evidence."

"How much clearer could it be?"

"There are alternative explanations," she said tightly.

"Oh? Let's hear one."

"The history suggests that the minor had some emotional difficulties in his home and school environment. Suddenly he was removed from that environment for a period of three or four months. When he returned, his circumstances might have looked much better to him. He might have realized how good he had it here. And that realization might have enabled him to knuckle down to his schoolwork and keep himself out of trouble."

Benjamin stared at her. "That's your theory?"

"It's an alternative explanation."

"Any clear evidence to support it?"

"It's an interpretation."

"In fact, isn't there clear evidence that refutes it?"

"I don't know what you're referring to—"

"When you reviewed the file in this case, didn't you come across an affidavit from a store manager?"

"Oh. Yes, I saw that."

"A week after the boy returned, he shoplifts, and you see that as evidence that he was thrilled to be home?"

"I discounted that affidavit, Mr. Benjamin. No arrest was made. No charges were brought. And in my experience, this is a fairly common misunderstanding that arises between store managers and teenagers who hang out in malls."

"When you reviewed the file, did you also come across the boy's testimony in Mr. Patterson's criminal court proceeding?"

"Yes, but again I discounted that."

"Sworn statements just don't carry any weight with you?"

"Your Honor—" Cam began.

"Mr. Benjamin," the witness cut in sharply. "It's my job to look through what people say to what they really feel. And it was obvious to me that Trey was troubled and confused when he gave that testimony."

"Wait. I thought he was thrilled to be home."

"You said that. Not me. I think the healing process took longer. In fact, it's still under way."

"You're referring to the boy's therapy with Dr. Imperato?"

"Yes."

"What exactly is it that she's treating him for?"

"She wasn't at liberty to say. All she could say was that he was making positive progress."

"Why wasn't she at liberty to say?"

"Doctor-patient privilege."

"Which the patient is free to waive. Or in this case, his parents are free to waive for him?"

"Yes, well, they chose not to."

"And that doesn't concern you? They're withholding information from you, and that doesn't concern you?"

There was a loud creak as the judge spun his chair toward the podium. "That's enough, Mr. Benjamin," he snapped. "You've been badgering this witness all afternoon, and I've just about had it."

"I withdraw that question, with apologies to the Court and to Mrs. Lawson. If I might ask just one final set of questions, I'll be done."

"Not soon enough," Miller said, but gave a nod.

"Mrs. Lawson, when you interviewed the boy, did you ask him anything about his own custodial preferences?"

"Yes, of course."

"What did he tell you?"

Senator Ramsay gave a pointed look to Cam, and she spoke out, "Objection. Hearsay."

Another skirmish followed. The rules of evidence were not strictly applied in Family Court, Benjamin argued, and besides, virtually everything the witness already testified to was hearsay.

"No, I'm going to sustain it anyway," Miller said. "If and when I decide to hear what the minor's preferences are, I should get it from the horse's mouth. In that case, I'll bring him in and talk to him here myself, alone."

"An excellent suggestion, Your Honor," Benjamin said. "In that case, I have only one more question. Mrs. Lawson, did you question the boy about his emotional ties to the parties?"

"Yes, but you have to discount his answer. Mr. Patterson is young and personable, he's physically active, he travels, he builds things. To an impressionable young teenager, he's new and exciting. The boy would naturally be drawn to the more glamorous alternative."

"I see. Much the way you were drawn to the Ramsays?"

Cam was on her feet again, the judge was banging his gavel, and Benjamin threw up his hands in surrender and took a seat with a smirk barely suppressed on his lips.

Beyond him Steve sat staring straight ahead.

* * *

Cam's turn. She rose to the podium and conducted an uninspired examination, reviewing and reinforcing every favorable comment Barbara Lawson had made about the Ramsays. They'd been married for thirty-six years, and resided in the same home for all of those years. Trey had gone to the same school since kindergarten and still had many of the same friends. If Jesse Lombard could be described as a caregiver for Trey, that would only be another factor in favor of maintaining custody; it meant there was a male presence in the boy's life even when the Senator was unavoidably absent. In any event, three caregivers he'd known all his life had to be better than one he'd first met this year. As for the doctor-patient privilege, wasn't it possible that the Ramsays declined to waive it out of respect for their son's privacy, as well as a desire that he feel completely free to confide in his therapist? Yes, Mrs. Lawson replied in relief, that did seem likely, and indeed was the wisest course.

Cam returned to her place but remained standing until the witness was excused. "Your Honor, may I present a motion?"

He nodded, expecting it.

"Respondents respectfully renew their motion for dismissal of the petition on grounds that the threshold requirement of Section 721 (e)(2) has not been established, namely that there is no evidence that it is not in the best interests of the child to remain in the custody of his parents."

Bruce Benjamin was on his feet now, too, waiting to be heard. Miller scowled down at both of them, then studied the clock on the wall. It was only four o'clock, too early to adjourn no matter how badly he wanted to.

"Perhaps the parties could be excused for the day?" Cam suggested. "Senator Ramsay needs to confer with his office in Washington before the close of business, and at any rate there's no reason for the parties to be present during legal argument."

Miller nodded. "The parties are dismissed for today, at least. Counsel report to chambers in ten minutes for argument on respondents' motion."

He left the bench, and Ramsay departed immediately after him, through the same door and down the same corridor, while Benjamin walked his client out into the public corridor. As Cam started to pack her briefcase, she realized that Margo hadn't moved.

"Mrs. Ramsay, should I call someone for you?"

"No. I'm sure Jesse's waiting downstairs."

"Would you like me to walk down with you?"

She shook her head. Cam snapped her briefcase shut and looked at the clock. She still had five minutes, time for a quick stop in the ladies' room.

"It's true, you know," Margo said, staring at her hands.

"What?"

"What he said—about me and Trey. I honestly can't remember the last time he kissed me good night or gave me a hug. I suppose he doesn't make eye contact either. I never stopped to think about what that must mean."

"It doesn't necessarily mean anything."

Margo got to her feet. "How would you feel, Campbell, if your own child wouldn't even look you in the eye?"

Miller was back in his shirtsleeves again, and the tyrannical bear was once more the timid mouse. Cam argued her motion quietly, touching all the right points but hitting none of them very hard. All the invective was contained in her written brief. The law was very clear: there was no authority to grant custody to a nonparent without first finding that it was contrary to the best interests of the child to remain in his parents' custody. Not only had Barbara Lawson not made any such findings, but she affirmatively concluded that custody should remain as it was. Case law required the court to give due deference to her opinion. Moreover, this was not a simple matter of comparing petitioner with respondents and picking out a favorite. In order to satisfy the statutory test, the court was required to find that the child's best interests would be better served *anywhere* but with his parents. In other words, his situation at home had to be so deleterious that the court would sooner place him in foster care than allow him to remain there. There wasn't a scintilla of evidence that would support such a ruling in this case.

Bruce Benjamin's arena had shrunk even smaller, but neither his voice nor his manner was pitched down to fit it. Barbara Lawson's findings were entitled to no deference whatsoever, he declaimed. The primary purpose of a home evaluation was to observe the interaction between parent and child, yet she'd failed to observe any interaction whatsoever between the minor and two out of three members of his household, who were notably the male members of the household. Moreover, she'd disregarded the negative aspects of his interaction with Mrs. Ramsay. She'd ignored the boy's criminal conduct and all of the other symptoms of his maladjustment over the past two years. She'd focused instead on a single month of good grades and good behavior and gave all the credit to the Ramsays, when it was far more plausible that the credit belonged to Steve Patterson. She'd failed to investigate the nature of the minor's psychological problems and the scope of his treatment. She'd overlooked the Ramsays' refusal to waive the doctor-patient privilege, and she'd disregarded their egregious omission to inform the boy of his own family history. Finally, and most fatally, she'd ignored the boy's own emotional ties and preferences, despite the fact that he was fourteen and entitled to be heard. All of these factors, Benjamin argued, combined with the court's earlier refusal to allow the petitioner's expert to conduct her own evaluation, would support an appellate court finding of reversible error if Judge Miller were to dismiss this case at this stage. Particularly in light of the witness's evident bias in favor of Senator Ramsay.

Cam had the better argument, but Benjamin had the bigger passion, and it was enough to sway a fainthearted judge fearful of accusations of his own bias.

"I'm afraid he's right," he said, flicking his eyes nervously toward Cam. "I can't make a best interests determination on this record. But tell you what, I won't deny your motion. We'll just put it aside until the rest of the evidence comes in."

He waited, tensing for her objection, but all she did was nod in silence.

"Good," he said. "Then we'll resume tomorrow at nine-thirty and Mr. Benjamin can call his first witness."

32

"Steven Patterson."

He sat down three feet from Cam's right shoulder, so close she could feel the tension coming off him like an electric crackle in the air. He kept his eyes on Bruce Benjamin behind the podium, and Cam did the same. But beside her, Ash Ramsay pushed his chair back and turned to stare at the witness. Beyond him, Margo sat very still with her hands folded on the table before her. Her iron-gray hair was pulled back in a bun, so tightly it stretched the skin at the corners of her eyes.

The preliminaries were over in a minute. He was Steven Patterson, age thirty-four, currently residing in West Chester, Pennsylvania, the biological father of James Ashton Ramsay, III, and the petitioner in this proceeding.

"Where are you from originally, Steve?" Benjamin asked. His voice was still too loud for the close quarters of this courtroom, but his tone at least was conversational.

"Carlinville, Illinois."

"What did your parents do?"

"My mother was a secretary at the college there, Blackburn College. My father was a carpenter. He worked construction jobs, usually in and around St. Louis."

"You say *was*?"

"My father died in 1990, and my mother last year."

"Where did you go to school?"

"High school in Carlinville. Then Cornell."

Benjamin raised his eyebrows, as if he were hearing this for the first time. "An Ivy League university," he said, impressed.

The witness shrugged. "I got a financial aid package."

"What did you study there?"

"Architecture."

"Did you graduate with a degree in architecture?"

"Yes."

"Are you a licensed architect today?"

"Yes."

"What kind of work do you do?"

"Residential."

"Do you earn a decent living?"

"Decent enough."

"What's your income been over, say, the last five years?"

"About a hundred, hundred fifty thousand a year."

Benjamin had exhibits to back it up, copies of his federal income tax returns for the last five years, and a financial statement detailing his assets and liabilities.

"Are you working on any projects at the moment?"

"Not since June. But I've still got the job waiting for me back in Maine, and one lined up in East Hampton after that."

"Did you meet Cynthia Ramsay at Cornell?"

The question was delivered in the same easy conversational tone as all the rest, and it took Cam half a second to realize how the focus had changed. She glanced at Ramsay, who was all but glowering at the witness, and at Margo, whose lips went white at the mention of her daughter's name.

"Yes," Steve said.

It was his sophomore year, he explained, and he was earning pocket money by leading orientation tours for incoming freshmen. Cynthia Ramsay was on one of those tours, and before it was over, they'd exchanged dorm names and room numbers. In a matter of weeks they were a steady couple.

"An intimate couple?"

He swallowed hard before he answered. "No, not until December, right before we went home for winter break. We were kind of torn up over the idea of being apart for four weeks. You know how it is when you're a teenager—everything's out of proportion. That night before we went home, we became—intimate."

A little noise came from Margo's throat, like a wounded bird fluttering.

"What happened when you returned after winter break?"

"We picked up where we left off, but this time it was more—deliberate, I guess. We were careful this time. Not that it mattered, though."

"What do you mean, 'not that it mattered'?"

"We didn't know it yet, but Cindy was already pregnant."

Cindy, Cam thought. He called her by the name the Ramsays never did.

"When did you discover that?"

"She told me after spring break, in early April."

"What did she tell you?"

"That she'd been to a doctor, and that she was pregnant. Past three months already."

"What was your reaction?"

Cam could hear him exhale beside her.

"Not very good. Or I should say, not very mature. Basically, I freaked. I was shocked and scared and angry."

"Well, let's go through those one at a time. Why were you shocked?"

"Because there was only that one time that it could have happened. And I was like every other teenager: I never really appreciated the fact that it only takes one time."

"And why were you scared?"

"I didn't know what to do. I wasn't even supporting myself—I didn't know how I could support a wife and baby."

"And why angry?"

"Because it all seemed so unfair, I guess, that this could happen to us. And I guess I was angry at Cindy, too, for keeping it from me for so long."

"Did you discuss any of this with her?"

"That's all we talked about, how could this happen and what were we going to do."

"Did you consider an abortion?"

"We talked about it. But before we could even make an appointment to see the doctor, she felt the baby move. And before long, I could feel it, too. And after that, there was no way."

"Why not?"

"I guess it stopped being a concept and started being a baby. And we decided to get married."

"What about school? And your money worries?"

"Cindy decided to drop out and start again later when the baby was older. And I spent the rest of the semester lining up jobs and fellowships and scouting out cheap apartments. I landed a great construction job for the summer, working on a desalinization plant in the Virgin Islands. I was going to clear ten thousand dollars in three months."

"When was the baby due?"

"Middle of September."

"What was Cindy going to do while you were in the Virgin Islands?"

"Stay with her parents, we hoped, until I got back. Then I was going to take her up to Ithaca in time for the baby to be born. But things got—complicated."

"How so?"

"This was 1984. The year her father ran for the Senate."

"I don't understand. Why would that complicate your plans to marry and provide for your family?"

"I'm not sure I can answer that. All I know is that Cindy said it changed everything. She said she had to go home at the end of the semester and talk it over with her parents. I went home then, too, for a week before my job started. The plan was that I'd meet her in Philadelphia and we'd get married there before I went on to the islands. But before I left Illinois, Cindy called and told me that she had to go to Europe with her mother."

"Did she tell you why?"

"She said that Delaware was too small a state for her to be walking around pregnant while her father was running for the Senate. It didn't matter whether we were married or not; everyone could do the math. So we came up with a new plan. As soon as my job was over, I'd meet her in Europe, and we'd get married there."

"That never happened, did it?"

He drew a sharp breath. "No."

"Why not?"

"She wrote me and said she changed her mind."

"Wrote from where?"

"The postmark said Geneva."

"Where did you receive the letter?"

"On the job in the islands. They had a barracks and a mess hall for the construction crew, and we got mail call before dinner every night. I remember I opened her letter at the table before we started eating, and I got up and went out and sat on the beach until the breakfast bell rang the next morning."

"What did she say in the letter?"

"That she wasn't ready for the responsibilities of marriage and motherhood. She wanted to continue her education. She didn't want to let one mistake ruin her entire life. The baby would have a better life with real parents, not with a pair of kids who were only playing at it. She was going to give it up for adoption."

"What was your reaction?"

"I was shocked and angry all over again. It didn't seem like it was only her decision, not after all the plans we'd made."

"Did you talk to her about it?"

"I didn't know where she was. No one ever answered the phone at her parents' house, and no one would put me through to her father when I called his campaign office. I tried writing to her, too, and wrote 'Please Forward' on the envelopes. I wrote to her every day and asked her to call me or to let me know where she was, so we could talk this all out."

"Did you ever get a response?"

"The only response I got was the day I came in at the end of my shift and found a man sitting on my bunk, waiting for me."

"Who was it?"

"Cindy's father. Ash Ramsay."

"Senator Ramsay came to the Virgin Islands to see you?"

"He wasn't a senator yet. But yes, he came to see me."

"What did he say?"

"He said that Cindy didn't want to see me or hear from me again. She wanted to get on with her life and put this episode behind her. He brought some papers for me to sign, and he showed me that Cindy had already signed an identical set of papers. He said I needed to sign, too, so the adoption could go forward, and Cindy could get on with her life."

"Did you sign?"

"Yes."

"Your Honor," Benjamin said. "I have copies here of Petitioner's Exhibit Six."

Judge Miller flopped his hand over his wrist and waited for it to be placed on his palm. He gave it a glance and a nod, then Benjamin handed it to his client and passed a copy to Cam. She ran her eyes over the pages. It was the same document she'd found in the adoption file last February: Waiver of Notice, Consent to Termination of Parental Rights, and Consent to Adoption.

"Is that your signature at the bottom of the second page?" Benjamin asked as he returned to the podium.

"Yes, it is."

"And is this the document you signed that day?"

"No, it's not."

Cam shot him a look; it was the first time all morning she'd let her eyes touch him. He kept his gaze on Benjamin.

"How is it different?"

"Most of what I signed was blank. All of these details here, they were added later."

Ramsay was leaning over, whispering to Cam to object, but she shook her head and held up a hand to silence him.

"Tell the Court which details were not set forth on the document that you signed."

"Okay, first, it said 'birth father,' but it didn't say 'of a male infant born in Geneva, Switzerland, on September sixteen, 1984.' Because I signed it in August, and he hadn't been born yet. Then on the next page, where it says 'consents to the adoption of said infant by' . . . ? It was blank after that."

Benjamin gave him an astonished look. "You mean to tell us that the document did not state that Mr. and Mrs. Ramsay were to be the adopting parents?"

"That's right."

"But Mr. Ramsay told you that, surely?"

"He told me it was blank because the whole thing had to go through an agency, and there were probably a thousand applicants who had to be screened before the selection could be made."

"You mean," Benjamin said, his voice rising with incredulity, "that he led you to believe that the baby would be placed with strangers?"

"Objection. Leading," Cam said.

"Sustained."

Benjamin shrugged. "Would you have signed this document if all the blanks had been filled in?"

"Not in a million years."

"Why not?"

"Because the only reason I went along with any of this was because I thought Cindy wanted to put it behind her. If I'd known she was keeping the baby in her life, I would've wanted to keep him in my life, too."

"When did you learn the truth?"

"In the fall of 1996. I moved to Rehoboth Beach then to work on a remodeling job, and one day I saw a campaign poster for

Senator Ramsay. And there, right in the middle of it, was my son."

"You didn't know that then, of course."

"I knew it the second I saw him. I recognized him before I recognized Senator Ramsay."

"But how . . . ?"

"I can't explain it. I just knew."

"What did you do?"

"I did a lot of research into old newspapers and magazines to piece together what happened. Then I went to a lawyer, a few lawyers in fact. But everybody told me the same thing. There was nothing I could do to overturn the adoption. It didn't matter if I was defrauded into signing those papers. If it was money or property—say, they'd cheated me out of ten thousand dollars and I didn't discover it for twelve years—then I'd be able to do something about it. But they cheated me out of my son, and there wasn't a thing I could do about it."

Ash Ramsay's breath hissed in his throat, and Cam laid a quick hand on his arm to keep him from speaking out loud.

"Then I tried the direct approach. I wrote to the Ramsays and told them I knew they had my son, and that I wanted him. They didn't answer. I wrote again and asked them to meet with me or my lawyer and negotiate some kind of arrangement. But they ignored that letter, too, and the next one and the next one."

"So what did you decide to do?"

"I figured I had three options. I could go to the newspapers and stir up a big scandal. But I didn't want to put my son through that, and I didn't see that it would really accomplish anything.

"Two, I could just give up and try to forget about him. And I did try that for a while. I kept myself busy on the Rehoboth job and tried not to think about him. But by that time he was more than just a campaign picture in my mind. See, I found out where he went to school, and I started to drop by, just to see him."

"Did he ever see you?"

"No. No one did. It really bothered me, how lax the security was—anybody could've taken him. And then one day I realized that *I* was the one who could take him. And that was my third option."

"Steve, on February twentieth of this year, what did you do?"

"I took him. I followed him and his friends that night, and I lured him into a van and drove away with him."

"Didn't you realize that a lot of people would view that as a criminal act?"

"Yes, but like I said, I only had three options, and that seemed like the best of them."

"You weren't worried about the consequences?"

"I was worried about scaring him, so as soon as I could, I told him who I was. It never occurred to me that he wouldn't already know who *he* was. But no one had ever told him he was adopted. He had to hear the whole story from me."

"If you'd known that . . . ?"

"I wouldn't have done it—not like that anyway. But see, I thought he knew he had a father out there somewhere. I even hoped that he might be halfway expecting me to come for him someday."

"You're aware that he testified in the criminal case that not only was he expecting you, the whole thing was his idea?"

"Yes."

"But that wasn't true?"

"No."

"Then why would he say it?"

"Objection," Cam said. "Calls for speculation."

"Withdrawn," Benjamin said. "Perhaps the Court can inquire directly of the boy later."

"Perhaps it can," Miller said peevishly. "Could you move along a little faster, Mr. Benjamin? We're coming up on the lunch hour here pretty soon."

Benjamin hooded his eyes. "Let's skip ahead a little, and talk about Maristella Island. Could you describe it for the Court?"

He could do better than describe it. He'd brought with him a portfolio of Trey's sketches of the island, and each one was duly marked as an exhibit and passed around the courtroom. There were sketches of the old house clinging to the edge of the cliff, and the meadow and the stand of spruce that swept down to the dock. There were scenes of gulls dipping their wings through the sky and seals sunning themselves on a rocky beach. There was a charcoal portrait of Steve at work, bent over a drafting table.

"Describe a typical day on the island."

Again Steve could do better than that. He brought copies of Trey's class schedules day by day; he brought the textbooks they'd used for history, math, and science, and a list of all the books he'd read for English; he had a folder full of the papers

Trey wrote, algebra worksheets, and photographs of the catapult he built for a science project. Recreation was documented, too, with photos of Trey paddling in a sea kayak, and sledding down the slope of the meadow, and stirring a pot of soup on the stove. Cam studied each one and passed them on to the Senator, who gave them a quick glance. Margo lingered longer over them. On one photo, she touched her fingertips to Trey's face.

"Steve, what are your plans if your petition's granted and you get custody of the boy?"

"First, we'll go back to Maristella, so I can finish what I started up there."

"How long do you estimate that would take?"

"Probably through the end of next summer."

"Would you continue home-schooling Trey?"

"Yes, but I've been looking into a couple ways to supplement that. I'm working out Internet access to the island, and I found a tutor in Baxter Bay who could give him a day or two a week if I ferry him over there. Then if we move on to the Hamptons at the end of the summer, there's a public school close by, and he could start high school there. I think I could line up enough jobs in the area to keep going for three years, so he'd be able to finish high school there, too."

"Are you able to provide food, shelter, clothing, and medical care for your son?"

"Yes."

"Can you provide for his emotional well-being?"

"Yes. We really connected when we were together. Almost from that first day, we seemed to be in sync with each other."

"Can you provide continuity in the boy's education, neighborhood, and peer relationships?"

"Not in the short run, obviously. But once we get to the Hamptons, I think so. I know it's not perfect, but it's no different from what a lot of kids go through when their parents get transferred and move around."

"But you admit that there will be a disruption of the boy's present situation, his education and friendships and so on?"

"Yes, but I'm not so sure that's a bad thing. Last February he was running with a bad crowd, he wasn't doing well in school—he might have been headed for some serious trouble."

"What do you mean, 'running with a bad crowd'?"

"They might all be good kids, I don't know, but together they were raising a lot of hell. Slashing tires, smashing mailboxes, smoking dope—stuff like that."

"Object!" Ramsay growled at Cam.

"Hearsay," she called.

"I saw it for myself," Steve said. "The night I took him. The truth is, that's what gave me the nerve to go through with it."

"Why?"

"Because I could see how much he needed me."

Ramsay flopped back in his chair so hard the wood creaked.

"That night," Margo said as they came out of the courthouse and headed up King Street to Cam's office, "when you said they were doing something they shouldn't have been . . . ?"

"Yes," Cam said. "I saw the same thing."

Ramsay strode on, half a step ahead of them, and didn't speak until someone called to him from across the street. "Hello, Senator! How are you!"

"Fine! Good to see you!" he shouted, his arm shooting up automatically into a wave.

They went another thirty feet before Ramsay decided that he wouldn't go back to Cam's office after all, but instead would stop in the federal building to see what his staff was up to.

"But Senator, we have lunch waiting."

"I'll get something here."

"I need to prepare my cross—"

"Yes, you do that." He was already starting to peel off toward the federal building.

"Ash!" a man shouted from the doorway, and Ramsay headed his way.

As Cam and Margo continued up the street, Margo said, "He's not what I expected."

Cam looked back at the man in the doorway. It took a moment for her to realize that Margo meant Steve Patterson.

That afternoon she went to the podium and took a slow breath before she turned to face the witness. She felt as if she'd been hurtling down a collision course ever since that night on Martins Mill Road. Now, here in Judge Miller's courtroom, she'd finally reached the intersection where the crash would occur.

"Mr. Patterson, when did you return from winter break during your sophomore year at Cornell?"

He sat with his hands gripping the arms of his chair and his gaze fixed on the front of the podium, three feet below eye contact. "The middle of January."

"Unbeknownst to you, Cynthia Ramsay was already about a month pregnant at that time?"

"Yes."

"When did spring break come that year?"

"I think it was the last week of March."

"During the period from mid-January to late March, how often did you have sexual relations with Miss Ramsay?"

He swung his head toward his lawyer, who said, "Objection. What possible relevance is there to justify such an intrusive question?"

Cam directed her reply to the judge. "It's relevant to petitioner's awareness of the pregnancy."

"Overruled. Answer the question, Mr. Patterson."

He moved his hands to the table and clasped them in front of him. "Very often. I was nineteen."

"Three times a week? Or three times a day?"

He grimaced. "About every night, I guess."

"So for more than two months you had a daily view of Miss Ramsay's unclothed body, and yet you had not a clue that she was pregnant until April?"

"Look, I was only nineteen. I wasn't tuned in to a woman's body enough to recognize the signs. Besides, she was only three months along by the end of that period."

"But speaking of periods, surely you must have been aware that Miss Ramsay wasn't having any?"

He bowed his head against the knuckles of his clasped hands. "I didn't put two and two together."

"Not until she came back from spring break and told you."

"That's right."

"When you were shocked and scared and angry."

"Yes."

"Scared because you didn't know how you could support a wife and baby."

"Yes."

Cam flipped a page on the podium. "And let me see. Your testimony this morning was that after you got her letter in the Virgin Islands, you were shocked and angry."

"That's right."

"But no longer scared."

"I—"

"Because—let's face it—this was a big load off your mind."

"No, I was past all that. I wanted to marry her."

"Then why didn't you?"

"I explained—"

"You explained why you didn't get married in Philadelphia or in Europe. But why didn't you get married in Ithaca?"

"Well—"

"April and May, Mr. Patterson. You could have had a lovely spring wedding in Ithaca. Why didn't you?"

"Cindy wanted to talk to her parents first."

"She couldn't talk to them any sooner than that? I mean, the clock was ticking, right? She was getting bigger every day."

"We wanted to have everything set first. So that they wouldn't be able to shoot us down with practical objections."

"But if you were worried about being shot down, wouldn't the wisest course be to get married first and tell them second?"

"In hindsight, yes."

"What were you really waiting for? For the Ramsays to set you up in a little house? Maybe get you a government job?"

"I didn't want anything from them. We didn't need them."

"Because you had things all lined up?"

"That's right, I did," he said defiantly.

"What was the address of the apartment you leased for your wife and baby in Ithaca?"

"I looked at a lot of places downtown—"

"No, but which one did you actually lease?"

"I didn't get that far."

"Wait, I'm confused. You left Cornell in May with the intention of returning with your wife in September. But you didn't actually have any place to return to?"

"I had to pay a security deposit and the first and last months' rent, and I didn't have the money for it in May. I was planning to work it out before the end of the summer."

"After you cleared ten thousand dollars from your summer job?"

"Yes."

"What *did* you do with that ten thousand dollars?"

"I paid my junior year tuition with it."

"Oh." She gave him a confused look. "Wait. How would you

have paid your tuition if you had an apartment and a wife and baby to pay for instead?"

He dropped his forehead into his hand. "I thought I had a fellowship lined up, but it fell through before school started."

"When did you find that out?"

"Sometime during the summer."

"So that's one more reason why you were secretly relieved by Cynthia's decision?"

"I wasn't, I told you. I was planning to marry her."

"What did your own parents think of those plans?"

"I never got a chance to tell them."

"From the beginning of April until the end of the semester, you never spoke to your parents on the telephone? Or wrote to them?"

"It's not the kind of thing a kid can say over the phone. 'Hey, my girlfriend's pregnant and we're getting married.' "

"You wanted to tell them in person?"

"Yes."

"You were home for a week before you left for the Virgin Islands. Or did it slip your mind?"

"Objection, Your Honor. These snide remarks are—"

"Because I was afraid, okay?" Steve burst out. "I was their big hope. They'd pinned all their dreams on me, and now I had to tell them that I blew it. It was going to tear them apart, and I was too much of a coward to see it through. I wasn't going to tell them until I was ready to get on the plane to Philadelphia. But Cindy called the night before and said, change of plans, so I never told them."

"Never?" she exclaimed. "You mean they died never knowing they had a grandson?"

He lowered his eyes and swallowed hard. "That's right."

Cam paused and pretended to flip a few pages in her notebook. She cleared her throat. "When you got Cindy's letter in the Virgin Islands, why didn't you come to Wilmington and pound on doors until somebody told you where she was?"

"I still owed the company six more weeks on the job."

"And what did you owe your girlfriend and your unborn child? Nothing?"

"I would have come looking for her eventually. Except that her father came to see me first."

"Oh, yes. And he brought those papers for you to sign."

"Right."

"And all the important information was left blank."

"Yes."

"But you signed it anyway."

"I didn't know any better."

"Oh?" She located a document in her folder and offered it to the judge. "Respondents' A, Your Honor."

He nodded, and she handed a copy to Bruce Benjamin, and then, gingerly, to Steve Patterson.

"Can you identify Exhibit A?"

He gave it a puzzled look. "It's my college transcript."

"I'm interested in a course you took second semester, sophomore year. The one called 'Basic Contract Documents'?"

"That was about building contracts. We went over the model AIA forms for bids and subcontractors and suppliers. It didn't have anything to do with this kind of document."

"After taking that course, would you have signed a construction contract without knowing who the other party was or when the work would be done or how much it would cost?"

"No."

"You understood even at the tender age of nineteen that those things had to be filled in?"

"Those things, sure."

"But the identity of the people adopting your baby didn't strike you as being as important as the cost of a building?"

"He told me nobody knew! I thought that was the way it was done."

"And you continued to believe that for the next twelve years? Until the fall of 1996?"

"Yes."

"You knew that somebody had your child, correct?"

"Yes."

"But it wasn't until you found out who that somebody was that you felt moved to do anything about it?"

"What could I do? I didn't know where he was."

"Did you ever consider hiring an investigator to find out where your child was placed?"

"I thought there were laws against that."

"Did you consult a lawyer?"

"Not then, no."

"Not until you found out that the Ramsays were the adoptive parents?"

He laced his fingers together again, and rubbed his thumbs against his temples. "That's right."

"When was the last time you spoke with Cynthia Ramsay?"

"The night before I flew to the Virgin Islands."

"You didn't speak to her again after the baby was born? To find out how she was?"

"I couldn't. I didn't know where she was."

"Why didn't you ask her parents?"

"They never would have told me. Her father made it pretty clear that I wasn't welcome in her life."

"But you didn't ask?"

"I didn't see the point."

"This was the woman you loved, Mr. Patterson, the mother of your only child, and you made no effort to see her or talk to her, ever again?"

His jaw clenched tight. "Look, if you want me to say I was a callow youth, I'll say it. I gave up, I went back to school, I tried to get on with my own life, too."

"But in 1996, after twelve years of inaction, you saw the campaign poster and suddenly a fire was lit under you. You did newspaper and magazine research, you consulted several lawyers, you wrote letters, you watched Trey at school. Suddenly you became very active, didn't you?"

"Suddenly I knew where he was."

"And who had him."

"Yes."

"It must have galled you, to see Senator Ramsay with his hand on your son's shoulder in that poster."

"It shocked me."

"Is that all? After the way he ambushed you in the Virgin Islands and trapped you into signing those papers? And lied to you about their intentions? After all that, all you felt was shock?"

"I was angry, too."

She searched for the reference in her notes. "Because as you say, they cheated you out of your son."

His chin came up and his eyes met hers. "That's right, they did. They cheated me out of most of his childhood, and there's no getting it back, no matter what happens here. He's fourteen years old now. He'll never take my hand to cross the street. I'll never hold him on my lap or tie his shoes or tell him stories at bedtime. Those years are gone forever. They stole them from me."

Cam kept her eyes down on the podium as he spoke, and when she finally looked up, it was at Bruce Benjamin where he sat with his arms folded over his chest, then across the aisle to the thunderous outrage on Ramsay's face, then to Margo beside him with her hand to her mouth.

"You want revenge for that, don't you, Mr. Patterson?"

"No. I only want my son."

"You took him because you saw only three options, and that one seemed the best."

"Yes."

"It was only a coincidence that it happened to be the option most hurtful to the Ramsays?"

"That couldn't be helped."

"Especially not if revenge was your principal goal."

"I told you, my only goal was to be with my son."

"Was it really? What if he *had* been adopted by strangers, as you'd thought? Are you telling this Court you would have taken him anyway?"

"I don't know."

"What if Cynthia were still alive? What if *she* were the one who'd be terrified and grief-stricken over the kidnapping of her child? Would you have taken him anyway?"

His eyes sparked furiously, his mouth already forming a retort, but then a look passed over his face like a shadow.

Bruce Benjamin watched him, waiting for his answer, and when he realized none was coming, he called out: "Objection! The question calls for rank speculation about a set of hypothetical facts so far removed from reality that no one could know how they might have behaved—"

"If he doesn't know, he can say so," the judge said.

"Your Honor, this is totally improper cross-examination, so far beyond the scope of direct examination—"

"As you're so fond of pointing out, the rules of evidence don't apply."

"But the rules of fair play ought to!"

Cam stood silent while the battle raged around her, and when it was finally over, she didn't know which way the ruling had gone, and she didn't care.

"No," Steve said heavily. "I guess I wouldn't have."

She closed her notebook with a thud. "I have nothing else."

Her hands trembled on the wheel when she drove home that night. A wall of black clouds was moving in across the northern sky. It would rain tonight, she thought, as a sudden gust sent a flurry of dry leaves scuttling across the road. A hard pounding rain that would wash out her mulch and topsoil and batter her tender plantings into the mud. But it was too late in the season to cover them; there was nothing she could do to protect them now.

Her car phone rang, and numbly she answered.

"Hey, babe." She could hear the dull roar of the campaign office behind Nathan's voice; the place was a beehive of activity these days. "Listen, we had a schedule shuffle. We have to head down to Washington tonight. Be back Thursday."

"Fine."

"You okay? You sound a little funny."

"I'm tired, I guess."

"Yeah, aren't we all? Hold on a minute. The man wants to talk to you."

"Cam?" Doug said a minute later. "You been home yet?"

"No."

"Wait'll you see. The plumber must have been by today. The pool's been filled and the fountain's on. Looks fabulous. The whole place does. You've done a hell of a job."

Storm clouds were rolling like tumbleweeds across the sky. She thought of pointing her car in their direction and following wherever they went.

"You know, I was thinking," Doug said. "We should move a couple of next week's functions to our place. Show the garden off."

"Fine."

The office babble suddenly cut off; Doug must have closed a door. "Ash tells me you're doing a hell of a job on this case, too, Cam. He's really grateful, and so am I. When this is all over, I hope I can show you how much."

She couldn't bear even the sound of his voice, and she pressed the button and silenced it.

At home she undressed and put on a robe, but she had no appetite for dinner, and there was nothing to do but drift from window to window and watch the storm roll in. The wind blew harder as night began to fall, and it started to lash at the water in the reflecting pool, making it swell and crest into little tongues that curved up and licked at the edges of the coping. The trees bent their backs to the wind, and the moon rose an icy white high in the sky behind the swift-moving clouds. It shone in shifting phosphorescent stipples across the churning surface of the pool.

She sat in the living room and paged through the gardening encyclopedia, but there was nothing left for her in it, and soon she got up again. A low rumble of thunder sounded in the distance, and she went to the kitchen for a pot and carried it upstairs to place under the leak in the ceiling. She moved to the rear window as another growl of thunder came and a quick strobe of lightning.

A jolt surged through her body and left her skin tingling. She gripped the windowsill and pressed her forehead to the glass, and when the next streak of lightning lit up the sky, she saw him again at the edge of the water.

She turned and ran barefoot down the stairs and outside with her hair and robe streaming behind her. The wind died abruptly when she reached the garden, the calm before the storm, and the water in the pool went so still that she could see their reflections floating on the surface, his at one end and hers at the other. She was in the dream again, moving sluggishly to reach him at the water's edge. But this time he was moving toward her, too.

"I thought I'd stop by," he said, his voice strained and tense. "See if the pool turned out all right."

Their reflections stopped, bobbing uncertainly six feet apart. "It's beautiful," she said.

"Yes," he said, though he didn't look at it either.

There wasn't a star in the sky, only the shifting shadows of the moon and the ponderous weight of the storm in the air.

"Steve, I'm sorry."

"No, don't be. It was true. Every word was true."

He closed the distance between them and took her face between his hands and turned it up to his. He hesitated a second, then bent and kissed her mouth, warily at first, then fiercely, breathlessly. They parted, and she turned and pressed her cheek to his chest where she could hear the pounding of his heart.

"Then you feel it, too," he said.

She nodded.

Another crack of thunder sounded, and this time a bolt of lightning came hard on its heels, and at last the skies opened and the rain pelted down. Steve grabbed her hand and pulled her after him down the length of the garden to the folly, and when the door was closed behind them, he took her in his arms and kissed her again.

Cam leaned back, gazing at him in the darkness, while the rain trickled down their bodies and pooled at their feet on the floor. "Come."

She led him up the spiral stairs, and they knelt on the futon and undressed each other while the rain pounded in a muffled rhythmic roar on the rooftop. The moon stole furtive peeks at them through the window as he kissed her eyes and her mouth and her breasts. She lay back and pulled him down after her, and the scent of pine needles and sea salt and wood chips rose up all around them.

"So there I was," he said afterward as they lay wrapped in each other, "being raked over the coals, my whole life sliced and gutted, forced to confess every bad act and stupid choice I ever made—and when it was finally over, all I could think of was how to see you tonight."

"Steve, I'm sorry," she said again.

"No, don't say that." He touched his fingers to her lips. "Say you felt the same."

"I felt the same."

He smiled and kissed her forehead. "Now tell me you're all right with what just happened here."

Thunder rumbled again, but this time the lightning hesitated before it flashed. The storm was blowing over. She looked at the window. There was only a wall of blackness outside.

"Cam?"

In one fell swoop she'd broken the vows of marriage as well as all the rules of professional conduct. But that wasn't what was setting off the alarm bells in her brain. Steve was a danger to her, she'd always known that. Now the danger was closer than ever.

"It's complicated," she said.

He rolled heavily onto his back and for a moment the only sound in the tiny loft was the ragged rhythm of his breathing. "You won't leave him," he said.

"I already did leave him, in every way that matters."

His face registered her meaning, but still he said, "Not in every way that matters to me."

She reached out and touched the stubble of beard on his jaw and moved her thumb over the little cleft in his chin. His arms reached around her and pulled her down close beside him, and they lay still and silent while the rain tapered to a slow, dreary drizzle on the roof.

In the morning the sun was shining, and the garden was wet and sparkling and filled with birdsong.

"So what happens now?" he said as they came down the stairs of the folly.

Cam turned to him at the door. The alarm bells were ringing louder than the birds could sing. "How can we possibly make any plans?"

"How can we not?"

She shook her head. "Until the election's over—"

"How long's that?"

She looked up at him, astonished that he didn't know, then by turns delighted. "Four weeks—no, twenty-seven days."

"And in the meantime?"

She hesitated only a moment. "Meet me here tonight?"

A smile lit his face, all the way back to the shadows in his eyes.

33

Bruce Benjamin put on three witnesses Wednesday morning. The first was Dr. Philomena Imperato, Trey's treating psychologist. She was appearing in response to a subpoena and clearly against her will. She answered all the preliminary questions about herself and her education, training, and current practice, but then invoked therapist-patient privilege and refused to answer any questions about Trey. Her own attorney was waiting in the hallway with a canned brief full of citations to cases delineating and enforcing the privilege, but as it turned out, neither he nor his brief was required. Judge Miller upheld the privilege and dismissed the witness.

The next witness was Trey's school guidance counselor, who gave a long, dreary recitation of Trey's eighth-grade record, including every disciplinary infraction and penalty, every unexcused lateness or absence, every C and D on his report card.

Cam had no questions.

The last witness of the morning session was the manager of the Gap at the Concord Mall, who testified that on June 11, 1998, he witnessed James Ashton Ramsey, III, remove a twenty-dollar, one-pocket T-shirt from a shelf of merchandise and stuff it down the front of his pants. He intercepted the youth on his way out of the store, recovered the merchandise and summoned the police, who took him into custody. However, later that day the manager received a telephone call from an officer identifying himself as Captain Broward, who asked as a personal favor that he not press charges against the boy. Not wishing to antagonize the police, he agreed.

Cam's cross-examination was brief. Did he notice whether Trey was with a group of boys before the incident? Yes, there were four or five others, who all scattered when he collared the suspect. How frequently had he witnessed incidents similar to this one? All too often, he was afraid; it almost seemed to be a suburban teen rite of passage.

After the luncheon recess, Bruce Benjamin rose and called Jesse Lombard as his next witness, and the bailiff went out into the corridor and returned with Jesse limping awkwardly beside him. He placed his right hand on the Bible, and it seemed all he could do to lift his left hand high enough to swear the oath.

"Please state your name."

"Jesse Lombard."

"Where do you live?"

"At 127 Martins Mill Road, Greenville."

"In the home of Senator and Mrs. Ramsay?"

"I have a room over their garage."

"How are you employed?"

"By the Senate Judiciary Committee."

"The U.S. Senate? In Washington, D.C.?"

"Yes, sir."

"But you live in Delaware?"

"Yes, sir."

"On a typical day, Mr. Lombard, how much time do you spend in the company of James Ashton Ramsay the Third?"

"A few hours probably."

"Can you break it down for us?"

"I drive him back and forth to school. On weeknights, we usually have some supper together. Maybe watch a little TV."

"Just the two of you?"

"Mrs. Ramsay's in and out."

"And where is Senator Ramsay?"

"In Washington weekdays. But now, weekends, it's totally different. He's usually right there."

"Before you went to work for the U.S. Senate, how were you employed?"

"With the Delaware State Police, for close to fifteen years."

"In fact, you were injured on the job, weren't you?"

"I sustained a gunshot wound to the head in 1985." He bent his head and pointed to the scar across his scalp.

"Did that result in any permanent disability?"

"Permanent? I don't know. It comes and goes."

"What does?"

Jesse waved a hand vaguely at the left side of his body. "Some numbness now and then. The muscles don't always work right."

"Do your injuries interfere with your job duties?"

"No, sir."

"What *are* your job duties?"

"My title is Law Enforcement Liaison."

"What does that entail?"

"I interact with local police, keep them informed about the work of the Committee, get their input."

"Do you write reports to the Committee?"

"No, sir. It's not that formal."

"Then how does the Committee know what you're doing?"

"I tell Senator Ramsay."

"He's a member of the Committee?"

"Yes, sir. Since 1991."

"Have you been Law Enforcement Liaison since 1991?"

"Your Honor." Cam rose from her seat. "I object to this line of questioning. The affairs of government have no relevance to this case. If Mr. Benjamin is out to expose improprieties on the Judiciary Committee, I suggest he find a more appropriate forum."

"My only intent is to expose improprieties in the Ramsay household," Benjamin said. "And my next line of questions should do just that."

"Why don't you get to it?" the judge snapped.

Benjamin turned back to Jesse. "Who employed you before the Judiciary Committee?"

"The Senate Committee on Veteran Affairs."

"What did you do there?"

"My title was Vietnam Veterans Liaison."

"Are you a Vietnam vet yourself?"

"Yes, sir."

"Where and when did you serve?"

Cam rose again, with an expression of strained impatience. "This is even farther afield than before. What possible relevance does Mr. Lombard's military service have?"

"Sustained. Move on to another subject. Now."

Benjamin raised an undaunted eyebrow. "Mr. Lombard, isn't it true that you suffer from severe post-traumatic stress syndrome as a result of your service in Vietnam?"

Cam shot a stunned look at Jesse before she remembered to jump to her feet again. "Objection! This is the same topic—"

The judge waved her silent. "It sounds a little different now. Let me see where this goes."

Cam stayed on her feet. "I also object on the ground that the question calls for an expert medical opinion. A lay witness can't answer as to psychiatric diagnosis."

"He can if it's a diagnosis he's been informed of," Benjamin said. "And if it's something he's being treated for. And if he can't, then perhaps it would help if I called his treating psychiatrist?"

Cam turned to her clients with the question on her face, but Margo dropped her head into her hand, and after a moment Ramsay shook his head. "Withdrawn," she said and sat down.

"Mr. Lombard?"

"I've never met a Vietnam vet who doesn't have post-traumatic stress to some degree."

"Let's focus on the degree to which *you* have it. You are being treated by a psychiatrist?"

"I see her now and then."

"That's Dr. Philomena Imperato?"

"Yes."

Judge Miller gave a surprised look to the witness stand, then to the Ramsays. Cam clenched her jaw.

"You had a particularly traumatic experience in Vietnam, didn't you, Mr. Lombard?"

"Everybody did. I don't know how you could say one was any worse than the other."

"But you survived one of the worst slaughters of U.S. troops in the entire war. Didn't you?"

The muscle jumped like a live thing in his face. "Yes," he said thickly.

"Tell the Court what happened in that engagement."

Jesse fixed his eyes on the table in front of him. "We got surrounded. They blew us out of the water."

"By *us*, you mean Task Force 118. The Brown River Navy, they called it?"

"Yes, sir."

"What were the U.S. casualties that day?"

"There were only ten of us who survived."

"And several hundred who didn't."

"Right."

"You still have nightmares about that engagement, don't you, Mr. Lombard?"

"Sometimes."

"In fact, they've gotten worse over time?"

"Only since my gunshot wound. The doc says it triggered something."

"Sometimes you scream out during these nightmares?"

"I guess."

"Sometimes you sleepwalk?"

"Yes."

"And sometimes you wake up and find that you've injured yourself?"

"A few times it happened, that's all."

Benjamin turned a page in his notebook, and Cam could feel the relief radiating off the Ramsays.

"And one time you woke up and found your hands around the throat of Trey Ramsay?"

The Ramsays sat up tense in their seats again.

"I never hurt him!" Jesse cried. "They moved me to the garage after that. I never hurt him!"

"After that incident, did the Ramsays continue to leave you alone with the boy?"

"They knew I wouldn't hurt him!" Jesse twisted in his seat, and his left arm slid off the table.

"What steps did they take to make sure you wouldn't?"

Jesse stared at his arm dangling over the edge of the table, and his face contorted as he struggled to raise it up again. Finally he reached across with his right hand and lifted it.

"Mr. Lombard," Benjamin said, louder. "Would you answer the question?"

Jesse looked at him with uncomprehending terror in his eyes.

Across the aisle came the sound of a throat being cleared. Bruce Benjamin heard it, too, and when his eyes darted to his client, Steve gave a quick, firm shake of his head.

"No further questions," Benjamin said.

The judge looked to Cam.

"No questions," she said quickly, before Ramsay could whisper to her.

"Mr. Lombard, you are excused. This court will be in recess for ten minutes."

The courtroom cleared at once, leaving only Cam and Margo

at the table. After a few moments of strained silence, Cam said, "You should have told me."

"But it was so long ago! I never imagined it would come up. I can't even imagine how they found out."

"Trey must have told him."

"Bruce Benjamin?" she said, confused.

"Steve Patterson. In Maine."

Margo sat back. "They talked about things like that?" She shook her head, dumbfounded. "Trey never talks about things like that."

Ramsay swung through the door and gave a quick look around to confirm that they were alone. "Campbell," he said, striding to their table. "When the judge comes back, you need to get this thing continued. I have to get back to Washington tonight."

"But Senator—I cleared these dates with you weeks ago."

"Can't be helped. Things have come up."

"But this case—"

"I think the business of the United States Senate takes precedence, don't you?"

She bit her lip and turned away.

When Judge Miller returned to the bench fifteen minutes later, both lawyers were on their feet waiting to be heard. Benjamin explained that the examination of Mr. Lombard was over sooner than he'd anticipated, and that his next and indeed final witness was an expert who could not make herself available until tomorrow.

Cam then explained that Senator Ramsay had been urgently recalled to Washington, and she requested an adjournment until next week. Benjamin made an indignant protest against such an unconscionable delay, but Miller called his bluff. "Fine. No delays. Call your next witness, Mr. Benjamin."

The hearing was adjourned until the following week.

Steve came to the folly at nightfall. Cam was waiting for him with a cold supper laid on the little bistro table. He brought a bottle of wine and two plastic cups and put them down to take her in his arms. They held each other a long time before either spoke.

"Are you all right?" he asked, tilting her chin back.

She shrugged. "It was so brutal, what happened today."

"Jesse? I know. It was my fault—I was too slow to stop it."

"It wasn't your fault. I just wish it could all be over."

"It will be soon. We only have one more witness, then the judge's interview with Trey."

She looked up at him with dull eyes. "We still have our witnesses," she said.

He winced. "Oh, right."

She could feel the tension in the muscles of his back. He was yearning to ask the question, but he knew that he couldn't. He kissed her instead, and they parted awkwardly and sat down at the table. They ate and drank in silence, but Cam had little appetite, and she was happy to push her plate away when he was done.

Upstairs, she'd dressed the bed with pillows and a comforter and set out candles that sparkled like tiny star points at the edges of the room. He rotated slowly, taking it in, then took her by the shoulders and pulled her to him, then pulled her down to the mattress.

"I love you," he murmured afterward.

Her body jerked with the unexpectedness of it. "That's impossible," she said bleakly. "You don't even know me."

"But I do. Because of Trey. I see the way you are with him, and how good you've been for him. I see you the way he sees you." His hand was on her face, and his thumb traced the edge of her jaw and the curves of her lip. "And don't tell me that's not the real you, because I know it is."

She shook her head sadly. "That's only part of me. What about the rest? Like the part that put you through hell on the witness stand yesterday? That's me, too, you know."

"Cam." He wrapped his arms around her. "Would you stop beating yourself up over that? You didn't do anything that any other lawyer wouldn't have done. In fact, you didn't even ask me the one question I was dreading most."

"Oh." She went still. "You mean—what happened on the island that made Trey radio the police?"

"Uh-huh. That's the one I was afraid of."

"Can—Can I ask now?"

"Yeah, though God knows what you'll think of me." He blew out his breath. "It wasn't exactly my finest hour."

He rolled onto his back and folded his arms under his head. "We had this old widow's walk on the house up there. Maybe you noticed it? It was all rotted out; I should have dismantled it my first day on site. Instead I just told him it was dangerous and to stay away from it. Which I guess made it even more tantalizing. I caught him up there once and gave him hell about it, and—stupid me—I thought that was the end of it. But damn if he didn't go up there again, and this time the worst happened. The wood gave way and the whole structure collapsed."

"Oh, God."

"I was working down at the dock, but somehow I heard him yell, or felt it or something. I raced up there, and there he was, clinging to the edge of the roof. Jesus—I think my heart stopped. Another couple of inches, another couple of minutes, and he would've fallen a hundred feet onto the rocks."

He lost his voice for a moment, and Cam touched her fingers to his jaw as he swallowed and found it again.

"It was a miracle I got there in time. I pulled him back inside and held him and all I could think about was how close he'd come to dying and what a stupid little fool he was, and then—then I guess I just lost it."

"What?"

"I spanked him."

Cam looked at him, wide-eyed in the candlelight.

"I know," he said, cringing. "Can you believe it? Over my knee, the whole nine yards. What an idiot. I knew it was a mistake the second it was over, but I was still too shook up and steamed up to apologize or anything. I just left him in his room to cool off, and I went downstairs to cool off myself."

"And that's when he went to the radio."

"If he'd been anywhere else, he would have just run away. Any kid would have. Hell, *I* would have. But he didn't have that option. He was stuck on an island. The only thing he could do was radio the police."

A cold, dead weight seemed to settle in Cam's chest. "And you forgave him for that?"

"Of course."

"But after all you went through—"

"Nobody suffered more than he did. Or regretted it more, either."

Cam sat up suddenly and turned away from him.

"Cam?"

She hunched her back and hugged her knees to her chest, until her shoulder blades jutted out like the wing tips on a flightless bird. She flinched when he touched her back.

"So, I was right," he said darkly. "I knew you'd think less of me."

"Not you," she choked. "Me. You'll think less of *me*."

"What?"

She drew a breath so sharp it sounded like a stab wound to her lungs. "There's something I have to tell you. About me. It's the truth about me. It's why you could never love me, Steve."

"Campbell, no—"

"I'm not Campbell," she cried. "I'm not anyone you think I am. My name is Camille Johnson, and my parents weren't killed when I was a baby. My father's alive and running a service station, and my mother—if she's alive at all—is running from the FBI."

"What?"

"Because when I was fifteen, I got pregnant . . ."

Darryl was waiting in his car with the engine running when she came out of the clinic. "Now, remember," the nurse said as she helped Cam into the passenger seat, "call us if the bleeding goes on longer than ten days."

"I will."

"And no intercourse for a month," the nurse said with a scowl at Darryl.

"No," Cam said.

She shifted to find a way to sit with the thick padding between her legs, then leaned weakly against the seat as Darryl pulled out of the parking lot.

"So—how ya feelin'?"

"Don't talk," she said.

"I was only askin'—"

"Don't ask. You paid your half and you drove me here, and that's all I want from you."

He worked his jaw as he stared ahead through the windshield. "Look, I said I was sorry. All right? I told you I never had this happen before."

"Me neither," she said. "And I never will again. And if I ever did, it certainly wouldn't be with you."

"Cunt," he muttered.

She made him drop her off on the highway, and he drove on alone to the garage for the start of his afternoon shift. He was already at work at the pumps by the time she walked past with her schoolbooks in her arms. She waved to her father inside the service bay, then shifted her books to the other hip and started the long trudge up the hill to the trailer.

She was halfway there before she realized that she'd left her purse at the clinic. She tried to think if there was anyone she could ask to drive her back to get it. But there was no one, and she resigned herself to losing it. It was nothing compared to everything else she'd lost today.

She climbed up the porch steps and shouldered the door open. Her mother was just hanging up the phone in the living room, and she turned around with an awful expression frozen on her face. Cam's first thought was that someone must have died.

Her second thought was that someone had, and that now her mother knew it, too.

"That was the nurse at the clinic," her mother said through white lips. "She hopes you're feeling all right, and don't worry about your purse. She has it locked in her desk." Her face contorted and was suddenly ugly with grief and rage.

"Mom—"

Her mother flew at her with a keening moan and both hands flailing. Cam's books spilled to the floor and she threw her arms up in front of her face. "Mom, wait!"

"You slut, you little slut! How could you do this? How could you throw away your life this way? You had everything—I gave you everything I could! And what did you do but spread your legs apart for the first boy you found? You filthy little slut!"

Cam's screams strangled in her throat but the slaps kept coming, raining down over her head and shoulders and back until she fell to her knees. "Mom!" she cried out with her hands over her head. "Wait! Stop! Let me explain!"

"It's Darryl, isn't it?" she shrieked. She wheeled to the door and wrenched it open. "I'll kill him! I swear to God, I'll kill him!"

The door banged shut behind her.

After a minute Cam pulled herself to her feet and staggered to her room. She dug through the boxes in the bottom of her closet until she found the tattered composition books that comprised her old Harriet the Spy files. She brushed off five years' accumulated dust and riffled through the pages until she found what she wanted. Then she packed a bag with as much as she could carry and walked out of the trailer for the last time.

She stopped at the first mailbox in town and dropped in a large manila envelope addressed to the FBI. Inside, in her best ten-year-old penmanship, was her mother's full name and Social Security number; the dates of her employment with the National Reconnaissance Office; details of her knowledge of spy satellites and capsule ejection and recovery procedures; and a description of her mysterious gentleman caller, along with the pencil rubbing of his note, a record of his cash gift, his license plate number, and his fingerprints.

Two weeks later when she called home from a phone booth in Elizabethtown, it was Charlene who answered, and she told Cam as much as she understood. Their mother had disappeared only three days after she did, and only a day before five carloads of FBI agents squealed up the hill and surrounded the trailer. They had handguns, shotguns, and rifles, and a warrant for the arrest of Abigail Zodtner Johnson on charges of espionage.

"Cam," Steve said, stricken. He was up on his knees behind her, trying to get her to turn to him, but she shook him off and hunched deeper into herself. "Cam, I hate it that you've been living with this all these years."

"Me? What about her? How has she been living? If she's living at all."

"She is. You would have heard something if she wasn't."

She reflected a moment and gave a slight nod to acknowledge his logic, then straightened with a ragged breath. He pulled her back against him until her head rested in the hollow of his neck.

"Did you ever find out what it was—that she did?"

"No. It's all classified. But this was 1968. People were blowing up draft boards that year; my mother leaked satellite photos to the enemy. I guess it was her idea of making a political statement against the war."

"What about her mystery caller? What did he have to do with it?"

"I don't know. At first I thought he must have been in on it with her. But as far as I can tell, he was never arrested, and there was never a warrant issued on him. I don't know—maybe he was one of those underground revolutionaries who helped out fugitives." She squeezed her eyes shut as another auger of pain drilled through her. "And there's more, too. It's not only the FBI who's after her." She turned on her knees to face him. "Two of the other women who worked at the NRO were murdered this year, by the same killer."

"What?" he said, staring at her. "Who?"

"Nobody knows, and the cops are following all the wrong leads. They're not even looking at the espionage connection. And the worst is that my mother doesn't know she's in danger, and there's no way anyone can warn her, because no one knows where she is." In a low voice, bitter and ashamed, she said, "Thanks to me."

"Cam." He pulled her to him and stroked the length of her hair. "This is what's holding you back from me, isn't it? Not your husband, not the case. It's this guilt."

"It's me. It's who I am."

"No, it's only what you did. One rash act half a life ago. You can't carry this around with you forever."

"I turned in my own mother."

"You were a kid in a highly emotional state. Anyone would understand and forgive you. It's not as if you made it up. Your mother did what she did. Cam, it's just like me and Trey. But I don't blame him, and I can't believe your mom blames you."

"I can't believe she doesn't."

"She forgave you years ago. She loves you."

"How can you possibly know that?"

He touched his thumbs to her cheeks and wiped at the tears, then leaned in and softly licked away their trails. "Because I love you."

She leaned back and searched his face in the candlelight, but she couldn't believe that either.

They talked and dozed on and off for hours, until the night took on the texture of a dream and Cam could barely distinguish between what she was telling him and what she was merely imagining. Toward dawn he asked: "What happened to that guy Darryl? Did you ever hear?"

"Charlene said Mom went after him with a tire iron. It took my father and two truckers to pull her off him before she bashed his skull in. As it was, he took ten stitches in his scalp, and nobody ever saw him at Johnson's Sunoco again."

After a moment Steve chuckled drowsily. "She must be something, your mom."

"Hmm?"

"She was like a she-bear fighting to protect her cub." He yawned and rolled over. "I like that," he mumbled as his voice faded off into sleep.

Doug arrived back in Wilmington Thursday afternoon and made a quick sweep through the office of Jackson, Rieders & Clark to press the flesh of his colleagues before heading to his campaign headquarters. Cam was at her desk, and she could track his progress through the corridors by the bursts of loud voices and laughter. She heard him nearing the corner five doors down, and when she heard him turn down the other way, she felt a shudder of relief.

Nathan popped his head in her office. "How's it going?"

"Ramsay bailed in the middle of our hearing. Other than that, it's going miserably."

"Yeah, I heard."

"Which part?"

"Both, actually. But, hey, don't worry about it."

"Don't worry about it?" she burst out. "I thought Doug's entire future hinged on my winning this case."

"That was last month. Listen, we're going to be holed up the rest of today prepping for Sunday's debate. So don't expect Doug home until late."

"I don't expect anything," she said.

His eyes narrowed, but Doug was calling him from the end of the hall, and he turned away.

Later that day Steve called. "Are you all right?" he said without identifying himself, as they'd agreed.

She swiveled in her chair and looked out over the streets of Wilmington. The maple tree on the corner had gone vermilion in the night. "He's back," she said.

"I figured. Come to my place tonight."

"And how do I explain that?"

"Then come now. This afternoon."

"I can't. I have a meeting."

"Have one with me, too. Name the place and time."

"I can't. Not today."

He was silent a moment. "Don't pull away from me, Cam."

"I'm not. It's just that—" She stopped and bit her lip.

"That you let me get closer than you meant to, and now you're pushing me away."

"No, today's just not good—"

"Tomorrow, then."

"I have to be in the Philadelphia office tomorrow."

Again he was silent, and it filled her with dread.

"Steve?"

"You know, Cam, the problem isn't that I know too much about you. It's that you don't know enough about yourself."

"That doesn't make any sense."

"Yes, it does. Take a few days. Call me when you figure it out."

Cam did have a meeting that afternoon, with Margo Ramsay.

Margo answered the door herself. She was wearing an apple-green kimono and waving a glass of sherry in her hand.

"Has Jesse gone to pick up Trey?" Cam asked as she followed her to the living room.

"Hmm?" Margo stumbled a little and clutched onto the arm of the sofa as she sat down. "No. Poor Jesse. He hasn't left his room since we got back from court yesterday." She took a swallow of sherry, then looked with surprise at the glass in her hand. "Oh, forgive me, Campbell. I forgot to offer you something to drink."

"Nothing for me, thank you." Cam sat down in an armchair and pulled out her trial notebook. "Senator Ramsay suggested I use this downtime to prepare you to testify next week."

"A cup of tea, then? Or coffee?"

"No, I'm fine."

"I'd offer you sherry, but I know girls your age don't care for it."

"I don't care for anything, thank you. I have an outline here of some points I hoped we might—"

"You ought to develop a taste for it, though."

"What?"

"Sherry." Margo held the glass to the light and squinted through it. "You'll have so many affairs to attend next year, and you know, sherry is still the only socially acceptable alcohol a lady can drink in the afternoon."

"Yes, I'll keep that in mind. I'm sorry to be abrupt, but I wonder if we could talk about the case now?"

"The case." Margo raised her glass and drained it. "He's winning, isn't he?"

"It's too soon to—"

"No, it's not."

"Yesterday was a bad day for us," Cam conceded. "I don't know—it might have gone better if I'd known."

Margo got up, went to the sideboard, and refilled her glass. "I suppose there's something else it might be better for you to know. Believe it or not"—she paused to take a sip—"Ash told him the truth that day in the Virgin Islands."

This was a topic from Tuesday's testimony, and it took Cam a beat to pick up the thread. "You mean about Cynthia wanting to get on with her life? Or about the adoption procedures?"

"All of it." She sat down again. "When Ash went there, it was everyone's intention to place the baby through an agency."

"Except for Cynthia?"

"Cynthia most of all. She didn't hesitate to sign those papers. She had no desire to be a single mother. If she couldn't have Steve Patterson—and Ash made it quite clear that she couldn't—then she didn't want any reminders of him, either."

"What happened to change her mind?"

"Campbell, that's what I'm trying to tell you. Nothing happened. She never changed her mind."

"I don't understand—"

Margo sighed. "That year Cynth went away to college—it was brutal. We'd always been so close, and suddenly I was at sea. I didn't know what to do with myself, rattling around in this old house. I felt so useless. And more dependent on Ash than ever. Poor company as he was, at least he was company." She tipped the glass to her lips again. "Then he announced that he was running for the Senate and moving to Washington, and that I was to remain here, alone, and maintain the fiction that he was still a Delawarean at heart. I didn't know how I was going to cope."

Cam stared at her. "It was your idea to keep the baby?"

"The moment I saw him, I thought, here's all I need. The second child I was never blessed with, come twenty years later."

"Senator Ramsay agreed to that?"

"He had no choice. He needed my money, you see, to finance his campaign."

"My God," Cam blurted, and dug her nails in her palms to keep herself from saying more. Tort reform, a newborn child—all fair currency in the game of politics.

"I know what you're thinking." Margo's fingers fluttered to her forehead as her eyes fell shut. "Such a colossally selfish act. My poor Cynth. She never went back to school that fall, even though Ash arranged her transfer to Penn. Here she stayed, having to live every day with the baby she didn't want. She used to look at him with tears streaming down her face—"

The front door banged in the hall, and Margo blinked and sat up straight. "Trey, darling!" Her voice was like metal, bright and sharp and hard. "You're home! How was school today?"

The only answer was the sound of his feet on the stairs.

For a long time Margo sat motionless on the sofa. Cam closed her notebook and put it away. "Shall we do this some other time, Mrs. Ramsey?"

She nodded mutely.

Cam rose and went to the door.

"Isn't it strange?" Margo said in a dazed voice. "Since it was my choice to keep him, you'd think it would be my choice to let him go."

Cam stopped and looked back at her. "Maybe it is."

Margo lowered her eyes and shook her head.

That night, Cam was in bed when she heard Doug's voice in the hall downstairs, and it was surrounded by a chorus of other voices. He was never alone anymore: for the past eight months people had been attaching themselves to him like sharksuckers hoping to share in the kill. But no, it was more symbiotic than that: Doug needed them at least as much as they needed him.

The chorus slowly faded, and at midnight she heard Doug's feet on the stairs. There was a hesitation as he crossed the landing, a brief hiccough in his step as he passed the closed door to her room. But he walked on.

She rolled over with thoughts of Steve swelling her heart, and on the edge of sleep it came to her that if all she could have of him was his baby, she'd take it, and count it as more than she deserved.

* * *

On Friday, Helen brought in a week's worth of accumulated mail, a stack of time sheets, and a package. "This just arrived by hand delivery," she said.

It was a small package wrapped in heavy brown paper. The name in the upper left corner was Pat Stevens, but it meant nothing to Cam, and neither did the address. She opened it and parted layers of tissue paper to find a book. It was an old one, with a tattered binding and no dust jacket. Law books usually arrived shiny new and triple-wrapped in plastic. Puzzled, Cam turned it and read the gilt letters on the spine. *Louise Fitzhugh,* it said, *Harriet the Spy.*

Her breath caught and she flipped it open. Inside was an inscription in blue ink and a strong hand: *Cam, I love you for all the things you are, all the things you will be, and all the things you ever were—including Harriet the Spy. Steve.*

Tears welled in her eyes. He must have scoured every used bookstore in a hundred-mile radius to find it. She ran her fingers over the heavy stock of the paper. It was once her most beloved book. It would be still if her own actions hadn't defiled its memory. She turned to chapter one, and it all came rushing back, the opening scene with Harriet spinning tales outside her brownstone house; her gruff, kind nanny scolding her from a third-floor window to get out of the mud; Harriet retorting, "I'm not in the mud"; the nanny shouting, "Harriet M. Welsch, you are to rise to your feet—"

Slowly Cam rose to her own feet. *Harriet M. Welsch.* The familiar name that she just couldn't place. *The Harriet M. Welsch Foundation.* An organization for motherless girls that was so anxious to have her join its board that they sent her three requests before they finally gave up.

And she'd sent all three requests to the trash can.

She sat down again and spun to her computer, her hands shaking so much that it took her three attempts to type in the search request without errors.

Not found.

The letterhead showed a Philadelphia address, she remembered that much. She dialed directory assistance, but after a minute the Bell Atlantic computer told her the same thing that her own just did. *No listing.*

Helen was standing in her office, and Cam looked up at her in a daze, only faintly aware that she'd spoken.

"Your time sheets, I said. If you could sign them today, they need to get them into the system over the weekend."

"Oh. Yes."

"Is anything wrong, dear?""

"No. Not at all." But before Helen left, Cam said, "You remember that foundation that kept asking me to go on its board?"

"Why, yes. The one for motherless girls?"

"Do you remember where it was headquartered?"

"Here in the city, wasn't it?"

"I'm trying to remember the street address."

"Sorry," Helen said as she left.

A cold knife of despair stabbed through Cam. She swiveled back to the terminal and let her hands hover over the keyboard, but nothing came to her. She'd reached the end of her search requests.

"Here. I found it," Helen said, bustling back in with a sheet of paper. "I kept a copy on file. I just knew you'd be interested someday."

It was the first of the Harriet M. Welsch Foundation letters, and across the top was the address.

"Helen, thank you!" Cam cried, and she jumped up and grabbed her in a hug that left the older woman sputtering with surprise and pleasure.

34

It was in the middle of a block of row houses three streets off Roosevelt Boulevard in Northeast Philadelphia. There was a mom-and-pop grocery on the corner, a chain-linked playground across the street, and a line of ten-year-old cars wedged bumper-to-bumper at the curb. The houses were one solid masonry mass, each unit a door and a window below and two windows above, with a patch of lawn beside a concrete stoop. Poor but clean, bleak but respectable, one block in a section of thousands that all looked more or less the same. A good hiding place, if this was it.

"You sure of that address?" the cab driver asked doubtfully as he slowed in the middle of the block. This was hardly the destination he'd hoped for when he picked up a well-dressed young woman with a Burberry shopping bag at the Ritz-Carlton.

Cam pretended to scan the street numbers. No heads appeared in any of the parked cars; there were no telltale wisps of smoke or puddles of liquid by the curb. If anyone was doing surveillance, they weren't visible to her. "I think so, yes."

She paid him and adjusted her scarf and sunglasses before she got out. A gust of wind blew as the cab drove off, and she clenched the scarf to her throat and waited until the cab rounded the corner before she went to the door. The curtain twitched at the window when she rang the bell, then the door opened.

Her hopes sank. Inside stood a man of sixty or seventy with grizzled gray-blond hair and a weather-beaten face. He cracked the storm door open. "Yeah?"

"I'm sorry, I have the wrong address." She turned to go.

"Who was it you were looking for?"

She took off her sunglasses. "Harriet M. Welsch?"

His ravaged face went blank as he looked at her. "What d'you know?" he said after a moment. "I'm out a hundred bucks."

"Excuse me?"

"I said you were never gonna figure it out. But Abby—she was sure that one of these days you would."

Cam drew a breath so sharp it sounded like a sob in her throat.

"Come on in," he said, pushing the door wide. "She's out back." He jerked a thumb at the rear of the house and settled himself in a recliner. "Go on out. You can't miss her."

In a trance, Cam walked back through the small living room and dining room, then into the kitchen. A pot of soup was simmering on the stove, and an array of prescription medicines sat on a lazy Susan on the kitchen table. She put her shopping bag down on the table and took off the scarf, then went to the back door.

Outside, the air had a sharp, clean fragrance like spring flowers, though fallen leaves rustled on the ground at Cam's feet. Two rows of clothesline were stretched across the width of the small yard, and they were hung with white sheets that flapped and billowed like sails in the wind. One of the sheets blew up against a woman's body on the other side of the line, molding itself like the wraps on a mummy before it lifted and blew free again. Cam came around slowly as the woman was bending to reach into the laundry basket. She straightened with a bath towel in her hands and a clothespin in her mouth.

She dropped both when she saw Cam. A question passed through her eyes and left them shining with tears, and her hands went to her face and her mouth moved, soundlessly forming *Cammy*.

"Mom?"

"Cammy!" she cried out loud and hugged her with damp hands and arms. "You're here! My baby! Oh, God, I prayed someday you'd come—" She took Cam's face in her hands. "Thank God you came!"

"But why didn't you come to me?" Cam cried. "There must have been some safe way you could have—"

"I didn't want to force myself on you, Cammy. I only wanted you to look me up if you were interested."

"Interested? Mom, I've been trying to find you, every way I know how. I've been trying so hard—"

"You wanted to find me?" She held Cam's shoulders and searched her eyes. "After what I did to you?"

"No," Cam said with tears streaming down her face. "After what I did to *you*."

Her mother's eyes squeezed shut as if a gun had gone off. "Dear God," she whispered. "Please tell me you haven't been holding that thought in your head all these years."

Cam pulled her lips tight to keep them from trembling.

"Oh, my poor baby," her mother cried, seizing her again. "It wasn't your fault! Do you hear me? It was never your fault!"

Cam sagged against her as fourteen years of guilt and yearning fell away. She felt dizzy and disoriented, like a child who'd been spinning in circles from yard to yard until she didn't know where she'd landed.

From the back door came a cough, and they turned to see the man at the screen. "Abby, you gonna stand out there all day?" he said. "After all these years, I'd think you could ask her to come in and sit down a while."

His name was Pete, they'd been as good as married for the past eight years, and he knew everything there was to know. Nonetheless, after a few minutes of small talk, he declared he'd go see Joe down the street for a bit.

"Don't forget your jacket. You'll catch your death with this chill in the air."

He rolled his eyes, but pulled on his jacket and pecked her cheek goodbye. "A hundred bucks," he said, shaking his head sadly at Cam as he left.

"You should let him win that bet," Cam said after the front door banged and he was gone. "He was right. I never would have figured it out on my own."

"But you did," her mother said, beaming. "Here you are."

"Only because a friend gave me the book this morning. I opened it, and there it was: Harriet M. Welsch."

Her mother smiled and reached across the kitchen table to pat her hand. "Sounds like a very special friend."

"But how did you ever find me? I changed my name, and my Social Security number—"

A smile broke like the dawn over her mother's face. "I saw your picture in the newspaper. Your wedding announcement."

"But that only ran in the Wilmington paper—"

"I looked at all the papers. All I could get anyway. Every

Sunday I used to go to the library and read through the whole week's stack of every paper they subscribed to."

"Every week? For all those years?"

"No, only until February, when I found out your name and where you worked and everything. That's when I got the idea of writing to you. Pete used to work for a print shop, and he had them run off that letterhead for me." She laughed. "I still have a whole box upstairs. But after the third letter, I didn't think I should write again. I just prayed that you'd want to come." She sat back and beamed at Cam again. "And you did. Here you are."

"Of course, I wanted to. But Mom"—Cam leaned forward intently—"there's a reason why I had to come. You're not safe. Gloria Lipton was murdered last winter—"

"I know! I was so shocked when I read about it. First that she was killed, and then that she worked at your firm. I thought, what a small world, and in the next breath, I thought, oh my God, that could have been Cammy on the street that night. I was so afraid for you—"

"But you're the one in danger. He killed Doris Palumbo, too—"

"I know. Poor Doris—"

"You could be next!"

"Oh, Cammy, no," she said, shaking her head dismissively. "There's no connection to me." She got up to get the coffeepot. "It was something to do with the two of them."

"Mom," Cam said severely, "they both worked at the NRO when that capsule was intercepted. It's not a coincidence."

A mask settled over her mother's face as she returned to the table and topped off their cups. "I'm not saying it was," she said tightly. "But I know it had nothing to do with me or the NRO."

"How can you be so sure?"

"Because—" She put the pot down and sank into her chair. "—anyone who knows what happened and knows that I was involved would have to know that Gloria and Doris weren't."

"Oh." Cam looked down at her coffee, then flicked her eyes up at her mother. "I wondered about that."

"What?"

"Whether they were part of the movement, too."

"What movement?"

"The antiwar movement, or whatever it was."

Her mother put down her cup so suddenly that the coffee

sloshed out into the saucer. "Is that what you've been thinking all these years? That I was some kind of activist? Making some noble sacrifice for the cause?"

"I didn't know what else—"

"I don't know how many more ugly truths you can take, but I can't let you go on thinking that. Cammy—sweetie—I did it for the money."

Cam's jaw dropped.

"Twenty thousand dollars. It was a lot of money in 1968."

"But—why?"

"That was how much Bud needed to buy the service station, and I didn't see any other way I could raise it. All I had to do was cable the coordinates to a contact in Oslo, and transpose a few coordinates in my cable to our people. It seemed like nothing at the time." She stared down hard at the table. "It didn't seem like something that would end up killing people."

"You did it for Dad?" Cam said, dumbfounded.

Her mother's eyes were brimming with tears when she looked up. "That was his price to marry me and give you a name."

It was as if Cam had been staring all her life at an optical illusion and now suddenly could see the hidden shape inside it. It was a feeling like, *Of course, I almost knew that.* At that moment, everything else seemed to fall into place, too, and all her childhood bewilderments and all the crisscrossed family alliances finally made sense.

"Oh, my God," her mother whispered. "You didn't know?"

"No, I did," Cam said. "I just never stopped to put words to it. It's funny, though. He was always so kind to me."

"He's a good man. You can't blame him for not wanting to raise another man's child without something to show for it."

"But then—" Cam looked at her mother. "Who . . . ?"

"I promised him I'd never tell a soul, and I never have, not in thirty years. But I always thought you'd figure it out on your own, a smart girl like you." She reached out and touched Cam's cheek. "I can't believe people haven't remarked on it. You look so much like him."

The light went out of Cam's eyes. "He was a politician."

"Still is, the last time I looked at the newspaper. But he was just starting out in Congress then. And married, of course. The scandal would have ruined him. But he was a wonderful man, and looking at you now—I can see all his goodness in you, too."

Looking at her mother, Cam could see how willing she was to break her promise. All she had to do was ask. Cam lifted her cup and took a slow sip of coffee and realized there was nothing more she needed to know. She put her cup down with a smile. "Let's go out and hang up the rest of that wash."

While they worked, Cam pumped her mother for the details of her life these last fourteen years. She'd gotten by on good, honest labor, cleaning and cooking mostly. In her off hours she got involved in service projects for disabled Vietnam vets. That was how she met Pete. He was a vet himself, and they were in the same van one winter night searching for their charges among the homeless men who slept on the steam vents in Center City. Something clicked between them that first night, but it took a long time and a lot of persistence on his part before she let him into her life. It was too much for him to take on, she'd thought, her and all her ghosts, but he never complained.

"I have a proposition for you," Cam said when they went back inside. "Let me get you a lawyer, the best there is, to negotiate your surrender and defend you against these charges. I know it's risky, but I'll be with you every step of the way."

Her mother smiled. "That's a wonderful offer, sweetheart. I've thought of doing it a thousand times, and I came close a time or two. To have you there with me—I really think I could go through with it. I'd do it, if it weren't for Pete."

"Why?"

"He has lung cancer. They cut out as much as they could, and he's had all the chemo and radiation they can give him. But it's no use. He's got maybe a year."

"Oh, Mom, I'm so sorry."

"He's a good man, Cammy. Too good for me. The least I can do is stick with him through this. But then—after he goes—I could turn myself in."

After that could be too late, Cam thought. "Then I have another proposition. I'll help you leave the country, you and Pete together. I'll get you somewhere safe."

Her mother laughed. "Pete's always after me about the same thing. Shoving these island brochures across the table at me all the time. But how can I go anywhere? I don't have a passport or any way to get one. Besides"—she smiled and squeezed Cam's hand—"I don't want to leave now, after I just found you. And look at you! So beautiful and successful, and happily married to such an important man."

Cam said nothing, but her face must have said it all, because suddenly her mother was on her feet and cradling her head against her. "Tell me," she whispered. "Tell me what's wrong."

They moved to the living room, and over the next hour Cam confessed all of her failures and all of the bad choices she'd made for all of the wrong reasons, and her mother nodded and held her hands and told her no, she hadn't failed, she was right to want more, she deserved every happiness in life.

"How can you say that?" It was the topic Cam had dodged earlier by the clothesline, but she couldn't suppress it forever, not after fourteen years of living with it every day. "How do I deserve any happiness after what I did to you? I separated you from your family, I sent you into hiding—"

"I did all that to myself."

"But if I hadn't tipped them off, today you'd be—"

"What?" she said sharply. "Hiding from the world in that trailer with a man I couldn't talk to? Why is this worse than that? I was in hiding either way. And now I have Pete, and there's not a day goes by I don't count myself blessed to have found him. You talk about undeserved happiness. I don't deserve Pete, but I grabbed onto him anyway, and I don't regret it for a minute."

She took Cam in her arms and said softly, "I want you to think about what it is that makes you happy. And I want you to grab onto it and don't ever look back."

Pete returned at the end of the afternoon, and the pot of soup that was meant to be lunch for two instead became dinner for three. At the end of the meal, when Cam got up to help with the dishes, Pete leaned back in his chair and lit up a cigarette.

Her mother caught her eye and shook her head. "It's no use. I can't get him to stop. Last time he was in the hospital he set off the alarm sneaking a smoke in the bathroom."

"There's two things I can't abide, " Pete said, blowing rings at the ceiling. "One's a reformed sinner, and the other's a reformed smoker."

Cam looked at her mother. "Reformed?"

"I quit fourteen years ago. They were looking for a smoker, so

I had to stop being one. You see?" she said, smiling. "Another good thing came of all this."

It was time at last for Cam to go. Pete said his goodbyes and left them alone, and after they worked out a code for the telephone and agreed on a place to meet, they hugged each other one last time at the door.

"You tell him thank you from me, too, would you?" her mother said.

"Who?"

"The man who gave you the book this morning."

"What? How did you guess?"

"Oh, Cammy." She smiled. "You always thought you were such a good liar. But I could usually see right through you."

Cam caught the bus on the Boulevard and rode it back to Center City, then cashed her car out of the parking lot and drove to West Chester, and at eight o'clock was knocking on the door to Steve's apartment.

He opened it. He was barefoot, wearing blue jeans, an unbuttoned shirt, and a look of curiosity that went quickly to uncertain surprise.

"Here I am," she said. "If you want me."

His surprise gave way to a slow smile. "I do," he said.

"And by the way," she added as he pulled her inside, "I love you, and I want to spend the rest of my life with you."

"I'll take that, too," he said, and closed the door.

At nine o'clock that night the final vote of the Senate term was recorded, and Gary Pfeiffer was in the gallery to see it happen. He sat in a kind of trance long afterward, and the floor was almost cleared by the time he remembered numbly to stand, then to turn and walk.

A million dollars, a year's work—gone. No, who was he fooling? It was a life's work he'd lost here tonight. ALJA would fire him within the week, and there'd be nobody lining up to take its place on his client roster. He'd been made a fool of, a laughingstock in a town with a short memory and a cruel wit. All his careful plans, all his hard work—everything was ruined. And it wouldn't be long before his balance sheet reflected it. So what now? He could sell the shore house and move into a shack with

Derek, but even if the money lasted, he had to wonder how long they would. Or he could stay with Eileen and her respectable income and let her support him until he struggled onto his feet again.

A Hobson's choice. Derek, the beach house, everything he loved was stripped from him, and a white hot hatred steamed up inside him at the people responsible.

He picked up his pace, and soon he was striding briskly across the Rotunda to the House Chamber with his footsteps echoing like the tolling of a bell. He beckoned to a House page and scribbled out a note, then took up position at the door to wait.

It didn't take long. The door swung open and Representative Hadley Hayes came out with the note in his hand.

"Good evening, Congressman," Gary said. "Can I buy you a drink to celebrate the close of the 105th?"

The old man waved the note at him. "You say here you have some information about Alexander?"

"I do," Gary said, leading the way. "I do, indeed."

35

Sunday was the first and only debate of the campaign, sponsored and moderated by the League of Women Voters, televised at the Channel 2 studios in New Castle and broadcast live throughout Delaware.

Meredith Winters and Norman Finn were waiting when Doug and his retinue arrived. Finn shook hands all around, but Meredith only had eyes for Doug. Critical eyes. "Makeup!" she yelled, and swept him away.

Cam endured her own hair and makeup check and was deposited in the lounge to await her cue. Someone had left the Sunday *Post* on the table there, and she sipped her coffee and paged through it. A special section reviewed the more significant laws enacted in the closing days of the 105th, and she started to flip past it when a single phrase caught her eye: *passage of tort reform legislation.*

She read it again. On Friday the Senate brought the long delayed S.4 to the floor, where it passed with a comfortable margin. Since the House had already passed it, the bill then went to the President, and he chose not to repeat his earlier veto. He signed it into law yesterday morning.

"Ten minutes, Cam," Nathan said, sticking his head around the doorway.

"Spare me one now?"

"Sure. What's up?"

She pointed to the newspaper. "Tort reform, apparently."

"I know. That's why we were called down there last week. The leadership wanted it to go to a vote."

"But you had a deal with Ramsay."

"He was getting a lot of flak, so we decided to let it go. Truth is, Doug was never happy being in bed with ALJA anyway."

"He was happy enough to take their money, though."

Nathan threw a look behind him, and came in and closed the door. "Okay, before you get up on your high horse about this—"

"About what?" She tossed the newspaper on the table. "Making a deal and sticking to it?"

"We needed that money, Cam. There wasn't any other way."

"Of course there was. Do without."

"And lose the election? Let Hadley Hayes stay in office? How's that the lesser of two evils?"

"How is your way?" she cried. "How can you justify this?"

"Easy," he said. "Doug's a great man, and he'll do great things for this country. So what if we have to pull a few fast ones to get him into office? It's a small price to pay."

"A great man," she repeated. "Eight months ago he was your ticket to a federal appointment, and now he's a great man? What is this, the cognitive filter at work? Or have you been listening to your own campaign ads?"

"You're too close to him to see it. Or maybe not close enough, I don't know. But he'll make a real difference. Think of Abraham Lincoln, or FDR. Wouldn't it have been worth bending a few rules to get them elected?"

She gazed at him and shook her head. "There's nobody so great that he's more important than basic morality and decency."

"Your problem is you don't believe in great men."

"I guess I don't. I only believe in good people."

He looked at her irritably a moment, then his expression changed and his eyes went wide. "Jesus. You've met somebody."

She glanced away

"Oh, God."

He wheeled to the door, but stopped with his hand on the knob. "We're close, Cam," he said, not looking at her. "We could actually win this thing. So, please—don't do anything stupid. I know you're going to split when this is over—okay, it's your life. Just leave him with his life, too. If not for his sake, then for mine. Don't screw this up for us."

She didn't give him an answer, and he didn't look back for it. He opened the door and left.

The next morning the *News Journal* gave Doug the win over Hadley Hayes in the debate, and the overnight polling gave them the spike they'd all been counting on. Doug picked up five points, and was now only eight points off the lead.

Monday was Columbus Day and the courts were closed. Cam went to the Wilmington office, announced that she was going to the Philadelphia office for the day, then walked three blocks past her car to the lot behind the Amtrak station where Steve was waiting for her in the Explorer.

"Talk to your mom last night?" he asked as they headed south.

"Uh-huh. For all the good it did. She still won't leave. I can't convince her that there's any connection."

"Then we just have to hope there isn't."

"What about you? Did you talk to Trey yesterday?"

He shook his head. "I hung around the garden all afternoon, but he never showed up."

She could see how deep his disappointment went. "He wasn't scheduled to, remember. There's no reason to worry."

"I know, but I want to tell him about you and me. He needs to know."

"Maybe that's not something he needs to know right now," she said uneasily.

Steve reached over and rubbed the back of her neck. "We're ready to start a new life together, the three of us. He's entitled to know that, too."

"On the brink of a new life," she said.

He grinned at her. "Yep."

Steve was fearless. He didn't know what she did about brinks. She took his hand in hers and tried to be fearless, too.

They drove to Lewes, where Steve had his boat moored now, and after Cam wriggled into jeans and a sweater in the backseat of the Explorer, they boarded the boat and took off out of the marina into the bay.

It was a pristine autumn day, the skies blue and clear and the wind just cool enough to sting their cheeks. They hugged the coastline around Cape Henlopen and into the Atlantic, then cruised south along Rehoboth Beach. Cam turned her face into the wind and unpinned her hair and let it stream behind her like a banner.

Steve was watching her with a smile. He cut the throttle until the engine went quiet. "That's it," he said. "That's the look I fell in love with. When you were pulling away from Maristella and your hair whipped loose like that. I stood watching you go, knowing you were the enemy, and still hoping like hell you would turn around and look at me one more time."

"Never your enemy," she whispered.

The boat rocked gently in the water, and the waves lapped softly against the hull. He lifted her hand and kissed her palm. "I know that now."

She leaned over and kissed him, then hooked her chin on his shoulder and gazed past him to the shoreline. "Know when I first fell in love with you?" she asked.

"You already told me. When the fog parted and you saw us working on the house."

"That's what I thought. But I just realized I was wrong. Turn around."

He twisted to look shoreward. They were drifting in front of George Westover's Shingle Style house on Lake Drive. Steve let out a laugh of surprise, then visored his hand over his eyes to study how it looked from that vantage point.

"It happened when I saw the house," she said. "I thought it was more beautiful than anything I'd ever seen made by man, and I decided that the man who created it must be the most wonderful man in the world." Her eyes twinkled at him. "And that was before I knew you were a dreamboat, too."

He grinned, but his eyes were still moving critically over the lines of the house. "I guess it turned out pretty well."

"Mr. Modesty," she teased. "If I could be as proud of my work, I'd be shouting it from the rooftops."

"You should be. You're very good at what you do."

"It's what I do that I'm not proud of." She opened their lunch basket and handed him his sandwich and bottled drink, then twisted the cap off her bottle and tilted it to her mouth. "My problem is that I became a lawyer for all the wrong reasons."

"You wanted to find your mother. There's nothing wrong with that."

"But it was more than that. I thought the law would be a kind of shield, and I'd be safe if I could just get myself on the right side of it and hunker down low."

"But it wasn't?"

"It turned out to be more like a cushion than a shield. Pretty flimsy protection, and in the end pretty suffocating, too."

He ran his fingers through the tangles in her hair. "I hope that means you won't have any regrets about leaving your practice when we go up to Maine."

"Not a one."

His expression was thoughtful for a few minutes as he chewed his sandwich and washed it down with a gulp of soda. "You know what you're really good at?" he said.

She gave him an arch look."If that's a sexual overture, sir—the answer is not here."

"No, seriously. Landscape design. You did a fantastic job on your garden. I think you have a real talent for it."

"Really?" She was embarrassed at how pleased she felt.

"I was thinking—just for the one year that I have you trapped on the island—I wonder if you'd like to try your hand at designing something for the grounds up there."

"Are you kidding?" she exclaimed. "Steve, I'd love it!"

Her face was shining, and he leaned forward and caught it like a sunbeam in his hands. "Know what I love?"

"Tell me," she murmured, and despite her statement a moment earlier, she let him show her, too.

Tuesday morning they were back in court, and Bruce Benjamin was calling his final witness, a Philadelphia psychiatrist who was on the faculty at Penn and had published extensively on the subject of adolescent disturbances. She'd reviewed all of the testimony in the case and all of the exhibits, and on the basis of that review, she'd formed an opinion to a reasonable degree of medical certainty as to the custodial best interests of the child.

"Doctor, in your opinion, is it in his best interests to remain in the custody of Senator and Mrs. Ramsay?"

"It is not."

"Why not?"

"He exists in emotional isolation from his adoptive parents. They are remote from him in every way. Physically in the case of Senator Ramsay, who can't be called a custodial parent in any meaningful sense of the word. And emotionally remote in the case of Mrs. Ramsay. His primary caretaker and companion is a man who has put the boy in actual physical jeopardy. These factors weigh very heavily in favor of removing the minor from this environment."

"Goddamn hired gun," Ramsay growled at the end of the direct examination.

Cam rose to cross-examine. The doctor admitted that she was being paid for her testimony, in an amount not yet calculated, although her normal hourly rate was three hundred dollars for preparation and five hundred dollars for testimony. She conceded that she had not interviewed the child or his parents or indeed any of the witnesses who testified before her. In fact, the only information she possessed was the evidence Judge Miller had already received, and, unlike Judge Miller, the doctor had no opportunity to view the witnesses' demeanors and assess their credibility. Her testimony here today offered the Court no new factual information.

Indeed, Cam asked, wasn't she simply stating her opinion on a subject on which the judge could easily form his own opinion?

"Not so," the doctor said indignantly.

"What's the difference?" Cam asked, baiting the trap.

"My opinion is an informed and educated one."

Judge Miller gave a fractious scowl and dismissed her.

Benjamin rose as his witness departed. "Your Honor, that concludes petitioner's evidence, with one exception. At this time we respectfully request that the Court interview the minor."

Cam made all the expected arguments, but in the end the judge could see no way around it. He studied the clock for a moment. "I suppose the boy's in school now, Mrs. Ramsay?"

Margo looked startled at having been addressed directly. "Y-Yes. He is."

"Then we'll adjourn until nine-thirty tomorrow. Mrs. Alexander, you will please present the child here at that time."

Cam nodded, and across the aisle, Benjamin turned to his client with a look of triumph.

Trey slept fitfully that night, and at four in the morning, he gave up trying. His insides were churning with the same explosive energy he felt the night before he testified in the kidnapping trial. But this time it wasn't fear or nervousness; it was the rush of pure excitement.

Not that he expected the judge to listen to him, any more than his shrink did. She told him once that his life wasn't a democracy, he didn't get a vote. Trey knew what that meant—as long as the old man was paying her bills, he got to make the rules. Trey didn't expect a whole lot more from Judge Miller. One way or the other, the old man was paying his bills, too.

But the point was that it was ending. It would all be over in a matter of days. That was what had him wide-awake and hyperventilating at four in the morning.

He got up and put on his gym shorts and running shoes and crept down the stairs and out the front door. Jesse had carved a pair of pumpkins for the porch, though his hands shook so badly that they ended up looking like some kind of demonic ghouls. Halloween was two weeks away. Trey wondered where he'd be by then.

The air was cool and a half-moon shone dimly as he plunged out onto the road. His arms and legs pumped and his feet pounded rhythmically on the hard black macadam surface. Everything seemed different in the dark. He could see all the shades of black in the night, and he thought of the painting he'd never gotten around to. *Greenville Night.* Soon he could paint *Maristella Night* instead. It meant *Star of the Sea*, he remembered. He pictured the sparkle of the silica in the sand and the gleam of the moon on the rocks. Yeah, he thought, he could do that.

The chill disappeared as he ran, and a trickle of sweat started between his shoulder blades and was rolling down to the small of his back by the time he turned into Cam's driveway. Her house was in darkness, and he slowed to a walk so he wouldn't wake her with the pounding of his feet. He circled around back and entered the garden. The half-moon shone down on the reflecting pool, and he stood a moment at its edge and tried to see himself in the black water. But he was only a blur, an undefined shadow passing over the ebb and flow of the water.

He walked toe to heel along the edge of the coping to the end of the pool, then went inside the folly. Everything was still and quiet, and the moon penetrated just enough for him to see his way to the spiral stairs. He climbed up and poked his head through the second floor as another head lifted sleepily from the mattress.

"Cam?" he gasped.

She gasped, too. Her arms and shoulders were naked where they rose above the covers. "I—I'm sorry," he stammered. "I didn't know you'd be here—"

Another head lifted behind hers and the moon shone enough for him to recognize his father and see that he was naked, too.

Everything held still for a second, like a freeze frame in a video, but in the next, everything was moving, whirling, a kaleidoscope inside his head spinning crazily out of control. He heard himself say something, but the words were all garbled, and then he was stumbling backward down the stairs and running out of the folly and across the garden to the street.

"Jamie, wait!"

He cut across the neighbor's yard on the corner. He needed to stop, he had to throw up, but there wasn't time. He hurdled over a flower bed but caught his toe on a garden hose on the other side of it and sprawled flat on the grass.

"Jamie—Trey, wait!"

He rolled up in a crouch, but Steve grabbed him before he could get away. "Wait," he said, panting hard. "Let me explain."

"What's to explain? You're fucking Cam."

"I wanted to tell you. She's going with us when we—"

"I'm not going anywhere with you! I never want to see you again!"

Steve jerked back like he'd hit him, and it was enough of an opening for Trey to take off again. He ran down Martins Mill and around Chaboullaird with his feet hitting the pavement so hard and so fast that his teeth seemed to rattle in his head. He ran a mile in darkness, until suddenly a circle of light appeared ahead.

It was his house, and all the outside lights were on. He stopped at the edge of the bushes and blinked the sweat out of his eyes. There was a cop car in the driveway, and Jesse was on the porch with a pair of cops. They must have discovered him gone; they must have thought he'd run away.

His throat tightened as he heard Steve coming up hard behind him. He threw a look back, then ahead to the circle of light around the house, then bolted out into the driveway.

"There he is!" Jesse shouted. "Where were you? We been looking all over—"

Trey ran up to the porch and looked behind him. Steve had stopped at the edge of the light, where no one could see him in the darkness but Trey.

"Are you okay?" Jesse said. "Where'd you go?"

Trey didn't answer. He was watching Steve.

"So everything's okay," one of the cops said.

"Guess so," Jesse said. "Thanks for coming out."

Steve was staring at Trey across fifty feet, and as the cops came off the porch and headed for their car, he suddenly stepped out into the circle of light.

"Hey, there he is!" Jesse yelled. "I knew it! See him?"

The cops fanned out and started to close in on him with their hands on their holsters.

But Steve didn't look at them. He kept coming forward with his eyes on Trey, until Trey had to run into the house and slam the door behind him.

36

Judge Miller came into the courtroom the next morning with his black robes billowing behind him like a noxious cloud from a factory smokestack. He took the bench and looked balefully at the two lawyers where they stood at attention before him. "The bailiff tells me there's been a development?"

"Yes, Your Honor," they said together.

"I hope that means you've worked out a settlement."

"Not exactly," Benjamin said.

The judge eyed the empty chair beside him. "Where's your client, Mr. Benjamin?"

He answered in a low voice, pitched at last to a level appropriate to this courtroom. "Mr. Patterson is unavoidably absent, Your Honor. He's in custody at Gander Hill Prison."

The judge's eyes bugged out. "On what charge?"

"Violation of a restraining order."

"You don't mean the one involving the Ramsay boy?"

"Yes, Your Honor."

Miller looked at Cam. "You're aware of this, counsel?"

"Yes, sir."

"Tell me what happened."

She glanced down at her clients. Ramsay sat with his arms folded and a look of righteous vindication on his craggy face.

"It's my understanding," she said in a voice as hushed as Benjamin's, "that Trey was discovered missing from his bed at approximately four o'clock this morning. The police were summoned to the house, but before they commenced a search, he returned on foot. Mr. Patterson was behind him, and because he appeared to the officers to be within five hundred feet of the boy, they arrested him at the scene."

"Well, what does the boy have to say about this?"

"Nothing, Your Honor."

Miller puffed out his breath and looked across the aisle. "Mr. Benjamin, it seems obvious to me that your client was attempting to subvert the procedures of this court."

"Your Honor—"

"He knew I was planning to interview the boy here this morning, and he met secretly with him in an attempt to influence the outcome of that interview."

"There's been no suggestion of that, Your Honor. If we could simply adjourn this matter until after Mr. Patterson's hearing on the criminal charges, then he can explain—"

"Do you have any idea what my docket looks like? How many law-abiding citizens are waiting for their day in court? While your client goes out and does whatever he damn well pleases? Enough is enough. Mrs. Alexander, I'm going to grant your motion. The petition is dismissed. This hearing is over."

He slammed his gavel so hard it bounced out of his hand and fell to the floor.

Why did you do it?

The question had been screaming inside Cam's brain from the moment she drove past the Ramsay house and saw what was left of the scene: Ash and Jesse on the porch; a police car parked in the circle drive; the cops shouldering Steve to the car and grabbing his head to push him down inside.

It was another thirty-six hours before she could ask it.

She was waiting in the parking lot Thursday afternoon when Steve got out of a cab at the door of his apartment building. She went to him, and they held each other in silence for a long time.

"What happened?" she asked as they went inside.

"Benjamin worked out a deal. A night in jail and a thousand dollar fine, and in return I had to agree to a modification of the restraining order. Now I can't go within a thousand feet of Trey, his school, his house, and—guess what?—your house, in case he ever happens to be working there. So now I can't even meet you there."

"I'll come to you," she said.

"Great, but will he?" He unlocked the door to his apartment and swung it in. "When it was all over, Benjamin told me to find myself another lawyer. I guess he's had it with me." He went to the living room window and opened it to let in some fresh air. "Not that I blame him."

"Steve, why did you do it?"

He sat on the sofa and rubbed his hand over his jaw. It was two days since he'd shaved; he had his wild outlaw look again.

"I mean, why didn't you stop when you saw Jesse and the cops at the house? You must have known this would happen."

"This was going to happen either way."

"What do you mean?"

"I knew what would happen if he had to go into that courtroom—what, five hours after he caught us in bed together? I knew what he was going to say to the judge. He was shook up bad, Cam."

She squeezed her eyes shut as the scene came back to her. She'd wished a hundred times since then that they'd gone to Steve's apartment instead. This was all her fault. She knew the folly was Trey's hideout, and she should have known there was a risk that he'd find them there.

A folly, something foolish or stupid. Or both.

Steve leaned his head back on the upholstery and stared at the ceiling. "In jail all day yesterday, I kept running it through my head, and I can see now what an idiot I was. After what happened with Beth last winter . . . He did his best to get rid of her. We were headed nowhere, anyway—it was no sacrifice for me—but I should have seen how things were with Trey. He wanted me to himself, or at least he didn't want me with a woman. Then throw in all his raging hormones and the fact that he's got a major crush on you—I mean, no wonder he got knocked for a loop. There's his father having sex with the woman he's been fantasizing about himself."

Cam cringed.

"So I knew he'd go into court and say things he'd regret later, just like he did with the radio transmission in June. I couldn't put him through that again. If I had to lose the case—and let's face it, that was a given—then I thought I should be the one responsible for it. Not him."

He heaved himself up and stood at the window and stared down into the parking lot. Cam came behind him and put her arms around him. "I know this doesn't help," she said quietly. "But I have to say it anyway. I love you. Even more now than before."

He turned with a sad little smile at the corner of his mouth. "That always helps," he said, and pulled her close.

She pressed her cheek to his shoulder as the tears burned in her throat.

"He'll get over this eventually, I know he will, once we're all together. But jeez—" He let go of her and paced to the other side of the room. "I don't know how we get there from here." He raked his hand through his hair. "Benjamin said I can't refile without showing some kind of changed circumstances."

"No, but—"

"What? You know a way around that, too?"

"No, there isn't one. I was going to say—I thought you were planning to take Trey no matter how the judge ruled."

He shook his head. "That was his plan, not mine. I didn't have the heart to tell him it wouldn't work. There's no way Ramsay would let us get away this time. Not now that he doesn't have anything to hush up anymore."

Cam looked up sharply. "But what if he would?"

"Would what?"

"Let you go. What if there's something else, something worse, and it's still a secret, and Ramsay wants to keep it that way? What would you do then?"

Steve stared at her. "You've got something on him."

She nodded.

"It's enough? To give us that kind of leverage?"

She nodded again.

"You'd do that, for us?"

She gazed at him. After a lifetime of hoarding information and keeping secrets, here at last was redemption; here was something that was worth the price. "In a heartbeat," she said.

Eleven days later she stood on the sidelines of the soccer field at the Tower Hill School. It was Halloween week, and the school grounds were decorated with pumpkins and scarecrows, while the boys on the visitor's bench were all wearing monster masks in a peculiar display of team spirit. For her own part, Cam had tried to dress inconspicuously, in jeans and a blazer like the other moms, though she was younger than the other moms and gained a few curious glances despite her efforts.

Though not from Trey. He didn't even cut his eyes in her direction when he sprinted past her down the field.

It was Monday, nearly two weeks since the folly, and though they'd heard nothing from him, Steve convinced himself that he'd be approachable by now. In her pocket was a letter from Steve, three pages long, full of explanations and entreaties that he'd worked most of the week to get down right. But it was the closing that made her heart pinch. *Love, Dad.* Two words, plain and simple, but weighted with a world of wishing.

Below it she'd added her own short note.

Dear Trey,

I'm so sorry for what happened. We never wanted to hurt or upset you. We fell in love by accident, and it caught us by surprise, too. Especially since the only thing we have in common is how much we both love you.

Your dad means everything to me, and you mean everything to him, and that means that the most important thing in the world to me is that the two of you be together again. He made a big sacrifice for you the other night, and now it might be my turn to make one for him. If you need me to step out of the picture, then that's what I'll do.

Call him. Please.

The game ended, visitors 4, home team 3, and while the visitors did a macabre victory dance in their monster masks, Trey went to the team bench and poured the contents of a water bottle over his head.

Cam started hesitantly toward him, waiting for him to acknowledge her, hoping to catch his eye if he wouldn't. One of his teammates said something to him, and he shook his head and turned to run off the field. He'd lost all his loose-limbed gawkiness; now he seemed taut and controlled as he ran, as if he were fighting to hold himself tight at the core.

His teammate looked back at her, and after a moment she saw that he was Jason Dunn, the boy she met last Christmas, the one she rousted from bed the night Trey disappeared.

"Jason?" she called, and when he loped over, she pulled out the envelope. "Do me a favor and give this to Trey?"

He treated her to a full-body ogle before he took it, but it was a small price to pay for the delivery. He turned and ran for the locker room, and Cam turned and nearly ran full-body into Jesse Lombard.

"Oh!" she gasped, stumbling back. "I'm sorry, I didn't see you there."

Jesse eyed the line of boys streaming into the locker room. "What are you doing here?" he said.

"I had some papers for Mary Ann Dunn, and since I was in the neighborhood, I thought I'd give them to Jason to take home."

"Papers for Mrs. Dunn?"

"She's a client," Cam said. "I'm afraid it's privileged."

When she got home that afternoon, there was a man on the porch and a strange car in the driveway. She peered at him as she pulled in. He was cupping his hands to his face to light a cigarette.

"Hello, Finn," she called, walking around to the front. "I guess Doug's not home yet."

"It's you I'm waiting to see."

"Oh?"

He stood silently smoking his cigarette.

She came up on the porch and rooted for her front door key in her bag. "Can I get you something to drink?" she asked as she swung the door in.

"Just point me to a VCR." He held up a videocassette. "I got something to show you."

Another TV ad, she thought wearily. "Right this way."

She led him to the TV in the study and sat down on the leather sofa as he loaded the cassette and turned it on. He stayed on his feet with the remote control in his hand, and after thirty seconds of dead air, a grainy black-and-white image appeared.

Cam squinted at the figures on the screen. They looked like combat troops in some kind of jungle setting. This was strange, she thought. The last thing Doug wanted to do was bring up military defense issues and play into Hadley Hayes's hands.

"On January eleventh, 1969," the voice-over announced, "Task Force 118, also known as the Brown River Navy, sailed up the Mekong River in search of enemy supply lines."

She looked up at Finn, but his face was impassive as he smoked and watched the screen.

A map appeared, tracing the route followed by the river patrol boats, then it returned to film and zoomed in on a few earnest young faces among the sailors. Abruptly the black-and-white footage went to blazing color as fireballs lit the sky and the boats erupted out of the water. The next image on the screen was black and white again, a photograph of Abby Zodtner at age nineteen.

Cam was on her feet, backing away wildly from the screen.

"Hold on," Finn said, fiddling with the remote control. "You might've missed something there. Let's go back and watch that part again."

"What is this?" she cried. "Where did it come from?"

"From the committee to reelect Hadley Hayes. Fifty thousand registered Delaware voters found a copy of this in their mailboxes today." He threw the remote into a chair and came toward her. "Imagine that. Fifty thousand. Why, that's more people than your Commie spy mother managed to get killed in all the years of the war."

She backed away from Finn as the announcer said, "Doug Alexander thinks national defense is a joke?" The video cut to campaign footage of Doug and Cam together on a dais, smiling and waving to the crowd. "We think it's a tragedy." The photo of Abby Zodtner floated onto the screen until it was wedged between Doug and Cam, and they stood together as an awkward trio. "A family tragedy."

Finn kept coming at her until her back slammed against the wall. "Do you have any idea what you've cost us? You worthless little tramp."

"Stop it. Please. Stop." She pressed her palms to the wall as the video reached its end and a loud static sputtering filled the room.

"Twenty years you've set us back. No, thirty. All our hard work, and you've ruined it all. Now we're the party of traitors and spies. Thanks to you." He loomed menacingly over her. "You had to inveigle your way in here, you little bitch—"

The doorbell rang, and she let out her breath in a gasp and ducked around him to open it.

On the porch were two men in dark suits. They stood before her with their hands out, an FBI shield in each one.

They took her downtown to the federal building and put her in a room that was ten feet square and windowless if she disregarded the expanse of smoky mirror along one wall. They pointed her to a chair and asked if she wished to have her attorney present, and when she declined, they asked her to sign a form to that effect, then another form consenting to provide fingerprints and handwriting exemplars. Then they gave her a cup of coffee and left her alone.

An hour passed before the door opened again. A pair of evidence technicians came in and inked her fingertips and pressed each one against a print card. Another technician came in after that and handed her a pen and paper and a block of text to copy. Then they gave her another cup of coffee and left her alone again.

Another hour passed. She looked at her watch and wondered if she'd been on the Philadelphia local news at six, perhaps even the network news at six-thirty. She hoped that she was, and that her mother had watched. There was no other way to warn her now. All the codes and meeting places they'd worked out between them were useless. Nothing was safe.

So close, she thought listlessly. She'd come so close. The election was only a week away. Another week and she would have been gone, and none of this would have mattered. She put her head down on the table like a weary schoolgirl.

When another hour passed and the door opened again, a man came in alone. He was slender and had thick gray hair that flowed back in waves from a delicate-featured face. "Sorry to keep you waiting," he said. "I hit some traffic on the drive up from Washington." He introduced himself, but the only part of it that registered was Special Agent, Counterintelligence Unit. He held out his hand, and Cam gave it an unfocused look until he withdrew it and pulled up a chair.

"You have to forgive me if I seem a little excited," he said. "This is sort of a momentous day for me. You see—I've been waiting fourteen years to meet you, Cammy Johnson."

He knew everything. He'd been on the case since the day her envelope arrived, and he knew all the key dates, the whole cast of characters, the financing of Johnson's Sunoco. He even knew where Darryl Pollack was living and what kind of scar he bore on his scalp. The one thing he hadn't known and couldn't find out was what became of her after she ran away from home. Today, thanks to an anonymous tip received by Hadley Hayes, he knew that, too.

There was only one blank left now, and it was the one piece of information it was his job to find out: the whereabouts of Abby Zodtner.

Over the next five hours he worked doggedly to extract it from Cam.

She performed a mental trick to get through the interrogation, a kind of self-hypnotic time travel in which she returned herself to the state of mind she'd occupied a week ago. She told him everything she knew as of last Thursday, in as much detail as she could dredge up. It was a story she'd never told to anyone until she told Steve last week, but now she related it to the agent in a monotone, as if she'd told it so many times she was bored by it all. She described all of her efforts to find her mother, every database she'd searched, every search request she'd launched. She even told him about Gloria Lipton and Doris Palumbo and how the anonymous tip that first linked their murders came from her, and she provided the reporter's name for verification.

At two in the morning the agent closed his notebook. "I'll be a few minutes," he said, and left her alone again.

The minutes stretched to an hour, and her lids sank heavier and heavier over her eyes. She was terrified of her fatigue, afraid it would make her careless in her answers. She was equally afraid to fall asleep, in case she woke in a daze and blurted the wrong thing. She forced herself to sit up very straight and take quick panting breaths to keep the oxygen flowing to her brain. She was almost hyperventilating by the time he came back.

"Thank you for your time and cooperation, Mrs. Alexander," he said. "You're free to go now."

She blinked hard and pushed herself to her feet. He opened the door, and his posture was almost courtly as he stepped aside and held it for her.

"Can I ask you something?" she said, stopping beside him.

He gave her an apologetic smile. "You can *ask*."

"The man—her partner or whatever he was—did you ever identify him?"

He shook his head regretfully. "For a ten-year-old, you did a terrific job of intelligence-gathering. But there wasn't enough to go on. The fingerprints didn't take, and the tags on the car traced back to a rental agency that purged their records after three years. So all we've got is his handwriting. Although"—he gave a hopeful shrug—"if we happen to find your mother and she happens to give him up, the writing on that note ought to be enough to nail him. In which case, the Bureau will be grateful to you all over again."

She bowed her head and walked past him. The office suite was in darkness, but she could see figures standing in the shadows of the doorways around and behind her. They were the other agents, the technicians, and they all stood at silent attention as she passed.

She went out into the elevator lobby and pushed the Call button, and when an elevator arrived, she stepped on wearily.

"Cam, hold up," a voice called.

Nathan trotted into the elevator after her and pushed the basement level button. "The press is out front," he explained.

"At three in the morning?"

"They've been camped out there since eight last night."

"Oh, God," she groaned.

"Come on, babe. You survived eight hours of FBI interrogation. This should be a snap."

"You were there," she said, unsurprised. "Behind the mirror."

"Part of the time."

"Doug, too?"

He shook his head.

The elevator reached the lobby level. He pushed the button to close the doors, and they rode down one more level to the basement.

"What's it been, Cam?" he said suddenly as they reached the rear door of the courthouse. "Eight years we've been friends?"

"Yes."

"Seems like after eight years, you could have told me."

The alley was deserted, but from the end of the block a shout went up, and before they'd gone ten yards, a throng of reporters was sprinting toward them. Nathan put his arm over her shoulders and steered her through, shouting, "No comment, folks."

He hustled her into the passenger seat of an unfamiliar car, then ran around to the driver's side and peeled out into the street. Within minutes a string of cars was following behind them.

"Where's Doug?" she asked.

"At home." His eyes were on the mirror as he made the turn onto Pennsylvania Avenue and headed for Greenville. The line of cars mimicked the turn.

"Maybe I should go somewhere else."

"We thought about that. But we decided to go for the family-united-against-adversity image."

She dropped her face in her hands. "What did Doug say about—all this?"

"Nothing that made sense. He just went ballistic."

Ballistic. Her mind registered dread, but she was too tired to feel it.

The only traffic was behind them, and they reached Greenville in minutes. Nathan slowed as they approached the house. A dozen men and women were standing on the front lawn of the place across the street. There was an air of anxious watchfulness about them, as if her house were burning down and they were the concerned neighbors. Nathan drove past them and as he turned into the driveway, a thick-bodied man in a black suit stepped out to block their way.

"We hired some security," Nathan explained. He lowered his window and called out, "Vance," and the man stepped aside.

Five or six cars were parked up by the garage, two of them on top of the flowers she'd planted. "Who's here?" she asked.

"Who isn't?"

All the lights were on inside, and the house gave off the low-pitched drone of a dozen harried voices. People were milling about everywhere: a frazzled Maggie Heller making coffee in the kitchen, Norman Finn smoking in the living room, barely familiar faces studiously avoiding eye contact with Cam as Nathan drew her down the hall and into the study.

Meredith Winters was on her feet in the middle of the room, alternately talking into the desk phone in one hand and a cell phone in the other. She glanced at Cam as she came in, then half turned away and said, "No, not live. No way. We don't see the tape first, it doesn't air."

"Who's that?" Nathan asked her.

Meredith mouthed something at him.

The desk chair was turned all the way around so that only its high back was visible. Cam sent a questioning look at Nathan as he took one of the phones from Meredith. He gave a brief nod.

Cam circled slowly around the desk and stopped six feet from Doug. He was leaning back in the chair with his hands laced over his stomach and his eyes wide-open and empty.

A family tragedy, the narrator had said in the attack ad. But the real tragedy, she knew, was Doug's alone. He'd waited all his life for this election, he wanted it more than anything in the world, and because of her, he was losing it in the most ignoble way possible. All because of her. He threw his hat in the ring, and she let him; he ridiculed Hayes on defense issues, and she stood silent; he opened himself up to contempt and derision, and all she'd ever worried about was herself.

"Doug, I know there's nothing I can say—"

"Nothing now," he said bitterly. "A year ago would have been nice, though."

"I know. I'm sorry."

"Sorry," he repeated with a harsh laugh. "Sorry doesn't quite cut it, Campbell. Or should I say, Camille?"

She could hear Meredith and Nathan in their separate conversations behind her, and there was still the drone of a dozen other voices from the rest of the house. But no one was eavesdropping on her; no one cared what she had to say anymore. "Doug, I tried to stop you."

"Oh, right. With those pictures. As if porn holds a candle to treason. A nice pair of tits versus hundreds of dead sailors."

"I'll go," she said. "I'll leave tonight."

"Oh, no, you don't." He came up straight in his chair. "You don't bail on me now. You see this through. You owe me at least that much, don't you think?"

She bowed her head and nodded.

"But come November fourth, when this is all over?"

She kept her head down and waited for his next words.

"I don't ever want to see you again."

It was Cam's own credo: go after the woman. And that was exactly what Hadley Hayes, Gary Pfeiffer, and all the political media had done.

The house became a fortress under siege, and instead of the Madwoman of Greenville, Cam became the Prisoner of Greenville. The army of reporters across the street never decamped, and so the private security force remained constantly on duty in the driveway. Every vehicle was stopped and its occupants screened. A caterer's truck arrived three times a day with meals for whatever number of people were holding the fort at the moment, and their trays were carefully checked for hidden microphones or cameras before they could be carried into the house.

The neighbors across the street reached some financial arrangement and took off for Florida, leaving the house to one of the network crews and the yard to everyone else. The video cameras were kept permanently aimed on the Alexander house. Over the next few days the most familiar face on every live news broadcast was Nathan's, since he made the most frequent trips in and out of the house. To fill in the air time between his appearances, the news producers dug out the footage from Doug's announcement at the Meyerwood factory gates, and they ran it with every update on the story, until Cam's pink suit became as familiar to TV audiences as Monica Lewinsky's beret. And if the beret was fodder for late-night jokes ending in *ooo la-la*, it was no worse than all the *pinko* jokes that emerged over Cam's suit. "An unfortunate color choice, in hindsight," Meredith Winters was heard to remark.

Meredith came and went. She was operating out of her usual suite in the Hotel DuPont, and she was also running a focus group at some undisclosed location near the university. Still, she arrived every morning with the overnight poll results. Doug lost twenty points the first night and a dozen more the next. The only glimmer of good news was that Hadley Hayes's numbers didn't move. All the points Doug lost had shifted to the undecided column.

Cam remained upstairs, usually in her room where she could gaze out at the dying foliage of her garden. Someone brought over her mail from the office Wednesday morning, and she put it aside without opening it. Later one of the staffers knocked on her door and told her a client named Stevens was on the line; did she want to talk to him? She didn't, and the footsteps retreated.

That afternoon, Nathan knocked on her door and told her she was needed downstairs.

The living room had been transformed into an operations center. A conference table had been hauled in, and half a dozen staffers were seated around it with laptops open in front of them and cell phones at their ears. Nathan cleared his throat and in thirty seconds they wound up their conversations and disappeared. "Have a seat," he said to Cam. "I'll round up the rest."

He went across the hall to the study, and Cam sat down at the table and waited. Since Monday night she'd known that something would be required of her. Now she would find out what it was.

The study door opened. Doug, Nathan, and Meredith were deep in the middle of an argument that they carried with them across the hall.

"Goddamn it, Sunday's too late," Doug was ranting as they took their seats. "Look at the way I'm hemorrhaging points."

"We'll pick up some points once the leaks start."

"But why not *Primetime Live*? Go on and end it tonight."

"Because *Primetime*'s got five million fewer viewers, that's why," Meredith said. "And this way we'll make all the Monday morning headlines, and it'll still be fresh in everyone's minds when they go to the polls on Tuesday."

Nathan glanced at Cam at the far end of the table. "You're doing *60 Minutes* this Sunday," he explained.

A hard lump rose in her throat.

"We'll tape it here Saturday afternoon—"

"Here?" Doug cut in.

"That's what Don Hewitt wants, and it works for us, too. The happy home and all that."

"Okay, but let's do it back in the garden," Doug said. "Make sure they know that's her hobby and she did everything herself. And get the sun to shine down on her."

"Halo effect, I like it," Meredith said. "Check the weather forecast," she said to Nathan.

"Got it."

"Meanwhile, we start the leaks," she said. "The *Times* first, so the Delaware papers can report that the *Times* reports et cetera."

"Leaks about what?" Cam asked.

"About what you did," Nathan said. "Your painful but unavoidable decision to choose your country over your mother."

Her heart stopped. "What?" she breathed.

"We have a few folks at the FBI willing to talk on deep background. We'll leak their names to the *Times*, and the story will start to dribble out by the end of the week."

"Then we've got the lead story on Sunday's *60 Minutes*," Meredith said. "You and Doug holding hands while he does the whole stand-by-his-woman routine." She looked at Nathan. "I tell you, I got a good feeling about this. I think we're coming out of this looking better than we did a week ago."

Doug gave a disgusted look at the ceiling. "Yeah, right. The man who fell for a piece of trash who only had to shake her ass at him to get him so hot and bothered he forgot to find out that her mother was a spy. Yeah, that makes me look real good."

"It does if you stand by her," Meredith said. "It's your performance that holds the key here, Doug. You treat her like trash, then you look as bad as you say. But you treat her like the woman you adore, it comes out the whole other way."

"Yeah, I hear you," he mumbled.

"As for Cam—" Meredith shifted her attention to the other end of the table. "You sit there and look every bit as shell-shocked as you do right now. Nobody'll expect anything different."

"That means Doug has to tell her story," Nathan said.

"Right."

"What story?" Cam asked in a whisper.

Doug picked up his notes. " 'My wife was only fifteen years old when she found out the truth about her mother. But even then, she had a strong sense of right and wrong and duty to her country. She knew that something this awful couldn't go undetected or unpunished. And even though it meant a tremendous personal sacrifice for her and her family, she went to the FBI and told them everything she knew. Thanks to her—' "

"No," Cam said through bloodless lips. "Please, no."

Doug gave her a cold stare down the length of the table.

"Please." Tears stood in her eyes. "Call me a tramp if you want. Say I'm a traitor myself, I don't care. But please, I beg you, don't say this."

"But this is the truth," Nathan said.

"Always easier to go with the truth," Meredith said.

"Doug." Cam closed the others out and looked only at him. "Please. If you ever had any feelings for me, don't do this."

But he'd closed her out so competely that he didn't even seem to hear her as he picked up a pen to edit his script.

"Cam, you don't get it," Nathan said. "You come out the hero of this story."

"No, you don't get it!" she cried, stumbling to her feet. "The most shameful thing about me isn't that my mother committed treason. It's that *I* was the one who turned her in!"

All three stared at her, and after a moment Meredith shook her head. "Nope. I can't work with that."

Cam bolted from the room with a sob rising in her throat.

"Oh, Mrs. Alexander," one of the staffers called to her. "Here's the message I took from your client."

She grabbed the slip of paper and crushed it in her hand as she ran up the stairs.

It was the end of the day before she smoothed out the creases to read it. *Pat Stevens,* it read, *wants to check on the status of his petition.*

The phone number was a local one she didn't recognize, but she knew the husky voice that answered.

"Mr. Stevens?" she said, her own voice shaking. "This is Campbell Alexander."

"Yes," he said tensely.

"I wasn't sure I had the right number. Have you moved?"

"I needed to be closer to my business interests. So I'm here now. Very close."

"I see."

"The reason I called—I'm wondering how you're coming along—with my petition."

"Well, I'm afraid things are a little uncertain. I mean, the law is kind of unsettled, and we have to expect the worst from our opponents."

"I understand."

"You remember there was another party we were hoping might file a friend of the court brief on our side of the issue? I haven't heard anything more from him. Have you?"

"No," he said heavily.

That meant that Trey was ignoring their pleas, or that he refused to read them, or that he never even got them, and she wasn't sure which of those was the worst.

"But I wanted to let you know," Steve said, "that despite all these uncertainties, I still feel very certain. I want to go forward with this. And I need to know that you do, too."

She closed her eyes. "I do."

"Good. Listen, somehow I'll work things out with the other party. If you'll be able to get around all the problems on your end?"

"I will. One way or the other. Within the week."

"If anything comes up, you know where to reach me."

"Yes. Thank you for calling, Mr. Stevens."

* * *

A landscaping crew arrived Thursday morning to rake the leaves and cut back the dead foliage in the garden, and a patio furniture truck drove up soon after with several selections that were set up and carefully photographed for comparison purposes. In the afternoon, a team of Meredith's image consultants arrived with a rack of dresses and shut themselves up in the bedroom with Cam. For the past six months they'd been working to make her look older than she was, but today the consensus seemed to be that younger was better. They settled on a gray wool jumper over a white blouse with a Peter Pan collar, and decided that her hair should be worn down and pulled back at the nape of her neck with a black ribbon. When they were done with her, she looked like a cross between a schoolgirl and a novitiate. "Perfect," Meredith decreed.

Friday morning the advance team from *60 Minutes* arrived, and while the technical people studied the garden layout, the segment producer conducted background interviews with Nathan Vance and Norman Finn. Ash Ramsay declined to be quoted or filmed, and sent a short apologetic note to Doug explaining why he couldn't afford to get tarred with this particular brush.

But whatever disappointment Ramsay's defection might have engendered was swiftly forgotten in light of the breaking development of the day. The agent who'd interrogated Cam for five hours had been authorized by the Bureau to speak, on camera, about the crucial information provided by a brave little girl and how it enabled the Bureau to crack one of the worst cases of espionage since World War II.

Another packet of office mail was delivered to Cam's room on Friday. She shuffled through it and came upon an envelope from Bermuda. It was a business envelope with *Bermuda Hospital Board* preprinted in the corner and Cam's name and address written in a crisp feminine hand. Inside was a letter in the same handwriting.

Dear Mrs. Alexander,

I am writing at the behest of Mr. Desmond Truesdale, whom I am nursing here during his most recent illness. He is in receipt of your letter dated 17 September 1998, to his late wife, Joan. Mr. Truesdale wishes me to inform you that he is her only heir, and that if Gloria Lipton bequeathed any sums to Mrs. Truesdale, that he would now be entitled to such monies in her place.

I must add my personal entreaty to this letter. Mr. Truesdale is quite infirm and very nearly destitute, so if there is any possibility of a bequest coming his way, it would be most welcome. Particularly given the tragedies he's suffered of late. You see, Mrs. Truesdale died under the most horrific circumstances. She was murdered while at prayer in St. George's—raped, in fact, and her throat slit on the floor of the church. As you can imagine, this came as a terrible shock to Mr. Truesdale . . .

The letter slipped through Cam's fingers and fluttered to the floor. Joan Truesdale, the fourth of the four, murdered exactly as Gloria and Doris had been. No one could claim it was a coincidence now. There was no vacation to Reno to explain it away, no explanation other than the unavoidable one: someone was hunting down and executing the NRO secretaries from 1968.

She listened at the door of her room, and when the coast was clear, she went to Doug's room and stood out of sight behind the drapes at the front window. The hordes of reporters were still down there. All the careful teasers leaked out about the FBI information had only whetted their appetite for more. Meanwhile, the security guards were still blocking the driveway and patrolling the perimeter of the four-acre property. There was no way she could get past all of them.

She went back to her room and looked helplessly at the bedside phone. She had to assume that the phones were tapped, which meant that she might as well draw the FBI a map as attempt to call her mother from here.

But that might be the only answer—to betray her mother a second time, to tell the FBI exactly where she was and get her safely into custody. Even if it turned out to be twenty years' custody, wasn't that better than an eternity of death?

When she couldn't debate the question any longer, she picked up the phone and slowly dialed.

"Hello?"

"Mr. Stevens? It's Cam Alexander. Jackson, Rieders and Clark."

"Yes."

"Mr. Stevens, I have your letter here, and I have to advise you that it would be very foolish for you to try to get visitation at this time. Ten months from now, it might be different. But it would be very foolish and stupid to attempt it today. Ten times more foolish than anything you've attempted before. Do you understand me?"

"I think I do," he said after a stunned moment. "We'll talk about it ten months from now, is that right?"

"Yes. Because today it would be something foolish."

"I understand."

At ten o'clock that night Cam crept down the stairs to the kitchen door and stood watching through the pane of glass until the pizza delivery car pulled in the driveway. The security guard posted at the street went to question the driver, and after a minute the guard posted at the back porch jogged down to join him, as was their routine.

She opened the door and ran soundlessly down the porch steps and through the arbor to the garden. She kept to the shrub borders, blending black against black and stepping where she knew the soft earth would deaden the sound of her feet. She positioned herself between two rhododendrons and waited and watched for the third guard to make his rounds. He appeared briefly in the reflection of light off the pool, and when he circled around the garage, she dashed across the lawn and into the folly.

She pressed her back to the door and listened, but it wasn't the sound of his breathing, it was the wood-chip scent of his body that told her he was there.

"Steve?" she whispered, and when his arms found her in the darkness, she sagged against him in relief. "Oh, thank God. I wasn't sure you'd understand."

"I wasn't sure I did. But it was worth taking the chance of being wrong."

She hugged him hard.

"Do you want to leave tonight? Is that why you called?"

She shook her head. "Steve, it's my mother."

They crouched on the floor of the folly and she told him what she'd learned about Joan Truesdale.

"You need to get your mother someplace safe," he said.

"I know, but I don't know where! She doesn't have a passport, and she'd be recognized anyway, at every airport or train station in the country."

He was silent a long time in the darkness, then he said, "Do you think she'd be willing to dye her hair?"

"What?"

"I have my mother's passport. She had black hair and glasses. It shouldn't take much to get your mother to match."

"Steve, that's—but—"

"Here." He reached in his pocket and pulled out a pen and a scrap of paper. "Write your mother a note. Tell her who I am, and that she and Pete need to trust me on this."

"But what are you going to do?"

"I'll take them south on my boat."

"No, it's too dangerous—"

"Cam, I've worked on houses up and down the Atlantic coastline. I know my way around, and I have friends where I need them. We'll go to the islands and find a safe place for them. My mother's passport ought to be good enough to satisfy the locals."

"Steve." She stared at him in the dim light, too overwhelmed to say more.

"Write," he said.

Meredith peered out the window as the cab crossed into Georgetown. A forlorn little group of trick-or-treaters stood on the corner, the children clutching their near-empty treat bags while their parents scanned the darkened streets in search of any sign of habitation. Lots of luck, she thought as the cab rolled past. It might be Halloween, but it was also the last Saturday night before the election, and Washington was a ghost town.

Even her own house looked uninhabited as the cab pulled up to the curb. Of course, it *had* been ever since Hadley Hayes's video grenade landed last Monday. The days since then were a blur, and all the details of the week's spin had bled like dyes until they ran together in a muddy mix in her mind. Only two facts stood out clearly: it was the worst political nightmare she'd ever encountered, and it was her greatest triumph. And perhaps a third: she was utterly exhausted.

After the taping was over that afternoon, she took the first train out of Wilmington, for it was already obvious that her triumph was complete. The setting was idyllic, with the muted autumn colors and the soft sighing burble of the fountain and the mellow glow of the sun as it shone down on Doug and Cam. Doug was a marvel as he told the story of his brave little wife in a strong, steady voice that was nonetheless full of emotion.

But it was Campbell's performance that was truly astonishing. Uncoached by anyone, she told Morley Safer that it was Doug's love for his country that first drew her to him. "I felt I needed to give something back," she said softly with her eyes cast down. "To try and make some kind of amends for what my mother did. And when I met Doug and saw how much he wanted to work for America and how hard he was willing to fight for it, somehow I knew that must be the answer for me: to work alongside him, and to support him in every way I can. To try and do my mother's penance through his good work." She'd finished with an adoring look up at him.

While the people behind the cameras were still picking up their jaws from that answer, Safer asked his next question: "What would you tell your mother if you could talk to her today? What if she's watching you now?"

Campbell lifted her chin and turned and spoke directly to the camera. "Mom? Mom, I love you, but you have to come forward and pay the price for what you did. You'll never have any peace of mind until you do. That's what you taught me, remember? Remember the book you used to read to me, *Sam the Slugger*? About the boy who hits a ball through the neighbor's window and won't own up to it, but then he can't get another hit until he confesses? That was my favorite book then, and it still is today. So, Mom, I beg you. End your torment and turn yourself in."

"I don't know how she did that," Nathan said wonderingly when it was done, but Meredith thought she understood. Campbell was a short-timer now; her days were numbered, in the campaign as well as her marriage. She'd wanted out since that first night on the staircase at Ash Ramsay's house, and now that the end was so clearly in sight, she was able to turn in the brilliant performance they'd all been hoping for.

Meredith trudged to the door and let herself in. The same rationale explained her own brilliant performance these past few days, for this would be her final campaign, too. She turned on the soft wash of lights in the hall and gave an appraising look around. Real estate was high these days; she ought to get a good price for the house. She'd become a print reporter again and cover zoning hearings and school board meetings. She'd wait for Bret to grow up and come and join her, and if she was too old by then for that little girl they wanted, well, they'd find one to adopt. However things worked out, she was out of politics for good.

It was the double-cross on tort reform that finally did her in. Doug seemed to think he could simply take the money and run. No, not run—stroll away with his hands in his pockets and a whistle on his lips. It was a venality surpassed only by Gary Pfeiffer's swift and stunning vengeance.

And there she stood in the middle, blood-splattered from her own butchery, the broker of iniquity.

She pulled herself upstairs and drew the bath and was just sinking into the bubbles when the tub-side phone rang.

No, she thought, staring at it. One night off, that was all she asked.

It was no use. It kept on ringing. She'd neglected Sutherland all week in favor of Alexander, and she knew she'd have to make it up to him, and she knew how.

"I'm right outside," he said when she answered.

"I'll be down in a minute."

She hauled herself out of the water like a sea cow, and plodded down the stairs knotting her robe around her.

"About time," he growled as he came in.

"Sorry."

He kissed her hard. "You see last night's numbers?"

"Of course. You've got a six-point lead."

"With a margin of plus or minus five. Damn it, Meredith, if I'm only ahead one point—"

"Phil! It's more likely you're ahead by eleven."

He was mollified by a drink in the living room and a quickie in the bedroom. Afterward, when she would have been happy for him to roll over and doze the way he usually did, he decided to become chatty. "Some week you had up there in Delaware, huh?"

"God, I'll say."

"Nobody in the campaign had a clue about any of it?"

"Nope. She kept herself to herself, Campbell did. Or Cam, I should say. I have to stop calling her Campbell."

She sat up. A thought had been buzzing around her head all

week and now it suddenly landed. "This explains why she looked so familiar to you, doesn't it?"

His eyes gleamed strangely in the dark. "How's that?"

"You must have known her mother. You were at the Pentagon while she was at the NRO. Your paths must have crossed sometime."

His body went stiff beside her.

"Phil?"

"Sssh." He slid from the bed and reached for his gun on the nightstand.

Meredith bolted straight up. "Phil, what—"

"There's somebody downstairs."

"Oh, my God." Her eyes opened wide in the dark, and she strained hard to hear what he had. But her ears weren't trained to pick up what his were. All she could hear was the traffic in the street and the heater in the basement.

Phil was gliding across the bedroom with the gun held up at his side. He darted a look out into the hall, then crept out and headed for the stairs.

"Wait!" she whispered, pulling on her robe as she flew after him. "You can't go down there! What if he recognizes you?"

He gave her a withering look. "I don't think a burglar's in any position to point fingers."

"But anybody can get a reporter to talk to him these days, whether he's in a cell or not. Or what if he shoots you and I have to call an ambulance? It'll be worse than Nelson Rockefeller."

He gave a curt nod and held the butt of the gun out to her. "Then you go."

"Me?" she nearly shrieked.

"What else can we do? We can't call the cops. They'd insist on searching the whole house. Or do you just want to stand here and wait for him to come upstairs?"

"All right," she said, wincing. "Give it to me."

"Safety's off," he said, putting the gun in her hand. "All you gotta do is aim and squeeze."

She sucked in a breath and blew it out slowly, then crept down the stairs. By the time she reached the front hall, she could hear what Phil had heard. There was a rustling sound, then a rolling one, and both came from her study.

She stole around the corner. The barrel of the gun brushed her thigh, and with a start she remembered to raise it to shoulder level. She took another step and cursed the silk fabric of her robe; when she moved, it swished like a thousand palm trees in the breeze. A faint pool of light glowed in the study, and with her breath rattling in her chest, she took another step forward.

"Oh, God!" she burst out as Bret raised his head from her filing cabinet.

"Meredith!" he said, straightening. "I didn't know you were home."

She hit the light switch. "What the hell are you doing here?" she yelled. "You scared the shit out of me!" She realized she still had the gun in her hand, and she hurried to put it down on the corner of the desk.

"I'm sorry," Bret said. "I needed to check this file, and I didn't think you'd be home until late tomorrow."

"Check what file? How dare you—"

Bret's eyes shifted to the doorway, and she turned to see Phil Sutherland standing behind her in his pants and an unbuttoned shirt. Suddenly her eyes opened wide. "Oh, God," she whispered as the nightmare opened up in front of her.

"Dad?" Bret's face screwed up with confusion.

"You better have a damn good explanation for this, boy."

"I—I—" He sent a dazed look around Meredith's study. "I needed to see the file on Campbell Alexander. I had to see it tonight. . . ." His voice trailed off.

"What in God's name for? She's nothing to you."

"I read in the newspaper that her mother was the spy at the NRO. I didn't know which one it was before. I thought it had to be the first one, the one who wrote you the threatening letter. But I couldn't be sure, so I had to find all of them. This is the only one I couldn't find. Abby Zodtner. I thought maybe her address would be here—"

His unfocused eyes wandered again until they landed on Meredith's bare feet beside his father's. He looked up at her with animal anguish. "I don't understand—"

Meredith spun away with her fist in her mouth.

"I don't understand you!" Sutherland shouted. "What the devil are you talking about? What letter?"

"Gloria Lipton. She sent us a letter right after you announced for the Senate. Remember? 'How dare you? Perhaps you've forgotten your own history, but others have not, and you can't expect us to remain silent forever.' I ran her down and found out about the NRO connection, and once I figured out what she was talking about, I knew she was right. We couldn't expect them to stay silent. We had to take care of their silence ourselves."

"You stupid fool," Sutherland spat out. "Gloria was talking about my private history. About the women I used to run around with thirty years ago, who happened to include herself. That's all."

"But—" Bret's eyes blinked rapidly. "The NRO, the satellite capsule, the interception—you set that all up."

"Shut up, you idiot!"

"No, but it's okay, Dad, I know why you did it. I mean—after the McIverson story backfired, what else could you do?"

"Wha-at?" Meredith said. "Phil, what's he saying?"

"Nothing! He must be drunk. He's talking like an idiot."

"He was a hero to do this," Bret said to her. "It was the only way to get them to stop scaling back the war. We needed some heavy losses to make people wake up."

Sutherland grabbed him by two handfuls of his shirt. "Would you shut your fucking mouth?"

"Phil, let go of him—"

"Get back upstairs," he shouted at her.

"Back upstairs?" Bret raised his stricken eyes to his father. "Dad? Are you—and Meredith—" His face seemed to cave in on itself. His eyes fell shut, and when they opened again, everything had changed.

"Bret—" Meredith cried.

He didn't look at her. He looked only at his father. "Gloria Lipton," he said slowly. "Doris Palumbo. Joan Truesdale—I had to go to Bermuda for that one. Dean McIverson. John Rocco—I bet you don't even remember who he was, do you, Dad?"

"What the hell are you talking about?"

"He was the Gulf Storm vet in West Virginia, remember? He was trying to blackmail you, so he had to go, just like those poor women and that old drunk McIverson."

Sutherland's hands fell away from Bret's shirt and he staggered backward. "Jesus Christ, boy," he whispered. "What are you saying?"

"I killed for you, Dad."

A scream ripped out of Meredith's throat.

Sutherland stared at him for one paralyzed moment before he spun out of the room. "I'll call somebody. A hospital," he gasped, stumbling for the phone in the living room. "We'll get him put away. Nobody ever needs to know about this. Goddamn it," he said to Meredith. "Don't just stand there. Get me a phone book. Or something. Jesus Christ!"

She stood in a stupor as he collapsed on the chair beside the phone. Bret came out of the study carrying something, and as he brushed past her, it registered dimly that he must have found the phone book in her desk drawer. Sutherland had the phone in his hand, and looked up as Bret crossed the room toward him.

"Bret. Son—" he began, before a crater opened in his face and the top of his head splattered against the cool white walls.

Meredith's scream roared as loud as the shot in her ears, and Bret turned on her, his eyes rolling wildly in his skull, the gun waving wildly in his hand.

"Bret, no!" she shrieked.

"I love you, too," he said, and his smile flashed at her before the gun got in the way.

"Bret—*no*!"

He pitched forward onto the floor, and the sisal rug drank up his blood like blotting paper, spreading swift and silent across the room until it touched her toes.

She was still screaming when the police arrived.

37

They moved in a pack—five hundred men and women, fevered and fractious, pressing cheek to jowl while clouds of balloons rose off the floor of the ballroom and roars of triumph burst from their mouths. They swarmed up from the tables and away from the buffets toward the dais, all of them cued by the rumor that was whipping like a live electric wire through the room. It was only ten minutes since the call had come in to the suite upstairs, but the news had spread like wildfire to the Party people waiting for it here in the ballroom. Hadley Hayes had conceded.

It was thirty minutes since ABC News declared the winner. With eighteen percent of the vote in, Doug Alexander was the projected winner with a ten point lead over Hayes. Already the pundits were opining that it wouldn't have happened in the absence of last week's scandal. Not only did Alexander emerge a hero, but Hayes was widely perceived as having overplayed his hand, shot himself in the foot, gotten greedy—a dozen clichés were offered to explain the upset.

Even Doug had a few to offer as they left the suite and made their way to the ballroom. "Cam, I know this campaign has been rough on you—it's been rough on all of us. And I know we're a little worse for wear, but we're a little wiser for it, too, aren't we? Because I know now that what we've got is worth fighting for. Don't you think?"

She didn't answer. She was striding briskly ahead of him and was the first to arrive beside Ash Ramsay at the podium. "And here they are now, folks!" he roared into the microphone. "The couple who've won your hearts and mine. I give you Cam and Doug Alexander!"

The crowd erupted, and the band struck up to add to the cacophony. Cam stood with a smile fixed on her face and scanned the frenzied heads that bobbed below her. Maggie Heller was front and center, her wiry torso wriggling out of control with excitement. Norman Finn was on the prowl, circulating through the crowd and slapping backs and shoulders as he went. Jesse Lombard stood at the exit with his arms crossed, and in the wings stood Gillian wearing a pale blue dress and a woeful expression.

The only notable absentee was Meredith Winters. She was in a hospital in Bethesda, reportedly still under medication following the traumatic murder-suicide in her home Saturday night. The pundits were all talking about that, too, and the consensus was that modern-day electioneering had spun out of control. The financial pressures, the negative ads, the dirty tricks—all the stresses had become so severe that it was really little wonder young Sutherland had cracked the way he did.

Doug's arm fell away from Cam's waist—her cue to start shaking the hands that were flapping up at them. He went to one corner of the stage, she to the other, and as she started to bend at the edge of the stage, she saw Steve slip in through the side door.

She gazed out at him over the heads of five hundred screaming people, and when he gave a nod and a small secret smile, the relief flowed through her like a warm pool of water.

Doug stepped up to the podium. At once the music stopped and the cheers began to dwindle and fade. "My friends," he said, his voice reverberating artificially through the room. "I've just had the honor of accepting the congratulations of Hadley Hayes."

In the explosion of applause that followed, Cam came down off the stage and threaded her way through the packed bodies of the crowd. No one noticed her; all they could see was Doug, and even of him, only what they wanted to see.

She reached Steve, and their hands met and joined down low between their bodies. "Ready?" he whispered.

There weren't words enough to answer that question. She nodded.

He opened the door behind him and pulled her into the service corridor that led to the kitchens. As the door fell shut behind them, the noise of the crowd faded into a faint dull roar like the sound of highway traffic over the next hill.

"How did it go? Are they all right?" she asked as they hurried down the hall.

"When I left them, Pete was surf-fishing on the beach and

your mother was in the kitchen trying to figure out how to clean a conch."

"Steve, thank you," she said, squeezing his hand.

The door banged, and a voice tunneled down the corridor after them. "Cam?"

She turned and took a quick protective step in front of Steve. "What do you want?"

Nathan came toward them. He glanced at Steve before his eyes settled back on Cam. "I guess all I want is to say—I don't know—All the best?"

"I wish the same for you," she said. "I always have."

He smiled. "And maybe someday I'll get it, too?"

Steve pulled on her hand and she started to go, but abruptly she turned back. "Would you deliver a message for me?"

Nathan lifted his chin warily. "All right."

"To Ramsay."

"Ramsay?" he said, startled. "Sure."

"Tell him that I know all about Kitty Renaldo. I know where she lives, and I know about the campaign funds that pay her rent. And if he sends anyone after Steve, if he does anything at all to interfere with him and Trey, the rest of the world will soon know about it, too, starting with the Senate Ethics Committee and the *Washington Post*."

His eyes widened and he slowly nodded. "I'll make sure he gets the message."

The house stood in darkness, and they had to navigate by starlight up the steps and past the pillars carved with *V* for *Victory*. Cam pointed to the lintel over the front door, and Steve reached up and ran his fingers along the edge until he found the key and unlocked the door. She hit the switch inside, and the two iron sconces flanking the door lit up and cast dusky amber shadows across the hall.

"Up the stairs, first door on the left," she whispered.

He hesitated. "You're not coming?"

"This has to be between the two of you, Steve."

She watched him go until he faded into the shadows at the top of the stairs. The house was full of old-house noises—creaks and cries and groans and rustlings—but she was thinking of another night, a cold winter night when it was full of music and laughter and voices pitched high, a night when nothing was what it seemed to be, least of all herself. She remembered standing on that staircase and watching her dreams of safety crumble, and she remembered how hard she'd campaigned to get there, to add another layer of protective coating over her identity, to become Mrs. Douglas Alexander of Greenville, Delaware, reduced to nothing more than the *s* in the title, so minuscule that no one would ever give her a curious look again.

But now all those layers were gone, and she was only Cam, with no last name that had any meaning to her, stripped down to herself at last. She gazed up the stairs and knew that if the verdict went against her when Steve and Trey came down, it might break her heart but it wouldn't change who she was. She'd still be Cam, and somehow she would go on.

The minutes crawled by, and as the night deepened, the stars grew brighter until they shone through the windows, a clean white light through the smoky glow of the sconces. There were more sighs and groans from the old house, then one sharp angry exchange from the second story, and finally a leaden step on the stairs.

Her hand went to her mouth as Steve came down, alone. He looked at her and shook his head in wordless desolation, and her heart thudded into her stomach and left a hollowing aching emptiness behind it. He took another step down, then another, descending slowly and bleakly toward her.

"Wait," came Trey's voice behind him.

Steve's eyes fell shut, but he didn't turn back. "What for?"

Trey didn't answer, but he emerged from the shadows and stood at the edge of the stairs.

"I know what you want," Steve said. "You want me to take you the way I did before. Right? That way the decision's out of your hands, and you're free to sulk and act up about it whenever you feel like it. But it's not going to work. It's gotta be your choice this time. Because this time you know what you're choosing."

He waited a beat, but still Trey didn't answer, and he took another step down the staircase.

"Wait," Trey said again.

"Your call, buddy."

Cam held her breath as Steve took another step down.

"Okay, wait. I'm coming."

Her breath escaped, and Steve's face sagged with relief before he turned and went upstairs. When he came back, he had a suitcase in one hand and Trey's shoulder in the other.

"I suppose it's goodbye, then?"

They all turned at the sound of Margo's voice. She was standing in the shadows of the living room with a glass in her hand and tears bright in her eyes. "I wonder," she said, gazing at Trey, "if I could have a farewell hug?"

He glanced up at his father, then swallowed hard and went to her for a quick, awkward embrace. When they parted, Margo stroked the side of his face and said: "Remember your mother, dear. Think well of her."

"Which one?" he said, confused.

"Why, both of them." Margo's eyes wandered across the hall and came to rest on Cam. "No. All of them."

Trey looked over at Cam, then back at Margo, and gave a nod.

Outside, Cam stopped beside the car. The November sky was full of stars, so bright they looked like the electric pinpoints on a campaign map. "Look how clear the sky is tonight," she murmured. "Isn't it beautiful?"

Trey threw a quick glance up before he crawled into the backseat of the Explorer. "Wait till you see the stars from Maristella. That's where they're amazing."

"I can't wait," she said with a smile as she climbed into the passenger seat.

Steve got behind the wheel. "Which one's the North Star?" he asked her.

She peered up through the windshield. "Right there," she said as she picked it out. "See the brightest one there? That's Polaris."

He started the engine and pointed the car that way.

ACKNOWLEDGMENTS

I'm grateful to Arthur G. Connolly, Jr., for guiding me through the courts of Delaware and for introducing me to the Honorable Barbara D. Crowell. I'm grateful to Judge Crowell for providing a behind-the-scenes look at the Family Court of New Castle County and for allowing me to observe her at work on the bench and in chambers. She serves as a model of judicial temperament and decorum, and her fictional counterpart in this book is purely that. Over the years, I've known a number of Delaware's judges and elected officials, and I can state with certainty that none of the characters in *Out of Order* bears any resemblance to any of them.

I'm also grateful to two of my close friends: Assistant U.S. Attorney Barbara E. Kittay, who advised me on federal criminal procedure and Washington lore, and Nathan Van Wooten, who lent me pieces of his persona along with most of his name.

And as always, I'm grateful to Joe Blades for his deft editing, and to Jean Naggar and her associates for all that they do.

A final note. All of the tort reform measures introduced in the 105th Congress were defeated, as were all attempts at campaign finance reform. In the summer of 1998, a bipartisan effort was made to end the Senate practice of "anonymous holds." It failed.

ANGLE OF IMPACT

by Bonnie MacDougal